LUCAS DONNELLY'S HAND WAS COOL, JUST LIKE THE INSIDE OF HIS LIMOUSINE. Glory didn't know how to talk to him. He wouldn't understand signing and she had neither pencil nor paper. His hand was still holding hers. Glory felt electricity flow up her arm, cold though, not hot.

"Don't be afraid," Lucas Donnelly whispered, except his whisper was loud, the words crashing against one another like cymbals.

The hand Lucas still held began to burn as if attacked by frost.

"There's nothing to be frightened of here," he said with a smile. "I've made a long journey to New Morning and it's taken me quite a while. I've waited, of course. But I'm quite patient. I'm known for my patience. Sooner or later everything comes to pass."

She turned to Lucas Donnelly, who merely smiled. His arms were spread wide, and Glory realized he must have released her hand. Now he wanted to pull her into him, to encircle her, and she threw up an elbow as if she might ward him off. He was inches away. How easy it would be for him to reach out and take her. Yet, he didn't. He laughed instead, and said clear as a bell, "You will."

By Diana Henstell

THE OTHER SIDE
FRIEND
NEW MORNING DRAGON

NEW
MORNING
DRAGON

DIANA HENSTELL

BANTAM BOOKS
TORONTO · NEW YORK · LONDON · SYDNEY · AUCKLAND

NEW MORNING DRAGON
A Bantam Book / October 1987

ISBN 0-553-26323-4

Published simultaneously in the United States and Canada

Bantam Books are published by Bantam Books, Inc. Its trademark, consisting
of the words "Bantam Books" and the portrayal of a rooster, is Registered in
U.S. Patent and Trademark Office and in other countries. Marca Registrada.
Bantam Books, Inc., 666 Fifth Avenue, New York, New York 10103.

PRINTED IN THE UNITED STATES OF AMERICA

KR   0 9 8 7 6 5 4 3 2 1

With love, to my son
Joshua Levine
for all the good times. . . .

"Love alone is the true seed of every merit in you, and of all acts for which you must atone."

Dante *The Divine Comedy*

"It is love not reason that is stronger than death."

Thomas Mann *The Magic Mountain*

NEW

MORNING

DRAGON

1

Alastair Wayne rested on a worn slatted bench in the midst of a patch of velvet green and tilted his head up toward a flickering sun. Light wove intricate patterns between the trees, striated his bony face on which the skin had loosened—though not so much for a man nearing seventy—cut benevolent streams along his closed eyes, and warmed him slightly. His chest felt tight, as it often did when he had strained himself, and his heart was fluttering in tiny, frantic drum beats.

When he was breathing normally and his fragile body with its withered, useless legs had ceased its involuntary trembling, he brought his head forward and opened his eyes. Through the foliage at the end of the square—not really a square but a long oval, flanked on one side by stately old colonial homes, and on the other by prim, white-painted shops and stores—Alastair could just glimpse his own house on an angle to the green. It was not far away, less than a block, but the journey on his crutches from the front door to this, his usual bench, might—for the energy it required—have been miles. Sadly, he recalled how once he had gone from the northern border of New Morning to the southern in much less time and with no pain. But that day was so long ago that no flight of imagination could bring back the solid feeling of firm ground beneath his feet, the buoyancy of that bouncing half walk, half trot. He had been so much younger then, before the landing at Omaha Beach, before his spinal column had been nicked by a splintering mortar shell, and the crucial vertebrae had shattered into useless fragments.

If you weren't such an old fool, he admonished himself, you'd give up this macho nonsense and resign yourself to the chair. Most days he wheeled about the sturdy clapboard where Waynes had lived from almost the founding of New Morning, and only used the crutches to labor himself up the narrow stairs on those nights when some yearning inside demanded he sleep in the room of his childhood, rather than downstairs in the old library. Still, he forced himself to make his daily pilgrimage to the square. It was a statement, the agonizing, lurching trek to the bench, but whether to himself or to New Morning, or both, he wasn't certain. He often went out in the chair, to the Public Market, to Simon's Hardware, or to the White Bear Inn at the other edge of Main just beyond the manicured park. The center of New Morning was level, and over the years, out of deference to him, though Alastair hated to acknowledge this, most of the shops and even the Inn had quietly erected ramps so he could wheel up and inside.

God damn soon, he thought, they'll be able to rip off the ramps because he wouldn't be around. When Alastair was in a snarly mood, his mortality hovered over him like a stone.

Do not go gentle, he muttered under his breath, recalling as he did, Dylan Thomas's poem, and knew with a sinking heart that that was just the way he would eventually go. Probably in his sleep to be found by Mrs. O'Brien on one of her three days. He envisioned her soft, powdery, unbaked muffin of a face tightening in anticipation and fear as she edged into the room, and inched in that overweight crablike shuffle of hers to the bed.

But not yet, he soothed himself, pushing aside the gloomy thoughts, his mood shifting in one of the mercurial changes that had come to be so common in Alastair's interior territory— soaring one moment, flat as a fizzed-out soda the next. When his heart wasn't thundering from the strain of his physical exertions, it was often galloping like a wild stallion from some inappropriate emotion. For more than forty years, since the war, he had lived a sedentary existence, had been frozen in a wasteland like a yeti in Himalayan ice. He had never married. There had been an occasional probe by some dewy-eyed spinster, but why let some female penetrate the defenses he had erected when he was capable of nothing more formidable than holding hands?

And, of course, he had never had children. That was the great sorrow. He cared about life with a ferocity that often shocked him, though that passion was what had kept him alive in the mud and chill of Normandy when a less determined, less fervent man would have died. Well, he had by sheer will and intensity saved himself, given himself as a gift all this time, but the years had been gray and lackluster no matter how full he had attempted to make them. Children, children would have made a difference. If only he had gone off to war already a father. Then he'd be sitting in the square with grandchildren to consider, to worry about. Perhaps if he were lucky, to watch playing on the grass. Instead the only growth in his life were the flowers in the tiny beds that scalloped his back lawn. And even those he didn't tend himself but left to Moses Llewelyn, New Morning's yardman.

Alastair was impervious to nature beyond the enjoyment of the sun on his face, or a cool wind dancing about his head. He enjoyed the look of it, true, but no more so than he did that of a painting or a finely crafted piece of furniture. Animals he cared about a bit more, but not unduly. He had sworn, when the full burden of his infirmity had become apparent, that he'd never be one of those doddering idiots who'd talk to a cat. No, his passion was what it had been when he could stride about the earth on his own two legs, throw back his shoulders and hold up his head a full six feet above the ground: people.

Alastair wasn't a gossip; he had little to say *about* anyone. Though his conversation brimmed with ideas, with scraps of odd information, he much preferred to listen. Others knew instinctively that he cared, yet at the same time that he'd never intrude. His concern was deep, a swiftly flowing underground current, but still, even when prodded, he never gave advice, but remained cocooned in an impenetrable silence. When he spoke, however, it was with a deep resonance.

He knew everyone in New Morning. Except for the two years he had put in at Dartmouth and the war, he had lived in the Berkshire hamlet all his life. His mother had died when Alastair was seventeen and now, after more than fifty years, she was a hazy ghost, insubstantial and drifting in the slow-moving tides of memory. His brother John had been swallowed up in the Battle of the Coral Sea and nothing remained to mark his existence but a name on a bronze plaque on the Route 20 side of the clock-tower monument.

So it was his father to whom Alastair had returned after the war and his father with whom he'd lived. His father—even then an old mournful widower who silently parceled out his days between the house on the green and the tiny cramped insurance office on the second floor of the First National Bank Building a block away at the corner of Housatonic Street.

Alastair had thought once of being a musician and he did, in fact, play the piano passably well. Only not well enough. So after the war he had slid without much thought and an absence of feeling into helping his father with casualties and damages and premiums. He'd only given up the agency five years ago, long after his father had joined his mother in the Congregational Cemetery. Now Alastair lived off his annuities and taught piano when a child or an adult interested him enough. It wasn't talent, or not great talent, that he searched for in his new pupils, but enthusiasm, the sheer love of sound.

Music was the one thing in Alastair's life that hadn't changed; the one constant. He trusted music, could give himself up to it, and in the stream of a concerto or the surging river of a symphony he would swim as though whole.

It was the music that drew him even then like a hooked fish to Glory Crowell. The sheer impossibility of her response, the wonder of it. That she heard the music at all was some kind of miracle; that she seemed to straighten, to rise up to her toes when, like an electrical current, it spun inside her, in her veins and along her bones, more than defied the physical rules of the whirling universe. Glory, nineteen and beautiful, was a perfect girl. But Glory didn't speak. Glory . . .

He caught a blur of motion like the flash of a wing, across and far off to the left, on Rowly Street. But it was only the Farrow's Bakery truck. Alastair knew it was Jordy Farrow behind the wheel making the daily deliveries for that truculent father of his. Thinking of Harlan Farrow, Alastair wanted to spit.

The baker wasn't so much a big man as one who seemed to be hammered from rock. He was wide rather than tall, with massive shoulders, and was solid muscle to the bone. A man whose heart was as granite-hard as his features.

Having worn out one wife who died gratefully, Harlan had for years now been eroding Jordy's mother. Worse, when Jordy and his older brother Tim were youngsters, there had been vague, unsubstantiated rumors as to how Harlan treated them. He was tough certainly, and he worked the boys as arduously as he did his wife. Then Tim ran off somewhere—town gossip had it, to join the Marines—and Jordy shot up tall as his father, then two inches beyond the old man. Not as strong, and soft inside instead of quarry stone, Jordy at twenty-four was still trying to calm his father's temper, usually to no avail.

Alastair shifted on his bench and charted the progress of the delivery truck as it pulled up in front of the Public Market. Banker Crowell on his way to the weekly board meeting at the First National where he was in charge, met up with Jordy just as the boy had flung open the back doors and was reaching in for a basket of bread.

Alastair imagined the sweet, newly baked scent, just as he imagined he could hear Theo Crowell's high nasal twang of greeting. His smile, if he allowed himself one, would be grim on his craggy face. Poor Theo, Alastair thought, knowing exactly how the banker was suffering. Uncertain about Jordy, wary. Glory was his daughter, after all, and Theo had the sweats over the boy's affection for her. Glory was Theo's princess, his Sleeping Beauty in a perpetual silence that in Theo's mind was hazily akin to a state of grace.

Evelyn, Glory's mother, was even more disapproving of Jordy's fumbling attentions. Puppy love, she'd sniff and roll her eyes, claiming it didn't mean a thing, while worrying that it might. Alastair wasn't unaware that Evelyn Crowell had grander plans for her daughter than a match with the baker's delivery boy. Even if Jordy was Harlan's son and one day the bakery would be his. Both parents agreed: Jordy was *wrong*.

Rearranging himself on the bench, Alastair let out a long, old man's wheezy sigh.

New Morning at 10 A.M., this day in June, played out its ritualized first act. Alastair could have closed his eyes and rocked in dreaming without missing a beat.

Will Austin, the minister of the First Congregational, came out on his front porch and stood for a moment, arms akimbo, hands curled into fists on his hips, then marched weightily down the front steps and over the narrow wedge of grass to his church.

Doc Trump's dark blue Buick shot out of the driveway alongside his house and sped along High Street.

Moses Llewelyn's pickup belched behind Alastair. Without even glancing around, Alastair knew the black man had lifted his hand in a wave. The truck, a faded gangrenous green, went left two blocks further on and disappeared into an alleyway. Emma Tydings's place, Alastair thought, gazing south to that end of the square at the house almost directly opposite his own colonial. Two men were washing the windows and there was a squat van out in front. Patterson Cleaning Service. From up Pittsfield way, Alastair supposed.

Emma Tydings had been a friend of Alastair's mother, ninety-two if she'd been a day, dead finally, six months before, not from old age but a header down her front steps.

Alastair wondered who would live now in Emma's house.

That was the big secret New Morning was buzzing about. Whoever had picked up the house from the estate wasn't talking, or not yet. But the colonial was redone, inside and out, its faded beauty restored with elegance. Ah, how Emma, long on family history but short on cash, would have loved to have seen that!

"Ha! Ha!" Alastair heard behind him. Charlie Calman, owner and publisher of the *New Morning Eagle*, editor-in-chief and sole reporter, full of himself, of the warm spring morning. Must be a rise in the subscription lists, Alastair thought, or a new ad. . . .

Carol, the youngest child and only daughter of Mike Boardman who owned the Public Market on Main Street, came off the perpendicular from Rowly Street, loping like a pony on her skinny denim legs. Mike must have taken her car away. Sense of a newt, he'd say. Twenty years old and drives that Chevy like it's a jet.

A cloud passed before the sun like a dark hand and the golden swatches of light paled to gray. A brief wind moaned through the treetops in a dirge and Alastair felt his head begin to stuff up. He yanked a neatly folded handkerchief from his breast pocket and blew his nose.

"Getting a cold, Alastair?"

"Damn it, Dee, don't sneak up on me!" he snapped at the short, tidy woman who had assaulted his flank in a sneaky maneuver. He was annoyed at himself for having missed her approach, but then, Dee Whittier seemed often to come up at him out of empty space. Unlike other New Morning citizens, Dee's movements weren't to be relied upon. Some mornings she was in the real estate office jammed into the first floor of the slender building next to the bank; others she stayed at home in her big house at the center of the square. Then again, she might be off showing a place to one of the summer renters or buyers up from New York, or occasionally down from Boston. In the two years, however, since she'd been home and "working the land" as she, wrinkling her nose, called it, fewer properties had changed hands than ever before. The business of real estate had come to a standstill though interest rates were sinking. But Dee, when Alastair pointed this out, only laughed, shrugged her shoulders and said, such was life. Besides, it wasn't as if real estate was her life, or that cajoling somebody into buying or selling was necessary for her to survive. So, more times than not, her office had a Closed sign swinging on the front door. Then, most likely, she'd be off wandering the Berkshires with her cameras. Or maybe up in the darkroom. Just fussing, she'd say when Alastair would ask what she found so interesting about New Morning to take pictures of. Just fussing. Playing, she'd say.

Only that wasn't true. She was too good a photographer. Her pictures had been in exhibitions, sold to collectors, and appeared often in magazines. Alastair always knew over the years where Dee was, more or less, by shuffling through the racks at the newsstand. She was well known enough to be called famous, and she probably had made pots of money, too. Alastair couldn't figure out for the life of him why she'd moved back to New Morning after so much time.

Dee plunked next to him on the bench and for an instant, before his vision cleared, he seemed to be gazing at her through a white mist. Eyes fogging up. Cataracts next, he thought despairingly.

"What are you doing lollygagging around this morning?" he asked. "No houses to show? No pictures to take?"

She crossed her long, elegant legs and jiggled a foot shod in a delicate, expensive sandal. Her tiny, pixieish face, indecently young for a woman Alastair knew for a fact was in her sixties, creased with a smile. But her gold-flecked brown eyes, as smooth and glittering as agates, were snapping.

Her eyes, Alastair thought, drawn in spite of himself, were her best feature. They were the eyes of a cat, and like a cat, Dee seldom blinked. She stared fixedly and seemed to be seeing with the same accuracy as her Nikon. There was no hiding from Dee's eyes any more than one could escape her unforgiving camera.

She had traveled all around the world—or as Alastair had once put it, "to hell and back." Dee, looking sour, hadn't been amused. She'd had at least three husbands (or was it only two?), won awards, banked a considerable fortune, experienced wars and moon launchings, hijackings and inaugurations, guerilla rebellions and terrorist attacks, the official crownings of several heads of state. And now, though Alastair would never understand why, when she had the whole globe to choose from and knew so much of it so intimately, she'd returned to New Morning where she'd been born.

"Doing your daily roundup of New Morning activities?" she asked.

"What are you talking about?" He was trapped by her curious stare. "And who invited you to dump yourself down on my bench anyway?"

"Ever think of working for the *New Morning Eagle*? You could do a first-rate gossip column. No!" She shook her head. "I take it back. You'd be wasted as one of Charlie Calman's hired hands. Buy the rag from him, Alastair, and make a decent paper out of it." Dee was laughing.

Alastair had to relinquish his frown and smile at last, as with Dee he almost always eventually did. Except for those times when she was broody and a tic flickered erratically in her left cheek and her clear eyes went muddy, she could usually sweep away Alastair's cobwebs.

The men brightening dead Emma Tydings's windows finished, stowed their equipment in the van, and drove off. Alastair, watching them depart, said, "So, are you going to tell me about this mysterious stranger who's bought Emma's house?"

"I told you, Alastair, he's some businessman, rich as Croesus, who's decided to settle here."

There was a thin coating of ice in her voice that alerted Alastair.

"Why? Why would some big financier want to bury himself in a sleepy backwater like this? How do you run a big business from here?"

She answered his second question. Only much later would Alastair realize that she hadn't replied to his first. "With computers, the same way you do in a Manhattan glass tower."

"Well, I'm not convinced," he said, and he wasn't. New Morning was the place he knew best, almost the only place, but he had no illusions. New Morning was small, though pretty, nestled in a Berkshire valley. The kind of town time swept over like a wind. Nothing much had changed in its two hundred and fifty-plus years, except for the appearance of a gaggle of jerry-built houses on the south side of town, two small shopping malls, a Ford dealership and garage, a car wash, and two gas stations.

A few outlying houses had been picked up by summer people and a cottage colony had gone up out at Garland's Pond. Tourists passed through saying "quaint," and then hurried on over to Great Barrington or up the Pittsfield Road.

Mostly everybody who lived in New Morning had been there since the day he was born. Many families were mired in a history not of years but of generations, and even the young, if they went off to college or the service, eventually found their way home after a while.

"Still seems peculiar," he said, half rising from the bench.

It was then that Alastair saw the limousine sweep around the curve, way down on Main, making the light. It was long and black and gliding smoothly toward them like an alien space vehicle, shiny under the glare of the New Morning sun. Light sparked silver jets off the chrome, ricocheted against the darkened windows, and reflected the street in a watery flow. When it neared the green Alastair sank back as if the air had been vacuumed out of him.

As the limousine oozed toward him and came abreast of the white colonnaded First National Bank, Alastair saw that the front, from the bumper right up to the hood, had burst into flames. A bright conflagration of orange and red fire was dancing, wavering, in sinuous spirals. By some trick of the light, or perhaps because of his faltering old man's sight, it seemed that Main Street was swept up in the blaze. As though the stores had been torched, and the park with its grass and flower beds, the benches.

Alastair sat fastened into place. He was helpless to cry out at the limousine's approach. Like Glory Crowell he had words in his head but not in his throat. The power had gone down in his system.

Inexorably, like an impending doom, the limo rolled toward him. The blackness of it above the flames was the pitch of midnight. The heat would be scorching; Alastair's flesh would metamorphose into ash.

The big black car drew nearer with its fiery, blinding light. He was gazing into a furnace, and for a moment when his entire life seemed a mere second in the vast weave of time, only one insignificant molecule in the continuum of eternity, his head pounded, threatening to explode. And then the car on its slow crawl inched out of the fire. A bank of clouds shouldered through the sky and Alastair was staring at a long, sleek limousine. The sun had set a dazzling, fireworks display of streaks and sparks off its highly polished surface.

"Alastair!"

The car's skin was once again as ebony-smooth as patent leather as the limo continued its silent prowl, the fire banked.

The tension that had set Alastair's nerves vibrating left him. Feeling suddenly limp and chilled, he sank back on the bench. Still, he couldn't give the limo up.

The car passed Alastair's house then slowly slid along the green's far flank like a fat, glistening nightcrawler, fascinating and repulsive.

The limousine continued its dark, antediluvian passage with Alastair unable to pull his glance away, hoping it would flash about the oval and go right back out of New Morning on Route 20 the way it had come in. But it purred instead up the driveway at the left of the Tydings place, and the two-story garage where for thirty years Emma Tydings had parked the Bentley she seldom drove.

"Alastair!"

Dee was shaking him, bending low, her face inches from his. He gazed into the liquid depths of her eyes and saw nothing. His breath rattled against his teeth and his head spun. He pulled away from her touch.

"Did you see that big black limo? Just came off Route 20, around the square, and nosed its way into Emma Tydings's garage," he said, shaken.

I'm hallucinating, like some drug-crazed kid. Wind and fire right in the middle of New Morning on a Thursday in June. Imagining flames from nothing but the glare of the sun on metal and chrome, he thought. All before noon and I'm sober as a judge and considered in sound mind if not body.

Despite his attempts to reassure himself the hair stirred at the nape of his neck.

"Black stretch with tinted windows so you can't see inside," he added.

"That has to be the new owner of the Tydings house. His wire said he'd arrive today."

"Why didn't you tell me?" But his accusation lacked force. He was feeling old and weak, half an inch from the first bore hole of senility. His imagination was indeed overblown and it had made him queasy, was still making him sweat. He supposed he'd have bad dreams over this.

"I thought I had," Dee was saying. Her voice swam at the edge of Alastair's hearing.

He asked her again, as he had before, as almost everyone in town had, sizzling with curiosity, "Just *who* is he?"

Dee repeated the same information she'd given over the past few months. An offer had come through the mail, only days after Emma's funeral. An offer so large the estate couldn't refuse—and why would they, anyway?

"I'm going over right now and meet him," she said as

Alastair climbed up to a shaky stance with his crutches. He swayed but stayed erect and Dee had the sense not to grip his arm. She paced her steps to his as they passed through the green, and came out on High Street. There, she left him. When he reached the curb at Rowly he gazed down the long leafy tunnel to Emma's house toward which Dee was purposefully striding. He watched her step onto the front walk and stop.

Alastair thought he glimpsed the front door of Emma Tydings's refurbished colonial swing open, but he couldn't be sure. The distant light was sooty, besmirched. But he was certain that Dee suddenly hesitated, that she even pulled back. He knew that she inched away to the sidewalk, and that she had turned around. For a moment he thought she was going to retreat to where he waited, but she didn't. In infinite slow motion, as if time had stopped, she once again swung toward the house. Alastair didn't stir, though his arms ached and his shoulders shrilled with pain, until Dee disappeared inside. It took her a very long time.

Feeling foolish and chilled by a draft of inexplicable fright, Alastair finally crossed the street in his wobbly way, toward home.

2

The morning the black limousine drove along Main Street, Evelyn Crowell was drawing up a family tree. It was Theo's ancestry, of course, that she was chronicling. The Crowells had arrived in New Morning in 1736 while her own people hadn't shown up until 1912.

Evelyn wanted to display the tree over the fireplace in the living room, but Theo obstinately refused to allow it further prominence than the front hall. He regretted the whole undertaking and would have stopped it if he could. But Evelyn's need for Theo's family was greater than his reluctance to have his lineage put on view.

Theo had a known genealogy while Evelyn knew nothing of

her heritage beyond a grandfather who'd come from some forgotten Baltic country in steerage and a grandmother fresh from the slums of County Cork. She tried never to think of them except in her worst dreams. Nor did she care to remember her own parents, now thankfully long dead, or an upbringing on one of the poorer, more outlying farms. As far as Evelyn was concerned she was a Crowell from her silvering curls to her polished toenails.

Evelyn had just happily sat down at her dressing table, where—with the curtains tied back—she could gaze out the window. So she witnessed Theo bobbing out of the *Eagle* office, a freshly printed newspaper in his hand, and loping along Main Street to get trapped before the Public Market by Jordy in his truck. Evelyn's pressure rose, sharpening her nerves. Sand flies nibbled under her skin. She was suddenly furious with Theo. How could he stand there chatting with that boy, right in the center of New Morning!

Evelyn fretted and wondered, as she had before, if it would make sense to talk to Harlan Farrow. Or rather to have Theo do it. But what could they say? That they were convinced Jordy was all wrong for Glory and they didn't—God forbid!— see him as a son-in-law? No, Theo was right, let it all just fade away. To protest, beyond letting Glory know how they felt, made more of the matter than it deserved. Still, Evelyn suffered a knifing pain under her breast when she thought, as she often did, that they hadn't made Glory their daughter for someone as inconsequential as Jordy just to come along and walk off with her.

The blackness appeared out of nowhere. Suddenly, it was just there on Main Street, silently paralleling the green, so glossy the glint of the sun striking its flanks was as sharp as a razor's slash.

Evelyn soared right off her chair and stood at the window watching the car. She lost it in the trees, then saw it flash as it turned at Rowly and slowly, processionally, crept by her house. Who? she wondered, feeling slightly dizzy as if the blood were draining from her head.

A tourist? A summer resident's weekend guest? No.

It had to be the new owner of the Tydings house.

New Morning was quiet, sleepy, the leaves on the trees barely shivering in the lifeless air.

Evelyn waited by the window, hoping for some glimpse of whoever was in the long black expensive car. But no stranger materialized, and after a while she returned to her sketch. Her attention, however, had ebbed, and finally, sighing, she threw her pencil down and reached for the phone. Somebody should know something, she decided, as she began to call around town.

Jordy Farrow also wondered about the limousine. His skin was still prickling from the icy darts of hostility sent flying by Glory's father. The hostility had come from the way Mr. Crowell looked at him rather than by what he'd said, which was nothing more lethal than, "Hello, Jordy, how are you today?" Jordy had climbed back into the driver's seat of the bakery truck, and was just about to turn the key in the ignition, when the limo appeared. The sunlight attacking the grill set off shooting sparks that pierced Jordy's eyes, and he barely had time to be surprised when the car slithered past. The windows were dark as night and there was no telling who it contained. Though it might be a mistake, a misplaced tourist having missed the Great Barrington turn, for some reason he couldn't explain, a bear trap closed on Jordy's heart. Perhaps it was merely longing, knowing he'd never own a car like that.

He craned his neck but lost the car as it turned right at the top of the green. He supposed he should get moving, but sat motionless anyway. He felt hot and sticky though both windows were rolled down. With his sleeve he wiped his forehead. He was as wet as if he had jumped into Garland's Pond with all his clothes on. He thought of going back into the Public for a cold Pepsi, and talking to the Boardmans for a while. But his old man would steam if he did that, and somehow Harlan always found out everything. He was worse than the CIA.

The next stop was Harry's, and then south along Route 20 to the Super Saver. Jordy pulled the truck out into the middle of the street, heard a shrill horn at his left fender, and pushed a heavy foot down on the gas. He took the corner on two shrieking wheels, driving with one hand, the other fumbling the dial of the radio, looking for something loud and clear.

Moses Llewelyn, in the alleyway behind the Tydings property, was scrutinizing a lowering branch of Miss Emma's elm that he'd been suspecting would have to be pruned back. It hung as though weary, unable to support the burden of its leaves. Diseased, maybe: rotting possibly from the inside out.

Moses had had his eye on the elm from shortly after Emma
Tydings's death, an event that saddened him more than he
cared to admit. Sooner or later the elm would need attending
to, Moses thought. But he wasn't going to take it on himself to
chop the sickly branch off. I know my place, he was always
muttering under his breath, which meant he didn't perform
work free of charge. For Miss Emma was one thing, but the
property didn't belong to her now.

Moses Llewelyn with his close-sheared grizzled gray hair,
his long skinny neck and shoulders, was a familiar figure in
New Morning, pushing his mower or bouncing by in his
pickup truck. He tended the green on a yearly stipend from
the town council and cared for lawns around town as well as
those of the summer folks. He didn't have much of a talent for
growing things, but his old gnarled hand was steady when it
came to clipping and pruning and he could always be relied
upon to appear if a homeowner had an understanding with him
to rake and burn the leaves in the fall.

Like Alastair Wayne's family, Moses's had lived in New
Morning for a long, long while: escaped slaves who had hidden
out in this very house in the secret crawl space between the
walls, or up in the attic, or in the root cellar, then stayed in the
village as freed men and women.

The Llewelyns had once been a large family that cooked,
cleaned, and handled the heavier work for the white people
who had originally given them refuge. Some had died, some
had moved to other places—now only Moses was left. He too
had drifted away for a few years and just as rudderless sailed
back. He had had three wives—in New Morning and outside.
He was certain they'd all gone to their graves by now. His
children, he didn't know what had become of them, not that he
much cared. He had never liked kids especially, either as
squalling infants with their wailing and bad smells, or as
teenagers, mean-spirited and sulky. Which might have been
why Moses wasn't concerned with the adolescents to whom he
sold pot—gage, as he still called it, having learned the term
from musicians he'd hung around with in New York City years
before. Now and again, he sold heavier stuff when he could
purchase some from his Pittsfield connection.

His sideline—what he privately called his "affairs"—brought
him far more money than mowing lawns. So much money, in
fact, that he was one of the richest men in New Morning now,
though he didn't know that and no one else did either.

Having lived through the big crash—he was that old and then some, though he didn't look it—he didn't trust banks. He remembered how the First National had closed its doors to the crowd that shuffled on the sidewalks, tearful and afraid, pleading and banging their fists futilely on the thick glass that separated them from what was rightfully theirs. His mother had been one of them, and when she had finally gotten what she had so painfully saved, it was only a few cents for each dollar. So he'd never given up his money to any bank again. He was only comfortable with his money hidden around the ramshackle, knocked-together shanty he called home at the edge of Bailey Cross's property on the New Morning side. It insulated him from the freezing winter winds that whipped across the scraggly acre, rustling the rusted relics of dead pickups rotting in the yard, the heaps of junk that had erupted like boils on his never-cared-for lawn. That the money also kept out the worst of the summer's heat was another of his superstitious conceits. Perhaps, however, it would have been closer to the truth to say he just liked to be able to reach out and take a big stack of bills from under the floorboards, out of the crawl-space attic, from between the two thicknesses of wood that formed the walls, and fondle them, smooth the fives and tens and twenties—fifties and hundreds, too. Moses Llewelyn, who reckoned he hadn't had a woman in at least twenty years, got his satisfaction from caressing his wealth. That he never used it to better his life, to make living easier, to fill up the house with possessions—except for a twenty-four-inch Sony color set and a Fisher stereo system on which he listened to Dixieland night after night—was irrelevant. Money wasn't the reason he drove up to Pittsfield twice a week and bought large quantities of gage and then distributed it through New Morning for double and triple the price. Or rather what money could buy.

Moses got a grim satisfaction from seeing the hungry pang in the eyes of those to whom he chose to sell his gage. It made him feel like an imperial monarch dispensing favors. The furtive wave of a hand from behind a closed window or a screen door. The hesitatnt shifting from one foot to the other, while Moses continued to mow a patch of grass. A blurred and hasty voice on the phone inquiring nervously if he could possibly drop by. Moses knew all the gestures, and what pleasure he got came from observing these signs. Joy came to Moses Llewelyn in swift spurts like sudden spring rain whenever he added a new name to his list of regulars, his happiness caused by the need, the dependency, which made his buyers cast down their eyes and be polite and extra nice. It was their knowing he could cut them off if he got a whim. That made customers jumpy, weak-limbed, and often excessively polite. It was one of life's big lies, he often thought, that the gage didn't get into the brain and set up drum beats like heroin or cocaine. Gage became God for some people like alcohol did, and if Moses could be said to love anybody, it was these particular clients of his.

There was a deep and abiding pleasure in knowing just who needed him most of all. With the citizens especially he liked the secrecy. Not one of them ever acknowledged the business relationship, the illegal, and the necessary connection with Moses. He was always the yard worker, the black man hired to do the outside chores. If a small plastic bag was slid across a kitchen table or handed into the murkiness beyond the back door, it was all done obliquely. At times he did want to yell at his citizens to *cut the crap!* He really didn't have any argument with the white people who bought his gage and now, increasingly, expensive small quantities of coke, it was just that he often got bone weary of all the subterfuge.

Lying was a disease that stirred up from the inside just like the elm's rot.

Moses scraped at the bark. It flaked in dry chips under his nail. He shook his head and looked away in disgust. That was how he came to see the limo head on. It had nosed into the driveway quiet as a stalking cat after a bird.

Just like most everybody else who'd caught sight of the endless car, Moses suspected this was the new owner come to take possession at last. A current of resentment tided through him at the notion of some stranger, some upstart rich nobody, living where Miss Emma had, where there had been Tydingses ever since the colonial had been built.

Moses glared at the car over the back picket fence, until the driver's door swung out. Then the driver emerged, stringy and lean as Moses himself, and dressed in undertaker black. But a honky for sure. Milky white from his collar right up to the top of his bald head.

Moses had just about decided he'd seen dead men who looked more alive than the limo's driver did, when his attention was snagged by the passenger who emerged from the backseat. This one was even taller, but all filled out, and with a full crop of black hair. Darker too, though still a honky, and with a dazzling toothpaste smile. Moses's first thought was: That's as attractive a human as I've ever seen. Which he immediately amended to mean, a powerfully good-looking man. New Morning's females are going to be more fluttery than birds in a high wind at the sight of this one, Moses thought, screwing up his mouth and sucking his gums.

He spat into the privet at the other side of the fence and would have stalked off to his truck, but the new owner was striding across the back lawn. With a heavy step that bent down the overgrown blades of grass, he came straight for Moses. The yardman would have turned and given this interloper the back of his rumpled green work shirt but the eyes got him, the large black eyes as sizeable as nuggets of coal. They fastened onto Moses's own, and though one scuffed boot toe pawed at the alley dirt, Moses didn't stir. Curiosity, he told himself afterwards, another regular customer he would add to that, but the truth of the matter was he couldn't move. He felt himself as firmly planted as the elm towering above his head when the stranger, smiling that brilliant sun-at-high-noon smile of his, called out his name.

Glory Crowell, the lynchpin in so many lives, was on Ridge Road biking out to The Gallery. Owned by the Greaves cousins—two fortyish women from Manhattan—The Gallery resembled a whimsical elf's home. With its thatched roof it sat, like a giant *Agaricus silvaticus* mushroom in a carefully groomed garden of larkspur and marigolds, bleeding hearts and baby's breath, dwarf tulips and sweet-smelling thyme.

Whenever Glory coasted down the final dip in the narrow road and pedaled up to that first sudden sight of the leaded windows and conical-shaped roof poking through the trees, she wanted to giggle. She did, but the sound of laughter was always locked in her head.

The wheels spun pebbles in the gravel parking lot, and

hopping off the bike, Glory pushed it along the flagstone path
to the rear and leaned it under the eaves of the sheltered
porch. She always half expected Dumpy or Breezy to open the
door and she hummed behind her eyes that silly "Hi-Ho" song
from the movie her mother had taken her to see a long time
ago. A movie she could roll up in her mind with total recall.

Glory remembered everything that entered the net of her
experience. Every sight and sound. Each word and detail. All
that had happened to her was tucked back *there* in some nook
or cranny, available like microfilm to be inserted into the
machine of memory and reviewed. Except for *that*. *That* was
the time—five years in all—that preceded the moment the sun
illuminated first her father's face, then her mother's, in a jet
stream of molten light. It all happened on a wooden dock that
jutted out in a white skeleton finger into the blue-green of the
warm Caribbean. There were boats at anchor on either side
and they were walking toward shore and the low-slung
building at the end of the dock. Glory was in the middle,
holding a hand of each though that made it crowded on the
narrow plank, made them bump into one another and forced
them to be *careful*.

An out island, south of Virgin Gorda, the other lip of the
Bermuda Triangle. It wasn't lush at all—dry, windy, dust blew
off a craggy landscape gorged with black, deep, never-ending
sea caves. Waves, even on hot, calm days, pummeled the
south coast with a spuming, white-roaring fury.

Snow White, her father had called her when she was little,
before her mother made him stop.

It wasn't that her mother didn't care that Glory's life seemed
to have begun at a boat harbor where in an instant she was
blinded by a golden, watery spear of the sun and *came to*.
Often Evelyn would ask her in the early years if she couldn't
remember something before that moment—a face, a name, or
even the littlest, the smallest detail. But Glory couldn't. There
was nothing, no matter how hard she struggled. When they
sailed from the island through the long slow days and the star-
drenched nights, she'd lie quivering in Evelyn's arms, Evelyn's
voice stinging her cheek as she repeated, "Try, try to reach
back and grab hold of a memory." But by the time they
reached New Morning and the big house, Evelyn was telling
her—Theo, too—never mind, just let it be. It would all return
to her after a while; but it never had.

Glory had been born at five, with straight blond hair,

wearing cutoffs and thong sandals. Though she wasn't unhappy, there was always a shadow drifting above her head, which was the knowing that her life had begun in an explosion of light on a dock in an anchorage of a southern sea. Mostly she ignored the blank in her memory that was as mysterious as a black hole in space, but sometimes the dark-entombed past sent out seismic quiverings that became eerie shivers of panic down her spine.

In the early years Evelyn continued to insist: don't worry, it's all right. When Glory grew older, however, her wondering annoyed Evelyn. Now if she mentioned it, Evelyn would narrow her eyes and hiss at her to stop thinking about it. And Theo, if Glory happened to tap out her questions to him, would murmur, his hand creeping across her golden head like a timid animal, that the only thing that mattered was *now*. But still, his eyes would smart as though he'd been struck by a sharp object.

At first Glory thought that if she could just speak, force the words out of her mind where they were *seen*, each syllable and sound, take them out into the open, hand them over to others, or just toss them loose in the wind, she would be understood and then answered. But that wasn't true. Because even when she had learned to tap out her words into the palms of her parents' hands, to craft them in air, or to write them down in neat block letters, then in round, fine script, nothing changed. Spoken words couldn't bring her more than those without sound. So finally Glory acquiesced and became who they said she was. Except that she still wondered. Now and then, she would peer into the darkness that lay at the back of her mind, trying to pierce it.

She opened the back door of The Gallery and entered the warren of small, gray-shingled rooms where heavy bubbled windows let in a milky light. What illumination there was came from silvery cylinders tucked away in the rafters. It was all very fairy-tale, and the tourists loved it. The summer people, or the ones who came like migrating birds year after year for the foliage in the fall flocked to The Gallery and bought delicate ceramics and paintings from the alternating roster of artists whose work the cousins took on consignment.

The cousins were not precisely cousins at all. They had once been connected by marriage that terminated in divorce. All that lasted was the affection of the women who had entered each other's orbit as gawky, teenage girls. From New York once upon a time, they'd arrived as summer renters and made the decision to stay. It had been almost eight years since they had converted old Silas Riff's barn into a Brothers Grimm facsimile.

One of the cousins—Eva, the taller, gaunter, older by two years—had painted. Francesca, pale and chubby, with woolly gray hair, a gurgling laugh and sparkling violet eyes, had worked for the Metropolitan Museum. She was the cousin who chose what was to be sold, and hung the oils, the sketches, the New England watercolors, and gouaches on the walls. The slightly daft demeanor and old-aunty appearance masked an inner core as metallic and intricate as an IBM-360.

Glory had worked for the cousins since high school graduation the year before. There wasn't much to do once the snows came and the tourists stayed home. The Gallery was closed from December through March, while the cousins wintered in Key West in an apartment by the sea. Glory, who distrusted the sea that had much to do with the lost memories, feared for the cousins when they were gone. She imagined them sailing off one day and getting lost, though she knew that was silly.

Glory liked the cousins, especially Eva. Glory liked everybody, her mother often pronounced as a statement of mysterious fact. She had no discrimination, no judgment, where people were concerned. But that wasn't true. She had a black feeling about Jordy's father, and a gray, unfocused one about Dee, a feeling that disconcerted her because Dee was important to Alastair Wayne, and Glory cared deeply for the old man. Her feelings for him were a bright, sinuous yellow, as they were for Theo, Jordy, too.

"Well, Muffet, here you are, right on time," Eva said, tilting back on the wood swivel chair, her legs—as always, in pants—terminating in scuffed clogs on the desk. She was not quite smiling. Eva's thin bloodless lips, in a horse's face as solemn as one of the carvings the cousins would be showing this season, never quite forged up into a real smile. At most they'd inch apart to display a glint of slightly crooked teeth, and that was how Glory knew Eva was pleased.

Glory, however, did grin, and tossed her long, straight white blond hair back over her shoulders. What should I do first? she was thinking, as Eva brought her feet to the floor with a thud, saying, "Pour yourself a cup of coffee before you get the feather duster and start making like a whirling dervish."

Our "dogsbody," Francesca once called Glory, and Eva was offended, saying that meant Glory was a drudge when she wasn't at all. She was a help and a blessing and they had been Hiroshima after the blast until Glory came to save them from chaos. Francesca had apologized, explaining that "dogsbody" was an English term that simply meant someone who did everything; and did it well, better, in fact.

Woof! Glory had thought the day they'd had that discussion, and both women had suddenly laughed, then asked each other whatever were they laughing about. *Because,* Glory could have informed them, if she had signed or written it down in black and white letters, *I made a joke.* Only then they'd have wanted to know how they could hear her joke when she never said it out loud. Glory didn't understand herself those quirky, unexpected moments when all of a sudden her thoughts had the reality of actual speech. Her mother, Glory suspected, occasionally caught the sound of what was silent. But Evelyn was too rational to give these moments any credence beyond coincidence. Alastair also might have been jolted by one of Glory's thoughts converted into a quick burst of sound, because sometimes he'd gaze down his beaky nose at her in bafflement, his shaggy brows arched into crescent moons. He often did call her miraculous because she could hear; and besides hearing music, could somehow carry it within her. She had tried to explain that to him, writing about it on a long, yellow pad, but still it took time before he grasped that the music to Glory was a river flowing under the skin, that it traveled the pathways of her veins and arteries. Occasionally— Mahler did this—it churned a surf in her head. The music was the only water Glory never found frightening.

"Glory," Francesca called, padding down the long corridor from the rear of The Gallery where the cousins lived. "I think we should move Giorgio's pots. I don't feel safe with them in the second room. They're too small and fragile. Somebody could break one and we'd never know. Or pop a few into a pocketbook. Customers are so unreliable. You have to watch them all the time."

Glory's thoughts were smooth as glass when she turned to Francesca, puffy as a hen, a fairy-tale character herself in dirndl skirt and bright, embroidered weskit over an organza blouse. Francesca's picture had been printed on the giveaway brochures. She stood in the doorway of The Gallery and everyone was reminded of Mother Goose, exactly as Francesca had intended. Eva had been embarrassed—she was happier with straight lines and white walls and no nonsense—but she

told her cousin she was very proud. Only Glory knew that Eva
wished Francesca wasn't always wearing clothes that were
more like costumes. But Eva would have also preferred selling
stark modern abstracts, sparse paintings that depended on
color and line. Eva spoke of certain artists with yearning and
reverence in her voice. Glory knew she struggled with her
own large canvases in the garage studio behind The Gallery.
"My talent is trapped inside me, just like your speech," she
once blurted out to Glory and then looked appalled.

Poor Eva, Glory thought, and sensed Francesca's annoyance. She sipped at the hot coffee and listened to the cousins.
They were not quite bickering, but were just a shade off-
center. Snippy with one another. They had had a fight. Glory
could almost see it, almost hear the unraveling edges of angry
voices though she could not make out the words. If she
pushed, let her thoughts dissolve like wisps of clouds until
there was nothing in her mind but a bottomless emptiness,
and concentrated, gave that shove as if leaning in on a warped
door, maybe, just maybe it would all come clear. But if so,
she'd be invading the cousins' privacy. That would make her a
Peeping Tom, someone who looked where she had no right to.

Glory finished her coffee, rinsed out the mug, returning it to
the small shelf above the hot plate, and followed Francesca to
the back of The Gallery. The delicate paper-thin bowls, as
tentative as eggshells, were carefully placed on a tray and
moved to a niche near the door, in sight of the register.
Francesca fussed in her chickeny little ways, hands feathering
like wings over the pottery. Glory followed her instructions,
but wasn't really listening to the fuzzy tufts of sound the older
woman made. Her mind journeyed back to yesterday. Glory
hadn't liked yesterday for no particular reason she could
pinpoint now. Just that the day made her uncomfortable in her
skin. Nothing had happened, nothing was much different from
the day before or this one now, except. . . .

Don't . . . the private voice in her head said. *Think about
it*, she supposed she meant. A spring day, warm, summer just
around the next bend.

*I don't know anymore about him than you do, Evelyn, and
that is a fact. The mortgage didn't go through the National.
Rumor is he paid cash.*

Yesterday, Glory remembered now, the stranger had come
to New Morning. Her mother had been so excited, patting her
hair in that nervous way she had, tapping her fingernail to her

bottom lip. At dinner Evelyn had drunk two glasses of wine and her cheeks sprouted tiny red veins like the routings in the fragile ceramics Glory was now rearranging.

Ava Trump said Moses Llewelyn told her he's as handsome as sin, Evelyn had said with a sigh, *and unattached. No wife or children.*

Though it was warm in the large room Glory was suddenly chilled. An iciness skimmed down her arms and moved along her backbone, through to her fingers. And the tiniest of the bowls—so finely wrought it weighed almost nothing at all—slipped from between her frozen palms and shattered in a dozen pieces on the floor.

Glory never remembered breaking anything in her whole life, not so much as a glass or a saucer. Even as a little girl, there had been no clumsiness in her. To have dropped the small bowl when she had been standing still, hadn't moved a micrometer or been inadvertently jostled, was shocking. For an eternity she gazed down at the shards, thinking: *I didn't mean . . . I don't know how . . . I'm so sorry. . . .*

Francesca was on her knees, her hands hovering over the fragments as if they were the broken bones of a child. As if she could heal. As if her grief would somehow mend the shattered bowl.

"Sorry never changes things, Glory. Surely you're old enough to know that," she cried. When she lifted her head there was an expression of fury lacquered in her eyes.

Later, biking home after an endless day bruised with tension, straining as she pedaled up the steep rise of Madder's Hill, Glory saw again the unstoppable slide of the bowl from between her palms, saw it forever falling in an instant frozen in time. Glory shuddered so violently the front wheel veered in an abrupt turn, striking the soft edge of the shallow gully. Her hands flew from the handlebars, and she went sprawling, tumbling across a spray of twigs and stones, of old leaves and prickly new growth.

Madder's Hill dropped steeply away. Below, the valley in which New Morning nestled was visible. Glory clung to a tangle of roots, afraid she would slide down Madder's Hill into Bailey Cross's plowed and planted field, along the new furrows, across the highway and into the old fairgrounds. It wouldn't be impossible from there just to keep going, tumbling like a snowball over the slopes of winter, right out of New Morning.

Stunned, Glory lay in the brambles. Tears filled up her eyes unexpectedly, and she realized her knee was skinned and spotty with blood. Her shoulder throbbed.

She rolled over on her stomach, swiped the swinging hair back off her brow.

Scrambling upright, she crouched on her haunches, the denim skirt rucked around, streaked with dirt, her blue shirt half-tugged loose, and stared at the emptiness that gaped between the bushes, still shaken by the fall. After a while she rose to her feet. She brushed the leaves from her skirt and climbed back on the bike. She coursed off over the top of the ridge, gliding, on the downside now, coasting, her hands firmly on the brakes. She rode through tunnels of foliage, around the sharp Dead Man's Curve where there was no guardrail and an unexpected precipitous drop, out into the sunlight. Below, New Morning rushed up to meet her as she came in looping circles off the mountain.

She cycled by the stripped wood fence, passed the shingled farmhouse and the red, paint-needy barns with their pitched rooves, the water hole, plowed, unplanted fields now spreading in a bumpy furl of rich land. On the right side, running behind the blurred motion, were the fairgrounds, dusty and scattered with gravel.

Glory wheeled to a stop, found the ground, and closed up to the wooden sawhorse in the entrance. She peered down the long tan sweep of emptiness. She remembered the carnivals that always came for Old Home Week. How she loved riding high on the Ferris wheel, the whole of New Morning visible when she reached the top. The swings, too. Holding the Peugeot steady between her legs, she spread her arms wide and imagined the high, lofting ride, rising to a dizzying ninety-degree angle, and the world below, lying on its side. And the merry-go-round. She heard the calliope music, "Daisy" one year and "Take Me Out to the Ball Game" another. Glory rode the splendid horses up and down in her memory.

It was late and she knew she had to go to Alastair's where the piano waited. Where Alastair was waiting too, perched by the front window, unconsciously toying with the curtain, pulling it through his fingers as his glance darted to the street then away to an opened copy of *Time*. She saw him so clearly, his back humped as a camel's, his face thinly etched with shadows.

The day was so queer, she thought, quivering with a sudden unexplainable shiver of fright that had her backing off from the

sawhorse. Wheeling the bike to the road, she tried to conjure
up the music that Alastair was undoubtedly listening to.
Deliberately she sought to possess this one element in a day
rift with unsought fantasies, and snagged a short passage of
what might be *Boléro*. She nodded, satisfied for no other
reason than Ravel just seemed right.

The comforting thought of Alastair got her moving, and
having gained a fluid, continuous motion, Glory swept with
the wind into New Morning. She swooped along familiar back
streets and finally came out on the green where she dropped
the bike by Alastair's front walk.

Before Alastair could struggle out of the chair and clamber
with the aid of the crutches to his feet, Glory dropped to the
carpet by his knees. She laid her head in his lap and grasped
his hand.

"Hush, hush," Alastair whispered, his tired breath warm on
her skin.

Glory's eyelids fluttered as the tight grip of fear began to
loosen in her chest. Slowly she settled and eventually Alastair's
nearness and the comforting familiarity of *Boléro* banished her
fright altogether.

New Morning, Massachusetts, lies snugged in a short oblong
valley where the declining Berkshires begin to slump, settle,
and roll in lumpy hummocks. Here a pocket of liberal English
settlers, fleeing their more rigorous compatriots to the north,
displaced the previous Indian tenants and built on their
leavings. Far down below the New Morning green, if any
archeologists were prepared to dig, lay flints and arrowheads,
shards of thick pottery, slivers of reed baskets, a broken human
bone or two.

Ebenezer Smythe, spiritual and actual leader, a gun-bearer
and a bully, was the first of these early English to find the
passageway around the base of Madder's Hill, entering into the
valley from the north in 1718. He and his party had awakened

"to the dawn of a new morning," and thus having given the town its name, Ebenezer Smythe had been buried beneath a now barely discernible stone, pockmarked and weathered, in a corner of the green. Under a spreading horse chestnut, at the curve of a winding path, Smythe's grave peeked out from behind a meandering bush. One had to look carefully to see the tilting marker at all, and then to decipher the queer intricate writing that identified the stone as not a peculiar discard of nature but man-made. Which was what the man, whom Evelyn Crowell recognized as the stranger, seemed to be doing. Bending that broad back and crouching over Ebenezer's final resting place, his pants tightened across narrow, masculine buttocks. The sight brought an involuntary catch to Evelyn's throat, as though she'd swallowed the wrong way, or gulped an icy drink too greedily. Her fingers spasmed on the window ledge, and she pressed her warm forehead to the pane, eyes wide, watching.

His name, she'd finally learned was Lucas Donnelly. He was, no doubt about it, a fine figure of a man, Evelyn thought, recalling that phrase Theo's mother had used to describe Theo, who'd never been any such thing. His shoulders were endless, Evelyn noted again as the stranger rose, tugged down his white suit-jacket over his white pants, and scratched the dark hair that curled low on his neck. Peering out the window, through branches overburdened with leaves that blocked her view, it was difficult for Evelyn to piece together his face. She moved a foot to the side and tilted her head, but Lucas Donnelly remained crosshatched. One large brown eye seemed to twinkle, but that might have been a trick of fractured light.

Evelyn was already elaborately dressed in her best summer outfit, a pale linen suit the color of Key lime pie. A frilly blouse ruffled at the edge of the puffed skin that draped under her chin. The diamond watch clasping her wrist in a slim gold band ticked away. The monthly Historical Society luncheon was in ten minutes at the White Bear Inn. Evelyn was chairing today, a not inconsiderable feat since she hadn't an ancestor through whose auspices she'd earned such an esteemed place, only a husband. But the fact that Theo held mortgages and loans on half of New Morning, perhaps more, had swung the necessary weight for Evelyn.

I don't want to be tardy, she was thinking, as she grabbed the white leather clutch and positioned the cartwheel strawhat, youthfully ribboned and sprigged with cherries, upon a neatly arranged chignon.

Outside her house with its carefully scalloped beds of petunias, and broad red front door boasting a brass eagle knocker, she squinted farsighted across the square, but though she could see right to the bank, she saw no vestige of Lucas Donnelly. If he was still there he was as firmly buried behind the foliage as Ebenezer Smythe was beneath the sod. She turned to the south and went along the sidewalk, past military elms on the march at the curb. As far as Evelyn knew she was the first person to see Lucas Donnelly—after all Moses Llewelyn didn't count—and, if she had her way, she would definitely be the first actually to speak with the man.

Overhead, lost in the leafy canopy, a jay shrilled, and Evelyn, startled, jumped, feeling suddenly spied upon. The elm stirred its arms and the jay, flicking dark wings, hopped to a low hanging limb. Jittery, Evelyn continued walking. As she swept beneath the jay's branch, it squawked and darted to the next elm. In this way it announced her passage, crying and warning with its deadly eyes. The jay's hysterical screams made her so nervous, she dropped her purse, and had to stoop to retrieve it.

It was unnaturally warm, even for late June, and a necklace of sweat pearled under the ruffled collar of her blouse. Even her breath seemed warm in her mouth.

At the corner of the square she swept to the right and halted before Emma Tydings's house. The colonial glistened with its shiny new coat of white paint. The windows sparkled, but backed by thick draperies, revealed no more than a blind man's eye. She waited hopefully for a minute, then swung around for the long view up the green, but there was no one she didn't know in sight. Alastair on his bench, later than usual, and nodding. Somebody's child skipping rope along one of the paths.

Time ticked rapidly on Evelyn's wrist and she dragged her high-heeled feet reluctantly along beside the fence that fronted Emma's house. But still there was no Lucas Donnelly, not anywhere she could see.

Where could he have gotten to so fast? Her stomach burned thinking the stranger could have wandered into the Public, or perhaps to the *Eagle* office where he might now be sitting uncomfortably on Charlie's sole visitor's chair listening to a barrage of questions—the same ones Evelyn would have asked

the man herself. Worse, he could have chanced into the
bookshop to be ignored by Vera, Aaron Stein's lachrymose
clerk, whose stubby nose was always buried in a romance.

Five minutes to the hour hurried Evelyn up at last. Waiting
at the signal on the corner of Housatonic Street, the Tydings
house now behind her, she had the annoying itch of having lost
something—without knowing exactly what.

"And rich as Midas, too. That's what I heard!"

"He'd have to be, the amount of work he put into Emma's
house. Practically tore its insides out, then put them right back
in, all polished up and fixed. Least that's what they're saying
over at Cardigan's Lumberyard." Old Mrs. Winslow dabbed at
a mouth sunken into bone and glared about the table.

"As I said, loaded with bags of money," Cora Montrose
pronounced, bobbing a head sparsely draped with white
strands. Cora was old, too, though not as old as Mrs. Winslow.
Mostly the Historical women were way beyond the half-
century mark, except for a few who were graying in that
swamp of middle age.

The conversation that skittered over muddied coffee cups
and the ruins of dessert—the usual apple pie from Farrow's—
was almost exclusively about the stranger. Evelyn had had a
moment's resentment that her short speech on New Morning's
first Fourth of July celebration, which had quietly occurred in
1786, had been passed by with only a few "how interestings."
But then she too succumbed to the lure of the stranger who'd
come so mysteriously into their midst, like an exotic tropical
creature. Now, she was simply biding her time.

"I hear he's about fifty," Melinda Edwards was saying.

Theda Barrington, Cora Montrose's sister-in-law, countered,
"No, he's a stripling, no more than forty-five."

"Wrong, Theda," one of the women called from a neighboring table. "He's still in his thirties, that's Joe Dombrow's
guess."

"Joe's never even seen him," one of the other women hissed.
"It's all hearsay."

Evelyn barely listened to the women speculating about the
stranger, his age, how rich he was and what he did to get his
wealth. Would he do it here? How could he? New Morning
had no industry to speak of. The drone of excited voices

pitched in speculation buzzed past Evelyn's ears. She thought instead of the man she'd seen crouching for a closer look at Ebenezer Smythe's grave. Even that truncated glimpse of Lucas Donnelly left her satisfied that he was *somebody*. A real man in height and girth. She tried to picture his face, but it swam in her mind unfocused, pitted only by those large dark eyes. Handsome, anyway, she thought, no doubt at all about that.

When there was a satisfactory lull in the conversation, Evelyn cut through the silence. "He's forty, I'd say, or possibly a year on either side of that. The point is that he looks forty." Evelyn wasn't sure, but it was a good guess. Besides, forty was a respectable age, neither too young nor anywhere near what one might define as old. Forty was an age that Evelyn liked in a man. Just right for Glory she thought suddenly. The idea of Glory and Lucas Donnelly hovered as Cora yelled what exactly did Evelyn mean by that. Another voice intervened, and then all the women were speaking at once, demanding that Evelyn tell them if she'd actually seen the stranger, and if so, what in heaven's name did the man look like. And how had she come to meet him? Had they really spoken?

A Cheshire smile worked at the corners of Evelyn's mouth as she leaned back in her chair and sighing, crossed her legs. The Historical ladies were salivating, like a pack of hungry dogs, but she stayed demure, murmuring that in her opinion Lucas Donnelly was a definite asset to New Morning.

"Really, Evelyn, can't you say anything that doesn't sound like worthless fluff!" Mrs. Winslow finally bellowed, and glared at Evelyn with the jay's nasty eyes. But Evelyn wasn't about to let the old woman annoy her into saying something she'd be sorry for. Such as she didn't really know a drop more about Lucas Donnelly than they did themselves. She had a head start in the race to form an acquaintance, and dubious though it was, Evelyn wasn't about to give up her inch.

"I really must be going," she said, gathering her purse and strawhat, which she'd carefully placed beneath her chair. "I promised Theo a soufflé for dinner and you all know what time and concentration that takes."

Since Evelyn was a superb cook who could whip up a soufflé while she slept, not one of the women believed her. "Delaying tactic," Cora Montrose was heard to whisper loudly when Evelyn, rising, turned her back and marched straight out of the dining room, stopping only to thank Herman September who owned the White Bear for a wonderful lunch. It had, on the contrary, been a mediocre meal, as any meal in the Inn usually was. But being polite to Herman was somehow intricately knitted into the scene Evelyn saw herself as playing with the women whom she had abandoned in the other room.

Once again out on Main Street, Evelyn looked right then left. New Morning, in midafternoon, was deserted, and no wonder, she thought. If anything, the day had grown even hotter; the air was motionless, solid as lead. Waves of heat brought a metallic glitter to the cars, and the parking meters seemed to dance in the watery shine. The newly paved stretch in front of the White Bear was bubbling with globules of sluggishly boiling tar.

Evelyn, walking on the shop side of the square, brought a hand up to swab her face, then veered sharply and crossed the street. Emma's house sat quietly on its lawn, shaded by elms, clothed in stripes of shadows, serene and cool looking. It invited Evelyn to enter through the gleaming front door, to set a firm foot on the parquet entrance-hall floor (unless Lucas Donnelly had shrouded it in carpeting). In fact, she took half a step down the walk before she pulled quickly back and asked herself, what am I doing?

Evelyn hurried around the blunt end of the green and pattered up the High Street sidewalk. Riverlets of moisture trickled down her rib cage. Her stockings were stuck to her thighs, itching disagreeably as she moved. She couldn't wait to shed her damp, sticky clothes, to lower herself into a cold tub.

Coming up on her own colonial, almost a twin to the Tydings house, but younger by nearly sixty years, she saw Glory come out on the small porch. On her way to Alastair's, Evelyn supposed, noting the leather folder for piano music tucked under Glory's bare arm. Glory was wearing a yellow pique dress they'd bought together last month in the boutique. She was uncreased and golden, her long straight hair falling neatly, not a strand stirring, over her shoulders. Even from the distance Evelyn could tell her daughter's face was dry, not dabbed with sweat. A smile formed when she saw her mother, and Evelyn, flushing suddenly with anger that made her hotter yet, thought: never needed braces and not a single cavity in her head.

Gazing up the short incline to Glory so young and beautiful, Evelyn wanted to howl *it isn't fair!* She thought of the way she herself was loosening—the rubber tire of flesh anchored at her waist, the veins popping out like turnpikes up and down her legs.

It's just not fair!

She would have wept, or raised her hand to her daughter, but Glory descended, kissed a fevered cheek with lips as light and cool as autumn rain and went on.

Lucas Donnelly didn't make a public appearance; he didn't appear at all, except to Moses Llewelyn whom he engaged that first afternoon to continue the necessary ministrations to lawn and grass, flowers and bushes. If he'd actually been in the square looking at Ebenezer Smythe's grave on the day of the Historical Society luncheon, no one but Evelyn saw him. He stayed, this stranger of the black limousine, behind his imposing front door, reinforced walls, newly washed windows, and allowed New Morning's collective curiosity to sizzle and flame. His "man," however, did venture forth, darkly suited like a glossy raven.

"Nameless" was how everyone referred to this cadaverous whiteness, pallid as flour, hairless down to an almost invisible fringe of lashes. His name actually was Jarvis Badderly though no one in New Morning knew that yet.

Lucas Donnelly's "man" slipped like a shadow along Main Street with his string shopping bag. After subscribing to the *Eagle*, delivered, he presented a list to Simon of Simon's Hardware and requested several items to be delivered, then made his way to the Public.

It was midmorning, nearing eleven, the dead time in the market. Mike Boardman, having done up the day's meat orders, had gone off to get his Volkswagen lubed over in Great Barrington. Bobby Pierson, the Public's weak-minded delivery boy, had swept, unpacked cartons, taken out the trash, and now was doing what he usually did when Mike Boardman wasn't watching. Bobby had wandered off. So it was only Carol Boardman behind the register, when Jarvis Badderly came in.

Carol, a tall, healthy girl with apple cheeks and dewy eyes, was Glory Crowell's best friend and had been ever since first grade. At five Carol had had a weakness for dumb animals and had immediately transferred her childish concern to a little girl who didn't speak. But unlike the Crowells and Alastair, she had never tried to coax Glory into sound. Carol still didn't think it was particularly peculiar that Glory couldn't utter a word.

Carol was reading about the latest antics of a leading soap opera star, luridly described in *The National Enquirer*, when the bell tingled over the Public's front door. Reluctantly closing the tabloid, she looked up and found herself confronted by an apparition who resembled the zombie in Saturday's "Creature Feature" at the Pittsfield drive-in.

For a moment as she stared into eyes as inanimate as prune pits, she thought here was somebody else who'd lost a voice. But Jarvis Badderly finally parted razor-thin bloodless lips and in a clipped English accent that sounded to Carol like footsteps over gravel, as he handed her a shopping list, said, "Fill this, please."

"Sure," she managed to whisper. "You want it delivered?"

"No, thank you. I'll wait."

As Carol raced about the Public, up one aisle and down the next, not even wondering why Jarvis Badderly didn't pick up the items on his list himself, she kept sneaking looks at the tall, skinny stranger. He never stirred. He stayed as immobile as a parking meter, not even shuffling from one foot to the other.

"Here you go," she said at last, as she dumped an armful of boxes and cans she'd collected on the counter and began ringing them up. "Fifty-four seventy-five."

"We wish to establish an account. Monthly bills, which will be paid promptly, to be sent to Mr. Donnelly."

"Ah . . . " Carol hesitated. Her father's iron rule was, no credit except to people they knew. Never summer residents or renters who had a way of forgetting to settle up when Labor Day came. Suddenly she wished Mike were in the store. Carol Boardman who drove her compact much too fast, who skated on Garland's Pond when everybody said the ice wasn't thick enough to hold her up, who still at nineteen was known to climb trees and hang twenty feet off the ground—fearless Carol Boardman did not want to tell this bony creature of the fish-belly white skin that he had to pay in cash.

Of course, she tried to reason, the stranger in old Mrs.

Tydings's house was rich. Everybody said so. And it wasn't like he planned to take off in the fall. So, it should be all right, and if it wasn't, then her father could tell him the next time Count Dracula came into the Public. "Okay." She shrugged and wrote up the bill, bagged his groceries and called out "Good-bye!" to his retreating dark back.

When the last reverberation of the bell echoed away, Carol still didn't return to *The National Enquirer*. For one of the few times in the years she'd known her, she just wished she could call Glory on the phone and hear what she had to say about *this*.

As Jarvis Badderly made his way up and down Main Street unsettling merchants and clerks, only Alastair noticed that the man didn't sweat. He looked, Alastair thought, as dry as talcum and just as white.

The unseasonable June heat had driven red-hot rivets into Alastair's joints. So inflamed was Alastair that today he was out in his chair. The weather had sapped the energy necessary to struggle with crutches; so had last night's bad dream. Contrary to his expectations he hadn't had any nightmares about the fiery car, but about eleven the night before he had dropped off to the drone of the television set and there was World War II all over again. He was lifted up bodily and transported back to that hellish miasma called Omaha Beach. The antiaircraft guns pounded, and his ears rang with the hair-raising screams and cries. There was a bass-drum thump that followed the fall of a bomb. Dreaming, Alastair, for one brief and agonizing instant, felt his legs spasm and jerk and go out from under him in his headlong pitch onto the wet sand. Still dreaming, he imagined himself sitting bolt upright in his bed whinnying with terror.

But it wasn't the bedroom to which Alastair, still asleep, opened his eyes, nor was it the Technicolor blur of the twenty-four-inch screen. It was the bluff beyond the beach and the rough, turbulent sea. It was the sand saturated with blood, carpeted by the dead. Alastair shrieked soundlessly as his ghosts did in the endless drowning on landing crafts and in the imprisonment of the sinking tanks.

Alastair came awake suddenly, trembling, to Johnny Carson's monologue on the RCA. He slowed his breathing and willed his heart to quiet the incessant thumping, to steady to its usual beat. But a spray of rain had spoken to him in the rapid-fire pattern of machine guns against the windowpane and then his heart went off again, a skittish horse, galloping hellbent for somewhere safer than it was here. Alastair fought for breath and wondered if he should phone Doc Trump. But eventually the final fragments of his dream Omaha dissolved. He switched off the set by remote control. Quieted at last, his memories safely returned to storage, he had bumped through the rest of the long night in a fitful, draining sleep.

So now, out on Main Street, suffering the unaccustomed heat, Alastair was snarly. The forty-year-old battle that had taken his legs and thrust him into an isolation existential in its depths, forcing him to erect bulwarks against the pain of life, was, he feared, returning to haunt him. Awake or sleeping, Alastair honestly hadn't thought of the landing at Normandy in decades. But now, even here under the glaring sun, he couldn't help thinking just at the moment Jarvis Badderly passed him by: *I could have died there in all that chaos. I could have been left broken and hurt in the muck to die. I could have given up!* That he hadn't, didn't, seemed not to matter as he rolled along the sidewalk to the air-conditioned office of the *Eagle*. Charlie Calman, owner, publisher, and editor-in-chief, kept beer in a small refrigerator out back, and though it was still the wrong side of noon, Alastair wanted a cold draft of it, and not only to soothe the burning in his throat.

"Well, did you see him?" Charlie cried excitedly when Alastair pushed through the doorway.

"See who?"

"For Christ's sake, you know who I mean! You couldn't have missed him. Donnelly's butler, or whatever he is. That ghoul in the black suit." Charlie shuddered.

"Yes, I saw him."

"Think he's an albino?"

"Nope. Albinos have those rabbity blue eyes. And they never could face that ungodly sunlight without dark glasses."

"I hear he's ghoulish."

"Where'd you hear that?" Alastair asked. He usually got the gossip via Mrs. O'Brien who insisted on pouring it relentlessly into his ear while she cleaned, but sometimes Charlie beat him to it. Charlie liked to boast that he had a good nose for news, but Alastair thought he was just the same kind of busybody Mrs. O'Brien was. Both of them enjoyed minding other people's business as much as their own, though Charlie often published what he'd heard. At least three or four times a year he had to print a retraction. Printer's error was what he invariably called a piece of news that had gotten written up all wrong.

"Oh, I don't know. Somewhere. Can't really remember." Charlie was being sly.

"Protecting your sources again?" Alastair asked. He suspected Charlie had the delusion he was Woodward or Bernstein.

Charlie tugged at the beak of the Red Sox baseball hat he always wore in the office. "You know, Alastair, if a newspaper editor goes around tittle-tattling, nobody will ever tell him anything." He attempted to look sagacious, but his moon face made him resemble an aging kid with his hand in the cookie jar.

"Don't tell me then. See if I care." Alastair took a swallow of beer and felt the pleasure of it trickle down his throat in a cold stream.

But Charlie hated not to share what he'd found out. Telling Charlie a secret wasn't much different from announcing it on the party line they'd had before New Morning was plugged into a central system. "Got it out of Dee. Boy, that woman is a tough one. It was like prying open a sardine tin with my fingernail."

Charlie went and got a beer, then propped his feet up on the big scarred desk that he liked to pretend had belonged to his father and his grandfather before him. The truth, however, was that he'd bought it at a tag sale.

Alastair rolled the sweaty Schlitz can between his palms and stared out the *Eagle's* front window at Main Street. New Morning was all washed out, faded like an overexposed photograph. Old towns, he couldn't help thinking, lose steam, go all doddery and sag, just like humans—meaning himself. He was as weak as tissue paper today.

With the background music of Charlie Calman gurgling his beer, sighing, scratching the roll of jelly fat through his denim shirt, Alastair sailed on a tide of mournful thoughts.

Glory Crowell came biking up along the green. Despite the vapid light, she stood out brightly. Her shirt was rose, her skirt a darker shade. Alastair could have sworn he could see the fine golden hairs like down on her arms. He watched her pedal out of sight, his spirits restored, satisfied as he always was by the sight of Glory. The sounds she could coax from the piano with those slender, graceful fingers of hers. Ah! Alastair recalled the Beethoven sonata she'd played at her lesson the night before. She'd held the final B-flat a hair too long, but the flourish at the close was as feathery as mist.

"What?" He realized Charlie had said something he missed.

"You seem out of sorts. Feeling the heat?"

"Who wouldn't be. It's up to ninety. Unseasonable, Charlie. Maybe you should write it up."

"Intend to. Hottest June in New Morning history, or since records started being kept. But I wasn't talking about the weather. I was asking if you'd heard about Fred Daniels."

"What about Fred?" Alastair wheeled around.

Charlie took another swig of the beer, making Alastair wait. That was Charlie's way. "Gone up to Boston for a bypass. Doubleheader. Doesn't look so hot," he said, shaking his head as if in his mind he was already writing up Fred Daniels' obituary.

"When did this happen?"

"Yesterday. I thought Lettie O'Brien would have told you by now." It stuck in Charlie's craw that Alastair's cleaning lady often had the news before he did. "It means we have to get another chairman for Old Home Week."

"Old Home Week's not until Labor Day," Alastair said. "That's three months away. Maybe Fred will be on his feet by then."

"Ah, com'on, Alastair, even if he is, he won't be able to run his committee and get done what needs doing, you know that."

Alastair lowered his head and brought up his shoulders like a turtle sinking back into his shell. He didn't like thinking about Fred who was his junior by fifteen years at least. "Don't plant him yet, Charlie."

"I'm just being sensible," he insisted. "Old Home Week's our big event. More money gets spent in New Morning those seven days than at any other time in the year. Even Christmas. And it's to nobody's benefit if it's screwed up."

"Fred won't screw up."

"A healthy Fred Daniels mightn't, but who knows how fast he'll recover. Only the good Lord could tell us that," Charlie said. "All I'm pointing out is that it's in the town's best interest to get another chairman."

"Then get one." Alastair tried to work up some concern, but he'd seen more Old Home Weeks come and go than he could remember. Every year there was always some problem or other, some breakdown in the tangled lines of communications, hurt feelings and stepped-on toes, events that didn't come off exactly as planned. The annual celebration was inevitably put together like a patchwork quilt.

"That's what I'm going to propose at the town meeting tomorrow night," Charlie was saying.

"Good." Alastair didn't have the energy to argue with Charlie. He just hoped Fred Daniels' feelings wouldn't be hurt. Fred was a punctilious accountant who had a high opinion of himself. "You got somebody in mind? What about Herman September? If I recall correctly he's never had the honor."

"Herman!" Charlie hooted. "He can't even keep the White Bear in the black. Forget Herman. Nope, Alastair, I was thinking about you."

"Me!" Alastair rose an inch from the wheelchair. "You're crazy, Charlie. I chaired four years back, and then five years before that, if I remember correctly. And another two or three times. And every time I did, Doc had to increase my blood pressure medicine." He was shaking his head from side to side. "No, Charlie, Old Home Week demands somebody younger than me."

"Stop acting like you're a dead turkey, will you, Alastair. You can do it in your sleep and that's a fact." Charlie had the bit in his teeth and was running. "Old Fred Daniels hasn't even gotten a parade marshal lined up yet, Alastair, do you realize that? And say what you will, but with so many events taking place on Labor Day all over these hills, a good chairman has his marshal tied and fettered by May at the latest. I know he asked the lieutenant governor and got a thanks but no thanks. And"—Charlie waved an ink-stained finger in Alastair's direction—"he didn't even bother to tell anybody about it. Furthermore, Fred let the whole matter drop—not that I'm blaming him considering the state of his health—but he could have drawn up a short list and made some inquiries, don't you think? Not Fred. He's just gone off to Boston without leaving one iron warming in the fire." Charlie spoke as though the accountant were off having a vacation instead of open-heart surgery, but he bristled when Alastair told him so and denied it. "There's just a proper way to proceed, and don't think this won't make me reconsider letting Fred do my taxes come next year."

Alastair was so mad at Charlie he snapped, "You don't make enough money to pay any taxes."

Charlie dropped his feet to the floor with a thump and tossed the empty beer can into the wastebasket. "Sticks and stones, Alastair. You're just trying to rile me because you know I'm right. At this late hour you're the only one who can get Old Home Week on the track. I'm going to propose you and you're going to accept because you care for this old town more than anybody. And that is that," he said with the same firmness he used in writing "The Editor's Opinion" in the *Eagle*.

Alastair rolled out of the newspaper office into a drenching sunlight that brought the sweat back to his brow. He felt lilke a fish caught on a hook. You can always say no, he told himself as he angled to the curb. He automatically glanced both ways for traffic before he rolled over to the green, but there wasn't a car in sight. New Morning slept peacefully in the late afternoon heat. Charlie was right; he couldn't refuse the town anything. He cared for New Morning probably more than ninety percent of the people who lived within the town lines. It was in his blood, his genes; it was his heritage. It was home.

Alastair loved New Morning, the look of it, the old white houses on the square—including Emma Tydings's which now, thanks to the stranger, no longer was a shabby sister—the square itself, the towering elms and their graceful sheltering embrace, the neat Congregational Church where a man felt at peace whether he believed or not, the bits of history like old Ebenezer's grave, the library built in 1835 and paining him because it so needed repairs, the gently rolling hills. . . . Yes, he loved New Morning, and wouldn't have allowed one single change if he had his way.

Alastair had worked up a full steam of sentiment by the time he reached his house and found Gina Papriakas waiting on the front porch for her lesson.

"Why didn't you go inside where it's cooler?" he asked, preceding her. Gina Papriakas stepped soundlessly over the hardwood. Plump without being fat, she was a dark attractive woman despite the purplish half moons beneath her almond eyes. Her olive skin was smooth, as unlined as the perfect fruit she and her husband Stanis sold from their roadside market out on Route 20. At the age of forty-something-or-other, her children grown, one grandchild, and a second on the way, she'd decided she wanted to play the piano. Without even asking the husband to whom she had deferred in all matters their entire married life, Gina Papriakas went out and bought an old upright from a dealer in Pittsfield and asked Alastair to give her lessons.

"I don't take many pupils," Alastair had explained. He hadn't wanted a plodder, especially one who'd gotten "musical" in middle age as an alternative to having an affair or running off, but he couldn't, of course, say that to Gina. In spite of his acerbic personality, Alastair was a kindly man.

Alastair had been surprised. Against his better judgment he allowed Gina two weeks at the piano so they could both see how she did. From the first she had handled the music with assurance. It took her a while to learn to read, but once she had mastered that skill, she progressed rapidly. Her touch was delicate, almost reverent. The short, pudgy fingers that should have fallen weightily on top of the keys flew instead. Stanis, when Alastair made his weekly stop at the market, always asked, in a mystified tone, what all this piano playing was about. He apologized too, each time, for Gina's behaving like a kid. For annoying him, he'd say to Alastair, as if Gina were throwing rocks on his porch. It only dawned on Alastair when he and Gina were six or seven months into the lessons that Stanis had never heard his wife play.

"You're getting pretty good," he had told her at the close of one lesson. "Why don't you give a little concert for the family? Maybe the Haydn we've been working on; they'd like that."

Her face had closed up, as if a door had slammed shut inside her somewhere. "Not yet, Mr. Wayne. Maybe later." But he sensed she didn't mean it.

Today, when she sat down on the bench, arranging herself with little womanly twitches and shuffles, smoothing her skirt, pushing the short black hair threaded with strands of gray behind her ears, Alastair noticed she was peaked, slightly off-color. Her skin had a faint greenish tinge to it, and the shadows beneath her eyes had deepened. But her execution of the Brahms he had given her the week before was flawless. He asked her to run through it again, and this time he leaned back in his chair by the window simply to enjoy the music. Only he couldn't concentrate. He watched Dee drive by his house and around the square in that foreign car of hers. He hadn't seen Dee in days, not since the morning the stranger had come to town. Alastair realized suddenly that he missed her. I'll have to call her and see if she wants to come over for dinner, he was thinking when a small black and white warbler that he had vaguely noticed darting in and out of the elm in his front yard did a nosedive. The warbler dropped like a bomb, hitting the ground, where it lay without moving. It was dead for sure, and

Alastair, surprised and wondering if birds could have defective heart valves like Fred Daniels, never realized Gina had finished the Brahms.

She cleared her throat in a shy little cough, and said, "Mr. Wayne?"

"Oh, yes, wonderful, Gina! Light, ah, light as a feather," he cried guiltily, darting a fast glance at the bird.

Gina rose from the bench awkwardly, all angles, a graceless contrast to her playing. "My hour's up," she reminded him, fumbling for her purse with one hand while with the other she smoothed herself with a quick arpeggio of motions.

"Next week practice the Beethoven sonata, page fifty-two in your book," Alastair barked, stuck to his chair as he watched her pass from the room and recede in the distance. She reached the door and whispered a "good-bye" Alastair never heard. His mind was on birds, or, more precisely, one dead bird. In his memory the Brahms played again, but this time accompanied by the rapid beating of wings and wind rustling through feathers.

There it was, yes, outside the window, a drab lump on the grass. Alastair stared intently at the unmoving mound of stilled feathers as if he had X-ray vision and could see the tiny, lifeless organs. Too peculiar by half, he thought, recalling the bird's dead fall, so straight and relentless.

Alastair turned in his chair, upset, and then thought, take a nap, get some rest. But no matter how firmly he shut his eyes, the persistent bird reappeared alive—only to die in its drop-dead dive all over again.

The town hall wasn't on the square but backed up behind the Barnes Memorial Library. It housed the small police station with its one whitewashed cell, the council president's office (seldom used by Howie Eumis), a licensing department that issued few permits since most necessary papers were gotten over in Great Barrington, and the large airy meeting room (adjoined by a kitchen) where most New Morning business was haggled over during monthly sessions that just about everybody attended. Tonight all the folding chairs were up and the hall was filled since word had gotten out about Old Home Week's customary birth pains.

"I hear it's a complete mess, that Fred's notes aren't clear at all. Charlie was complaining that nobody can make head nor tail of them," Theo Crowell was saying behind his hand to Simon Hooper, owner of the Main Street hardware store. They were up on the platform waiting for the meeting to be called to order by Howie Eumis.

"It's a fact," Simon agreed. A fussy little man who constantly rearranged his store so that it was almost impossible to find anything smaller than a lawn mower without help, Simon toyed nervously with his wire-rimmed glasses, as he glanced about the hall. "Big turnout tonight. I hope that means it won't take forever to get things done."

Since Simon himself was usually responsible for drawing out the meetings by constantly challenging every point raised, Theo coughed sharply and turned away. On his left sat Will Austin, darkly severe, his bony face settled in a scowl. "How's the musicale shaping up, Reverend?" Theo asked.

"Perfectly!" he said. Will Austin had the sonorous voice of a television newscaster. "The church choir will sing six selections, and believe me, not one of them will be off-key." Further along the table Alastair let out a groan. A yearly battle raged between Alastair and Will Austin over just which selections the Congregational choir should perform.

Will Austin was conservative for a Congregationalist and one Old Home Week he'd had the choir doing Gregorian chants. He'd also dressed them in monks' robes made out of heavy sacking which were far too warm. An alto soprano had fainted. That should have taken the starch out of Will Austin, but it hadn't a bit. The following year he had wanted to do the *Messiah*, but Alastair had found out early enough to bring it up at a town meeting, and the minister had been voted down on the basis that the Handel was more appropriate to Christmas. Will Austin had been so furious with Alastair that the two men didn't speak until Easter. He was still frosty and so suspicious that he was cagey about revealing the program of the musicale until it was too late for changes. Now, when Alastair called out, "What are they singing?" the minister abruptly shook his head. His profile was sharply chiseled with a hawk's beak and a jutting chin. Alastair suppressed an urge to take a poke at that arrogant jaw.

When the clatter of chairs scraping hardwood had ceased, and the flood of voices had dried to a trickle, Alastair—shuffling uncomfortably in the wheelchair, the small of his back achy as though jabbed by hot pins—whispered to Howie Eumis, "For God's sake! Let's get on with it!"

Howie, who reacted to any hint of authority like a trained retriever, rose with a jerk, banged his gavel on the table, and called the meeting to order.

"You should of seen him! Thin as a stick and in that black suit. Without any hair, I mean like a baby. All white, too. Yuck, he was spooky!" Carol Boardman raised the wine bottle to her mouth and took a swallow of Gallo red, then held it out. "No, Bobby, you can't have any. You know it makes you even funnier than you already are," she scolded kindly as the bottle swung away from Bobby Pierson's waving fingers. Carol handed it to Jordy who offered it first to Glory before he drank.

"Didn't any of you guys see him?" Carol continued. "I mean, was the dubious pleasure all mine?"

Carol, Jordy, Glory, and Bobby were all sitting on blankets in the back of Jordy's van in the fairground parking lot, sharing a pizza and drinking wine. They had been at the drive-in outside of Pittsfield and normally would have stopped at one of the roadhouses on the way home, but Bobby got agitated by crowds and smoke made his eyes water. Though he was only seventeen and mentally stranded forever around eleven and a half, Carol dragged him along whenever she could. Carol felt sorry for Bobby and had a theory that the more time he spent with normal people the more he'd learn to be like everybody else.

"I guess it was, Carol." Jordy shrugged. "I saw that Cadillac limo the day it drove into town. But I haven't caught a look yet at this Donnelly or that spook of his."

Glory reached up for Jordy's free hand and tapped out something in his palm.

"What? Do it again, Glory. I'm a little slow tonight. Okay. Glory says her Mom said Donnelly is a pretty good-looking guy."

"Ooooh! Just what New Morning needs, a real hunk! But how does she know, Glory?" Carol asked excitedly.

"Ah, apparently Mrs. Crowell saw him in the square one day. Tall, dark, and handsome," Jordy translated. "But who knows what that means. Older women have queer ideas." Jordy knew what Evelyn Crowell thought about him and found her disapproval worrying. He was serious about Glory; so in love with her that most times they were together he felt feverish as if the blood boiled in his head. He remembered the first time he had ever seen her, right after the Crowells had come back from their sailing trip—the trip on which they'd found Glory somewhere.

It was in the bakery. Timmy was waiting on customers and Jordy was helping. He had tried to get his brother to sit behind the register and let him do the running around. But Timmy acted stubborn, refusing to give in to the pain that must have been fearsome in his left leg. Their old man had whacked Timmy hard with the iron shovel he used to take the loaves from the big oven. "I don't think he broke anything," his brother had said. But he was black and blue from his hip to his knee.

Jordy had been working up a sweat because there hadn't been any air conditioning in the bakery back then. It must have been over a hundred. The heat poured from the kitchen through the doorway into the front of the shop. It pounded at Jordy's back and his T-shirt stuck glued to the skin. Yet, when he looked over the counter at the little girl, it was just like diving into the cool waters of Garland's Pond. Jordy had never seen anyone quite as beautiful before, but then at ten he hadn't actually thought of beauty much. His attention focused on struggling to find a safe passage through the mine field of Harlan Farrow's anger, and of dragging his brother with him. Though Timmy was almost thirteen and bigger, stronger than Jordy, he didn't have as highly developed a streak of self-preservation and often blundered into their father's rage. Jordy suffered more for his brother than for himself and tried, as best he could, to draw Harlan's fire. He had his own collection of bruises—even a broken arm once—but they hurt less because some of them had been meant for Timmy.

That day, as he hustled, panting from the heat and the fear, he looked at the little girl who was Glory Crowell (whoever she might have been before), with her cloud of white blond hair, those violet eyes, and was stopped cold. Even now Jordy could recall vividly what he had thought: There's a whole other world out there.

Remembering that long-ago day started Jordy thinking about his brother. "I wonder where Tim is," he said, putting his arm around Glory and drawing her close. "He never wrote, not once, after he ran off. You'd think he would of sent a postcard or something. Just to let us know where he was and that he was okay." Still, after so much time, the memory of Timmy caused a knot of anguish to unfurl in his throat. "Ma's never been the same since Timmy up and went off in the middle of the night."

"Maybe he joined the army and has been traveling around the world ever since. The army has bases just about everywhere," Carol suggested hopefully. She had liked Timmy Farrow and even honored him with one of her fleeting schoolgirl crushes once. Not that Timmy had ever noticed. She reached out for the wine bottle, feeling the wave of Jordy's sadness like a chill wind. "Don't you think Timmy might come home one day, Glory, bringing presents from all those strange places he's been?" Glory nodded her head. "See, Jordy," she said, "even Glory thinks so. It's not impossible."

"Yeah, neither is taking a space ship to Mars," Jordy snapped back at her, for he'd given up believing long ago that some afternoon when he got home from delivering and sorted through the mail there would be a postcard from Timmy. Palm trees and dancing girls. Big waves coming into a white sandy beach. *I'm fine and doing okay. Feeling good and happy. Wish you were here.* Still there were times as he'd drive into the yard, when he'd think, why shouldn't there be a message from Timmy? Some word. But it had been almost ten years now.

Glory said with her fingers, *We should go.*

"Guess so," Jordy agreed, scrambling into the driver's seat. "Com'on Glory, get up beside me. Bobby, be sure to remember and sit back and not try to stand up again."

"That was my fault. I was daydreaming and forgot to watch him," Carol said.

"Won't stand," Bobby promised, nodding his head and sending hair over his eyes.

Carol pushed Bobby's hair back from his face and clucked. "You need another trim. Tomorrow when things are slack at the Public I'll remind you to go down to the barber's, okay?"

"Okay."

As Jordy swung the van into a wide U-turn, Glory settled against his shoulder. Beyond the rolled-down side window, the woods and fields passed darkly as they headed back into New Morning.

At the town hall the windows shone with yellow rectangles of light; Brewster Street was still hosting a crowd of parked cars lined end to end.

"Wow! That must be some meeting." Carol crawled half over the front seat and craned her neck. "Wonder what the fight's about this month."

"Who says there's a fight?" Jordy asked, slowing.

Carol laughed. "Com'on. Normal meetings are just like cat brawls, but when they go this late . . . wow! Hey, guys, let me off here. I want to find my folks and see what's up. You can drop Bobby, too. It's only a couple of blocks to his house. You'll make it home okay, won't you, Bobby?"

"I'm no baby!" he protested, clamoring after Carol out the back of the van. "I deliver everywhere, don't I?"

"Sure you do, sport," Jordy called around, "but you're not delivering now. Straight home and no wandering in somebody's yard." Bobby, lifting his feet high, stalked off into the puddles of streetlamp light.

Carol went around to the driver's side. "Why don't you two come with me? Might be better than that awful movie we saw. God! I've seen enough green slime to last me through my next incarnation. You can pull into Mr. Wayne's alleyway. He won't mind. Besides, he's probably at the meeting."

"Glory?"

She raised her shoulders in a shrug that meant, why not? "Okay, Carol. Wait on the corner for us.

Carol Boardman was right. The New Morning monthly town meeting had taken a sharp swing from the usual bickering and orbited off into chaos where it had been stalled for almost an hour.

About the only issue that got resolved smoothly was naming Alastair Old Home Week chairman. After the requisite murmur of regret for Fred Daniels's ill health, Charlie had thrown Alastair's name out, and within minutes *that* motion was passed. Sure, Alastair couldn't help thinking sourly, use me again. No considering that I might be tiring, running down after so many years. But he also found he was touched and a little bit flattered that the town simply assumed old Alastair Wayne was the man for a crisis, the one person who could put things right.

Vera Dickson, who clerked for Aaron Stein at the bookstore, had the floor and was stuttering. It took a while for Alastair to figure out what Vera wanted, but gradually it became plain that Vera was proposing the sidewalk sale be held Friday as well as the customary Saturday. However, since Friday was traditionally sports day, with a baseball game at the high-school field and swim events over at Garland's Pond, Vera Dickson flailed around to no avail. The willowy spinster in her Sears polyester two-piece dress looked ready to collapse like a Japanese fan. Taking pity on her, Alastair grabbed the gavel from Howie, who seemed to be off in his own daydream somewhere, rapped it sharply on the table, and got a sudden quiet in return.

"Sorry, Vera, I'm voting you down," Alastair said, not unkindly, as the woman sank with an audible sigh of relief to her seat. "We always do sports on Friday as everybody knows, and there's no reason to change this year." As the meeting resumed, he glanced across the room toward the door at the back. And so he was the first person to see Lucas Donnelly enter the hall.

There was an oblong of darkness and then the tall, broad-shouldered stranger appeared, framed in the doorway. His curly head almost brushed the top of the jamb and he smiled to display flashing teeth. Dressed in a white suit with a white shirt and, as if that wasn't glowing enough, a white tie, he reminded Alastair—except for the black ringlets—of Mr. Clean.

In less than a second everyone at the meeting was aware that Lucas Donnelly had arrived. Silence greeted his entrance until Charlie Calman burst off his chair at the side of the hall where he'd been taking notes for the *Eagle*. "Mr. Donnelly, what a pleasure to have you join us!"

Magically, like the Red Sea parting, a passage opened for Lucas Donnelly to the front where he proceeded in a triumphant march. The big man nodded and smiled, shaking a hand here, tapping a shoulder there, as if he were running for election. How does he know so many people? Alastair couldn't help wondering. He's been in town only a little more than a week, and never out of Emma's house, except maybe that afternoon in the square playing tourist at Ebenezer's grave.

"You all know Mr. Donnelly," Charlie said, preening like a talk-show host introducing a star, "the new owner of the Tydings house, which he fixed over so beautifully Emma would be proud."

"It was nothing, nothing at all." The stranger grinned, more abashedly now, ducking his serpentine locks and shrugging those massive shoulders. Too humble by half, Alastair thought, sucking his cheeks. He had a sour taste on his teeth as though he'd bitten into a lemon. But he seemed to be the only one at the meeting who wasn't beaming idiotically, primping and fussing, even the men, even farmer Bailey Cross who normally revealed less emotion than an isopod. Bailey was tugging his collar, shoving out a callused paw to have it swallowed by one manicured Donnelly hand and clasped with the other, muttering a "Pleased, I'm sure."

"Reverend Austin, Mr. Crowell, Mr. Eumis . . ." Lucas Donnelly had all their names, as he greeted each individual along the table. "Ah, Mr. Wayne, this is a pleasure, truly it is!" The hand Alastair was forced to shake was cool, almost chilly, and he yanked away none too politely from the stranger's touch. Like stroking a snake's belly, he thought, hissing through his nose, glaring, but managing a brief grunt of hello. Lucas Donnelly's charm oozed in an oil slick, but Alastair was curiously unaffected. On the contrary, his muscles tensed and he felt threatened as though Donnelly's charm was adhesive, that if he allowed it to lap over him he'd be glued fast, as the others seemed already to be. Alastair noticed that the stranger's eyes were so dark the irises and pupils merged in inky pools. Then the hand released him and Lucas Donnelly moved on.

All the Old Home Week arguments became ancient history though Lucas Donnelly urged that the meeting continue, that he'd sit quietly at the end of the first row and just listen. Then, when they were finished, he had one or two little things he wanted to say.

Howie Eumis had perked up and was enacting his role as council president in earnest now. He tapped the gavel neatly, though it was so quiet in the meeting hall the proverbial pin could have dropped and resounded with the thud of an exploding grenade. "You have the floor, Mr. Donnelly," Howie said.

"First of all, I want you to know how delighted I am to be settling in your midst. How perfect New Morning is! In the whole world, it is the only place I choose to be." He spread his arms wide, preacher fashion, and swooped them in, as if he was gathering up the whole group of attentive residents—the women, even Vera Dickson, who was now in high flutter—like a gaggle of geese. At Alastair's elbow Howie Eumis emitted a long sigh.

Alastair groaned, closing his eyes, only to be jolted into alertness by Lucas Donnelly saying, ". . . And I will donate the necessary funds." *For what?* he scribbled on a notepad and shoved it toward Simon. It took a second for Simon to shift his attention away from Donnelly. Finally, he whispered, "The Barnes."

The Barnes! Was this stranger going to pay to have the library restored? Impossible! Alastair fumed, recalling that in the last election a bond issue to do just that had been voted down overwhelmingly. Too much money, the voters had complained en masse.

"Whatever it costs," Lucas Donnelly was saying.

Who is he, Rockefeller? Alastair knew a hundred thousand dollars could be sunk into the Barnes without leaving a trace. "Get the blank check before he comes to his senses," he hissed to Howie, but his comment was drowned in a clatter of applause.

The stranger, apparently a cross between Santa Claus and the good fairy, was toothy with pleasure, striding back and forth in front of the table where no one, it seemed, was sitting in judgment but Alastair. Though he loved the Barnes as much as the next person and even had read most of its books, Alastair was discomforted by all this largesse. *Beware of Greeks*, he thought, while at the same time trying to subdue his doubts.

Lucas Donnelly wasn't ready to sit down. He continued to hold the floor with yet another promise, this one concerning the grounds of the Barnes. Reseeded, planted, bushed, and flowered up, he was telling the meeting. "A contract which, in the spirit of New Morning, I'm sure you'll all want to go to Moses Llewelyn." No one was going to dispute any suggestion Lucas Donnelly offered though everyone knew Moses was notoriously bad with flowers.

Maybe if Lucas Donnelly, as cool and fresh as an Italian ice, had stopped with the Barnes, apprehension wouldn't have been dancing a tango down Alastair's spine. After all, such munificence might have been motivated by a lopsided tax situation, and better New Morning than the IRS. But Lucas

Donnelly wanted to fill up the cracks in every New Morning sidewalk as well as recobbling the back streets from Brewster on. He offered to have the elms on Rowly that the blight had hit so badly the year before chopped down. And even then his bag of goddies wasn't empty, because he was donating a traffic light out by the high school. New benches in the square . . . painting the town hall . . . a second police car in case the town's single black-and-white had to go into the garage, as it often did. After a while Alastair lost track of all the stranger's promises. He grew weary, as if he'd been watching a game of shells and trying to keep the pea in sight. Theo Crowell, however, was writing everything down, as was Charlie. Will Austin started making notes when Lucas Donnelly threw in a new roof for the church. Doc Trump got a wing for the hospital and Alastair felt like throwing up. He seemed to be the only one at the meeting who wasn't as excited as an orphan meeting Daddy Warbucks on Christmas morning. Nothing for nothing, Alastair knew in his bones. What was the stranger going to want in return? What, for that matter, could New Morning offer that Lucas Donnelly didn't already have in spades?

Once Lucas Donnelly had run out of gifts to shower on the town, there was no getting back to such an ordinary matter as Old Home Week.

With a hasty motion the meeting was brought to an abrupt close. Like iron filings to a magnet, there was a landslide of bodies forward. Lucas Donnelly had stood up and there was Charlie tight on one flank. Evelyn elbowed Ava Trump aside to claim the other and her eyes glowed. In a pack, the council abandoned the table to cluster about New Morning's benefactor who topped even Theo Crowell by a good couple of inches.

Geese! Alastair thought, but then he too rolled down the ramp. "Your Mr. Donnelly could get elected God right this minute, unanimously too, if somebody'd put his name into nomination," he said acerbically to Dee who had suddenly appeared by his chair. It came to him fleetingly that he hadn't noticed her before, but with all the hoopla a pink elephant mightn't have been obvious.

"He's not *mine*, and you're not funny, Alastair."

"I've just got a New Englander's suspicion of too much generosity," he said. "Not that I'm turning down any of his offers—"

"You'd be stoned to death if you tried!" She laughed, *caw, caw*, as if something had caught in her throat.

"It's such a lovely town," Lucas Donnelly was intoning to his rapt admirers. "Quite perfect in its way. Still small and not yet bludgeoned by tourists with their knickknacks, gift shops and ice-cream stores . . . all those horrible pizza stands." He shuddered, and the crowd shuddered with him, the sisters of The Gallery, particularly Francesca, bobbing her curls. Alastair wanted to remind somebody—though who would listen?—that Gino's Pizza was standing room only on Saturday nights. "Not so many weekenders either. It does need work, of course, particularly that glorious old library of yours. I don't know"—he shook his head in disapproval—"it's just been let go so badly."

Stung, Alastair cried out at last. "Do you know what it'll cost to fix the Barnes up? We had to put in a new gym for the high school, and then buy another fire truck to replace that old relic we had. Money, sir, all those expenditures cost a great deal of money. Do you think New Morning is paved with gold?" The crowd had parted. Lucas Donnelly loomed over Alastair, who hunkered in the wheelchair.

"Now, now, Mr. Wayne," the stranger soothed, though his balm agitated Alastair even more, "don't worry about it another minute. I promised and I always keep my promises, you can rely on that. Everything will be taken care of." He smiled broadly, displaying those flashing white teeth.

Alastair started to shake, and one hand crept to the other holding it tightly captive in an effort to bring the tremors under control. "I still don't understand why it is you've come to New Morning," he snapped.

"You've lost your mind, this time I swear you have!" Charlie Calman had inserted himself between the two men, as though Lucas Donnelly needed protection from attack, while Alastair just gazed right over Charlie's balding head. But while he was considered persisting in his challenge, Dee gave him no choice. She grabbed the back of his chair and, whipping it around, rolled him to the rear of the room. "That's it," Charlie mumbled under his breath, "get him some coffee before Donnelly decides to move bag and baggage over to Monterrey."

"Really, Alastair, you have no sense," Dee chided above him, hovering, like a rain cloud.

"Why do you say that? Seems I've got more sense than the rest of these lemmings. Just because some city slicker turns up and promises us the moon doesn't mean I have to like him."

"If he give you the moon you still don't have to like him."
She sounded so strange that Alastair craned his neck to glare
up at her, but her chin was tilted, pug nose in the air. All he
could see was her neck, tight as a girl's, no drape to it. Dee's
too young looking for a woman of her age, he thought as he
often did.

Through the social half hour that always followed a meeting,
during which wounds could be stanched and bruises healed,
harsh words apologized for, and tempers cooled—a recupera-
tive period often necessary after the rough-and-tumble democratic process had taken place—Alastair kept back from Lucas
Donnelly. Not that he could have rolled within three feet of
the man without crushing somebody. Evelyn Crowell hung on
every word as if she were being kept from drowning.
Francesca of The Gallery stared adoringly at him and ignored a
sad-eyed Eva. Reverend Austin was blathering on about
liturgical music, a subject that seemed to interest Lucas
Donnelly. Maybe it was his imagination, more vivid lately, but
he thought that despite the attention that dripped like melted
butter, the stranger kept darting long, direct, and wondering
glances his way. As he sipped his coffee and crunched cookies,
he felt himself being impaled by Lucas Donnelly's stare.

At last, the crowd began to shed, people tearing themselves
loose—farmers first, like Bailey Cross, then Doc Trump with
an 8 A.M. gall bladder to remove. Doc had Ava's arm in a
viselike grip and was tugging her backward as her face flushed
and she squealed.

People started to drift outside. Alastair saw Carol Boardman
at the doorway as she called to her father and tunneled into the
hall. Behind Carol was Jordy, then Glory, her violet eyes wide.
She seemed startled, like a rabbit exposed suddenly to the
light. Always, the first glimpse of this girl, whom Alastair loved
as though she were his own child, sent his heart lurching
against his ribs.

Glory! He was about to summon her, to ask that she wheel
him home. His arms ached and lead ingots weighed on his
shoulders. He didn't think he had enough strength to move by
himself. There was Dee, of course, and Charlie who would
never leave him in the lurch no matter how angry he got with
Alastair. But he wanted Glory, he wanted her to play for him—
perhaps the Brahms—before he descended into sleep. As a
child wants his mother, he realized with an acute tremor of
embarrassment. And at his age! And for a girl, no less, a child!

But Evelyn caught Glory before Alastair could, waving her
to the cluster of people by the coffee urn. Obediently Glory
slipped loose from Jordy whose face knotted as he watched her
go. Alastair watched her also, her blond hair flowing in a
stream of soft light.

"My daughter, Mr. Donnelly." Evelyn smirked, proud of
herself, proud of owning Glory whom she nudged in the small
of the back, inching her closer to Lucas Donnelly. Theo was
more reluctant, hanging behind, doubt smudging his face.

Lucas Donnelly seemed to straighten, grow even taller, and
in his whiteness he glowed incandescently. When he lifted
Glory's hand he took it all the way to his mouth, kissing first the
knuckles and then slowly turning it over and lingeringly
caressing the palm with his lips. As he watched, unable to shift
his eyes away, a wave of nausea rose from Alastair's bowels and
flowed up to his chest. He had to clench his teeth to keep from
being sick or crying out. No! he shrilled, and then prophetically: Damn you to hell, Lucas Donnelly!

7

The day after the town meeting New Morning hummed as
though electrified. The talk was of nothing but Lucas Donnelly
and his wondrous generosity. So popular was the newly arrived
Lucas Donnelly that if he emerged from Emma Tydings's
colonial for a stroll along Main Street, most of New Morning
would have sidled up to him for a few words, questions really.
But the stranger stayed hidden away, and as the days passed
without even a glimpse of him, more than one citizen felt
uneasy. What if it was all a hoax, the Barnes and the cobbled
streets, the traffic lights, the new benches for the green, never
mind Doc Trump's hospital? Then, on a Thursday afternoon,
Jarvis Badderly slipped from the big white house like a dark
shadow and flowed through the dazzling June sunlight over to
the council president's office and presented Howie Eumis with
a check.

"See, I told you it wasn't a dream. The man's good as his

word," Howie crowed when he called around to the council members, though he'd started to worry as much as anybody.

Alastair only snorted when he heard what Howie had to say. He almost suggested not counting chickens until Theo cleared Lucas Donnelly's check, but Howie had already hung up leaving Alastair with a dead line and an anxiety he couldn't pin anywhere. He settled in for a satisfying evening of J. S. Bach instead. But as he prepared for bed, he remembered Howie Eumis saying: *It wasn't a dream*. Which spun Alastair off into thinking about nightmares, and the fright that had assailed him a few days before. How come, he wondered, I've started dreaming about Omaha Beach after all these years? An aberration, he decided, and turned off the light.

Alastair might have made a conscious decision not to dream, but dream he did.

He found himself, dressed in everyday clothes, outside in the green, sitting on his usual bench, the crutches propped by his useless knees. The sun shone insistently, and Alastair, asleep, was limp from the heat.

As had happened before, in real life, Lucas Donnelly's limousine slithered into New Morning. But this time, the long black car stopped near the curb. Right then, even dreaming, Alastair knew he should leave, rise and totter off on his crutches. Only he couldn't. He was held fast by the car, by the men who climbed out on leaden feet from the darkness beyond the limo's rear door.

Captain Markowitz had only half a head. The whole left side was splintered fragments of bone, frayed edges of skin. The one brown eye remaining stared at Alastair.

Horse Keleidas was next, or what was left of his six-feet-four after Omaha. He walked on one leg, the other gone at the thigh. From the waist up he remained the identical Horse with his gummy smile, canary hair ruffling from the out-of-nowhere breeze. Alastair heard the familiar midwestern farmer's voice.

Behind Horse was Bill Wright, a bright poinsettia of red flowering on his chest. And then Whiskey Rubin holding his head in his khaki arms. Sergeant Breener was mapped in blood from stomach to groin. George Moran had no hands attached to his jutting wrist bones. And Major Morgan was as precise and pressed as he'd always been even in battle dress, except his face had been blown off. Where his eyes and nose and mouth should have been was a sponge of raw meat.

One after another the long dead unfolded from the black

embrace of the car and lined up at attention. Discounting their
wounds, missing limbs, ravaged and shredded flesh, they were
all as Alastair remembered. He cringed, stranded on his
bench, immobilized as much by grief as terror.

No matter how helpless the war had left him, they were
worse. They were underground, or should have been. Only
they seemed to have risen and come to New Morning in the
limousine. Now they stood silently beckoning to their old
comrade-at-arms. Alastair's sleeping body flamed with a need
to reach the men. It was a burning laceration, and in his hurry
to rise, he tripped, sprawling on the path, gasping for breath.

The very air was on fire. His heart was pounding furiously
when he lifted his head. As he struggled to gain his feet, to be
once more rushing toward them on ruined legs, the men
blurred, fragmented.

Oh, why did you all die, he wept as he grabbed a crutch and
tried to anchor it so that he could pull himself up. The rubber
tip skidded and he fell back. No matter how much energy he
exerted, nor how much will, or again, how fueled by anger at
his helplessness, still he was unable to rise.

Alastair beat his fists on the hard-packed earth. Mysteriously
it seemed to soften, the brown earth turning to the cold blue-
gray of the English Channel, the water rising over him.

Alastair, awakening from the nightmare, found himself on
the bedroom floor. He lay twisted in a painful angle upon the
Oriental rug a traveling Wayne had brought home from the
Far East.

The men had vanished. Tears lingered in Alastair's eyes.
Shuffling to the bed, he levered himself up. Something
irretrievable had slipped out of his grasp there in the dream,
and he lay back anguished.

I should have died then, he thought, the forty-year guilt
surfacing, belly-up like a dead fish.

But you didn't . . . didn't . . . didn't . . . his inner
voice metronomed through the rest of the night, not that
Alastair found that much comfort at all.

There's nothing quite so frightening as a bad dream, for the
worst such terrors have the punch of reality. Strangely enough,
Carol Boardman was trying to make Bobby Pierson understand just that in the Public the next morning when he arrived
for work as white as a sheet.

"Wasn't a dream," Bobby stubbornly insisted for the third or fourth time. "Was real like . . . real like"—he stumbled, then lifted his hand and swept it in a wide arc around the market—"*now!*"

Bobby Pierson, who was addicted to peeking into New Morning windows, was just as obsessive in refusing to admit it. He stonewalled, in his dim-witted way, any attempt to force him to admit his Peeping Tom activities. But today he was eager to tell Carol Boardman what he had viewed.

The story Bobby related had him on his usual ramble peering beneath Miss Emma's drawn shades. Only Miss Emma had died over six months before and her house belonged to the stranger. It was through *his* windows that Bobby Pierson saw flames. The whole living room blazed in tall columns of fire as the stranger sat in his rocker, puffing a long black cigar and watching Bobby watch him.

"Miss Emma's all burning, 'cept for that guy inside." Bobby sniffed, starting to shake as he'd done when, hunkering down in the bushes, he found himself unable to rise. The man wouldn't let him, holding Bobby to his peeping with dark, unblinking eyes. He'd been staked to the ground for hours, the room on fire, but nothing incinerating away. The flames burned hot and steady, like logs in a fireplace, until Bobby swooned, as much from the heat beating against the closed window and filtering through the glass, as from fright.

"A bad dream," Carol insisted again, not knowing what else to say.

"No! No!" Bobby puffed up his cheeks, his face turning magenta. "Real!"

"Most dreams seem real," Carol said. "But the Tydings house never burnt down, did it? See"—she pushed him toward the door—"isn't that the top of it through the trees? If it had caught fire it wouldn't be there right now," she soothed, trying to reason him out of his fear. But Bobby clung obstinately to his conviction, and for the rest of the day he was so unnerved that he stayed close to the Public except for deliveries.

It was funny, Carol kept thinking as customers came and went, that both of us should have bad dreams the same night.

At breakfast when her mother had put a mound of pancakes glistening with honey in front of her, she'd pushed the plate aside too queasy to eat. Surprised, Mrs. Boardman had said,

"What's the matter with you?" Then Carol had almost blurted out the nightmare, but didn't.

There was a '78 Toyota Corolla, identical to her brother Jack's, coming around Madder's Hill much too fast. As the speeding car hit the bend of Dead Man's Curve, it went straight instead of left, taking a long header out into emptiness. For an unbelievable moment it sailed like a kite before it crashed to the valley below, igniting on impact with one explosive burst of flame.

All day, the nightmare stayed vivid and frightening, until Carol decided to share it with Glory when the Public closed.

Tell him to get the brakes checked, Glory advised, when she and Carol were seated in Glory's bedroom.

"I guess you're right. I mean, I can't say, 'Listen, Bro, I had this absolutely awful dream of you going off Dead Man's Curve.' He'd laugh his dumb head off. But it was just such a bad dream, Glory, you know what I mean?"

Glory nodded, listening to Carol and doodling on the tablet. Under the tip of the ballpoint a tiny sailboat took shape and rode calmly on an inky sea. Glory shoved the tablet to the floor and abruptly slid off the bed, waving her fingers.

"What?" Carol concentrated. "Oh yeah, I'll stay for supper if it's okay with your mom."

Carol was glad she stayed, because while Mr. Crowell was quiet, heavy-lidded, brooding, she supposed, about affairs at the bank, Glory's mother kept talking—though she hadn't two words for any subject except Lucas Donnelly—and that stopped Carol from thinking about her bad dream.

"Your mom's really cuckoo about the stranger," Carol said later as she was leaving. A shadow flitted over Glory's face, but she simply shrugged. "Yeah," Carol agreed, "I know, mothers are a drag." She tied her sweater around her shoulders and stepped out into the night. It was just then that they heard the rat-ta-tat-tat of the horn, immediately followed by the squealing brakes and the screech. Carol craned her neck for a glimpse of the speeding Toyota. "If Jack's going to drive like that I will tell him to get his brakes checked, and up his if he tells me I should mind my own business." Swooping suddenly to plant a light kiss on Glory's cool, alabaster cheek, Carol smiled. "Thanks for listening to my worries about old Jack." And with a wave she was off.

Don't dream, Glory would have called after her friend, moving out of the splash the porch light threw, if she were able

to translate the thought into sound. Don't dream . . .
because there was something about dreaming, Glory sensed,
but she didn't know what. She too had been restless during the
last several nights, buffeted by frights, though none as vivid as
Carol's. Glory's dreams had to do with water, patches of open,
endless blue. A sea somewhere and a boat, the skeletal
instability of a dock, though not the one where she'd come to,
walking between Theo and Evelyn in a jet of melting sunlight.
Somewhere else, a different marina, maybe the one from
before. . . .

Glory wanted to remember, yearned to retrieve that part of
herself that had sunk into memory and lain hidden like buried
bones, but she didn't like the dreaming. She was as scared of
her water dream as Carol was of Jack's flying Toyota.

"Why don't you play for us, Princess?" Theo asked, when
she had shut the door and returned to the living room.

Glory mouthed a silent *no*. She didn't feel like music. She
didn't want to see Jordy either, and when he called ten
minutes later, she had Theo say she was going to bed early, a
message Theo—not displeased—relayed.

"I think she's coming to her senses, finally," Evelyn said after
Theo had hung up the phone. "Realizing that there's more in
life than a baker's son. Especially now, after the town
meeting . . ." she added.

"After the meeting, what?" Theo lowered *Business Week*
just enough to peer over the top.

"Really, Theo! Don't be so dense. You were there and saw
what happened just as I did, as everyone did. How Lucas
Donnelly was charmed by Glory. I mean, kissing her hand that
way, and just staring at her!" Evelyn smiled remembering,
once more hearing the whispers of envy from the other
women.

"He's a good twenty, twenty-five years older than Glory,"
Theo protested, but mildly. He'd learned to tiptoe carefully
with his wife when her mind was set.

"Older men make the best husbands," Evelyn pronounced,
ignoring the fact that she and Theo were only a year apart in
age.

Unrolling the Crowell family tree on the coffee table, she
began to outline Jonah Crowell's descendants in red, oblivious
to Theo's glare of annoyance. No matter how much he
objected, Evelyn was going to hang it on the wall. One should
take pride in one's heritage.

But they're not yours, the voice she could never quite suppress snickered in her head. *Glory's children won't be either*.

Evelyn's hand swerved so sharply a trail of red jutted off course. "Damn!" she cried.

Theo crinkled his paper. "I wish you'd give up this nonsense."

Carefully covering over the offensive streak with Wite-Out, Evelyn replied, "You have got to stop acting like some poor immigrant without any past to speak of."

Theo sighed. "Not that silliness, this other business with Donnelly and Glory." Evelyn arched her brows in innocence, but he hurried on, "Oh no, don't play dumb with me because I know you've got the wedding all planned. Probably named the babies, as well. I simply don't understand this rush you're in to do something about Glory. Settle her some place. Why can't she stay home with us where she belongs?"

Evelyn was torn between wanting to yell at her husband to stop being a donkey, to grow up!—Grow up! was what you always screamed at people whose behavior disconcerted you— or go perch on the arm of his chair and soothe him. The truth was that, in her way, she loved Theo. And so she replied evenly, "It really isn't good for my back to bend over like this. I think I better move everything onto the dining-room table."

She wasn't going to discuss Glory with Theo any more tonight. His Victorian protectiveness kept him locked to a single point of view, as stuck as the hands of the clock tower, committed to ten past the hour of three and unable to change. Still, settling at the table, Evelyn was certain she'd eventually get her way. After all, she always had before.

Jordy Farrow lay in his bed unable to sleep. It was a warm, soggy night. When the last shimmer of dusk had crowned Madder's Hill and seeped away, the heat remained. The sky purpled, then deepened to a velvety black where the stars sparkled in tiny quarter carat chips and the temperature barely dropped. No wind curried across the valley and ruffled the New Morning elms. And the air, especially toward the edge of town where the bakery and the Farrow house were, was gelatinous.

As he lay naked under the sheet, his muscles tense as steel

cables, Jordy's memory yanked him back to the rear of the bakery around five in the afternoon. He'd been over by the ovens where Harlan had grabbed Beryl, one of the two hired girls, and sandwiched her into a narrow corner. Beryl's boyish, breastless body, a construction fragile as chicken bones, dangled, sneakers frantic to find the floor as she hung suspended in space from Harlan's hands.

Beryl purpled in Harlan's grip. Her eyes threatened to pop loose. Once again the scream rode up Jordy's throat and he almost let it out now in the darkened bedroom. *Pa, you're going to kill her if you don't let go!*

Jordy had pried Harlan's fingers free and watched as Beryl dropped in a sprawl on the bakery floor. What came next Jordy just downright refused to see again, struggling against the unwanted memory of Harlan's kick to Beryl's ribs. His father's foot had shot forward, producing a loud and definite crack when it connected with Beryl's bones. Jordy thrust the image and the sickening sound of bone snapping out of his mind. With a tremendous effort he pushed himself through the early mist of sleep, down to the dark silent depths where at last he escaped the one image from those terrible few moments in the afternoon that with all his heart he didn't want to recall. When it had seemed more than likely, indeed was a hair from being certain, that Harlan was about to strangle Beryl to death, Jordy had seen not the hired girl's tortured face but his brother Timmy instead. By some quirk he'd never be able to explain, it was Timmy swinging up in the air, and the veins in his brother's eyes had popped. Timmy, as Jordy watched in horror, had cried blood.

8

"No grass grows under his Adidases, I will say that," Doc Trump was saying to Alastair. From where they were sitting companionably in Doc's private office, Doc in the high-back leather swivel behind the desk, Alastair in the lower, less comfortable patient's chair, they could see the behemoth construction trucks rumbling by on High Street.

Doc scratched what tufts of hair still grew like baby grass on his head, and sighed. "I suppose every blessing is mixed. We've got to be thankful to this Donnelly fellow, no doubt about it, for picking up the slack, redoing the Barnes and all the rest of it, in particular that new hospital wing he's building for me." Doc was as happy as a chicken in a feed store. It was almost possible to see the dream take shape in the still office air as Doc dreamed it. Only then, being Doc, he had to point out the downside, too. "But the noise, the inconvenience! You know, I waited twenty minutes at the light by the White Bear yesterday. Regular traffic jam." He shifted his attention from the window to Alastair who sat hunched like a crab. "Your blood pressure's up!" he complained peevishly, a frown sliding down his face.

Alastair was having a bad morning. His regular six-month checkup would have occurred at three-month intervals if Doc had his way. Doc was less than delicate in his examinations, and Alastair had emerged sore and achy. Now he shifted in his chair, stung with guilt that his blood pressure had climbed. "Haven't been sleeping too well," he mumbled, staring off into a corner so he wouldn't have to meet Doc's eyes.

"Why haven't you told me!" Doc cried. He poked the wire-rims perched on the tip of his nose to the bridge and snapped, "A doctor's like a priest, Alastair. You're supposed to confess everything!" Doc stewed, as if Alastair's insomnia was a personal affront. "It might be the weather, or maybe your age, but whatever, I don't like it, Alastair, damn it, I don't."

Alastair wasn't wild about not sleeping long and dreamlessly either. He coughed when Doc lapsed into a sulky silence and mumbled, "There's probably some reason, but I doubt it means much."

Doc bristled. "There's always some reason. Nothing happens haphazardly, at least not in the world of science." He shook his head so emphatically his wire-rims whipped off-center and he had to straighten them out. "And you're not the type for psychosomatic symptoms." He grabbed his prescription pad and began to scribble in his illegible handwriting. "Here, have the drugstore fill this for you. Take one about twenty minutes to a half hour before bed. See if it helps."

"Sleeping pills!" Alastair barked.

"Well, what do you think, gumdrops?" Doc waved the prescription at Alastair. "Com'on, Alastair, don't be a fool. They're mild as mother's milk. Only to take the edge off."

"Doc . . ."

"Don't 'Doc' me. With your heart at the gallop you need all the rest you can get. And I want you back here in two weeks."

Though he was accustomed to being strong-armed by Doc Trump, who gruffly bullied all of his patients out of love and the fear that they'd die on him, Alastair equivocated. "I don't enjoy being treated like an old man."

"You *are* an old man. And it's my job to see that you get older. So do as I tell you." Reluctantly Alastair accepted the prescription and tucked it into the pocket of his shirt. "That's better. And give me a call in a couple of days to let me know if they help." But Alastair didn't look convinced. It was only after he was back in the wheelchair and puttering out onto the walkway along the side of the office that he thought maybe it was foolish not telling Doc about the dreams of Omaha Beach.

The heat was drenching, and a shaft of light flashing through a break in the High Street elms sparked the arm of the chair. Alastair's fingers stung when he touched the sizzling metal. The frustration he'd felt in Doc's office transformed into anger. He straightened from his slouch, deciding that neither heat nor bad dreams would keep him away from the green.

All the benches sat empty. Nobody but a mad dog would be out in this heat and the town drooped in the brilliant white light. The traffic, nothing more serious than a few cars, crawled sluggishly. Most people, Alastair thought, had probably hightailed it out to Garland's Pond.

It was too sizzling and close for Alastair to keep from slumping. His eyelids fluttered and he slid into a light doze.

There were things he should have been doing, not the least of which was routing out Dee. Her phone didn't get answered, no matter how many times he'd let it ring, and he hadn't seen her around. Once a day, if he was out of his house, he'd run into Dee somewhere. Only not lately. The last time he'd seen her was at the town meeting where she had groused at him, thinking he was a fool for being testy about Lucas Donnelly's generosity.

He supposed later it was because he was lightly snoozing that he wasn't aware of the man's approach. Unlike so many older people, Alastair's hearing was acute. But now, before he realized it had happened, Lucas Donnelly was ensconced on the nearest bench. Dressed in his usual white, without so much as a wrinkle or a smudge of dust, he exposed himself to the sun without apparent concern. It needled Alastair that Lucas Donnelly didn't seem fazed by the heat. The man looked almost chilly.

"Ah, Mr. Wayne, lovely day, isn't it," he chimed in his lusty baritone when Alastair could no longer feign sleep. "Though perhaps a bit hot for a man of your frail constitution to be outside?"

It seemed a polite inquiry, solicitous even, but Alastair leaped as though he'd been broadsided by a large, scaly claw. He fairly yelled, "Sturdy, healthy as an ox!" Thinking, what business was it of Lucas Donnelly's, the condition of his health? But though he tried to ignore it, his heart was pumping overtime. He feared it would explode.

"Well, I am just delighted to hear that, Mr. Wayne, absolutely delighted," Lucas Donnelly chimed again, blow-torching Alastair with his smile.

Alastair had an infernal urge to simply roll right off on the man. I'll drop by Dee's, he thought, glancing surreptitiously toward her house. Maybe invite her to dinner.

"I make it a point to be on friendly terms with my neighbors. And so few of us, Mr. Wayne, do live right on the square. Do you realize your house and mine face each other directly?" He was so earnest that Alastair, relaxing his military posture, settled back and winced. He was trapped on the green which had grown hotter yet. Even the grass steamed. To leave the stranger would be to give offense.

Snapping his words, Alastair said, "That is true, Mr. Donnelly, but the New Morning square seems a strange place for a man of your obvious accomplishments. Why have you come to New Morning, if you don't mind my asking?" And the hell with it if you do, Alastair couldn't help thinking. He was making an effort to be affable, but the truth was, he didn't like the man. For no reason, he thought, as Lucas Donnelly crossed his legs and continued with that smile of his.

"I am passionate for things New England, and as I said at the town meeting, New Morning is simply the right place to settle down. Right for me, that is."

"There's a whole lot of New England besides New Morning," Alastair rejoined, attempting a smile of his own. But what unrolled on his face he sensed was more like his response to Doc jabbing a needle in his behind.

Either Lucas Donnelly had the hide of a rhino or he was determined, as he said, to get on with the neighbors. Not one hair of his curly head fell out of place as he quickly replied, "But I like it *here*."

Too perfect, too perfect by half, Alastair thought, narrowing his eyes. A flesh and blood version of Michelangelo's David. "New Morning's not for you," he spat out, "Why not get into your limo, Mr. Donnelly, and go save some other town from wrack and ruin?" The whole town will have my scalp, Alastair thought with a shudder, suddenly appalled by his rudeness.

The stranger, however, simply laughed, a rich crackle like dry wood on a fire. "Just move on to Great Barrington or somewhere smaller, like Monterrey?" He appeared impervious to Alastair's surliness, and Alastair almost regretted what he had said. Still, for no apparent reason, he wished Lucas Donnelly away.

Quieter now, Alastair sighed. "New Morning's only a village, Mr. Donnelly. Bigger than some, smaller than most. People get themselves born here, grow up, go to school, work, marry, have children, and, if they're lucky, wander into old age—" *like me!* "And die." *Not yet!* "The cycle of life's so different from anywhere else." He felt the glare of those dark, smoldering eyes and turned aside. "There's been Waynes here from almost the beginning, you know," he added.

"Oh yes, I do know. I've studied up on New Morning history."

"Have you now." Even this interest grated on Alastair like sandpaper. Inwardly he shriveled, wondering if there was anything this man, who appeared so sociable and at ease, could do that wouldn't set his teeth on edge.

The heat was so stifling the air seared up Alastair's nostrils and fired down his throat when he took a breath. Sweat rivered along his spine, pooling under his skinny shanks. His eyes felt heavy in his skull, and Alastair was having trouble staying alert.

Like a buzz saw spinning in the distance, he could hear Lucas Donnelly saying, "I hope to rest, to put my feet up. Though not all the time. I still have rather formidable responsibilities which can't just be thrown to the wind." Alastair, starting to doze again, caught ". . . computers . . . new walls . . . a first-rate humidifying system . . . rewiring for added usage . . ."

What could the man mean? He tried to ask what it was Donnelly did for a living, but the words were lodged in the cotton-candy stickiness of a dream. He struggled to cry, to

awaken from this unwanted attack of sleep. But he was
sandbagged by weariness, all his energy draining away with his
sweat. His last conscious memory was of Lucas Donnelly
leaning close, and as he did, of a great cloud of steam churning
out of all that whiteness and swallowing both of them.

The heat had scourged channels in his bones, and he came
to panting like a dog in need of a good drink. His eyelids flew
up like snapped window blinds and he twitched his nose. One
good sneeze cleared all his passages, and he suddenly remembered Lucas Donnelly, cool as an icicle, sitting next to him on
the bench.

The man was nowhere around. Alastair rolled a short way
down to the center of the green where the meandering paths
met like spokes in a wheel. Still, no Lucas Donnelly. Well,
what do I care, he thought.

Suddenly remembering his intention to rout out Dee, he
angled off toward her house. New Morning continued sleeping, shimmering under the lapping waves of heat as though
immersed in water. Something squawked in the leafy umbrella
that arched greenly over his head, but there was no bird
visible when he looked up. Glancing around hesitantly,
Alastair half expected another dead bird to plummet to the
ground before his chair, then wondered if in fact there had
really been a dead bird. When he'd sent Mrs. O'Brien to
dispose of the small feathered corpse midway down his front
lawn, that bird was gone. Lately real life in New Morning
seemed flimsy.

In front of Dee's he shifted into high and chugged up the tilt
of the drive. The Porsche wasn't outside, but the double doors
of the garage were closed.

Around the back he banged on the screen, hollering her
name. Beyond, the kitchen was empty, unused, a model
kitchen from a magazine. Above the refrigerator the moon-
faced clock was ticking, he could tell by the lurch of the red
minute hand. But everything else was motionless, battered in
gloom, for the light seemed to stop at the windows. Never
noticed how dark this house is, Alastair thought as he backed
out of the shade.

He was even grumpier and more out of sorts than he'd been
when he awakened in the square. Again marooned on the

High Street sidewalk, he waffled, not certain where to go. There were any number of people he could drop in on, places he could wander to. But he was on the wrong edge of the green now, for the drugstore, too.

Maybe tonight sleep would be even, unfurrowed with dreams and he could forget the pills. But it wasn't likely; still, he rode the wheelchair in the opposite direction, toward home.

Upstairs in her bedroom Dee Whittier lay on a white silk upholstered chaise and listened to Alastair below knocking and yelling, just as she had suffered through the incessant shrilling of the telephone. She hadn't answered the phone, nor was she about to trail downstairs in her caftan and open the door and let him in. Sooner or later she would see him, but not right now. The pounding continued, and she swore, *damn it, Alastair, give up!*

The ormolu ashtray was overflowing. It offended her sense of perfection, but she hadn't the energy to dump the cigarette stubs and ashes into the trash. Dee shifted away from this flaw in the artful composition and gazed about the rest of the lovely room she had arranged for herself, trying to ignite the pleasure she usually found. But all she saw were twisted bodies on the pale satin bedspread and heaped on the thick blue rug, the dead, meticulously arranged, brown skins sooty and lined with inky pen strokes of blood.

It was Africa, the massacre along the Lualaba River that Kurm, a fat shiny colonel, Buddha-like in his impassivity except for mad-dog eyes, had engineered in order to quell it. Praised by the people as well as lauded in the foreign press, Kurm had won an army then a nation for such deviltry.

Dee, in central Africa on assignment for *Newsweek*, had photographed the rubbishy remains. Emaciated bodies with roseate curls of entrails dragged in the muck, hacked limbs with projecting shoots of polished ivory bones, dark heads squashed like overripe plums. She wanted to be sick, but couldn't, too coldly dispassionate really to care. Of course she didn't cry either, for she hadn't wept, not once, since Barcelona.

Kurm. She had taken his picture too, and had him still on a negative somewhere. He had been smiling—well, why shouldn't he?—yellow spangles of gold like buried nuggets glittering in his mouth.

She groaned, shivered from a chill that unfurled in her chest. It was too warm, even with the air conditioning humming on high in the window, to feel so cold. She slipped her hands up the wide sleeves of the caftan and rubbed the goose-pimpled arms. Her arms had no slippage of skin to pinch. Young arms, a girl's, and she knew that if she rose and studied her face in the mirror above the dresser, that flesh would be young, too. No smudges or pouches shelved beneath her lids, no webbing of wrinkles on her cheeks. Her lips were plump, soft, not striated with thin lines as old women's were. Lipstick blotched on the mouths of women as old as she was. There was always something new being advertised for that telltale sign of age. Only Dee didn't need it; she never would.

Alastair had finally ceased his banging and it was when silence filled the house at last that Dee realized the dull thump-thumping had resounded in her head like the flat pulsing of one of Kurm's tribal drums. She pressed her fingers to her temples just as the phone rang. It couldn't be Alastair, and without thinking she lifted the receiver.

"Dee, darling, I called to see if you'd thought over what we talked about."

She couldn't identify the voice that crinkled like cellophane. "Who is this?"

"Why, it's Francesca, Dee. You do remember, don't you, dear, how we discussed your doing an exhibition for The Gallery? Something energetic to hang during Old Home Week. Such a wonderful idea, I'm really so proud of myself for thinking of it. Just imagine what a *civilized* tone your pictures would give to what I for one, well, consider rather hokey proceedings. So small-townish, this fuss with fireworks and parades."

"New Morning is a small town," Dee interjected icily.

Francesca ran on without listening. "It would be a very profitable exhibition, too. Why I know we'd sell every single picture."

Dee sat up, and cradling the phone against her shoulder, lit a cigarette. The smoke burned in her mouth, tasting of charcoal. Lucas Donnelly's little black stogies smelt sulfuric, she thought, wincing, as Francesca continued to babble. "It would be such a cultural event . . ."

Through the window Dee saw Moses' truck pull up. He

lumbered out and stood inspecting the flower beds at the edge of the yard.

"Dee! Dee! Are you still there?"

"Listen, I've never taken a civilized picture in my life, and there's nothing cultural about a bunch of photographs hanging on the wall. And," she hurried on breathlessly, framing in her mind's eye Moses Llewelyn as he stooped to his knees, admiring the curve of his back, "furthermore, I always worked in the media, for magazines, newspapers. I'm not God damn Ansel Adams!"

The phone was slammed down in fury, and Dee was surprised. She didn't lose her temper any oftener than she cried. *1950.* Again Barcelona flashed like a neon sign, and the small hotel tightly wedged between taller neighbors on the Rambla.

Dee thought at first that the Spaniard—who looked like a Cervantes grandee with his pointy beard and hawk's nose— was a crazy person who had somehow insinuated himself past the porter's post at the foot of the stairs. Worse, she feared he was one of Franco's henchmen, even if more elegantly dressed than a Guardia. She'd been afraid he'd come to arrest her for some crime or crimes unknown.

Now, remembering, she swirled away from the window, the sleeve of the caftan sweeping a Dresden shepherdess off a table to break on the floor. Dee ignored it. She could buy a dozen more, a hundred if it came to that, and thinking still of the Spaniard, said, as she fumbled her way down the stairs, "If only he had been something simple like a fascist!"

9

New Morning, Massachusetts, wasn't a town that had witnessed many great or momentous events in its three hundred years. Time came and time went with the predictable seasons. If prodded, the old-timers could recall some grandparent had mentioned a bad winter or a spring so devoid of rain that the crops failed and the usually prosperous farmers were hard-pressed for a year or two. There were memories of hailstones the size of baseballs, of a traveling circus where after the evening show the midget stabbed the fat lady, of some Whittier or Wayne or Crowell or Tydings relative so peculiar he or she had to be locked in the house. But by and large, history seemed to have passed over New Morning like that "October of the crows" around the turn of this century when for several tawny days the sky was blackened by a steady stream of birds. Blackbirds cawing as they flew south without ever landing or bothering to look down. All the crows in Massachusetts were reputed to have flown over New Morning that year.

It was a town blessed with unusually good weather, perhaps because of the declination between the hills in which it was nestled, tucked up like a child in sleep. Harsh winds sailed above it, and though New Morning was snugged in a valley, there was seldom a flood. Excessive water drained off into the Housatonic, wide and deep and swiftly racing on the other side of town. The snow fell ponderously, of course, for this was, after all, New England, and the cold midwinter bared its teeth and snapped, but there was seldom, even during the long gray days of January, that raw wind that seemed to flail the skin from one's bones.

New Morning was lucky and for a long, long time nothing touched the town or made the slightest dent in its soporific calm.

So it was most peculiar that the town had become involved with runaway slaves. Perhaps it was simply an accident, the first black in flight from the onerous bonds of servitude coming to New Morning. But others followed. It was the Tydingses who offered sanctuary; that big old house served as a way station on the underground railroad. How many poor refugees hurrying from bondage, like the Hebrews on their historical trek, to be fed, clothed, hidden in the airless cubbyholes, would never be known. They trailed through the nights, dark and bent and silent, shadows headed even further north. Once across the Canadian border, no bounty hunter could drag them south in leg-irons and chains.

A scattering of slaves, however, remained in New Morning, to be hastily secreted when danger came cantering up the one road from Connecticut in a cloud of dust. Moses Llewelyn's family, for example, having reached New Morning, stayed. It took the vicissitudes of the twentieth century finally to rout them out by death—or in Moses's own case simple orneriness, though Moses had returned.

Moses seldom considered his family's beginnings in New Morning, except for the tie of genetic memory that secured Miss Emma a soft spot in Moses's otherwise stony heart. Her death had afflicted him with the achy persistency of a February flu.

What did you expect, old woman like that. Near the century mark. Nobody lives forever, he'd mumble, not quite believing it. Bury the dead and get on with the living, that's what he had to do, but still Miss Emma preyed on his mind. He became plagued, asleep and awake, by dead Emma Tydings.

Moses dreamed vividly one night of Miss Emma and her house on fire, burning up. His great-grandmother appeared too, out on the lawn clawing at Moses' arm, her sharp nails hard as horn scissoring through his sleeve, yelling all the while: "You can't leave her in there to charcoal. You is promised to save Miss Emma! You is!"

"Promised nothing, woman!" Moses howled in his sleep to the old granny with the mahogany skin. But she shoved Moses, walloped him with a wicked hand between his shoulder blades. Sleeping, Moses stumbled up to the second floor of the Tydings house, where in his waking memory he knew he had never been, to Miss Emma, who sat serene and with the goofiest grin, cross-legged in the middle of the iron-framed bed. She cradled a shotgun, holding the twenty-gauge the wrong way around, the muzzle posed to blow off a knee-cap.

"Miss Emma, watch out!"

Stupid, being agitated, worrying that the old woman was going to maim herself, because the house was in flames. Tufts of fire were winnowing through the mattress already. Besides, Miss Emma was dead. Moses picked at the loose thread of remembering as it snaked through his sleep: *She is already gone, just another parcel of old bones now.*

Still, asleep, Moses was forced to drag Miss Emma out of that house where his ancestors had been hidden behind the walls.

There was another dream Moses had, of diving into Garland's Pond—though he'd never learned to swim—to yank Miss Emma off the muddy bottom. Yet a third had Miss Emma being asphyxiated in her antique kitchen, her head cushioned on a dish towel by the open oven door. There didn't seem an end to the ways Miss Emma—dead six months going on seven—could die in Moses Llewelyn's sleep.

When awake, Moses would find himself driving by her house. Whenever he trimmed the back lawn, he mowed near the windows and furtively peeked inside, half expecting to see Miss Emma and at the same time expecting to catch the honky, Lucas Donnelly, doing something weird.

Right now, mowing the lawn though it already had a crew cut since he'd gone over it only a few days before, Moses Llewelyn was fuming. Never trust a machine! he snarled as the mower leaped once again out of his grasp, revving off like a rabid dog. It spun in circles as he gaped in surprise before he scooted after his machine.

The mower was new, too, though past its warranty so he couldn't take it back to Sears. Damnation! He gripped the handles tightly and together—though not quite—with the mower tangoed across the lawn.

Moses was in a terrible sweat, his heart thumping with the thunk of hammer blows, his lungs aching. His teeth chattered in spite of the soppy June heat. Get it finished, he kept telling himself, feeling put upon, not admitting that the grass might have been left for another two or three weeks, and that he was in Miss Emma's yard for no other reason than a long nose—that and a draggy feeling that Miss Emma, though dead, was still living in there somewhere. Though he had attended the funeral himself, in his one dark suit, he was still attached to the impossible notion that maybe Miss Emma hadn't died.

As Moses pushed the mower alongside the High Street hedge, he saw Bobby Pierson's head bobbing on the other side. Bodiless, the boy rolled along like a bowling ball, staring wide-eyed at Moses. Moses pushed past him, but Bobby kept pace at the other side of the hedge.

"Get on with your deliveries!" Moses shouted. He reached the end of the lawn and swung the mower in a half circle, trimming once again toward the house. Bobby Pierson's head jounced on the left. Moses muttered to himself under his sour breath and yelled, "Get away! Shoo, beat it Bub!" as though the boy were a stray dog.

On the third turn when Moses glared over at the hedge the molten sunlight struck his eyes, temporarily blinding him. He passed his hand across his forehead, wiping at the sweat that streamed down his face. When he looked up, the green hedge swam in front of him. Bobby Pierson still stood before him, but instead of the dirty-blond thatch and big unblinking eyes, Moses saw the flesh had gone, as had the hair, and where the eyes had been were two boreholes gouged into the bone.

Lord, love me and save my soul! Moses swore and stopped short a foot from the privet. Tendrils of fear were vining in his bowels.

The naked jaws gaped wide on their hinges, and even over the clatter of the machine Moses heard the raspy grate. "Hello, Moses," Bobby Pierson's skull said, his voice echoing.

Aaaaah! The cry bounced in Moses's head.

"It's pretty hot," the skull continued. "You don't look good. Maybe you're overheated. Carol says it's not smart to stay out in the sun too long. Your brains will bake."

Moses, horrified, screamed, "Go away!"

The bony jaws snapped, and from the empty sockets two silvery tears, viscous as mercury, slipped. "I'm only being polite, Moses, like Carol says I should be to people, 'specially if they're old."

Moses shuddered and looked over his hunched shoulder at the old colonial. He remembered Miss Emma down on her knees by the flower bed, clucking to the peonies and the vincas, encouraging them to grow and stand tall. He wished her back to life, up and out of the grave, the stranger forgotten along with all his funny-looking antiques that Moses glimpsed when he sneaked up to a window. Moses Llewelyn had never witnessed apparitions when he worked for Miss Emma, nor heard them speak, not in broad daylight anyway, not when he was both sober and straight. When Miss Emma was up and walking the only event of import had been the day a branch from the elm was split by lightning and crashed to the ground.

"Now you just listen to me, Bub," Moses said, stiffening his spine. "I don't know what kind of funny game you're playing with old Moses"—some game, making his stomach do flip-flops!—"but you stop it now!"

"What?"

It wasn't Bobby Pierson's skull on the spiny ends of the privet, but Mrs. Montrose's gray temple of curls and tufts, her puffy face crimson with outrage.

"Excuse me, Missus Montrose," Moses yelped. "I promise I get over to you next week." Quickly giving Cora Montrose his laddered back under the sweat-soaked work shirt, he hurried for the other end of the property and the short grass beneath the dripping willow. Usually he snipped that patch with the

shears, but ruthlessly now he rolled the heavy mower flat over
it, then thumped the fuzz with his heavy work boots, not
caring if he stunted the delicate growth. He had half a notion
to load the machine into the truck and finish up Lucas
Donnelly's gardening another day, maybe when it was cloudy
and smelled like rain.

Stoically, however, Moses mowed on. He still had the lilacs
to prune, the dahlias to tidy. I'll be here till supper, he snarled
with disgust. Next thing that skinny honky who looked more
lifeless than Miss Emma in her coffin would come to the back
door and hummph! at him for not being done. Moses would
give that long piece of chalk whatfor if he did! Well, not really,
for that bald-headed black-clad ghoul spooked Moses more
than he cared to admit.

Moses mowed faster now, snipping the edges.

Sour milk, that was what Miss Emma's house with its new
inhabitants made him think of these days. You couldn't tell the
milk had turned until you squeezed up the little spout and
stuck your nose down close. Then the rank smell hit and got
you queasy.

Finally he was finished with the grass. Heaving, breath
exploding like cannon balls in his chest, he switched off the
machine. Just for good measure he gave it another kick before
he rolled it out to the alley and lifted it into the back of the
pickup truck. He wiped his sweat-streaked face with a damp
sleeve and considered leaving the rest of the gardening and
going home where he could crawl into bed. But even with his
$49.95 fan from Woolworth's in Pittsfield sputtering on high,
the shack would be as stifling as one of the Farrow Bakery
ovens. Still, there was a nice cold six-pack of Bud sitting in the
fridge and with his tongue swollen and his head spinning like a
pinwheel he could use the beer.

When he pushed through the back gate that shrieked like a
fingernail scratching glass, to retrieve his shears, his eyes were
drawn to the attic window like iron filings to a magnet. Moses
could even feel his eyeballs strain in his skull.

There was Lucas Donnelly, filling the window with his
white-clad figure. He was not smiling. As Moses watched,
Lucas Donnelly was wreathed in smoke, too much smoke for
such an itty-bitty stogie. And not wanting to, not fully aware of
why he was even doing it with that glistening image of a cold
brew dancing in his thoughts, Moses found himself down on

knobby knees, the dirt hard as a cement slab, weeding the beds.

As he moved away from the window Lucas Donnelly expelled a long breath that would have passed for a sigh of contentment in anybody else.

The devil's work is never done, he thought, his smile returning, as he glanced around the attic of what had once been Emma Tydings' house and where she continued her tenancy in Moses Llewelyn's dreams. The attic was completely open under eaves that were now masked by an acoustical ceiling. The walls were of no-nonsense plain wood painted stark white, and the extra-thick Thermopane windows hung solid in their new aluminum frames. The latest IBM computers filled up much of the space, but there was also a long conference table and one black leather executive chair, adjustable. On the polished mahogany rested a long pad of dimestore paper, a neat row of sharpened number-two pencils, six Bics in navy, and a brass ashtray in the shape of a uroboros.

Lucas Donnelly had been working on a mine disaster in Canada when he heard the mower start up. His eyebrows rode up his dark face and two rivers of sulfuric smoke streamed down his nostrils at the sound. The room was normally so silent, except for the slight and not unpleasant hum of the IBMs, that only Lucas Donnelly was able to hear.

From the window to which he had strode, Lucas Donnelly gazed down, expecting to see symmetrical highways mowed through the grass. Despite an unwarranted reputation for chaos and illogic, he had a keen eye for shape and form. Straight lines soothed him like a cool hand to a fevered brow. So the imprecise, snaking paths that Moses trimmed as he wended from the house to the privets and along the rear of the property by the picket fence shook Lucas Donnelly's usual composure. Agitated, a bitter taste clung to his tongue and lips, and he seethed, smoke pouring from his ears. Moses Llewelyn didn't understand his task! Furiously, he threw the old black man a fast fiery curve that yanked the machine out from his grasp. Then, as if sending the old man galloping about the lawn in the midday heat wasn't enough, he defleshed Bobby Pierson's head upon the hedge.

The cigar glowed red, a smoky cloud billowed as Lucas

Donnelly puffed, and formed an aureole around his head. And he thought, his official eye fixed on Moses: *death by incineration*.

Finally, Moses having settled to what he paid him for, Lucas Donnelly turned his attention once more to the murky underground cavern in Ontario slowly filling with toxic gas, where thirty-two men, all in mortal terror, were trapped. Rafters cracking, shaft walls of shale crumbling, trickling with the slide of dust.

Canada arranged to his satisfaction, he retrieved the latest printout from the fourth IBM on the left—Southeast Asia—and scanned it quickly, made a few rapid calculations with a Bic on the pad, thought for a second and scratched his chin, then put the printout and his notes into the shredder and moved on to Africa.

Lucas Donnelly, no different from an ordinary executive, labored on long after Moses below had finally finished up, right to the second when day abruptly changed to night, the last curve of vapid light having crawled from the sky. Only then did he drop his Bic and ease back, stretching out his long legs, thinking about New Morning, about how much he was going to enjoy having an heir . . . a son.

10

Reverend Austin looked impressive as he did every Sunday in his black robe, exactly like the one Glory wore for her graduation from high school. Solemn as the middle of the night, he stood by the front doors of the Congregational Church shaking hands with each member of his flock. There was never any escaping him; wind, snow, or rain, he planted himself on the narrow porch to take your hand and give it one good pump. But as the long line slowly snaked forward, and Glory inched nearer to the minister, she saw that his face was slick with sweat.

Glory, following behind her father, felt the stir of air at her neck as Evelyn fanned herself with a wide-brimmed strawhat.

"God's grace upon you, child," Will Austin intoned to Glory as he always did, watering her hand with his. His warm skin felt slightly unpleasant, sticky, and Glory pulled away from his touch.

"Such a lovely service this morning," Evelyn was saying, "so uplifting!"

Her mother said this often to Will Austin on Sundays, and Glory never knew what she meant. Nor did she understand Evelyn's other traditional comment to the minister, the one traded on Sundays for the handshake: "Inspiring."

The hour and a half it required for the service to unroll from beginning to end was all blank time. From the moment Glory sat down in the Crowell pew a mist seemed to descend. Consciousness vanished as though she had fallen asleep. She knew she hadn't actually because the pages of the book she'd hold in her hands would turn and she must have stood to sit again along with everyone else. Over the years Evelyn surely would have scolded if Glory had been suspiciously out of step. Still, she never remembered one word of the service.

Most of New Morning attended the Congregational Church, except for the few Catholics like Mrs. O'Brien and the Papriakas family. Or the Jews, Aaron Stein and his wife, and the Myerses. "Even if they don't believe," Alastair once told her, "people feel obligated to go." A touch point in the week, he called the service.

Now there was somebody else in New Morning who didn't show up to rise and pray when the big doors banged shut and Will Austin strode imperially up the three steps to the pulpit. Lucas Donnelly hadn't come to the Congregational in his white suit—the only outfit anyone had ever seen him wear— not once all these weeks he'd been living in New Morning. He was conspicuous by his absence, or at least that was what Evelyn said. Glory could tell that it annoyed her mother, this lapse on Lucas Donnelly's part. When Theo suggested "maybe he's Roman," Evelyn reddened and said with a cough, "Don't be ridiculous!" Glory had asked Alastair why it was ridiculous, her father's suggestion that the stranger might be Catholic.

"Because she doesn't want him to be," Alastair had explained.

Do you think he is?

"He's a heathen, whatever else he calls himself," Alastair had said, and Glory sensed that his reaction to the stranger was

as strong as her mother's. But Alastair disliked Lucas Donnelly,
as much as Evelyn admired him. As Glory had heard her say
more than once to Theo, "His coming to New Morning's the
most interesting thing that's happened here in God knows how
long."

A crowd clustered on the steps of the church and stretched
down the sidewalk, spilling over the curb onto High Street,
which was as empty as a dry riverbed on this Sunday morning.
Even in the swaddling shade at 10:45 A.M., it was warm. Too
warm for a closed-up unair-conditioned church. The congregation, finally released, staggered out of the church and stayed,
clinging together, glued.

Theo was murmuring to Howie Eumis, and Evelyn was
leaning over Mrs. Winslow who looked as skinny and withered
as a leafless twig. If her mother swooped forward she'd grind
poor Mrs. Winslow to dust. Sometimes Evelyn made Glory
feel like that, too—small and in a dangerous position—as
though her mother could pulverize her, crush her under all
that certainty and assurance.

Nervously Glory glanced around for Alastair. Somehow just
the sight of him emboldened her. She saw he had rolled down
the walk to the side of the church and come to a stop at the
fringes of the crowd where he was arguing with Charlie
Calman.

She would have gone over to Carol but Mike Boardman had
his daughter firmly captured by the arm. He was talking
rapidly to Mrs. Montrose and her widowed son, Delmar.

All of a sudden there was Dee Whittier whispering, "You're
a very beautiful girl, Glory. Do you know that?" Dee had
sneaked up on her, just as Alastair sometimes accused Dee of
doing to him. Like a cat, rubbing your ankle or hopping to
your lap before you even know it's around. Glory didn't like
cats much. Always silent and sly. Dee was too, she couldn't
help thinking, and her cheeks flushed. "Very beautiful," Dee
repeated, regarding her the way a customer would one of the
watercolors on The Gallery's wall. Considering if it was worth
the price. "Perhaps," she added, "I should take your picture."

Glory shook her head no! She didn't want Dee Whittier to
photograph her, not ever, no matter how much it would please
Theo and Evelyn. In front of Dee's camera, Glory would be
helpless, trapped and drowning, going down. . . .

Driftwood pointing up and out of the water . . . waving
. . . white, bleached.

The dream image erupted into memory, rupturing her vision. Hanging there before her wasn't Dee's upturned face, smooth and unlined as her own, but the arm in the water, vivid as white bone, until it dissolved into foam.

With a sharp swing, Glory slipped through the crowd.

The arm in the sea, fingers dancing, had surfaced from sleep. In the dream of a boat that was barely moving, just waiting on the glassy top of the water. Glory was dreaming. Of the blue sea somewhere and the sailing vessel and the cloudless canopy of sky. It was a day not unlike one of these now passing in endless formation here in New Morning, except for the silence, and the frightening quiet, when the crying stopped.

Facing away from the church and the people who buzzed and hovered behind her, Glory saw the arm float downward, shimmering. There hadn't been an arm before. That limb was attached to something (someone!) who Glory sensed but couldn't see, already far below. The arm was new. Each night, sleeping, dreaming, another piece got added to the picture puzzle that was filling in.

It was the *before* time and though she had yearned for it, now Glory wished she could let it go. Or rather that the images wouldn't come to her. Evelyn had been right: "Forget it; don't even try." Only she hadn't been trying. The dream had arrived on its own.

Looking up through the trees, she saw Lucas Donnelly's house. It glowed with a white fluorescent light, like a sail on the sea.

From an upstairs window Lucas Donnelly gazed out at her. She saw him clearly though a good block or so separated the two of them. He was staring at her, the way he had after the town meeting when he'd kissed her hand.

Glorious, she could hear Lucas Donnelly saying, as if his lips were pressed to her ear. The cool breath tickled her neck, and she jumped, stung.

Glory darted across High Street, oblivious to Evelyn calling, "Where are you going off to?" and ran through the green. She sank down to a dusty patch of parched grass near Ebenezer Smythe's final resting place, not caring if she dirtied the beige skirt her mother complained was so hard to clean.

Behind her she knew Lucas Donnelly watched like a night owl, though surely he couldn't find her crouched as she was so low to the ground and sheltered beneath the trees. Her fingers dug into the grass and her knuckles grazed the edge of the marker. Still, she felt his burning X-ray glare. It sliced the foliage, beamed through the tree trunks. The hair on her head felt singed.

There didn't seem to be anywhere Glory could go where Lucas Donnelly wouldn't find her.

Sunday afternoon was a quiet, almost a drowsy time in New Morning. After services ended most everyone wandered home to a heavy midday meal or over to the White Bear for Herman September's "Brunch—Special, including a Bloody Mary—$8.95."

By 3 P.M. when Lucas Donnelly strolled off to the Bear, the Inn had disgorged its last customer and a lull settled until the bustle began before dinner. The wood-paneled barroom was empty, all the ice-cream parlor chairs were pulled up around the Formica-topped tables, and Herman, on a high stool, his elbows propped on the bar, watched stockcar racing from Indiana.

With the television announcer screaming an incomprehensible description of the careening race cars and their drivers, it wasn't surprising that Herman September never heard Lucas Donnelly's light-footed approach. Lucas Donnelly, despite his size, traveled soft as the wind, and when he drifted in his white haze up behind Herman to stab his back with two fingers like a pretend gun, the Inn owner levitated half an inch off his chair.

"Scare a man to death!" Herman cried, his eyes round as coffee cups. Not that he would have heard an elephant's trumpeting with the T.V. blaring so loudly.

Lucas Donnelly's gaze flickered to the speeding cars and he blinked. The T.V. hissed, popped, and a tiny curl of smoke spiraled up from behind the set. "God damn!" Herman said, "I just had the mother put to rights." He stomped around to the other side of the bar and reaching up, began fiddling with the dials. "It really burns my ass, the way nothing works the way it's supposed to. Know what I mean?" In a second or two Herman gave up in disgust and asked, "What's your poison, Mr. Donnelly?"

Herman September, a grungy little character, no more than five four—a measurement about which he lied—with long untidy hair and aviator glasses, was a latecomer to New Morning. He'd settled in around 1972, off a commune in northern Vermont. An unexpected inheritance had propelled Herman from a lackluster career as a soybean farmer into the inn business. He worked erratically to make a go of it. Some days he rushed around the Inn frantically, a tornado in full blow; other days he malingered in bed (Herman's home was the second floor front room) until after lunch and then went back up before dinner. Herman was a steady customer of Moses Llewelyn's, having become acclimated to certain stimuli during his time at the commune.

His pale, damp eyes stared sadly from behind the aviators at Lucas Donnelly, but whether because the T.V. had gone on the fritz again or because he suspected that this customer was about to name some elaborate concoction that he'd have to search for in his bartending guide, it was impossible to tell. As it was, Lucas Donnelly ensconced himself on a stool and ordered a ginger ale, no ice.

"Easy enough," Herman said with a smile. Though he made most of his money not from meals or the occasional rented room, but from alcohol, Herman disapproved of hard drink. Liquor wore out the heart and diseased the liver, he often announced to his unrepentant customers. Herman believed in clean living, vegetarianism, eight glasses of purified water a day, in megavitamins and meditation, in Yoga and proper breathing.

Naturally Herman also frowned on cigarettes, cigars as well as pipes (marijuana was different, of course, being therapeutic), and when he placed Lucas Donnelly's ginger ale on a coaster in front of him, Herman glared, rather cross-eyed, at the thin black cheroot. "Doesn't do much for the circulation, the heart, never mind your poor lungs. And I read there's some connection between atrophying brain cells and nicotine," Herman said.

"Is that a fact," Lucas Donnelly replied, puffing away, before he swung around on the plastic stool which shrieked under him and gave the White Bear barroom consideration. Into the silence he said, "You know, this Inn is over two hundred years old. Look at those beams."

"Yeah, I guess I got to start thinking about getting them replaced."

"And the walls, the floor, even the door lintels."

"Uh huh." Herman September sighed, not having the

foggiest notion what Lucas Donnelly was getting to, and not caring too much.

"Even this bar," Lucas Donnelly went on, running his hand over the worn wood.

Herman coughed from the smoke that seemed thicker than one slim cigar might generate. "What about it?"

"What about it?" Lucas Donnelly directed a rather frightening look his way, but Herman's eyes teared too much for him to notice. He blew his nose in a cocktail napkin and took another to wipe his glasses dry. "Why, the White Bear's a true jewel!"

Without the aviators, though Lucas Donnelly sat less than a foot from Herman's eyelashes, he had the disintegrating hazy look of a planetary body in distant space. "You're just going to have to put out that stinking weed!" Herman wheezed. "I'm allergic to smoke." Which wasn't exactly true, but he did seem hypersensitive to whatever brand of cigar Lucas Donnelly enjoyed.

Not only was his request ignored, but Lucas Donnelly puffed all the more, or at least Herman September thought so. He was about to raise his voice when Lucas Donnelly said, "These tables and chairs have to go. Those curtains, too." He shuddered. "Antique Sears Roebuck. Furthermore, those Van Gogh reproductions . . . no, no, no!"

The smoke ruffled as Herman shouted an approaching cloud of it away. "What are you talking about?"

"New Morning, Mr. September. And getting the White Bear back to where it was."

"It was always right here, as far as I know. And if I'm supposed to toss out the chairs and the tables, where are people going to sit?" Herman jammed the glasses on his nose, but he saw no more clearly. There hung between him and his customer a scrim not dissimilar to inner-city smog.

"Authenticity," Lucas Donnelly growled.

Herman, holding tight to his temper, snipped, "You're not making sense."

Lucas Donnelly growled louder, and perhaps it was merely coincidental that there came from outside a rumble of thunder. Surely the sky had been as clear as a well-scrubbed dinner plate, and Herman, gazing upward, wondered about jets. Not that he'd ever heard anything supersonic pass over New Morning before this moment.

While his head was averted, Lucas Donnelly continued, "We must return the White Bear to its original state."

"Original state!" Herman laughed so hard he choked until his face flushed a deep plum shade. It took a minute or so before he found his voice. "It was only a barn way back when, and over where the dining room is was a pigsty, or so I've been told. What are you thinking of, Mr. Donnelly, my getting in some hogs and tossing pig slops and cow pads around? The Department of Health would have a thing or two to say!"

"We're failing to communicate, Mr. September," Lucas Donnelly said, stating the obvious. "I mean that I don't enjoy man-made materials such a Formica or linoleum tile." He shuddered. "Nor do I appreciate imitations."

"Well, I'm sorry to hear that, Mr. Donnelly," Herman said, having finally caught his breath. "But I've got bigger fish tugging at my line right now. Like that weed of yours. I'm not kidding, either you or it has got to get out of the Bear." Lucas Donnelly blew his thickest cloud yet into Herman's eyes. "Agh!" Herman cried, as liquid dribbled from his nose, eyes, even the corners of his mouth. He wheezed in such acute discomfort he never heard Lucas Donnelly insisting on new tables and chairs—meaning antiques—and the floor redone down to the original wood. Shutters hung, real ones too, not skimpy pine recently made.

Herman September sneezed, sniffed, blew, wiped, coughed, and had a terrible time of it until he thought to throw cold water on his face. When he could breathe seminormally once again, he turned around and yelled into the middle of Lucas Donnelly's suggestion about kerosene lamps, "I like it this way! And this is how the White Bear's going to stay. *Funky!*" He reached out and snatched Lucas Donnelly's cheroot from his mouth. He plucked it clean away and threw it into the stainless steel sink behind the bar.

"Now, Mr. Donnelly, you were saying!" Herman snapped like a maddened turtle. He was ready for a good screaming match, but in the one second that he turned to the sink, Lucas Donnelly had—impossibly—vanished.

Herman glared around the Bear suspecting Lucas Donnelly of hiding somewhere before he started sulking. His Sunday lay in ruins. His head ached, too, and his back molars. His glasses, no matter what he did, kept fogging. Finally Herman just gave up, and leaving the bar unmanned, he stomped up to his bed, thinking unhappily, as he never had before, *life's not worth living*.

* * *

"Well, I don't see what's wrong with inviting somebody to Sunday dinner!" Evelyn had been stuck in the same groove for the last twenty minutes and wouldn't let up. "Alastair's here, isn't he?" she insisted, nodding her head toward the window by which Alastair sat, reading the papers.

Again to the kitchen to return with yet another of the elaborate courses she served each Sunday exactly at five o'clock, she repeated, "It would only be neighborly."

"Alastair's not a stranger!" Theo snapped from the couch like an old dog aroused. "Alastair's a friend."

Alastair coughed sharply then smiled. "Thank you, Theo."

"Of course he is," Evelyn said, reappearing. And to Alastair, "A dear one, too!"

Syrup from the candied yams must be stuck in her bridge, Alastair thought. Not that he paid undue attention to most of what Evelyn Crowell said. A jabberwocky if every there was one. But this obsession with dragging Lucas Donnelly into the family, making him one of her own, had Alastair worried.

A rich son-in-law, that's what Evelyn was after. A trophy to burnish her reputation. How she would crow over the Historical ladies!

As for Glory, there was no telling what she felt about her mother's desire to toss her into Lucas Donnelly's arms. Alastair had half a mind to ask right out loud, "Glory, what do you think about all this?" But he didn't, he just went on reading the obituaries as Glory fiddled with a Schubert sonata on the piano.

Suddenly Alastair's head came up out of the newspaper. He had *heard* a bell, deep, resonant, a dull twank. The Congregational bell. Glory plucked at his sleeve, weaving sentences with her fingers in front of his face. Alastair glanced over at Theo, but if he heard it too, he never wavered. Theo read on. From the kitchen Evelyn's voice rose and fell, drifted unmelodiously.

The Congregational bell, sure as cows give milk. Somebody's died, Alastair knew that right away. Somebody's departed. His own flesh shivered and hugged his bones.

But why was Will Austin ringing? He never had before. The bell hung silent in the belfry, used only on holidays and times of unnatural events. The town hall fire a few years back had

had the minister swinging, even though the flames fizzled out with only minor damage done.

The left hand . . . can't do it right . . . listen . . . He saw what Glory was saying but asked her instead. "The bell. Will Austin's clamoring. Did you hear it?"

Glory frowned, puzzled. *What bell?*

Alastair sighed and slipped back in his chair as the bell's echo faded in his head. No tolling actually sliced through the Sunday calm, but still he knew, there was one less soul alive in New Morning. He wondered who as he listened to the strains of the last passage of the Schubert.

The who turned out to be Herman September, hanged by his own hand from the rafters under the White Bear roof. It must have been hot as Hades up there, stuffy and not much light, Alastair thought at the funeral and later during the gathering at the Inn itself.

"Heard Herman was spending more money than he was taking in," Charlie Calman said, as he munched a deviled egg and checked the crowd scattered about the White Bear dining room. The Historical Society, in memory of so many monthly meetings, had thrown together the lunch. "Bankruptcy . . . receivership . . ." Charlie was mumbling. "Who knows what will happen to the old barn now." He groaned. "We'll have to do something, or the Bear will turn into a Holiday Inn."

"No problem, Mr. Calman." Lucas Donnelly came up behind their backs. Looming over Alastair, he cast his white shadow.

Good God, the man doesn't even change that suit for a funeral! Alastair disapproved. He was resplendent as always, vanilla except for his swarthy skin. Smiling—as Alastair supposed he did forever, even in his sleep—Lucas Donnelly was as Mediterranean as the Papriakases.

Man's only been in town a spit of time, yet here he is at Herman's last rites with the supposedly bereaved. Gall, unmitigated gall. It peeved Alastair that Lucas Donnelly had turned up to pay his respects, though why, he couldn't say except that everything the stranger did was irksome. Can't stand the fellow, he thought as he always did, watching Lucas Donnelly shift and slide without really moving a muscle. Looking for Glory he was, and when he found her, his gaze followed Glory, cast a net, and trawled the girl about the room. Except that Glory kept her back to him.

"How's that, Mr. Donnelly?" Charlie Calman was asking, whipping the pencil from behind his ear. "About the White Bear, I mean?"

The smile broadened. "New Morning doesn't want a Hilton or Marriott. Do they? Or *we*, if I might be so bold. Glasses in plastic wrap. Muslin sheets. Flowered carpets. And those tinny dime-store lamps. That's the kind of thing hotel chains specialize in." Lucas Donnelly was ponderous in spite of the smile. "There's no individuality, no craft, and even an inn—especially one as old as the White Bear—should be special, unique. Why it's part of New Morning history," he added.

"Smythe's barn, that's what this place was," Alastair instructed him, unaware he was reprising the conversation Donnelly and Herman September had had. "We're sitting right where Ebenezer's ancestors had to shovel up pig slops, if you want to be historical about it."

"Shut up, Alastair," Charlie hissed. He had his notebook out and was trying to scribble Lucas Donnelly's every word.

"Which is why I've bought it," the man said, lighting one of those infernal cigars. "So that it remains authentic and doesn't get trivialized."

"Herman wasn't exactly running a trailer park." Alastair, needled, felt the urge to protect the dead man's name though, considering that the man had tied a rope around his neck and jumped from a stepladder right above where they were eating, drinking, and forgetting, Herman's reputation was pretty shot anyway. Suicide wasn't a socially acceptable finish to life.

Charlie, shocked by what would be a banner headline for the *Eagle*, bellowed for Theo who hastily crossed the room. "Mr. Donnelly says he's buying the White Bear. Did you know about this?" It was an accusation, not a question.

"Since I hold the paper, it would be impossible not to, wouldn't it." Theo was discomforted, sucking in his cheeks. Put out by this he is, Alastair surmised. Maybe he doesn't care for the man's interest in Glory either. Alastair wanted Theo Crowell to dislike Lucas Donnelly more than Jordy. The boy's the right age and more fitting for her disposition, Alastair decided, enjoying his view of Jordy and Glory, close together, at the far end of the room.

Charlie was haranguing Theo for not having told him about the White Bear before.

"We just put Herman in his grave," Theo countered. "There hasn't exactly been much time. Besides, it's not for me to send out news flashes about who buys what. A bank keeps confidences, same as a doctor."

"That's not the issue, Theo, and you know it. Town's got a right to all the news all the time."

"Well, now the town has it," Theo snapped.

"Gentlemen," Lucas Donnelly crooned.

Theo shoved his hands deep into pockets and hunching forward to see through the smoke of Lucas Donnelly's cigar, said, "Tell him anything you want to; but expect to see it in print."

"Now just a minute, Theo. Don't you start acting so high and mighty with me! There's still freedom of the press in this country, and New Morning's a part of the good old USA. Keep that firmly in mind! This isn't Russia, least not yet."

"Are you accusing me of being a communist?" Theo's eyes bulged.

"Watch your temper, Theo. No good getting excited on a hot day," Doc Trump hollered, rising from his chair, but Charlie and Theo had started to squabble in earnest while Lucas Donnelly puffed away. Alastair caught the glint of laughter in his eyes. Set the two of them onto each other, damned if he hasn't. Deviltry, that's what it is.

Bicker and complaint ricochetted back and forth as the men's voices escalated, until Theo marched off, midsentence, leaving Charlie staring after him. Huffing one last long exhalation of breath, he drew himself up and asked, editorially, "Will you be running the Bear yourself, Mr. D.? Or do you have plans to hire a manager?"

"Actually Jarvis will tend to it. It's just his sort of thing."

"Jarvis?"

"Jarvis Badderly. My majordomo. My man. He does everything for me. Quite a capable chap, reliable as, well, as I am myself. My familiar you might call him." Charlie looked blank.

Alastair knew what a familiar was, but Will Austin, who hoved to in ministerial fashion, had something else in mind. "The fellow who arrested heretics, unbelievers, and threw them in the slammer during the inquisition," he intoned. "An extremely important position."

Before anybody could stop him, the reverend was launched on the Inquisition, heresy, the need for a consensus of belief as a bulwark against the hordes rioting at the gates. Hands clasped behind his back, he rocked heel to toe, droning and staring glassy-eyed over everyone's head. Listening to Will Austin was like reading the encyclopedia, page after page.

When Will finally paused for breath, Charlie, never the fearful angel, rushed ahead. "I heard there was some talk of not burying Herman in the cemetery because of"—he jerked his thumb upward—"doing himself in like he did."

Will Austin's cheeks swelled out so that he resembled a puff adder ready to strike. "A sin! A transgression that cannot, must not, be forgiven. As the Lord giveth, so the Lord taketh away. It is not for man to choose his time, not to desecrate the flesh by his own hand."

Alastair, on crutches instead of in the chair for Herman's funeral, finally had enough. "I've got to sit down. I can tolerate almost anything, but when you get all tripey about religion, Will, my bones ache."

"Let me help you, Mr. Wayne," Lucas Donnelly offered solicitously. Just being insulting, pointing out my infirmity, Alastair thought, forgetting he'd brought the subject up himself. Yet he said with Yankee firmness, "Don't need any help, thank you kindly." Wasn't a kind gesture, just infringing on personal territory, like the other day on the green. Anger spumed in Alastair, and he demanded of no one in particular, "Why did Herman September kill himself anyway? Huh? Somebody answer me that. And don't give me any gobbledy-gook about business being bad. Or the Bear sliding into the red. Herman could have borrowed the funds, taken in a partner, raised prices even. He might have done a lot of things besides jumping off a stepladder with a rope necktie. No need, no need at all for *that!*" This death whittled at Alastair's existence. And why shouldn't he feel diminished? He had known Herman September. This wasn't some John Doe they had just planted in the cemetery.

Old Mrs. Winslow objected. "Don't let's talk about it!"

"About what?" Alastair cried. "Herman's dying? What the hell are we here for if not because the poor gopher's gone? Do you ladies think this is another Historical Society luncheon and right after the pie one of you girls gets the chance to jabber? Is that what you think?"

From a distance, Alastair viewed himself having a tantrum. He should have been horrified at his bad behavior, at the awful things he heard himself saying, but he was in a full-rigged temper, fanned by the stuffiness of the Bear, Herman's death, and the silliness of his friends. Lucas Donnelly, he thought in the one small corner of his mind that hadn't filled with fog, set a match to us. This was all the stranger's doing. He was taking over New Morning like a syndicate committed to profitable redevelopment. *But what does he want us for?*

Alastair suspected he'd be hustled off, just as Dee and Charlie had rolled him right out of combat after the town meeting, but nobody grabbed at his elbows, and yanked him out of harm's reach. Too much was going on.

Alastair was fettered in a strange, almost catatonic state. He had stopped shouting, but he remained angry and confused by his own bad temper, unsure what had caused him to vent his spleen on his neighbors, who were arguing now among themselves. Theo was haranguing Stanis over a mortage when the town knew that the Papriakases' word was as solid as gold. Charlie was running around with his pencil poised. Alastair wanted to hit him in the head with a crutch before he had a chance to chronicle all the goings-on.

Alastair heard Aaron Stein telling Cora Montrose she was an anti-Semite if ever there was one.

"You're damned right I am, and proud of it, too!" the old lady bellowed.

Evelyn Crowell cornered Jordy Farrow, at long last having her say on this "unsuitable relationship that's to stop right now!" Evelyn was shouting, but Jordy, to Alastair the witness, seemed the only sensible person left in the room. Dragging Glory by the hand, he struggled to tug loose from Evelyn's clasp on his arm.

Somehow Lucas Donnelly managed to slip between them, Alastair wasn't sure how. A sliver of silver light shot out of nowhere and speared Jordy's hand. He yelped as though bitten and suddenly he and Glory were detached. Lucas Donnelly had Glory now, and was walking her serenely away as though they were merely taking a stroll, cleaving a passage through the middle of New Morning's arguing citizens. A cone of silence surrounded them as they went out onto the White Bear's broad front porch. Alastair twisted painfully to stare out the window. Lucas Donnelly and Glory had taken to the wicker rockers.

Behind him now Alastair—having swiveled to ease the crink in his neck—saw Evelyn, her red-dabbed lips pursed like those of a catfish on a hook. Jordy sucked the fleshy side of a hand that was ugly and inflamed. "Like I caught the edge of a tray coming out of the oven," he complained to Alastair, displaying the burn. "Hurts," he whimpered, seeming ten years old, no more. Jordy's eyes were filmy, and like the rest of them he seemed fogged in. Alastair didn't have the heart to cry out at the boy: *Do you know where Glory is? Out on the porch with that Donnelly fellow, rocking and getting wooed*. If Jordy heard him, Alastair worried about what the boy might do. What would be done to him. As sure as he was of anything in the bedlam swirling through the White Bear, he was sure of this: Lucas Donnelly played a significant part in setting the town at sixes and sevens, in riling tempers, and unlatching gates that people almost always kept locked tight. The unspeakable was suddenly voiced all over the dining room and the bar. Drunks, the whole bunch of them, Alastair thought, but he was grabbing at wind. Not one of them was really stewed.

Lucas Donnelly, he knew it . . . *knew it* . . . was at fault. As clear as he'd heard the Congregational bell tolling, when in fact Will Austin hadn't rung the bell, Alastair heard Lucas Donnelly say: *I can't plant acorns, Mr. Wayne, I can just help the trees to grow*.

Lucas Donnelly's voice crashed and clanged in Alastair's head as if the man had spoken loudly right into his ear.

When he craned his neck again for another look through the window, Alastair confronted Donnelly smiling at him. One quick swipe of light and black eyes blinking fast like the click-click of Dee's Nikon shutter.

Alastair imagined himself thrusting a heavy-bladed sword through the glass and embedding the point in Lucas Donnelly's chest. The image was so vivid he could feel the hilt in his hand, so thick that he could barely close his fingers around it, so heavy the weapon was impossible to lift. But then he saw his arms encased in metal, filigreed with a winding design of leafy vines.

St. Alastair! Lucas Donnelly, still paying him attention, laughed.

Alastair couldn't turn away, not until Lucas Donnelly, inclining his head in a courtly nod, unfurled one last banner of smoke that floated right up against the window and clung like Saran wrap.

Alastair felt his soul quiver like a three-year-old in a dark closet, and closing his eyes, he entered a black night. When his heart stuttered to a slower drum roll, he stiffened his resolve and peered out through half-closed lids. Lucas Donnelly no longer rocked sedately. Glory was gone, too.

"Go find her!" he croaked to Jordy, and spent the last of his energy giving the boy a shove.

Jordy obeyed Alastair's orders, dashing to the hall. In minutes the Inn emptied, people slinking out to the sunlight. But everyone went hunched over, shoulders cranked up half a notch, eyes cast downward.

Alastair, too, made his shaky departure, the last to leave. For one of the few times in his long tenure as a cripple in New Morning no one offered to help him.

11

Don't make a whole cloth from a few scraps. Stop being dramatic, this isn't something on T.V., Alastair protested in an ongoing interior monologue. But no matter how diligently Alastair clung to his denials, he knew something wrong was going on. And the reasons had to do with Lucas Donnelly.

Alastair was not satisfied that the brouhaha following poor Herman's funeral could be attributed to logical causes. Poison gas more likely had seeped into everybody's pores. Lucas Donnelly had puffed it from that little black cigar of his.

"Disgusting, all that yelling, and people insulting one another, being downright mean," Alastair said to Charlie Calman as he sat in the *Eagle* office drinking a can of Diet Pepsi.

"What are you yapping about?" Charlie gazed out at Alastair from the shadow cast by the brim of his Red Sox cap. His face reminded Alastair of a crushed paper towel.

"Herman September's funeral."

"A funeral's a funeral's a funeral."

"You can't say that about Herman's." Though Charlie had, Alastair continued. "By the way, you showed good sense for once when you wrote it up. Nothing about the buffet at the Bear later except for the food."

"Hmmm?"

If it wasn't the early side of noon, and if Charlie hadn't been sipping Pepsi, Alastair would have suspected the editor was soused. He had that fuzzy air of someone who was not exactly clear upstairs. "The White Bear, Charlie," Alastair prompted, holding back from rolling closer and shaking Charlie by the arm.

"Good thing Donnelly bought it, otherwise, who knows . . ." Charlie drifted into silence. Midsentence he sagged. The swivel chair creaked as he lolled, a Raggedy Andy spilling his stuffing.

Alastair fretted. "You feeling okay? Charlie?"

Charlie was whistling, a whispery sound like a kid playing a tune on a blade of grass.

I'm not the only person going soft with age, Alastair decided, unable to extract more out of Charlie than the little tune he kept working over his teeth.

Disgusted, Alastair rolled out of the *Eagle* office and onto the sidewalk. He tried to ignore the blazing sunlight and the sludgy air which made breathing a torturous exercise. He started thinking about lunch instead. He wasn't inclined to go home to have it, not while Mrs. O'Brien was working up World War III with the broom and making the dust fly. Keeping within the shadowy lip thrown by the shops on Main, Alastair rolled on.

Main Street bubbled a bit more actively now though the sun was higher, brighter, and the gauzy light obliterated the meanest wedge of shade which was all this side of the square got until later in the day. He gazed into the glare of New Morning with watery eyes and wished he could take himself out into the country for a long walk. A good tramp, clambering along the rocks on the short spike of Madder's Hill, wandering through those leafy caverns, fresh air pungent with the scent of pine, of earth, a green aroma that refreshed a man, made him feel clean and healthy as he went along. Arms swinging, muscular legs scissoring.

Alastair yearned so for an arduous long walk that he stifled a moan. He hadn't felt that achiness in his limbs that comes from healthy use, only soreness and outright pain, for more than forty years. The desire rose now as much from regret and lingering anger over his injury as a longing to escape a New Morning so whitened and flat, a town that seemed as fleshless as he was.

There *was* something wrong with New Morning, something that went beyond tempers frayed by the heat. A pulse of fear throbbed inside him, urging Alastair to flee, to escape. But he hadn't run on the beach at Omaha, only those fatal few feet— the last he ever walked unaided—and he couldn't run now.

Lunch . . . food in my stomach. That's what I need. He nudged the fear aside as he wheeled along Main, eyes on the pavement. It was when he looked up that he encountered Horse Keleidas.

Blood dripped down the singed edges of his torn combat pants. Horse's blood was brighter than anything else in New Morning. The blood jeweled, glistened, but then Horse did, too. His teeth sparkled with the same Colgate glow as Lucas Donnelly's. And his bright button-eyes twinkled as he called out Alastair's name, shaking his head and waving back a mane of tousled hair.

"Hey, old buddy, how come you got so small? You use to be tall as me, Al." Horse was shining, haloed in a golden vapor like some medieval saint. The apparition lurched closer, leaving a spore of blood along Main Street.

Alastair's fear rode the roller coaster up from his stomach and caught choking in his throat, as Horse's hands reached out. They were callused in stony ridges. Horse's hands had always frightened Alastair. Hands capable of killing. Now the sight of them panicked him as he imagined those hands crushing his windpipe. But as he stared, immobilized by fear, Horse's corporality began to melt like candle wax, skin and muscle loosened until nothing was left but a skeleton held together at the joints with stringy pieces of sinew. The stench of death, of rot and decay rushed up Alastair's nostrils, and fear mixed with a sour mash of vomit in his mouth.

The naked phalanges hovered over Alastair, ready to clamp him in a bony grip that would stop all circulation. He shuddered, recalling Horse's strength before a mortar shell had pulverized his left leg, most of his thigh, half his buttocks, and more intestines than he could afford to lose. The mortar had knocked him flat into a gully at the steep rise of Omaha Beach where, shocked silly, unconscious, pain mercifully wiped clean from his mind, he had bled to death, to this stinking cadaver, this rattling cage of bones. Only now, Horse seemed just as strong after forty years as he'd been in life.

Like a puppet hoisted on strings, Alastair was sucked upward until his face was inches from Horse's naked grinning jack-o'-lantern skull.

Noooooooooo . . .

Fear sprayed out in a gurgle, as smelly as Horse's graveyard stink.

A creaky jaw snapped, "How come you didn't drag me out of that sand, Al? We was good friends, that's what I thought anyways. Huh, Al, why didn't you save me?"

Because I was hit, too, Horse. I took one in the spine and went down. I didn't even know where you were once we got out of the water. Or the captain. Or Sergeant Breener, either. Whiskey's head was blown clean off his neck, that one I saw! And next to me, Bill Wright was shot in the chest. Went back flying, like somebody punched him, and it was right after that I got hit. Alastair's mind jabbered, though the words were blocked by the fear in his throat. *Help!* Why had no one come to help him escape this . . . this *thing* that held him in its grasp? There were people everywhere on Main Street but no one stopped. Alastair felt the surge of terror inside his chest.

"Horse, I'm sorry!" Alastair wept. "For me . . . for you, even though there was no way to save you. I never heard, not 'til later, back in the hospital, that you were dead at all. That most everyone in the unit was."

The skeleton's grasp was crushing him now, the pain unbearable. He felt himself launched into space, upended on his side, spinning. Blackness blinked on and off like a neon sign shorting until Alastair realized his nose was flattened against the Main Street curb. Something heavy pinned him in a pretzel twist; a naked end of something else gouged his shoulder. He thought it must be Horse, holding him fast. A red trickle rivered by his left eye. Blood. His most likely. He supposed he'd bitten his tongue. Salt leavened the taste of fear in his mouth. He could feel the stiff North Sea wind battering behind him, hear the trumpeting waves and the drumming of mortars, the syncopated popping of antiaircraft guns. A thud-thud booming. He recognized Omaha and the strip known as Dog Green.

There was a crash like the noise of a bowling ball on a fast wing down the alley slamming into the pins: Airplanes firing.

Oh, Lord, dead and gone finally. Went to hell on Omaha Beach that was hell itself, died there . . . oh Lord, forgive me!

This—all of it, New Morning, Charlie Calman and his red Sox hat, Evelyn's gourmet menus, Glory, dear Glory—was the dream. The dream was not Horse Keleidas; no, Horse with his severed leg, his blood-soaked rotting body was real. Alastair smelled the dead man's stink yet, Horse rotting, already rotten flesh, even as he became aware that he was lying sprawled near the curb, in front of him a fresh mound of dog's feces. Suddenly, he was aware of his pain, and of the fact that he was being hoisted up again.

"Mr. Wayne, you should be more careful. Terrible, this accident you had. This would never have occurred if you'd stayed home, in that nice cool house of yours," Lucas Donnelly was saying, as with one swing he raised Alastair off the ground as easily as if he were a bag of potatoes, and popped him back into the wheelchair.

Alastair—scraped, skinned, blood-spotted, joints shrilling from unaccustomed abuse, a ringing in his head—still had the acuity to notice that even the task of lifting him hadn't dirtied Lucas Donnelly's suit. Alastair was besmirched and wrinkled, sweat-streaked, smudged. But Donnelly was as pristine as ever, a mannequin in a Boston department store window, untouched by life. Lucas Donnelly wasn't the least bit ruffled. Now that his head had cleared from the stench of death, Alastair smelled the faint sweet aroma of after-shave.

"Go to hell!" Alastair croaked. And don't tell me, he cried silently in that crawl space behind his eyes where he tried to secret his thoughts so Lucas Donnelly couldn't snatch them away, don't tell me I didn't see Horse dead! Because I did. As much alive as the next man, as the man towering above him.

The terrible memory carried with it sulfuric vapors and Alastair, coughing, sputtering, weakly thumping his chest, started to swoon. He lulled, jerked back to wakefulness, wary of oblivion, but consciousness had unmoored, slipped loose in his head. Alastair slid forward, fast asleep.

"Heat prostration, you old fool!" Doc Trump seethed at the edge of a tantrum. His eyes bulged behind glasses tilted off-center, and he sucked his cheeks.

The skinny neck stalking above his collar was crepey, and Alastair, having swum groggily back to consciousness, thought before he thought anything else: Doc's getting old, too. Older than he was last week. Doc seemed battered, wonky, as he trembled, fists clenched, by the side of Alastair's bed.

"That ticker of yours could've just gone splat!" He hissed so sharply that Alastair mumbled incoherently, *"I'm sorry about that, too."*

Sorry about Horse. Sorry about Omaha, and woeful for

those other men who had never made it back. Sorry for himself as well, his shattered spine, his insignificant legs, and sex that was less than a memory. He couldn't even remember how making love with a woman felt. The texture of pleasure, the smells and the sounds. He did recall the vision of Horse, however, and blinking rapidly scuttled his regrets. "Too hot," he groaned.

"You're damn right it was too hot. That's what I said. You should've been in the house with the air conditioning, not wandering around town falling out of that chair on your head. Good thing, too, Mr. Donnelly, you snatched the idiot off the pavement or he might have been squashed by a car." Doc Trump stamped his foot for emphasis.

Alastair realized suddenly that he wasn't alone in the old sewing room with his physician. As a matter of fact, there was quite a crowd. Lucas Donnelly, naturally, because like Alastair's shadow the man was everywhere, either before or behind. Right now he was being modest, saying it had been nothing; anyone would have rescued Alastair without a pause.

Alastair was ready to shout, damn it, I wasn't in the middle of Main Street traffic. Just resting on the curb. A car would have had to jump the sidewalk if it wanted to get me. Alastair said all this, but nobody listened. They were all clattering— Doc, Lucas Donnelly, a teary Mrs. O'Brien wringing her hands, Gina Papriakas who must have arrived for her lesson, and Evelyn Crowell, never one to miss a trick, certainly not when it meant a chance to socialize with New Morning's star turn. It was some kind of miracle that Charlie Calman didn't barge in, prop himself down on a chair, and flip his notebook open. Alastair sprawled on Main Street was a news item, and Charlie should have been hovering like a vulture.

"I don't know what you went out for anyway," Mrs. O'Brien chastised. But Alastair was hypnotized by her fingers, one of which danced on a carved pineapple that capped a bedpost. He knew she was thinking: *Better dust!*

His voice returned in a shout. "Because I always go out!" Why in tarnation did he have to justify his habits to these people who invited themselves unwanted into the privacy of his bedroom? Interlopers!

Evelyn oozed, her eyes attached to Lucas Donnelly like suckers, "Dear Alastair . . . not as strong as you once were. Time passes, and one simply must slow down."

Alastair was disgusted with everyone staring at him as

though the Belwether brothers, the town's undertakers, had laid him out in a box, ready for burial. He glared down the useless length of himself to his toes. Somebody had taken his shoes off, and a pink orb winked from a hole in a black sock. For some reason this petty detail mortified him.

"Rest," Doc ordered. "Flat out here on the bed. Lettie, keep an eye on him—better make it two eyes—until you leave."

"Then Glory's coming by," Evelyn gushed. "To keep you company and play the piano. Which she does so beautifully!" This last to Lucas Donnelly. "And she'll make you supper. Glory's such an accomplished cook. After all, she learned from her mother!" Alastair thought she'd break her neck, swinging back and forth between him and Donnelly.

Mrs. O'Brien, not to be outdone, chimed in, "I've already got a chicken potted. And Dee Whittier called, said she'd bring soup."

"Call Dee," Alastair instructed Mrs. O'Brien, "and tell her to make it pea with some fat chunks of ham."

"Broth. Chicken," Doc prescribed. "Nothing heavy on your stomach in this heat."

Alastair choked back a protest. Pointless to argue over a bowl of soup. Not when they'll all gang up on me.

Lucas Donnelly was rumbling with laughter. Alastair saw the quivers, caught the seismic shakes that seemed to unsettle the floorboards and cause the bed to toss. He grabbed at the spread. Nobody else, however, sensed anything, busy as they were recommending home remedies. Even Doc suggested sweet tea, but not so much sugar since he was ever leery of diabetes in a man Alastair's age.

"You'll be fine, Mr. Wayne." Lucas Donnelly had stopped laughing and was nodding his head sagely. "As long as you remain home. Resting, of course. Perhaps napping in the afternoon. Listening to music. Music is such a friend. Soothing. Quiet, Mr. Wayne, that's the ticket. Staying out of the thick of things. *Let this be a lesson to you!*" His advice was logy with meaning, and Alastair's flesh crawled. Lucas Donnelly warned him, at least to keep off the streets. "Not too much excitement. Or visitors. You might even consider suspending piano lessons for a while."

Gina Papriakas paled. She imagined Alastair falling dead in the middle of her scales; a clunky left hand giving him a sudden coronary. "I won't come until you're feeling good!" she promised.

Lucas Donnelly congratulated her with a smile that sent Gina right to the door. "That's perfect!"

"Man should have been a doctor because he prescribed exactly what I would've myself." Doc tossed out the compliment airily, but his attention fixed on his patient. He snared a wrist and took Alastair's pulse. "Well, you've slowed down some, I will say that. But don't get any bright ideas about getting off this bed. Least not until I say so."

"How do you suggest I perform my bodily functions? In a bedpan? Like an invalid?" Alastair howled. Anger pumped so much adrenaline into his system that he shot up on his elbows, jerking away when Doc tried to hold him back. "Why don't you call the fire department ambulance and truck me over to Great Barrington? Then you can hook me up to some machine. Or better still"—he turned on Lucas Donnelly—"maybe you can hurry up that new hospital."

Lucas Donnelly didn't respond and only the slightest whisking of long spidery lashes signaled his annoyance, but then, all at once, Alastair was sucked into a maelstrom. He peered not into dark eyes flaked with granules of gold dust, but down a chute of fire. Flames darted in the holes gouged through bone, and Alastair saw Horse burning, Captain Morgan going up in a puff of smoke. Whiskey's head seared as the infernal heat singed skin to flakes of ash. His mother, his father, too. They looked god-awful, as if they'd been buried underground for years. Of course, they had. His brother John swayed by, waterlogged and stripped to the essentials by sharks. There was so little left of him Alastair, for a moment, failed to recognize him. Then John passed on and Timmy Farrow, just as anciently dead, arrived. Boy won't return from his travels, unless he arrives like Horse, Alastair reasoned, falling back onto his pillow.

Doc, not the least upset by Alastair's attack, whipped a stethoscope from his pocket and got the cold little cup under Alastair's shirt, searching for a clangy heart.

Lucas Donnelly did not move a muscle. He said, "Didn't I suggest, Mr. Wayne, that you stay calm?"

"You should apologize to Mr. Donnelly." Mrs. O'Brien leaned over the pillow to poke Alastair's chest with her finger.

Doc pushed her back. "Leave my patient alone, Lettie." But Doc must have been satisfied that Alastair's heart was at least marginally functional, because he snatched the stethoscope away and stuck it in his jacket pocket, from which it dangled like a snake.

"Mrs. O'Brien's right." From the corner of his eye Alastair saw Evelyn sidle around the bed and pat Lucas Donnelly on the sleeve.

"Don't listen to Alastair. He doesn't mean a thing he says. An ornery man by nature, that's how he is."

"Throw in senile, why don't you!" Alastair muttered.

Evelyn clapped her hands like a schoolteacher. "Can't you behave yourself, after all Mr. Donnelly's done for New Morning, and for you?"

The dead Bear owner bobbed up in Alastair's memory like a cork. He hissed through clenched teeth, "What about Herman September's funeral?"

"What about it?" Doc wanted to know.

A concrete slab bore down on Alastair's shoulder and arm—Lucas Donnelly's presence, weighty with the burden of all those dead. Still he rushed on, determined to have his say.

"A mess, Herman's funeral. Back at the White Bear, after the cemetery. The whole town arguing with one another, and acting crazy—"

Doc interrupted. "Alastair, you must be hallucinating. Herman September's proceedings were boring as ditch water. Even at the Bear. The same dreary whispering regrets. Just a bunch of soggy sandwiches, Alastair, and some drinks. Nobody could cough up more than a sentence or two about Herman, no matter that the man hanged himself."

Doc paused for breath and there occurred a sudden quiet into which Lucas Donnelly stepped. "You know, New Morning should be perfect, a town frozen in time."

Alastair locked eyes with Lucas Donnelly and was swept with relief that they were just ordinary pupils he stared into. Then, with a gesture that from anyone else would have been a man-to-man touch of affection, Lucas Donnelly gripped Alastair's arm. A red-hot poker sizzled through the shirt to his skin. He roared in pain, flinging himself over.

The eyeball-to-eyeball contest ended. Alastair most certainly had lost. Worse, he'd been cheated because there wasn't so much as an ash on his sleeve.

"That's it!" Doc ordered in an attempt to take charge. But Alastair stubbornly refused to give up; he determined to convince just one of them that the picture was wrong. Whatever had gone on in the White Bear, boring it wasn't, though he shouted himself hoarse saying so.

Evelyn, simpering, pursed her lips. "Ask Mr. Donnelly,"
she said. "He was there."

"Ask him!" Alastair shuddered, not courageous enough to
raise his eyes again. I know my limitations, he thought,
recalling hell's fire smoldering in a four-alarm somewhere on
the other side of Lucas Donnelly's corneas.

The dragon, that's who he was. The dragon had come to New
Morning and settled in. Acting friendly and throwing money
around like confetti. John D. Rockefeller Donnelly, outfitted in
human trappings, he had the town hoodwinked. Only the
dragon didn't fool him. And *why not?* The question was
frightening, as scary as the dragon himself. Alastair wished the
wool had remained draped over his eyes, too. But, like so
much of life he missed out on over the years, blissful ignorance
deliberately passed him by.

Though the dragon he might be—the devil, in other
words—he performed Lucas Donnelly expertly. Concerned,
soft-spoken, showing thoughtfulness too by not smoking his
stogie in a sick man's room.

"Mr. Wayne has to get some sleep." That was Lucas
Donnelly, shepherding them to the door, leaving Alastair alone
to bury his head in the pillow and try not to think his terrible
thoughts.

12

Glory Cromwell knew that sooner or later she would have to
do something with her life—as though life consisted of flour
and eggs and salt and milk ready to be blended together and
baked.

If you were a girl and almost twenty there was first of all the
never-never land of marriage.

So Glory thought about getting married and having children, and living in her own New Morning house where she'd
line the window ledges with pots of marigolds. When Glory
considered marriage, that was what came to mind—marigolds,

bright, plump with petals, nodding their heads in the early sun.

Jordy wished Glory would marry him; he'd asked her often enough. Only she hadn't said yes. But she hadn't said no, either. Her hands remained in her lap, fingers quiet and unmoving, when Jordy brought up marriage.

It wasn't that she didn't love Jordy, since in her heart of hearts Glory supposed that she did. There was, after all, the tremolo quiver beneath her breastbone when Jordy kissed her. But still, that sort of love seemed mysterious. She recognized how different it was from the sort of feeling she had for Alastair.

Glory had never told Alastair of her feelings for him; never unsettled the air with the words or written them out. *I love you* being the sort of thing that had to be said out loud. Somehow handing over *I love you* to Alastair with her fingers had a peculiar feel to it. And appearing from the tip of a pen or a pencil, *I love you* came out silly. The words had no more weight than "I'm cold" or "please close the window." *I love you* on paper might be only another item on Evelyn's grocery list. Soap powder, syrup, a head of romaine, two pink grapefruit— if ripe!—shelled walnuts, two packages of chicken breasts, and I love you.

Written, *I love you* got lost.

Yet, she wanted so much to let Alastair know that she would roll the words around her mouth, practicing, as if some miracle would occur and there they'd be, ready to send to the old man. It was somehow more important to tell Alastair she loved him than it would ever be to tell Jordy.

Now Alastair had had an attack, falling out of his wheelchair on Main Street. Glory, rushing home from The Gallery, the strain of pumping the bicycle pedals so rapidly tightening her legs, was afraid Alastair might die. He was old and frail and if not actually sick with some disease he was certainly fragile.

Glory, young, in glowing good health, never thought about dying. Death belonged to the future, even for Alastair.

Of course one day Alastair would die, so would Evelyn and Theo, Jordy, the cousins, Carol, and Bobby Pierson. She would die, too. Everybody did. Glory might be mute, but she wasn't foolish.

Dying was one of the few things Glory didn't fret over. She was, as a matter of fact, quite a worrier in her quiet way. About The Gallery for one thing, though The Gallery never had been one of her frets before. Glory liked her job, dog's body or not. The funny old building, hushed, and always cool as a cave, was a friendly place. Then, Glory enjoyed the art, some pieces and paintings more than others, and Eva instructed her how to, as she said, "separate the wheat from the chaff." Giorgio's ceramics, for example, though not important enough for the thinner cousin, were, in their way, special. Light as air, more breath than substance, they could almost float up by themselves. Breaking one the other day—Glory shuddered remembering—had been bad enough, but a slim sliver of a plate had slid from her palm just minutes after Evelyn called. Upset and afraid, that's what she was, Glory told herself after the plate had gone, taking off, a delicate saucer into space. It was worry over Alastair that caused the fall. Yet there had been a stirring in the bit of clay; the plate had moved all by itself, no matter how much Glory wished to deny it.

It wasn't just Giorgio's works that escaped Glory. A painting not secure in its frame fell when she lifted it to the hook. And that wasn't all. This morning, when she'd opened it, the front door had crashed into the wall, the reverberation unsettling the nearest coat-hanger structure which lurched from its stand. Neither of the cousins saw that, and the bend in the metal, though severe, might have been intentional.

Awkwardness, never one of Glory's failings, was coming to be matter of fact, and she worried so much over it and the resulting damage that, perversely, she didn't want to think of The Gallery at all.

Glory's list of worries was long. This summer Glory worried more ardently than she usually did. Perhaps because the whole town was in a turmoil with all the renovations. And strange things were happening. Like Herman September's suicide. And Lucas Donnelly he worried Glory to the point of dizziness. That look of his came at her like one of Doc Trump's needles, and she worried it would stab right through her, or fill her full of something terrible. Then, there was the dream.

The dream flooded her sleep with an endless sea and the boat, sails unfurled. The arm, rising, trailing like driftwood. The net of pale gold hair so like her own draping in a web of seawood on the water's skin.

Glory pumped faster, pushing the bike up a rise, almost horizontal over the handlebars, her hair flying forward in a banner. The hair in the water and the face she caught only a glimpse of, white and flat. Tonight or tomorrow night, the face would surface, Glory knew that, and she was even more afraid.

The effort of propelling the bike so fast rushed the blood into song through her veins, and her ears rang, so that she failed to hear the car creep up behind her. Suddenly there it was, Lucas Donnelly's black limousine, the windows shrouded with night. It paced alongside her whether she slowed or speeded up, the engine purring catlike, the tires whisking on the macadam. Glory pretended it wasn't there, that car that made her think of some prehistoric beast, but the limousine refused to drive by.

Her lungs squeezed painfully. Rivets stitched her side just below the ribs. Finally, she had to stop. The limousine stopped, too. The back window slipped down and in the smoky interior Lucas Donnelly's face hung like a cameo.

"You'll wear yourself out, my dear," he said, smiling. "I think you better ride here with me."

My bike.

As if she actually spoke, or maybe he intuited her thoughts as Alastair did, Lucas Donnelly said, "Jarvis will put your bike in the trunk."

Jarvis Badderly oozed out the driver's side and slithered around the front of the car. Glory longed to yell *go away!* but even if she were able to speak, she knew he wouldn't leave.

In a moment the Peugeot was swallowed up in the cavernous trunk and she stood on the soft shoulder. Then Lucas Donnelly opened the limousine's door and drew Glory inside as though she were a stream of water flowing downhill, unable to slip backward.

Once in the car, however, embraced by a seat so soft it must have been stuffed with feathers, and cooled by a draft of chilly air that whispered from some secret source, she eased slightly. It was really much nicer to be carried along than to bike in the heat. But it was unsettling too, riding in a car when you couldn't see out the windows. A pallid glow barely lit the interior, a grayish light that gave Glory the sensation of traveling in smoke.

The enclosed space, dark and cushioned in leather as soft as skin, was like the belly of some being. It was a womb and she was somebody's child carried effortlessly, unborn. There were no choices in the cocoon of Lucas Donnelly's car.

For the briefest moment, a moment that lasts no longer than it takes for a tear to fall, Glory wondered about her mother. Her real mother, not Evelyn. Who was she?

Suddenly Glory Crowell thought she might have been born from the sea.

"This is much better." Lucas Donnelly rustled at her side. He sounded to Glory like a breeze at night whispering against her window. She resisted turning to look at him and stared at the sheet of black glass separating Jarvis Badderly from the backseat. Not being able to see the driver behind the wheel keeping the car on the road added to her feeling of dislocation.

Unlike Evelyn, Glory didn't think Lucas Donnelly was something wonderful, a miraculous event that New Morning had been blessed by. His generosity and his renovation of the town meant nothing to her. Glory was almost unmoved by Lucas Donnelly's handsomeness. She realized he was a beautiful man, better looking than anyone she'd ever known or seen (even Jordy in his robustness paled beside the stranger), but that mattered nothing to her.

As for his polite demeanor, his sophistication, his style, Glory couldn't have cared less. She'd grown up in New Morning where, except for her mother, people seldom put on airs. People were simple in New Morning and Glory considered Lucas Donnelly's manner peculiar. He belonged in a novel by Jane Austen or Charlotte Brontë, seemed more a character in a PBS epic beamed down from Boston than a real person. She couldn't imagine going to the Pittsfield drive-in with him, or dancing out at Harry's on a Saturday night. Lucas Donnelly wouldn't eat pizza with his fingers or drink beer from a can.

Lucas Donnelly simply made her uncomfortable. She wanted him to leave New Morning, or if he insisted on living in old Miss Emma Tydings' house, just to keep to himself, as indifferent as a summer resident.

Unhappily, Lucas Donnelly decided to pay her attention in his strange way, as he had at Herman September's funeral, when he'd taken her out to the porch. He'd fastened his hand to her elbow and cleared a path, though she wanted to stay inside with Jordy. Then he'd sat by her side, the two rockers keeping pace with each other, and talked melodiously of the weather. Glory still didn't understand why those few, really boring minutes had made her blood run cold.

In their encounters Glory never gazed straight into his eyes, not even the night he kissed her hand, so she had no experience of Alastair's fires and the spasmed dancing of the damned. If she had been forced to face Lucas Donnelly directly, and if there was no escaping those dark eyes, Glory expected she'd recognize admiration and desire. It was lust she assumed would beam out intensely. And Glory knew about that. Jordy, after all, wanted to make love with her, though so far she had resisted despite their passionate fumblings in the van or on a blanket at the top of Madder's Hill.

If it was only desire that shone from Lucas Donnelly so radiantly, Glory wouldn't have worried about him at all. But there was something else that escaped defining. He smelled wrong for one thing, though as a matter of fact he smelled just fine. His odor was masculine, like Jordy's and Theo's, Alastair's too, though Alastair was more musty. But under that lurked another aroma.

"You're going to Alastair Wayne's to play the piano and to cheer up the old man." He had taken her hand as everyone who wanted conversation with Glory did, unless he listened by watching or reading what she wrote. Though she dwelt in a particular isolation, Glory was accustomed to being touched.

Lucas Donnelly's hand was cool, just like the inside of his limousine.

Glory didn't know how to talk to him. He wouldn't understand signing and she had neither pencil nor paper to write down: *How do you know about Alastair? Is he all right?* It was because of the old man that she had entered the limousine, because she was in such a hurry. That's what she told herself.

His hand was still holding hers. Glory felt electricity flow up her arm. Cold though, not hot, as if that part of her had been plunged into icy water. She would have drawn loose, but Lucas Donnelly held her firmly. He wasn't going to let her tug free, so Glory tried to widen the distance between them, shifting to the corner of the car. The seat wasn't soft now; she wasn't sitting on feathers but rocks. And he still continued to hold onto her hand. Glory thought, he's going to swallow me up. Like the shark in *Jaws*, Lucas Donnelly was preparing to consume her piece by piece, to do away with her flesh savagely, and when there was nothing left, Glory suspected he'd have what he wanted most of all—her soul.

"Don't be afraid," Lucas Donnelly whispered, except his whisper was loud, the words crashing against one another like cymbals.

Something in Glory overrode the fright of Lucas Donnelly's nearness, and all at once she found herself facing him in the gloom. His white suit in the pallid light wasn't chalky, but a faint lemon yellow, and his skin seemed darker below the black hair. And for a change a smile failed to tug at his mouth. He was handsome as ever but without any warmth. He seemed to Glory terribly cold, an ice figure sculpted to resemble a human being.

The hand Lucas Donnelly still held began to burn as if attacked by frost.

"There's nothing to be frightened of here," he said with a smile. But Glory knew in her bones he lied.

If the car hadn't been moving, if she hadn't been secured in Lucas Donnelly's grip, Glory would have jumped out. Then she'd be saved from his whispering, and the strange, old-fashioned way he spoke as he said, "I've made a long journey to New Morning and it's taken me quite a while, though the years have been no more than a minute flicker on the curve of time." He smiled quickly, a flash of lightning in the dark confines of the Cadillac. "I've waited, of course. But I'm quite patient. I'm known for my patience. Sooner or later everything comes to pass," he said with what Glory would have described as a sigh, had it come from some other person. Coming from Lucas Donnelly, that slow exhalation of breath sounded like the rumble of earth turning, rocks loosening their grip in the dirt and beginning to slide. The car might have been ready to plunge over a cliff, taking Lucas Donnelly and Glory, too, with it.

Though she didn't move, not so much as an inch, Glory felt herself falling through space. It was the same terrible sensation that came during sleep when her body would be hurtled into emptiness and she'd rush all at once in a sudden, alarming wakefulness. Then her heart would thunder, just as it was doing now, and her breath would be short and painful.

Yet a witness to this scene in the limo would have noticed nothing amiss, certainly not a flailing, terrified girl. In fact, a witness would only have been charmed by the man's courtliness as much as by the girl's quiescence; his dark handsomeness and her golden beauty.

The world seemed to settle; the limousine traveled smoothly on, but Glory was even more frightened. Her free hand was clenched, the nails digging trenches in the palm. Yet all he was doing was extolling her beauty, and promising eons of enjoyment for the two of them.

Then, in the murkiness of the limo Glory suddenly saw Emma Tydings' house, as if a movie screen had unrolled from the ceiling. The glossy floors shimmered where they weren't

covered by dazzling Oriental rugs. The furniture was delicate
Early American. There were silver bowls everywhere and a
tea service Glory knew her mother would faint over, and
flowers, baby orchids so lovely Glory caught her breath in
spite of the fear clutching painfully beneath her breastbone.
Marigolds in china pots lived on the window ledges. Marigolds
just as Glory imagined in that house where she was married to
Jordy. But Jordy didn't live there. It was Lucas Donnelly in a
silk smoking jacket at rest on the settee.

She saw herself in something long and tissuelike, the
material threaded with fine golden strands, so that she
sparkled as she moved like a prism turning slowly in the
sunlight. Her hair was piled high and studded with pearls.
Diamonds flashed on her fingers and in the lobes of her ears.
She was a magical apparition in Lucas Donnelly's parlor, a
princess, and that was what he said. "Princess," he called her.

In the limousine Glory shivered, chilled by the deep
freezing gusts of air, while *there* she was incandescing,
burnished yellow to orange. Tiny flames skipped over her in
mothlike flickers.

Glory ached to scream and cry, to throw herself at that image
of some other Glory who wasn't there. Panic rode up in her
throat and for a moment would have some foreign, harsh
sound to it. But nothing emerged, only a small puff of breath.

Wildly she turned to Lucas Donnelly who merely smiled in
his usual fashion. His arms were spread wide, and Glory
realized he must have released her hand. Now he wanted to
pull her into him, to encircle her, and she threw up an elbow
as if she might ward him off. She closed her eyes.

Glory put her fists against her eyes, and curled as far from
the stranger as she could get. Still, he was only inches away.
How easy it would be for him to reach out and take her. Yet, he
didn't. He laughed instead. And Glory, so frightened she
thought she'd crack into tiny fragments, heard Lucas Donnelly
say, clear as a bell, "You will."

Later, when Glory arrived at Alastair's, the old man failed to
notice she was shaking. The others had left and he had been
complaining, fretting invalid fashion, for the last hour or so to
nothing more substantial than air.

Glory kissed his cheek, straightened the covers he'd

mussed, and went to play the piano in the living room. Pleased though he was by her presence, Alastair had a lot to think about: Horse Keleidas appearing on Main Street, Horse who had to be a ghost even if he did appear in broad daylight because Alastair *knew* Horse was forty years dead; New Morning's amnesia; and not the least frightening thing that had occurred in only a few hours, the fire burning behind Lucas Donnelly's eyes. Or the fire in them. Alastair felt some confusion about what he had seen, or rather *where* he had seen it. What he was certain about, however, was that Lucas Donnelly had given him a sign. The man who wasn't a man but a dragon—the devil, the Prince of Darkness, Beelzebub, Satan, Mephisto—was warning him off. That much was plain anyhow.

If Lucas Donnelly was actually the devil who'd come to settle in New Morning, Massachusetts, this summer of 1987, for whatever nefarious reason—and as far as Alastair knew the dragon never did a thing without some grand scheme or plan—the message was simple. *Mind your own business. Lay low. Play dead. Stay home in bed. And shut up.*

Whom could he tell anyway? That was the thing. Trying to explain it would earn him a straitjacket for sure. If the dragon didn't fry him with his fiery breath, Doc would commit him. Either way, Alastair would be of little use to the town. Not that New Morning seemed concerned about being turned upside down like a paperweight in which snow fell when you inverted the glass. Not when the Barnes was being fixed up, streets, too, benches painted, new traffic lights, and a modern hospital with fancy equipment for Doc. And all the other improvements Lucas Donnelly was paying to have done. By the time the dragon finished, New Morning'd be the prettiest postcard town in the entire state of Massachusetts.

Though he was frightened and worried, sore from the bumps and bruises—his thigh was purpling already—something new nagged for his attention. That was when Alastair realized that Glory's rendition of a Strauss waltz resembled a dirge. He had suffered once through Will Austin's forcing him to listen to a Gregorian chant that was livelier than Glory's Strauss.

What's this?

The waltz was an easy piece. Glory had played it perfectly for months. "What are you doing in there?" he shouted, raising his head. But the Strauss thunked on. Nerves scratching,

Alastair scrambled upright. Wobbly or not, he'd transport himself to the living room and see what was wrong with the girl. Glory's draggy performance was worse than lifeless. He'd never heard her play so badly before, even when she'd first started her lessons.

He leaned halfway over the side of the bed, unbalanced, so that it was questionable which part of him would reach the floor first, when mercifully the waltz ended. He breathed a sigh of relief at the quiet, though for a moment he worried that Glory like Mrs. O'Brien had left without a good-bye.

But there she was, long hair swinging as she fussed him back against the pillows, tidying him, hands winging like small birds. "What was that caterwauling! Mutilating poor Strauss! I've heard peppier funeral marches."

Glory didn't answer. She sat in the chair by the window and stared out. It was one thing to goad somebody who could speak into sound, it was another to force Glory's hands into replying. *I don't like this; I don't like this at all*. Alastair was as frightened by Glory's moody stillness as he'd been by Lucas Donnelly's fire. I love this child, he was thinking, though he'd never been capable of telling Glory so. It was foolishness to tell somebody else's child you loved her as if she were your own, though Alastair was aware that Glory belonged to the Crowells by accident rather than design. He'd never gotten the whole story out of either Theo or Evelyn, where they had found Glory, nor how it happened that they'd brought her home. She had been a two-week wonder when the three of them drove back into town in a rented car and the Crowells took up life in New Morning as if they'd never been away. As if they hadn't taken a sabbatical to travel in a childless state and suddenly, poof! popped up with a five-year-old.

"We decided to adopt, and so we got Glory," was all Evelyn offered. Theo said much the same. If you twisted his arm Alastair doubted another word on the subject would have been forced out of his mouth.

After a while no one bothered to ask about Glory, and she slipped into New Morning's currents just as though she had been a fish the Crowells snagged.

Glory wasn't much help to Alastair, not cheering him up in the least. The waltz had been awful, her fingers on the keys heavy as hammers. Now the rest of her sank just as lifeless in the chair.

Glory needed to tell Alastair about Lucas Donnelly and the

trip in his limousine, but she couldn't think how. She could write it down, of course, but the idea of seeing the words take shape on paper terrified her. On paper, words were real; they remained on paper, leaving an impression even when erased.

Alastair hadn't an inkling of what Glory was worrying over, for contrary to what she believed his powers were, he never actually read her mind. Knowing her well, he was often able to catch the tail end of a thought. That was all. Had he known she credited him with an intuition he didn't enjoy, he would have explained as much to Glory.

"More fuss about Jordy?" he suggested.

She shook her head. The light bleached her. Alastair, whose distant vision was sharp, swore a watery glint of tears sparked in her eyes.

Love has the power to slice through one's preoccupations. Every fear but this one blew out of Alastair's thoughts. "What's wrong?" he shouted.

Glory's fingers played with one another, not saying anything.

"You've never cried, never that I recall. And I swear those are tears now. Glory?" But she swung her head emphatically from side to side in denial. "Now that Carol Boardman, she's a real weeper," Alastair babbled on. "I bet she blubbers over every little bump. Movies, too. Didn't you tell me once Carol's a waterfall in the movies?" Maybe he could joke the tears away and coax her into signing a couple of words. But Glory wasn't a two-year-old, not that Alastair was a big success with babies either. He grinned anyway, lifting up his lips over old teeth like a horse. Only the grin felt peculiar, stiff and unyielding, and Glory didn't offer a smile back. Her hands hung limply, and though he waved the pad of paper from his nightstand, she stayed huddled in the chair.

Alastair's back ached, up on his elbows as he was, propped, struggling to defy gravity. He longed to move off the bed. And do what? Take Glory in his arms and pat her awkwardly on the shoulder, smooth her hair? Her hair he noticed for the first time was frizzed. An aura of little threads wisped about her head. She seemed to bristle with static electricity.

Well, I've got to do something. I can't just lie here like a side of beef. But Alastair was an amateur in comforting.

From the first time he had seen the beautiful little mite, Glory ruffled his insides and made him sorrow for all that might have been but never would. Oh, dear Glory, his angel, his dream. Her unhappiness caused Alastair to cringe, especially now as misery came off her in waves. He struggled for some inspiration on how to cheer her up, but nothing came to him. Alastair slouched with a pain in his gut, powerless.

God damn! He wondered all at once if this was more of Lucas Donnelly's evil business. The memory of Glory captive in a rocking chair on the White Bear porch had seized him. Alastair just *knew* the child's unhappiness had to do with the dragon in the tapioca suit.

He flopped back to the pillows recalling that Lucifer was a fallen angel who'd once sat at the left hand of God. He had never had more than a vague humanistic belief in the Almighty, more Unitarian than Congregational even before Will Austin began dragging his flock to the edge of orthodoxy, and now he found himself forced to believe in the Devil Incarnate. Mephistopheles had assumed the shape of a human with dark good looks, suave, cultured, rich as a sheik, and oh so charming, this human embodiment of a beast, a dragon with sharp dangerous teeth.

He considered that he should take this problem to Will Austin who, after all, was the authority on faith. On the Lord and his fallen angel. But Alastair had a good idea what Will Austin would say. "Bonkers, that's what you are, because the devil's inside us, in evil thoughts and desires, or outside in terrible actions. The devil's not living in Emma's house. The devil's not Lucas Donnelly walking around New Morning, or riding in a limousine. Why would the devil want to renovate the Barnes, or spruce up the green?"

Oh yes, that would be Will Austin, after Alastair had unscrambled the conversation, erased all the arcane references, and gotten rid of the asides on liturgical music.

Alastair, wheezing, drooped with exhaustion. This sudden collapse—or some landslide in what she was thinking, Alastair had no idea which—got Glory moving. She fussed again in whispery motions. He thought she was trying to say something, but weariness overcame him and he couldn't stay awake to hear. His eyelids kept lowering like faulty blinds. And so, no matter how diligently he struggled to keep from sleeping, Alastair, yet again, slept.

While Alastair slept . . .
Moses Llewelyn rode high on the seat of his pickup into the

square, parked on the no-parkng side of the green, and took out his mower. Grass-cutting time. Time to trim the hedges. The gravel walks needed a raking, and the trash—mostly cigarette butts, gum wrappers, shreds of paper, hardened curls of dog feces—had to be cleared away. The small beds of flowers were looking ragged. He'd have to feed the soil and throw some grass seed on the barren paths of earth.

The green should be lovely, an oasis . . . was what the Donnelly man said. Well I ain't a miracle worker. Moses would have snapped like a snarling dog at anyone else, but the retort went unspoken with *him*. A bogey for sure, Lucas Donnelly dried up the saliva in Moses Llewelyn's mouth.

Moses didn't scare, Moses heavy-footed it through life with other people scared of him, or almost. In the time he'd spent out of New Morning, he'd always carried a knife in his pocket, a mean switchblade he referred to as Willy and which Moses was fast with. There was no delicacy in his manner of wielding the blade, but he was definite with it. Home again, Moses put Willy away in a bottom drawer because in New Morning he needed nothing beyond the hardness of his scowl and the raspy tone of his voice.

Moses thought of the switchblade as he wrestled the mower off the bed of the pickup and onto the grass. Maybe he should take it out, oil it, and carry Willy's reassuring weight against his thigh. Not that he'd ever flash the knife at anybody in town, never certainly at Lucas Donnelly. Moses shuddered, no, absolutely not at some honky with weird blinkers. Coals flaming in the stove, only Lucas Donnelly's eyes threw off no warmth. It should have been funny, but it wasn't, and Moses didn't laugh thinking that the only place to find any relief from the noonday sun was to stand in front of Lucas Donnelly and receive a freezing blast from his eyes. Spooky, that's what it was.

The sun purpled and Moses Llewelyn's sciatica gave him a swiping pain down his left leg. His knobby knees trembled, and just like some old darky who'd been hid in one of those hidey-holes of Miss Emma's house, he nodded his grizzled head and barked, "Yessus!" He could have puked.

Moses didn't know how but Lucas Donnelly had him behaving like someone he wasn't, laboring extra hard at his yard work, for example, when any sane soul his age would be taking things easy, winding down. Worse was finding himself selling some coke to Jack Boardman, the youngest Public son.

A hellion in that Toyota, he sure didn't need any help speeding up. Besides, trucking with the white lady wasn't Moses's style. He even had to go outside his normal contacts in Pittsfield to buy some. Now why was I troubling myself so much?

Lucas Donnelly suggested it.

Well, the honky hadn't right out pushed his face up into Moses's and ordered, *Sell that boy cocaine!* He hadn't been anywhere around when Jack caught up with Moses on Ridge Road, honked him down, parked off the shoulder, and climbed into Moses's pickup.

But Lucas Donnelly's presence was hunkering in his head somehow, filling up his passages like a bad cold. Moses heard him and had a lightning-fast vision of the man in the Wonder Bread outfit blazing like an ivory flame, and this got him agreeing to supply the pleasure Jack Boardman was so excited to buy.

Craziness, just plain craziness, Moses mumbled as he rolled the mower over the blades of grass.

Dee took yet another picture of the old black man, though she had more than enough, too many, and what did she need them for anyway. Just because, which had been the answer to every question since 1950.

Evil, Dee had learned over the years, is random. There's never a plan to it.

Not for the first time since Barcelona, Dee asked herself if it wouldn't have been better to have taken the plane to Majorca, the midday Iberia flight that winged off each noon. The flight that hadn't arrived. Maybe she should have chosen to fly, and to plunge from the clouds to the floor of the Mediterranean in a fireball.

She slipped her arm through the straps of the camera and swung the Nikon to the side where it bumped her ribs as she walked. Dee had watched the limousine deposit Glory and her bicycle on the sidewalk in front of Alastair's. She waited until the girl left before she went over with a jar of soup in a shopping bag. Alastair had been sleeping, sunk far into unconsciousness like a turtle in its shell. He didn't stir while she stood beside his bed and charted his breathing, so she left him a note.

Moses Llewelyn's lawn mower whined though the yardman

had disappeared behind the trees. Dee was thinking of her old friend, mouth open, snorting little puffs of breath, and trying to remember him as a boy. But the slide of a young Alastair, tall, rangy, a real bean pole and coltishly clumsy with his long legs, stuck in her memory, scuttled by the mower's shrill. That's what a plane dropping to the water would sound like. She shivered, and Alastair's picture slipped away. Dee saw the Spaniard instead. She never saw Jerry Holmes who had flown off to Majorca without her and hadn't arrived. Or she never caught him completely. His back, or a fuzzy slice of his profile, or the blurred, too-close nearness of him when his lips came in search of hers. But she couldn't bring to mind one good eight-by-ten glossy of his face. Count your blessings, she often told herself, but still she would have liked a clear image of Jerry Holmes. After all, that fall in Spain, she thought she loved him.

The Spaniard, he had burnished skin. Shadows grooved his cheeks and wedged below his eyes. It was strange that she could see him still when she couldn't see Jerry Holmes. Maybe that was another clause in the contract, written on parchment, she'd signed in the cheap little hotel. It seemed unreasonable that she hadn't read the document she put her signature to, but she hadn't. Fear made her willing. Who wants to die at twenty-eight? Who wants to be hurled in the fiery wreckage of a plane to drown in the sea?

Dee had just passed the Crowells' when Evelyn appeared on the porch. "Yoo-hoo! Dee! I was picking up the phone to call you!" Evelyn laughed. "Isn't this a funny coincidence?"

Dee hadn't the slightest urge to take Evelyn's picture. Evelyn Crowell's presence was nothing, a big fat zero, only empty space in Dee's thoughts. "Some coincidence, Evelyn. I only live next door."

Evelyn's smile dripped icicles. "I wanted to invite you to a small dinner party a week from Saturday for Mr. Donnelly."

Dee was too far away to see Evelyn's eyes, but she'd give odds they were shining. "I'll check my calendar and see if I'm free," Dee called up the Crowells' front walk.

Evelyn laughed. "Oh, Dee, you're so funny!"

Dee started to walk away, but Evelyn came a few feet nearer so that if Dee went ahead to her house, it would be simply rudeness. Not that Dee cared, but even this negative gesture demanded energy. It was easier to stand still and listen to Evelyn being pretentious.

"It's just a few people. To make the man feel welcome in New Morning. I mean, it's criminal that in all this time no one's entertained him. Considering who he is and what he's doing for the town. Honestly!"

I can tell you who he is and what he's doing and you won't like it one bit, Dee considered saying to Evelyn. The woman was plumped with importance like a prize hen. But what for, the stupid bitch won't hear me, or worse, won't listen. Her mind's locked tight as the First National's vault. Believing that Lucas Donnelly's the last hurrah. And everybody in town agrees. Except Alastair. Dee thought of Alastair, so insubstantial, a sheet of tissue paper on his bed. Thin and ailing. His old man's body a flimsy shadow. It was a wonder he didn't fade away in the light. Forget Alastair . . . still, I could tell him. Not that Alastair possessed any magic capable of driving Lucas Donnelly away. What could one shriveled, wasted old man with unusable legs and a failing heart do?

Evelyn's voice, insistently flowing as the Housatonic, broke into Dee's thoughts. "You'll have to dress up a bit, though nothing formal. The usual black with pearls, I think."

Imperious bitch! Dee sniffed, sorting through an album of memories for a snapshot of Evelyn Crowell as a girl. But Dee failed to find her. Evelyn had been too faceless, a nobody, no matter if she deemed herself a New Morning Brahmin now. In Dee's recollections Evelyn possessed no real presence, and she overdeveloped her, whited her out with too much light as, finally, Dee went on.

13

Word of the Crowells' dinner party for Lucas Donnelly blew through New Morning like a stiff wind. The telephone wires sang and the gossip became feverish in the stores, on the sidewalks, at the White Bear among those who didn't know a soufflé from a mousse. In a town the size of a thumbprint everybody knows everything the moment it happens.

"Oh, I'm keeping it small. Only a few friends," Evelyn said with sly pleasure to Cora Montrose. Neither Cora nor her Barrington sister-in-law had received an invitation.

Theo, at the bank, caught out of his office and on the floor by the tellers, said to Charlie Calman, "It's just Evelyn having a couple of people in." Charlie hadn't been asked either.

"Well, maybe I ought to drop over for the details. To write up in the *Eagle*. You know, guests, the menu, about the flowers . . . that sort of thing."

Theo, embarrassed, drew in his head like a turtle. "It's not that important."

"It is!" Charlie whistled.

Theo, however, did suggest to Evelyn that Charlie Calman might be included, but Evelyn obstinately remained firm in her refusal. She hadn't forgotten the article on mortgages, which in Charlie's mangled prose came close to accusing Theo of usury. Which wasn't what Charlie'd meant, it was just what he'd written.

Inviting Charlie wasn't worth arguing over. Theo decided he'd just call the editor the day after and give him the facts. Alastair, however, was an entirely different matter. "I'm sure," Theo said innocently, "you simply forgot."

"Never! I'm never going to ask him!" The knife slicing potatoes whacked the chopping board. Theo winced. "Never!" Evelyn repeated. "Alastair will throw a scene!"

Theo felt forced to say, "I like Alastair. He's my friend. Our friend. Probably like him better than anybody else in town." He might have added that he was comfortable with Alastair, but that wouldn't have cut any ice with Evelyn either. This dinner party of hers wasn't a friendly gathering for food and conversation and relaxation. This was shaping up to be one of Evelyn's "social events." So he offered instead, "Alastair's interesting. He keeps things jumping."

"Jumping!" Whack! Whack! The knife assaulted the wood. "He certainly keeps things jumping all right."

"He'll feel slighted."

"Frankly, I couldn't care less!" Evelyn cried.

Not everybody in New Morning wanted to spend a social evening with Lucas Donnelly. Bobby Pierson, for one, had very mixed feelings about the stranger. Having gazed into the

Tydings house on more than one occasion, Bobby knew he never dreamed about what he glimpsed through the windows.

Bobby Pierson had often spied on old Miss Tydings whom he found interesting. He saw her upon several evenings remove her hair and lay it atop the kitchen table, something Bobby found amazing. When he told Carol, she scolded him for peeping, but then she explained that Emma Tydings was just old.

"Old people are weird," Carol said. Weird meant funny; weird was strange. Lucas Donnelly acted strange too, even if he was much younger than Bobby Pierson ever remembered Emma Tydings being.

As Bobby also reported back to Carol—who believed Bobby was dreaming—Lucas Donnelly set fires blazing. He started them up in the middle of the living room in the same way Moses Llewelyn built autumn bonfires for leaves. Only once the conflagration was doused, nothing lingered, neither smoke nor ashes. There remained no charred wood.

Often people wandered through the big old colonial, or as much of the downstairs as Bobby Pierson could peek in at. But no one from New Morning; not a person he knew. Strangers in funny outfits. Bobby, watching Lucas Donnelly's visitors, was reminded of the movies or T.V.

Like so much of what happened to him on his rambles, Bobby mentioned the costumed foreigners to Carol who said, "If Mr. Donnelly finds out you're peeping he'll get mad at you."

It was then not unprecedented for Bobby Pierson, New Morning's own Peeping Tom, to go creeping through the streets, a ghostly shadow of himself, when darkness settled, as he was doing a week prior to the Crowells' dinner party. Bobby's sneakers whisked across the green, passed lightly over Ebenezer's grave. He crossed High Street and swirled low to the sidewalk like ground fog.

He meandered by Alastair Wayne's house, gray with nighttime cobwebs.

A full moon of a white light shone over Doc Trump's office door, but that globe always did at night. In the living part of the house the shades were raised, only no one paraded about inside.

The Crowells, Glory's mother and father, argued with each other. Red faces and shiny eyes like fireflies, hands swinging carelessly in space. A fight for sure, he thought, and moved away to Dee Whittier's house which rode still as a rowboat on an early-morning Garland's Pond.

The real moon climbed in the night sky round and white as Doc's office light. An icy glow seeped over the town though it wasn't cold. Not a breath of wind stirred the trees. Dead silence muffled New Morning like heavy winter clothes.

Bobby frog-stepped around the lawns and ambled back to the High Street sidewalk feeling lonely. When he reached Lucas Donnelly's picket fence, he heard Jack Boardman's Toyota down by the Route 20 traffic light. Jack's car for sure, roaring like an angry lion, and Jack's tires screeching when he made a two-wheel corner. In a second the Toyota burst in on the square, Jack hitting the horn in a tap-tap trumpeting.

Too fast, Bobby Pierson thought, as the Toyota swooped through the town center in a whirlwind. Though he turned in the shadows to chart the flight of Carol's brother, he sensed a throbbing at his back, as if the ground moved unsteadily. When he looked around he saw something odder than anything he'd ever seen through a window. The Tydings house pulsed whitely, swelling then contracting. The sides bulged in a regular spasming, the pyramid-shaped shingled roof stretched flat. Bobby, surprised, rubbed his eyes.

His Pumas, laces dangling, carried him along the fence and around the side. The pulsating house held him magnetized. By the time he reached the alleyway at the end of the black lawn, Bobby realized that the shadows, gauzy ribbons of gray, had slowly ceased their ruffling. The house, as if synchronized with the Toyota's shrieking—now fading away—stilled.

Bobby stepped back into a stream of moonlight lying in a thin covering of frost across his toes, and thought of the Housatonic where Jordy had taken him fishing once. He liked Garland's Pond better, where Jordy had also taken him. Garland's Pond sparkled clear as glass, clear as a window right to the muddy bottom.

Thinking about fishing with Jordy Farrow made Bobby almost forget the house and the funny way the walls swelled out. The house sat now on its corner as if it had never moved. Bobby tried to think of a reason a house would do what old Miss Tydings's colonial had done, what he knew it did—though Carol would tell him this pulsing house was dream stuff, too— but nothing even remotely reasonable presented itself to his slow and cloudy mind.

A brightly lit window glowed in what Bobby Pierson—who

was, after all, an expert in the house's layout—knew for certain was the living room, or the parlor as some people like his mother called it. The light that poured out of this particular window spun in a golden riverlet, warm, inviting, not cool like the moon's whiteness. This light shone yellow, almost amber, and it made Bobby want to touch it, to dip his hands in it and feel the softness trickle between his fingers.

By this time Bobby had come down the alley, his Pumas scuffing up dust, and he pushed through the gate. The house filled Bobby's vision and he drifted toward it, to the square of burning window, as if he hadn't a choice. When he arrived, tiptoeing into a bed of jonquils, he touched the wood, his hands creeping around to the sill. The house felt warm, but not unpleasantly so, and his fingers left the siding and went to stroke the pane.

At the other side of the window Lucas Donnelly gazed right out at Bobby Pierson. A curl of electricity slowly sizzled from Lucas Donnelly's pupils. The charge, cutting straight through space like a carving knife and through the glass without even cracking it, tore into Bobby's chest. He sailed off from the window, flopped to the ground where he lay, wide-eyed, watching the moon, oblivious to everything, while Lucas Donnelly stared for an endless moment down at him, appearing—not that Bobby saw him now—satisfied. Then Bobby Pierson, more mindless than he was on his blankest days, rose like the dead.

No meandering. Bobby cut a steady course over fences and down alleyways, onto the highway, out Route 20. Once, he was almost pulverized by a station wagon as he crossed the white line.

When Bobby met the river he waded in to his knees. The warm, lazy water nuzzled him as his sneakers slid on the rocky bed. Still he plunged ahead, to his thighs, past his crotch. The current embraced his waist.

The Housatonic at the point Bobby Pierson entered it was only half the width of Main Street. The far bank, drenched by moonlight, was ragged with choppy bushes. Gnome firs, arthritic beeches scalloped the edge. A large, amputated oak trunk collapsed half down the slope. The tree might once have bridged the current. Now nothing linked one side with the other. Still, the river wasn't wide, and a cloudless summer devoid of rain kept the level low.

Bobby never learned to swim but it was no great feat to walk through the water, for the moon-struck river drifted in a lazy swing. If only Bobby Pierson hadn't lain down upon it, as sleepy as though he were home in bed.

No one found Bobby Pierson right away. Only his mother and Carol Boardman even realized he wasn't where he was supposed to be, not that either of them worried overly much. Bobby often wandered off, and always returned. So Glory, when she biked out to The Gallery, couldn't know that Bobby Pierson was sleeping eternally, in the Housatonic.

Though the morning was beautiful, warm, the sky unsullied, a blazing blue, Glory, rapt in thought, as she pedaled off, never noticed. Her mother's party hung over her head like an incipient rainstorm. Glory would have been much happier if Evelyn never decided to entertain at all. Or if she hadn't invited Lucas Donnelly. Or last, if she could avoid attending the party. This, of course, was impossible. Ever since Evelyn had seen her emerge from the dark interior of Lucas Donnelly's car, she'd been beside herself.

"What did he say? And how did he happen to give you a lift?" Evelyn had been feverish with curiosity by the time Glory had returned from Alastair's.

Glory shrugged vaguely, for what could she explain? If she found herself incapable of telling Alastair what went on in the gloomy cavern behind the darkened windows, she certainly couldn't describe to her mother the Technicolor visions that bloomed like real life.

Lucas Donnelly terrified her. Lucas Donnelly and his car. She'd never enter the limousine again, not ever; she'd run first. Her mother proved right: Don't ride with strangers!

Evelyn, who had no notion of what went on in the limousine, and wouldn't have been disturbed anyway, felt they should strike while the iron was hot. Before, she meant, Lucas Donnelly took a liking to somebody else. Evelyn convinced herself that Lucas Donnelly had serious intentions. The ride and kissing Glory's hand as he'd done seemed signposts to Evelyn on a road to the altar.

"Don't worry," she said to Glory, "there's not any girl in New Morning who comes within a mile of you." Evelyn misread her own ambitions and desires for those of her daughter.

"Still," Evelyn added, "we better hurry, because a man like

Lucas Donnelly must know thousands of women. Women from all over." Lucas Donnelly might decide that one or another of those women who'd arrive one day, just passing through New Morning, ought to stay. The unknown glamorous women haunted Evelyn's imagination.

Lucas Donnelly, for all his attributes, aroused pity in Evelyn Crowell. He lived alone in Emma Tydings's house and Evelyn believed as an article of faith that there wasn't a man alive who wouldn't be better off with a wife. Men needed to be bonded to women, and if a man lacked a wife, it was because no female would have him. Like Alastair. This was so patently not the case with Lucas Donnelly, that to Evelyn it was only a matter of time.

Glory, pedaling over the hills, wished Lucas Donnelly would drive away as quietly as he'd come. She preferred a shabby New Morning. She liked the town as it had been before, the way it was changing from.

As Glory came up on The Gallery, as she had each morning since she'd begun working for the cousins, her muscles tightened. A warmth, then a slight wetness started under her arms and at the small of her back.

What will I break today? she asked herself. What damage will I do?

"Graceful Glory's become the proverbial bull in the china shop," Francesca had joked with Eva the day before, but the look she sent straight at Glory was lethal.

Leaning the Peugeot against the side of the building, she moved slowly, her steps leaden, worrying for the moment more about the sculpture and ceramics, the paintings, about the cousins, and her job, than Lucas Donnelly.

Bobby Pierson still hadn't been found by noon when Alastair, in his chair, cruising Main Street on the way to the White Bear for lunch, almost ran over his prize pupil Teddy Myers as the twelve-year-old tore out of the Public.

"Why haven't you been coming for your lessons?" Alastair barked. Teddy hadn't shown up for weeks now, and every time Alastair called his mother to ask how come, he got her mechanical voice on the answering machine. And no matter how many messages Alastair left, or requests to call back, he never heard from her. Now here was Teddy. Alastair half expected the boy would jump around him, and scamper down the street, but Teddy stopped.

"How come?" Alastair asked again. Teddy stared at him with eyes as cold as distant stars. He seemed, this small boy in torn blue jeans and too-small Disney World T-shirt, plus a turned-around Yankee cap, too still and watchful. He might have ceased breathing. Though he spent most of his after-school hours and every weekend playing ball, a liverish whiteness colored his skin and set off the freckles splashed over his nose and about his cheeks like measles spots. Alastair thought he looked less healthy than he had when he played the piano.

The old man and the boy glared at each other until Alastair honked into the silence, "Well, cat got your tongue? Or maybe you're too ashamed about sneaking off from your lessons."

But Teddy Myers was neither embarrassed nor ashamed, for he said in a voice so low he might have already passed through the usual change from soprano to bass, "Mr. Donnelly said I don't have to take piano lessons. He promised I'll be a famous baseball player when I grow up."

The words flung Alastair, who'd been leaning forward, back with a slam. A ruffle of fear winged to his heart and he might have barked at Teddy Myers, *What did you say?* and tried to corral him with the wheelchair if Teddy had stayed. But he went up Main Street, not running or rushing to escape Alastair, but at a normal pace, hands in his pockets. Alastair, who had swung around to watch him, saw Teddy blur in the midday light, blur right away, until it appeared that the boy had vanished in thin air. Was he here at all? Did I hear what he said? Alastair asked himself, inexplicably chilled and afraid.

Alastair was certainly off his lunch. The mere thought of food swirled the gaseous unrest in his stomach. He pushed the lever on the arm of the chair to forward motion, and rolled in the same direction Teddy Myers had taken, though he never thought of finding the boy, surely somewhere ahead of him. For the briefest second Alastair considered the awful possibility that Teddy had become—through some violent action he'd yet to learn of—one of his ghosts. But he instantly rejected this. He had no course other than to believe the boy. It was just as he said, more doings of the dragon. Lucas Donnelly had stolen Teddy Myers away.

This realization made it all the more urgent for Alastair to talk to Gina Papriakas who also had stopped her lessons. And again, he never got her on the phone. But he had reached

Stanis who only relayed the information that Gina had decided to quit. Stanis wouldn't say why, but he sounded relieved, even pleased that an end had come to his wife's musical education. Right to this moment Alastair assumed it was Stanis's doing that Gina quit. Now he thought, now he *knew*, Lucas Donnelly had stilled the music Gina struggled for. But as he rode around the northern curve of the square and onto High Street, heading for home, he realized he had to be sure.

Ten mintues later Alastair was driving his specially equipped old Dodge down Route 20.

Either he hadn't been out to the Papriakases' stand in a month of Sundays—though he would have sworn it hadn't been a very long time since he'd stopped for early apples and sweet corn—or he had to revise his memory. He remembered the stand as a large shed with a tin roof.

On the shoulder of the stand, the edge nearer New Morning proper, was an open space for cars, where Alastair parked his Dodge, not as close to the door as possible, his usual location, but further back, on the perimeter of the tarmac surface. That hadn't existed before! Alastair remembered clearly the bare earth lot filled with stones and rocks, deep ruts dug in by the trucks that brought produce from the farms. A man wobbly on crutches could go flying if he sank a rubber tip in one of those channels. Now Alastair journeyed safely to the stand. It was newly painted. The sturdy building glowed like a wedding cake except for the roof. The old tin roof no longer existed, it was cedar shingled now, each rectangular wedge looped attractively over the lip of its neighbor.

The year so far hadn't been particularly good for produce, a lack of rain mostly, and a late frost in early May. The fruit and vegetables grown locally were, therefore, rather skimpy and overly expensive. People grumbled and complained and bought most of what they consumed at the Super Saver rather than from the Papriakas stand or the Public, both of which provided little produce from such far-off places as Florida and California. So Alastair, coming from the crowded parking lot around to the front of the building, couldn't believe what he saw.

The tables groaned under a bounty of brilliantly colored apples, so red as to seem artificial, pears crisp and mouth-watering, cucumbers, squash, zucchini, radishes, too. All beautiful, big, succulent. The strawberries burst from their baskets; the blueberries weren't marble-sized but large as

mibs. Even the potatoes demanded you take them out of the
bins, home to be baked or mashed or fried and eaten.

Nobody would be able to resist this Papriakas cornucopia of
plenty, and nobody was. The narrow aisles between the tables
were jammed with people. They must be coming from as far
away as Pittsfield, Alastair thought.

Inside was just as crowded, with fruit and vegetables as well
as customers. Little spare space remained for either, and
Alastair noticed Stanis, his sons, a daughter-in-law, a Monterrey girl promised to one of the boys, and several white-
jacketed helpers whom he didn't recognize, all whizzing
about. Busy, busy. Mostly the stand was filled with strangers.
Strangers everywhere, he fumed, almost jarred from his
crutches by a well-dressed female with two tiny diamonds, one
atop the other, punched in her earlobes.

He was reassured, however, to catch a glimpse of Gina on
her stool behind the cash register totaling up. That hadn't
changed anyway. An Enderman teenager was bagging. Still,
the line weaving through the stand was long. Even for a
handicapped person, and one of venerable years, to thump
past so many customers patiently waiting, would have meant
murder. They'd kill him for sure.

He wasn't going to beard Gina behind her register, and
when she glanced up, squinting at him with no more
friendliness than she offered the strangers, he knew he's never
have a chance at all to ask why she *really* stopped the lessons.

A small black mole sprouting a nest of spidery hair spotted
her cheek. Had she always had that? Alastair had never
noticed it before. How could he have missed it? It wiggled like
an insect when she spoke.

Alastair swung aloft from his stoop and tottered out of the
stand in his whooping-crane lope. He didn't even bother to
buy any produce; he'd eat frozen. Behind him, over the shuffle
of voices and the scuffling of feet along the sawdusted aisles, he
heard a sigh of relief.

Alastair had been home for some time when Bobby Pierson's
water-logged remains were found. He'd been brooding by the
front window, searching the quilted patches of sky stitched
between the trees for birds. But while no robins or finches,
cardinals or blue jays, not even one crow above a town where

crows had historical significance, took flight, his thoughts winged wildly. Teddy Myers and Gine Papriakas. Alastair struggled but failed to chase either from his mind.

At the same instant, Glory was biking a return from The Gallery to the green, feeling useless, incompetent, for having shattered two more works of art. One, and she couldn't believe it even now, was another coat-hanger construction. Glory's arm had swung wide, swung out of her control, and sent the piece soaring. Still, it shouldn't have collapsed, not something created from curls of metal wire and welded into intricate bends. Metal never snapped and crackled like a dropped icicle, yet this sculpture did. It lay in severed pieces on The Gallery floor. The other accident occurred to a framed pen-and-ink sketch that lost its glass when she'd hung it. But the glass didn't merely splinter, it gouged deep slashes, somehow, in the crinkled paper.

Even Eva had gotten angry at Glory today, though she said little. Her eyes gave her away and the sharp jut of her jaw. As always, Francesca admonished Glory. To the cousins' regret, Glory was being warned. Just one more accident . . .

Glory was biking homeward and Alastair was brooding by his front window at the exact moment that two teenagers who were fishing and drinking beer in a rowboat on the Housatonic hooked Bobby Pierson. Since they drank more than they fished, the bobbing handful of dark material appeared at first to be a log. But as they neared the soggy hump, their befuddled minds quickly cleared and they snagged Bobby with an oar. One boy held him close to the stern while the other rowed. They couldn't tell immediately who it was, since poor Bobby Pierson faced downward in the water, and they whispered excitedly all the way to shore.

The current tugged at the boys when they scrambled from the boat finally and into the river. And they were less than reverent when they yanked Bobby over the stones and up on the grassy bank. Turning him over they were, for a moment, disappointed that it was only Bobby Pierson and nobody important. "The dummy," one boy said, and the other added, "So stupid he fell in and drowned himself."

14

Even in death Bobby Pierson commanded very little attention. As more than one person remarked, it was surprising Bobby hadn't gone and done something dumb like drowning before. What with his vacant mind and his meandering, it was amazing he had lasted so long.

So, poor, dumb Bobby Pierson passed from memory, except for those few who really cared, like Carol and Jordy, Glory, and the essentially decent Alastair Wayne.

New Morning paused over Bobby's death for half a beat and went on. Life was too urgent with so much happening. The Crowells' party, for instance, waited just ahead on the calendar. The town continued its jealous buzzing, while those who were invited preened, stuffed with self-importance.

Many people, however, were unhappy about the Crowells entertaining Lucas Donnelly. Jordy Farrow for one. From the back of the bakery he couldn't help overhearing the customers as they came and went, all having much to say about the dinner party.

Harlan worked behind the counter this afternoon instead of his wife. Harlan's domain was the kitchen; Grace had charge of the customers. But across the drive in the house, Jordy's mother lay upstairs on the bed, shades drawn, an ice bag pressed against her temples. Grace had one of her headaches, a migraine too bad for her to stay in the bakery.

The bakery was short one girl, and so Jordy, between deliveries, scrubbed the burners, listening to the tide of conversation ebb in from the front. In the pantry the remaining girl, Sarah, boxed pastries for Jordy's next delivery.

Jordy was surprised Sarah hadn't left with Beryl who couldn't run fast enough after Harlan almost killed her with his bare hands. They were friends, or at least though the girls arrived separately—Beryl came first—they seemed to get along in the narrow room they shared above the garage.

Jordy, thinking of Beryl again, saw her face purpling above

Harlan's hands. And then, just as had happened when he was struggling to tear his father loose, Jordy thought of Timmy, and all at once Jordy imagined he heard his brother whispering, as he once did every night when they lay in their separate narrow beds.

"Chop off his toes, one at a time, that's what I'd do," Timmy sang. "Then I'd take an ax to his fingers. When he was all stubby I'd do his ears and his beak. Yeah, his nose." Harlan, enraged, once punched Timmy in the face and his brother bled something fierce. "Then . . . then, I got to consider about the rest." Timmy shuffled lopped legs and arms like a juggler until they'd fly through Jordy's sleep. Even now an amputee took Jordy instantly back to those nights in the dark when Timmy terrified him with dreamy images of mutilation.

The little bell tinkled and broke Jordy loose from his memories. Glory's mother entered the bakery and almost immediately she engaged in a tug-of-war with Harlan. Jordy kept to the side of the stove where Evelyn couldn't see him. He never went out of his way to make himself visible to either of Glory's disapproving parents.

Jordy, bending over and scrubbing extra hard, listened to his father acting mulish with Evelyn Crowell. *Dumb*. Harlan should have learned by now that he frightened Evelyn Crowell about as much as a water bug in the kitchen sink. Jordy had to admire her, though he did so begrudgingly, for her lack of fear. After all, Harlan Farrow made an awful lot of people quail. In fact, Harlan Farrow forced almost everybody into collapsing like paper fans. But not Glory's mother.

Moving to the sink, Jordy could see, on an angle, into the front where Harlan leaned on the counter. Jordy imagined a wicked light in his eyes as he was saying, "I do the dills in the morning."

"I want fresh ones baked in the afternoon," Evelyn Crowell replied, pursing her lips.

Harlan bristled like a pit bull. "I got my schedule." That was ridiculous Jordy knew, and Glory's mother must have known it too, but she didn't contradict Harlan Farrow, she merely repeated, "Three loaves baked in the afternoon."

"No can do."

His father was a fool, standing there facing down Evelyn Crowell for no reason. Just plain meanness. It was no trouble to save some dough and put the dills in the oven in the afternoon.

"These dills, Harlan, are for Mr. Donnelly. Who is coming to my house for dinner." Evelyn was bearing down.

"For all I care you can have the pope and the president, too," Harlan snarled. And that at least was true. It was impossible to impress Jordy's father.

"Perhaps I better take my business over to that new baker in Great Barrington," Evelyn Crowell threatened. Harlan stiffened, not liking that a bit. He liked it even less when Evelyn added an extra bit of pressure. "And maybe Mr. Donnelly will give them the White Bear's business, too."

Jordy ran the water over his finger, drowning out the argument. When he shut it off he heard his father say, "I'll have to charge extra. If I do it, that is. Which I won't." Harlan Farrow was adamant, and when Jordy took a quick look up front, he saw the two adversaries eyeballing each other.

The moment hung in space, lasting forever, until Evelyn Crowell's upper lip curled. "Three loaves in the afternoon, Harlan. I want Mr. Donnelly to have the freshest bread."

"Well, that's too effing bad, what you want. Go over to Great Barrington, who gives a damn." His father was playing hardball, but Evelyn Crowell just dug in her high heels. She knew how the Farrow Bakery game was played, so she stretched across the counter until her face was half an inch from Harlan's and shouted, "Three dills. In the afternoon. For Mr. Donnelly. And don't give me any of your folderol about charging extra!"

Harlan's mouth gaped, some curse or insult about to be spoken. But he was too late, for Evelyn Crowell stormed out the door slamming it so hard the pie plates rattled.

"Did you hear that?" Harlan asked, coming into the back, looking uncertain, slightly dazed. It was a rhetorical question and neither Jordy nor Sarah, the hired girl, answered.

To glance casually at Harlan Farrow, there was nothing much to see. A medium-size man, square and rather beefy. Under a baker's white coat it wasn't possible to tell that his arms were thick as trees, hard with muscles. Many women had thighs smaller than Harlan's arms.

A close gray crew cut capped his head in steel spikes. An ordinary face thinned in slabs of flesh from his narrow brow to a blunt chin. Thin lips stood out against the dark shadow he was never able to shave completely clean. It was Harlan Farrow's eyes, however, that froze people dead in their tracks.

Small, pitted deep into bone, piggish. Harlan Farrow had the mean BB-eyes of a boar.

Now he was glaring at Jordy with those black-nugget pig eyes of his. His hand curled into a fist. And he was smoking. When Harlan Farrow got mad it was almost possible to see a white vapor clouding about him. His nose twitched and the cordons in his thick neck tightened. "It stinks in here!" he cried.

Sarah rolled her eyes, and since she stood boxing the White Bear order, behind Harlan where he couldn't reach her, she twirled a finger at the side of her head.

"Nothing smells," Jordy said after sniffing the air.

Harlan screamed, "Don't you tell me! I can smell it! The whole place is a sewer!" His nostrils flared and he swung around, confronting Sarah, grabbing her arm. Startled, she tripped, and when Harlan yelled, "You, you smell it?" Sarah received a fine spray of spit on her cheek. She blinked, tugging backward, too frightened to speak, but shaking her head negatively. Harlan swore, "God damn it!" and let her go with a snap.

Harlan moved through his bakery, throwing open cabinets, flinging the pantry door back so forcefully it slammed against the wall.

Jordy and Sarah froze as Harlan stomped down to the basement, while Sarah repeated her "screw loose" gesture halfheartedly. Her eyes fogged with wariness. She'd missed seeing what Harlan had done to Beryl, but she'd heard about it, and even if she was bigger than the other girl, she was frightened. Jordy thought about calling his mother, but she'd only be another victim of his father's rage.

They could hear Harlan down below in the cellar. Something crashed, and Sarah uttered a sound midway between a giggle and a cry. Quickly she covered her mouth, but her eyes found Jordy's. He shrugged, as if to say, just more of my father's craziness.

In a minute Harlan barreled back up the stairs and burst into the bakery like a thunderstorm. "God damn place smells like a toilet!"

Jordy inched toward the pile of bags and boxes, the deliveries, saying, "I got to go." He kept a watch on Harlan. His father might not have swung on him for years now, not since Jordy got big enough to hit back—though he hadn't, not

once, but still, he didn't trust him. Harlan vented his anger
with loud words once Jordy had gotten tall and fleshed out,
with insults and threats. If Timmy had stayed, Jordy often
thought, he would have outgrown their father's rage, too. But
Timmy hadn't waited; Timmy ran. In the night. In the dark.
No note. Nothing.

But had he?

"I suppose you think this is funny. Some trick to pull on the
old man, huh!" Harlan stood in the middle of the floor, his
hands knotted on his hips. His face mottled red, and he
churned, steaming, an engine set to explode at any moment.
"What did you do, let some milk sour?"

"Pa, I got to go," Jordy said. The temperature seemed to be
rising in the bakery. It was hot as a blasting furnace. Sarah
mewed now, like an animal in pain, as she inched to the side,
her glance moving restlessly from Harlan to the door. She was
readying herself to bolt.

"Answer me!" Harlan howled, his fists coming free now as
he swung his arms.

Jordy jumped. "Pa, nothing stinks! It's your imagination!"
That was the wrong thing to say, for Harlan, white beads of spit
foaming on his lips, leaped. He threw himself at Jordy with a
hair-raising shriek, but Jordy moved too fast, darting around
the counter. Harlan slammed into the metal shelves, and
Sarah, seeing her chance, fled. No hired girls now, Jordy
thought as he ran, rushing through the door after her. Without
stopping he hurled himself into the van, and when Harlan
staggered down the one step to the drive, grabbing at the
fender, Jordy shifted into reverse. He ripped away from his
father who fell to the ground. The last he saw of him, in the
rearview mirror, as he sped off, was Harlan running down the
rutted drive between the bakery and the house, shaking his fist
and screaming unheard curses.

Imagining, Jordy kept telling himself all the way into New
Morning proper. Imagining the thing that's not there, the
smell. He turned left and bumped the van over the ragged
second block of Brewster Street. It was all torn up, chunks of
tarred surface ripped free for the construction crew to ready
the bed where the cobblestones Lucas Donnelly was paying
for would lay. Lucas Donnelly . . . Jordy remembered suddenly that the smell rose up and out of Harlan's imagination

right after Evelyn Crowell left, after his father had given her a hard time about the party dills.

Traffic stopped and Jordy hung over the wheel, thinking. It was only coincidence, his father's argument with Glory's mother. It didn't mean a thing. More likely a tiny blood vessel had gone pop in Harlan Farrow's head.

Coincidence, Jordy struggled to believe as he swung into the square. Harlan had always had a thing about the bakery being clean as an operating room, that was all.

Down on the right, coming out of the Public, Jordy saw that long drink of milk, Jarvis Badderly, and shivered. He couldn't help himself, for his own imagination he sometimes thought was as overburdened as his father's. Jarvis Badderly, or rather the man who employed him, gave Jordy the creeps. Oh, how he wished Lucas Donnelly had never come to town, that the limousine had just kept going when he saw it that first morning on the square.

Slowing on High Street Jordy gazed up at Glory's house. He wanted to see her so badly that very moment his heart skidded painfully in his chest. He needed to touch her, to put his hand against her cheek. He needed Glory to erase Harlan's bad smell, the fragmented memories of Timmy and the hired girl, but most of all to put away the fear of Lucas Donnelly, to bury it.

It didn't matter that he'd risk her mother's anger—after his father's hysterical attack, Evelyn's temper would be no worse than a squall. He stepped on the gas and drove far too fast around the alleyway at the rear of the Crowells' where he parked. Leaping out of the van, leaving the door not quite closed, Jordy ran across the grass. He tried to imagine that inside Glory was running, too, toward him, ready to hurtle herself into his arms.

15

The day of the night of the Crowells' party came up with thunder rumbling to the north of the valley. But by noon the storm had passed over, heading south to Connecticut. The scattered rain dried up quickly and the sky returned to its summery blue.

Evelyn, with the casualness of a Prussian general, suggested seven-thirty as the arrival time, but long before that her guests were dressed and waiting. As for Evelyn herself, she stood before the dressing-table mirror in a new chartreuse silk and admired her elegant reflection. Arms held slightly akimbo, so she wouldn't sweat and stain the expensive dress, she walked rather like somebody who'd just risen from the dead down the hall to Glory's room. She found her daughter sitting on the bed, in jeans and an old work shirt, staring out the window.

"You're not dressed!" she cried.

Glory turned and gave her mother the blankest of stares. Her violet eyes were pebble-flat. But Glory's hands lifted up from her lap and fluttered languid as butterflies. Evelyn missed it.

"What's this? Tell me again." This time she paid closer attention, and as she read Glory's message her spine grew straighter. "What do you mean you don't want to come downstairs? How absolutely ridiculous!"

I don't feel well, Glory's fingers said.

Evelyn rushed to the bed and placed the back of her hand to Glory's brow. "Nothing. You're fine. Now get up and go take a shower."

On her way out of the room, Evelyn approved once again of the dress she'd bought for Glory up in Pittsfield. It was white, a chambray-cotton trimmed with lace about the hem and around the bodice. Low cut, it had short cap sleeves and a pink grosgrain ribbon at the waist. Though Evelyn had been unable to capture Glory long enough to take her shopping, she'd purchased the dress anyway, and of course it fit. Glory was a perfect size five. She'll look gorgeous, Evelyn thought as she had when first sighting the dress. Almost like a bride.

At the doorway Evelyn glanced back over her shoulder. Glory's fingers flew wildly. "No," she said firmly. "I don't want to hear it. Get ready!" Really, the girl was becoming impossible, wanting to throw away the chance of a lifetime. "And hurry up. There are last-minute things to do," she added before she marched down the hall to check on Theo. But her thoughts dragged behind her, lingering with Glory. So obstreperous lately! Evelyn blamed Alastair Wayne with whom she considered herself no longer on speaking terms. Not after the other day. How ungrateful that man was, how wretchedly he carried on! Those scurrilous accusations, and maligning poor Mr. Donnelly who only went ahead and saved his puny life! No, Alastair was impossible, if not downright senile, and Evelyn had told both Theo and Glory as much.

Theo, his jacket off, vest unbuttoned, tie loosened, sat on the edge of the bed reading *Business Week*. Evelyn drew in a deep breath, then exhaled angrily. "I don't believe it!" she cried.

"Hmmmm," Theo replied, rustling the magazine.

Evelyn shouted, "Theo!" and her husband finally lifted his head. "You have to get ready!"

"What do I have to do?" he asked in surprise.

"Shower and change, shave, comb your hair."

"Oh, really, Evelyn, this is too much!" He flapped the magazine, turning a page. "We're only having a few people in for dinner."

"Theo . . . go . . . change." Evelyn's tone sank dangerously.

Theo tucked in his chin and gazed down to his belly. "I look fine," he said, returning to meet her eyes. But something in her face made him back off from arguing. He closed the magazine and muttered halfheartedly, "Oh, all right!"

Jordy hadn't delivered the dills because Harlan Farrow remained adamant about the afternoon baking though Evelyn Crowell had called that morning, saying, "I don't want any misunderstanding."

"No misunderstanding at all," Harlan shouted down the wires. "Dills get baked in the A.M., not at some half-assed hour like four o'clock. If you want your three loaves delivered before noon, I'll see what I can do." Then Harlan slammed the receiver down on the cradle and continued sniffing around the bakery like a hound dog.

If it weren't for the fact that they all suffered from Harlan's new obsession, went on tiptoes in anticipation of his yowl— "The stink!"—Jordy would have enjoyed his father's agitation. Harlan seldom allowed himself to be gotten the better of, but the bad smell had shaken his balance. Jordy appreciated his father's discomfort, because he didn't like him much; hated him was closer to the truth.

At least the smell kept Harlan so occupied he stayed off Jordy's back about Glory. More than once his father had yelled, "Dummy, wait and see if the Crowells don't marry that pretty girl of theirs off to somebody rich. You think they're going to let her tie up with some poor geek like you?" His father turned outright nasty when his mother one dinnertime said, "But if they're in love . . ."

"Love! Love!" The word "love" infuriated Harlan Farrow. "What's this love nonsense everybody yaps about? Is it white like flour and nourishing? Does it have a taste to it, like salt? Answer me that. Tell me love is as real as the dollar eighty-nine I get for a loaf of bread!"

There was enough truth in Harlan's comments to keep Jordy quiet. It frightened him, Glory being handed over to some man better than he was. An educated man, rich, a professional. But no single male of the right age and with the necessary qualifications existed in New Morning, or hadn't. Now there was Lucas Donnelly and he'd been invited to the Crowells' for some fancy sit-down dinner.

That Glory was reluctant to attend her parents' party caused Jordy's heart to pound wildly. She couldn't think much of Lucas Donnelly if she had no interest in sitting down to dinner with him.

Jordy, agitated and at loose ends this evening, drove around aimlessly in the van, having no place special to go. Loneliness bore down on him like a coffin lid, and he pounded his fist on the steering wheel. Part of him felt like poor Bobby Pierson, wanting to peek into the Crowells' windows once it got dark.

Why, he wondered sometimes, didn't he simply walk into Glory's and take her away with him? Just simply carry her off? He shook his head, disgusted with his hesitation and plain cowardice, and accelerated along the newly cobbled stretch of Brewster, going much too fast.

Jordy slowed coming around High Street for another pass by Glory's. He felt no different from a sixteen-year-old. As he neared Alastair's he saw the old man come out his front door in the wheelchair. Jordy slowed even further and tapped the horn. Alastair, beaked and wide-eyed as an owl, looked up, raising his hand when he saw the van. Then Jordy passed on thinking that if he wasn't at the Crowells' to watch over Glory at least Alastair Wayne was. Only why should Glory need watching over in her own home?

Alastair shook his head as Jordy went on by. Boy's going to drive himself up a tree, he thought. Crazy for love. Well, why not? What better way to be at his age than yearning after a beautiful young girl?

Maneuvering the wheelchair over to the driveway and then down the short incline to the High Street sidewalk, Alastair rolled toward the Crowells'. He'd been more than a little bit surprised when Glory told him Evelyn wanted him to come to dinner. Naturally he'd heard gossip about the upcoming party. He'd have had to be either deaf or dead not to, but supposed Evelyn was still in a snit with him. Half a mind not to attend at all, he'd thought, but still said yes to Glory. The look in her eyes told him he had to. Besides, he was obligated to seize every chance to keep watch on Lucas Donnelly.

Alastair arrived at the Crowells' in the wake of the Eumises. Rita had on a flashy silver dress, and Howie, his cheeks scraped red, smelling like a floral bouquet, was being slowly strangled by his polka-dot tie. Behind his back Alastair heard a familiar rattle and turned just before he vanished inside to wave a hand at Moses.

Moses smiled at old Alastair Wayne, but then the smile shriveled into a scowl as he rumbled by the Tydings place. *That house*, he thought, filled with bogeys these days; it hadn't been when Miss Emma was alive. It was now possible, if a body listened carefully, to hear the tramp of boots, the rustle of skirts, a furtive whispering between the walls. Mice, any sane person would have decided, but then to Moses's sharp ears would come the ghostly shuffle of something much larger than rodents being hurried to the cellar.

Moses recalled the other day when he'd knocked at the back door to ask for his pay, and Jarvis Badderly, tall and freezing as an icicle, ordered him into the kitchen where Lucas Donnelly waited.

"Moses!" Lucas Donnelly sparkled.

"That's my name," the old yardman snorted. Fright clutched his intestines, but he held his ground. Known more than one big-shot honky, and nothing's so different about this white man, he reassured himself.

"How are you getting along, Moses?" Lucas Donnelly asked. Fluorescent tubes tracked across the kitchen ceiling emitting an unblunted hospital light. Still the man's face was webbed with shadows, thin as razor blades. "Doing your job?"

"What job is that, Boss?" Moses heard somebody say, some old darky, shuffling, sliding skinny legs in his chinos.

"Why the lawn and the flowers, the trees, too."

"Yessir! Yes, Boss. Moses does good work, don't you worry none about that!" Now who was that idiot, that fearful whiner, pawing the ground, chilled to the groin where his testicles had shriveled up like last fall's walnuts? Moses dared to look up at Lucas Donnelly. Shadows crawled over him. Not shadows but spiders, traveled in all directions across the man's skin. Tiny spiders trailed the cheeks and up the nostrils. Meandering on top of his eyelids, dropping off lashes. They skittered out of his mouth, to tap dance on his chin. Climbing the mountain of that imperial brow, the spiders disappeared into the black curly forest of Lucas Donnelly's hair.

Moses whimpered. He was dead-scared of spiders, and even more frightened of the man upon whose face they crawled.

"Now, Moses, it has come to my attention that when you mow the lawn the edges are left ragged. And that elm by the back gate is diseased. As for the azaleas, why Moses, I like them blooming in unison. I want to look out my window and witness a river red as blood!"

"Yessir!"

"As for the green, you've neglected it shamefully. It's shaggy as a mongrel, and that simply won't do." He grinned broadly now, allowing the spiders to march across his teeth.

Don't the man know there is insects in his mouth?

"You're too independent, Moses," he was saying, though Moses didn't know how he could speak with the baby spiders carpeting his tongue.

Moses wheezed. "True, I is a traveler by my own clock, Mr. Donnelly, and I beg your pardon for it, truly I do."

This isn't me! This be some nappy-head! A hundred-plus

years had been stripped back from time. Or perhaps three centuries of genetically patterned fear had freshly blossomed to give Moses Llewelyn the rash that was enclosing him like a body bag.

"Prune, weed, cut away the dead wood, rip out the deformed, replace the ugly with the beautiful, Moses. After all, New Morning is home. And the look of it must be sheer perfection!"

"Yessir, yessir," Moses cried, his tongue so badly swollen in his mouth he could barely speak. His parts jiggled, knees knocked, joints rap-a-tattled like rivets come loose.

Moses found himself dismissed with a shake of Lucas Donnelly's head that sent the spiders flying, winging off him like a swarm of wasps. He went high-stepping out of the kitchen, clanging, a tin woodsman, right across the grass that was barely flattened by his work boots, through the back gate, to the pickup where he collapsed on the seat, clutching the steering wheel to his heaving chest.

Moses was shattered. Was he, Moses, an independent man as he had assumed for decades without thinking about it, or one of his ancestors?

Past and present, the dead man and the living, Moses struggled on the front seat of the Ford pickup truck where, in the watery glow of the dash, he saw a brand scourged, scarred over and ridged up, on the underside of his forearm.

PP . . . two men noosed and hanging. Potter Plantation. The flesh smoked, skin, muscles burning. In terror, his whole arm seared with pain, Moses gunned the engine and shot out of the graveled back alley, tires squealing. The motor roared like a beast.

Howie Eumis had been looking forward to a social evening with Lucas Donnelly. It wasn't every day that he got to sit down at the dinner table and converse with a successful entrepreneur. Then, as council president, he had drafted a small speech that he meant to give over the wine. But only the day before, Howie's prize male Persian had to be put down because of feline leukemia. As if the grief he suffered over this stroke of ill fortune wasn't bad enough, the Pittsfield Veterinary Hospital phoned just as Howie and his wife Rita were leaving the house to inform them that Pussims, their remaining darling, also had to go.

Howie was devastated, Rita no less so. Being childless, the

Persians were, as Rita Eumis said, "our lives!" Neither husband nor wife knew how they'd manage to survive without the cats.

"Buy a couple more," Doc Trump had suggested. "For God's sake, Howie, buck up, they're only cats, not people!"

Doc Trump didn't understand, nor did Will Austin who said, "God's will." But then no one comprehended what the Persians meant to the Eumises. "Luckily we have each other," Howie said, weeping, to Rita, ignoring the glint in her eye, because he thought he knew what she was thinking. It was what he was thinking himself: I'd rather have the Persians.

Now Howie was trying to explain to Lucas Donnelly. "I'd give anything if this hadn't happened." He looked ready to cry. And, truth be told, he wondered if he should even be attending. Maybe it would have been better, more sensitive, to spend Pussims' last night at home. Tomorrow, together, they'd hold onto their cat, as they had with Horatio, when the vet sent the Persian into the next world.

"Heartbreaking, Mr. Donnelly. Just like losing a child." Howie sighed.

Lucas Donnelly, for once not smiling, appeared thoughtful. "Perhaps, Mr. Eumis, we can make some arrangement to rectify this unhappy situation."

Howie, a foot shorter than the dragon, rose up on his toes. "Anything! I'd do anything, Mr. Donnelly, don't you know, to get my babies back!"

Dee sat in the corner by the bookshelf leafing through an old *National Geographic*. Of all the unexpected things for the Crowells to possess was, as far as Dee could tell, several years of the magazine. Why? she wondered, flipping the pages. She stopped to stare at a New Guinea native in full regalia, war paint and an intricate headdress, holding a lethal-looking spear.

Relentlessly silent, she collected more than a few glances as she sat, dressed in one of her caftans, upon a straight-back chair, her legs crossed, looking at pictures. She came upon one she'd taken herself, or so the credit line stated. She failed to remember the photograph, a snowy alpine setting.

At first Dee debated not attending at all, but she had business with *him*, and the dinner party was as good an opportunity as any.

Sipping a vodka martini, a touch too dry, Dee kept watch on

Lucas Donnelly over the top of the magazine. It would take no mean trick to talk to him with any degree of privacy. All attention focused on him. Even Alastair, in his wheelchair at the room's farthest perimeter, held Lucas Donnelly in his sights.

The guest of honor, however, was more interested in Glory than anyone else. His glance, which kept falling on her, seemed careless. She might have been in his path as he searched beyond her for something else. But Glory wasn't fooled any more than the witnesses to Lucas Donnelly's interest. She sat, stiff as a board, her legs and feet firmly together, trying to look somewhere, anywhere but at Lucas Donnelly. But again and again their gazes snagged and Glory would pale while the dragon sizzled. Sparks of electricity came off him; he appeared about to eat Glory alive.

Only Jonah Enderman, New Morning's attorney, asking in his stuffy, men's club voice, "What business is it exactly that you're in, Mr. Donnelly? I don't recall having heard." Got him to let Glory go.

Everyone froze, leaving bits of conversation dangling. It was possible to hear the hall clock. *Tick! Tock! Tick! Tock!* Evelyn, coming from the kitchen with a platter held aloft, kept one foot in the air.

Save your curiosity, Dee could have told them, turning a page of the magazine so savagely she tore it slightly.

But the dragon only laughed, and even his laughter had a certain attractiveness to it. "People, you might say. My business is people." Before Jonah Enderman, poised with another question, could respond, Lucas Donnelly tapped the back of his hand with a manicured nail. "And buying and selling, Mr. Enderman. I am a great one for making deals."

It was when Evelyn called everyone to the table that Dee got her chance. She sidled up to his flank and nudged his arm. "Ah, Dee." He smiled, gazing down. "You look as young as ever."

Oh, how she wanted to strike him, or to yell at the top of her lungs. But there were other people about so she had to restrain her temper, secure it like a wild beast. She hissed through her teeth, "I didn't know about forever."

This remark caused the dragon to throw back his head and laugh even louder than he had before, which startled all the other guests but only infuriated Dee even further. Her fuse was shortening by the second. Though before she could explode, Evelyn said, "You here, Mr. Donnelly, on my right as guest of honor. With Glory to your left."

Dee got sent to Coventry, down the table by Theo. Alastair, noticing Dee's face, black as a rain cloud, had no chance to wonder about her bad temper as he was ordered to his own spot. Evelyn stretched out her arm and pointed straight at Alastair's chest as if she were aiming a rifle. There was something wrong with Evelyn, too. Alastair had been thinking that, since he'd rolled into the Crowells'. Evelyn's fuchsia lips had parted in a gasp of surprise and it took a full thirty seconds before she gushed like a geyser, "Alastair, how nice to see you!" Alastair wondered if he'd actually been invited to this gala of the Crowells', and smiled behind his own stony countenance thinking Glory had pulled a fast one on her mother. Who'd have thought the child had it in her! But then he realized Glory must have been that worried. Despite the pretty dress, she appeared weak, undernourished, and had clung as near to him as she could get. Away from Lucas Donnelly was what Alastair meant. Even now Glory was shaking her head, the long, shiny hair like spun gold slapping against her as she moved in a white flutter off from where Evelyn wanted her and next to Alastair. Once again Evelyn was forced to bite her tongue and smile, but it was obvious that inwardly she raged.

No one missed Glory's reluctance to go near Lucas Donnelly, but if the dragon himself was peeved, he didn't show it. He wove enchantment all through the meal, liberal with his entertaining stories, and his charm, so thick it was a wonder, Alastair mused, that they weren't drowning in treacle.

Evelyn was particularly pleased, her party a success, but her real pleasure would be to link Lucas Donnelly in matrimony with Glory. The women had whispered of Evelyn's intentions before sitting down to dinner, and now Alastair heard Cece Enderman hiss, "She'll get them married or else!" Evelyn must have caught that comment herself, because she licked her lips.

Really swallowed the canary, Alastair thought glumly. He left his food virtually untasted. He poked at tiny pieces of chicken in a cream sauce, stabbed a floret of broccoli, nudged a broiled tomato. The cooking was first-rate; Evelyn had out-done herself. Still, nothing tempted Alastair's appetite. He felt acutely depressed, and a heaviness like a thick woolen enclosed his heart. His mood wasn't lightened by each current of conversation flowing his way. All this talk of Glory marrying! He groped under the table to pat her hand.

The weight of his years hung on Alastair like steel.

"Off your feed?" Doc Trump, by Alastair's other elbow, prodded professionally.

"Why, you want to drag me into the office and abuse my poor body with some of your witchery?"

"In your usual mood," Doc joked. "Been sucking lemons again?"

"Very funny."

Across the table and down, Jonah Enderman said something to Ava Trump that had her throwing back her head and braying like a donkey. Doc, his eye on his wife, beamed, saying, "I have to admit Ava gets better looking with age. Don't you think so?" The question was rhetorical. Not better, broader, Alastair couldn't help thinking. Ava had gained thirty pounds in the ten years since her marriage. Doc didn't care, he had such a thing, still, about her. He had adored a much skinnier Ava from the moment he'd wandered into an ice-cream parlor up in Pittsfield and saw her dishing out a hot fudge sundae. Barely twenty when Doc, a confirmed bachelor of forty, asked her to marry him, Ava quickly said yes. And marriage had done nothing to dim Doc's infatuation, though no one in New Morning ever understood Ava's fatal attraction. Alastair, however, explained away Ava as Doc's Achilles' heel.

Howie Eumis now gripped the conversational bit in his teeth and, leaning around Rita, cried, "Some of the square's benches are going to need replacing. Wood's too rotten to simply throw on a couple of coats of paint. So I was wondering. Maybe we should get all new ones. Maybe wrought iron. You know the kind. Ornamental, New Orleans style, like they sell up in the garden shop at the mall. And white. What do you think, Mr. Donnelly?"

"I like the same old benches," Alastair sputtered, but no one paid him any more attention than a derelict relative. Excluding Lucas Donnelly, who smiled.

"I agree with Mr. Wayne," he said effusively. "Let's keep the benches. We'll just redo them, for better or worse."

Who asked the man for such smiley good humor, Alastair fumed. Oh, so expansive, so good-natured. Alastair's teeth set on edge. Besides, there was no denying the manner in which he concentrated on Glory. *Stop!* Alastair almost cried out. *Get out of here!*

"Not this year, Mr. Wayne. Not ever," Lucas Donnelly said, once more an uninvited guest in Alastair's head. He was as intrusive as a viral infection, and just as deadly.

Glory, her head lowered, guarded her eyes so that she

couldn't be trapped by Lucas Donnelly. But, after dessert, she was startled into looking up with the wide, terrified stare of a rabbit, when Evelyn said, "Glory will play for us."

Glory would do no such thing, which was what she cried with her fingers. But Evelyn, refusing to hear her, forged on. "Do that little piece you played for Daddy and me yesterday. The Beethoven something or other."

Alastair snorted. "Can't you see she doesn't want to, Evelyn?"

"Alastair!" Evelyn stormed. "Mind your own business!"

A fight was brewing, but before Alastair could exhale another breath and tell Evelyn Crowell that teaching the piano *was* his business, Glory flung back her chair, signing, *I'm tired, going up to bed.*

Evelyn read that all right and snapped, "Oh no you're not! You're going to play the piano!" But Glory turned her back and ran, oblivious to Evelyn crying after her. Anger so winded her, it required a minute for Evelyn to calm herself. She said, finally, "I must apologize for Glory's inexcusable behavior."

Lucas Donnelly, for once, had nothing to say, but he wasn't smiling either. He had, in fact, darkened like a dangerous squall. Hurricanes blew in his eyes.

As though Lucas Donnelly gave off a frightening charge of electricity, everyone at the table drew back from him, looked the other way. All but Alastair, who seemed joined to the dragon for the brief flicker of time. In this second Lucas Donnelly did nothing more than light up one of his little black cigars. The moment, however, happened so slowly the hands on the clocks froze and time stopped altogether. For Lucas Donnelly used neither a match nor a lighter, and he didn't lean forward to catch a flame from one of the candles in the center of the table. No, he simply clicked his thumb against the nail of his index finger and ignited a small jet of fire.

One quick motion that it would have been so easy to miss, and horror clutched Alastair's bowels. This magician's trick that Lucas Donnelly in his fury didn't seem aware he was performing tipped the balance for Alastair. He knew beyond any reasonable doubt. Horse Keleidas in the flesh, the dead so fantastical and frightening, proved less than Lucas Donnelly snapping his fingers and igniting a flame.

Lucas Donnelly wasn't Lucas Donnelly at all, but the dragon, the devil, Lucifer, the Prince of Darkness himself.

Alastair's heart missed one beat, then another, and he did something that later he wouldn't or couldn't for the life of him explain. He lifted up the still-full plate of cherry cobbler and chocolate-mousse cake smothered in whipped cream and threw it with enough steam to send it sailing. He was gratified to see his aim was still good, because he hit Lucas Donnelly just as he meant to. The dragon flung himself back, but for once Alastair had caught him napping.

"I refuse to lay down like a dying dog and let you prance off with my remains!" Alastair yelled to a startled smoldering Lucas Donnelly who was mopping at his face and white suit.

Alastair had only a vague idea what he meant, and when the dragon lashed back, "Mr. Wayne, this time you've gone too far!" he almost agreed. A slight suspicion niggled in his mind that maybe he should, at least perfunctorily, apologize, but a sudden tornado rattled the windows in their frames, blew out the candles, knocked over glasses and toppled the floral arrangements in their vases. Napkins sailed about the table like a swirl of autumn leaves. A chair overturned.

Alastair, plumped with self-satisfaction, rolled out of the dining room beneath a Star Wars of china spaceships. If a man's a man then he's got to take a stand even if it's the dragon . . . the devil . . . Lucas Donnelly.

Everyone yelled after him, but Alastair hustled to the front hall and as he struggled with the door, trying to swing it open and move the chair out at the same time, the handles were grabbed. He tensed, ready to swing around in some paltry old man's attack. But it was Glory, pale as the rising moon.

"And just where do you think you're going?" Evelyn loomed up behind them.

Alastair cast one final glance over his shoulder and came near to fainting. Evelyn hulked fat and bloated; her eyes dangled on flimsy threads. Her lipsticked mouth bled. The silk dress stretched tight as sausage casing on her ballooning frame and split; curling entrails spilled out. Evelyn trod right over her own intestines in her rhinestone sandals, almost tripping.

Alastair shrieked, "Run!"

The warm night hit him in the face like a wet rag after the air-conditioned coolness of the Crowells'. He gasped for air, hanging onto the arms of the wheelchair and wheezing.

Glory pushed him fast, running, the chair bouncing in the hurly-burly flight up High Street.

New Morning, somnolent, a dreamy ghost town, eleven at night, lights doused but for the pale puddles dribbling off the street lamps, was suddenly disorderly with sound. A second wind, as pounding as a blizzard, lashed around the square, flailing through the trees, battering at the bushes on the green. Flowers whipped by the unexpected current lost their heads. Fragile gladiola tops, tiny impatiens, bleeding tea roses, dark peonies gusted. Dust swirled in frantic desert dervishes, and a pebble struck Alastair in the eye.

The night vibrated with screaming, unidentifiable voices shrilling in dread, moans, chains clanking, the thump-thumping of horses' hooves, the Neanderthal crunch of tanks rolling on sand. Humans shrieked in agony until the bodiless cries reached the limits of sound and died. Birds dropped from the sky.

Alastair was an old sack of flour, flung side to side in his trusty, reliable chair. Then Glory got him up to the porch. It was Glory who had to get the door unlocked because his hands shook as violently as the elms. Finally, they were inside.

Quiet descended and Alastair, gasping, pushed against the heart riveting with jackhammer gyrations in his chest.

Glory hung over the chair, her arms dropping to entwine with his. Her cheek nuzzled his in a silky caress. "Now we've done it," Alastair fussed, but he didn't care. For all his aches and pains, all his fears, he was exhilarated, as though he'd taken that long hike up and over Madder's Hill.

16

Glory spent the night rolled up in a quilt on Alastair's bedroom floor. Alastair listened for the *clickety-click* on the ancient Singer in the old sewing room his mother had used, but didn't hear it. His ghosts weren't familial ones, which he would have welcomed. A cool motherly hand sweeping the cowlick off a boy's brow. Alastair could have used that. But Alastair slumbered and awoke, dropped off again, sank, then startled with a jerk, and supposed in the drift of not quite dreaming that he should be grateful none of his old army unit crawled out of their various graves to haunt him. Or that he envisioned none of the living as though they were already dead, as he had Evelyn Crowell before he and Glory fled into the night.

Once safe inside the house, Alastair had Glory lock all the doors—some bolts so intransigent from disuse they took a struggle—and flip the catches on the windows. No flimsy pieces of metal would stop Lucas Donnelly if he wanted to get in. Through the cracks, into the keyholes, down the chimney, there were hundreds of ways the dragon might enter. If need be, he'd blow the walls down. That he didn't come was some kind of miracle, though the dragon could wait. Time was on his side. When the telephone rang on and off for an hour Alastair knew it was the Crowells. He half expected them, too, Theo in his banker's suit, Evelyn dressed in her rage, pounding on the door and threatening Alastair with a kidnapping charge.

Halfheartedly he suggested that Glory return to her own home. He thought she'd be safe, that Lucas Donnelly had no intention of snatching her away, of running off with her. Not so precipitously. Lucas Donnelly had something more traditional in mind. Or he wouldn't have bought Emma's house and gussied it up. He wouldn't have bothered restoring the town. A New Morning New England perfect, that's what he fixated on.

Glory refused to budge. She signed she wouldn't leave him, that he wasn't well enough even if he wasn't sick. So how could she let him stay alone?

"Not sick, you're right. Just scared to the marrow," Alastair confessed.

Glory was, too, bloodless as Jarvis Badderly with fright. She told Alastair then about Lucas Donnelly's limousine and the ride she had gone on. She whispered it all with her fingers, the whole trip from the moment the Peugeot was swallowed in the limo's trunk until she was let out in front of Alastair's house. She moved so slowly at moments, as if she had forgotten what came next or how she would sculpt the words for it. Her gestures were unusually awkward and at one point, when she described Emma Tydings's house and how she had seen it right there before her, in the belly of the limousine, she spasmed, shaking like someone with a nerve disease. Alastair had to take her hands and hold them, saying, "Shush! Quiet now. It's all right." Only it wasn't, of course. It was wrong as wrong could be, this wanting, this insane desire or need Lucas Donnelly had for Glory. A child, that's all she is, let her be! Alastair cried silently.

When she settled finally, Alastair—though he knew it would only scare her further—had to share with her the appearances of the Omaha dead. Horse Keleidas without a leg and the others. But first he was forced to go back and explain about the Normandy invasion. "A blistery morning, bone-chilling, wet. But we were all so scared and spilling our guts out from seasickness, it wouldn't have mattered if it was a hundred-and-ten in the shade. Nothing really mattered except staying alive. Nobody was even thinking about killing Germans. The sea was wild, but maybe it wasn't. Maybe it just seemed that way. We all crowded together in that LST, which is like the flatbed of a big truck, but with high sides, and the front lowers like a tailgate. We had to go off that and into the water and get across the beach. Getting across the beach whole was the name of the game. Horse and the others didn't make it. Me, you could say I was luckier. I got halfway over with the sand sucking at my boots like wet cement, before I was hit. It was terrible at Omaha, terrible," he whispered.

And he told Glory about hell's fires in Lucas Donnelly's eyes where the dead danced and burned. "Jordy's brother Timmy was there. Gruesome." They looked at each other thinking: *no postcards, not ever.*

"But it was when, at the table, he flicked his fingers together to light that stogie of his. A cheap stage magician's trick. Any carny can do it. Yet somehow that tiny burst of flame . . ." He shook his head. "That did it. Maybe because it was so awesomely small after Horse and the rest of the dead. One quick little burst of fire." He didn't tell Glory that he had seen Evelyn rotting. Such a revelation wasn't necessary.

Their confidences exhausted them. They were by the table; Glory had brewed up a pot of tea. The leaves stirred uneasily on the bottoms of their cups. Alastair wished he could read them, wished he'd paid more attention to such things.

The only light was the sixty-watt over the sink. Gray, evaporating images climbed up the window. Glory, her arms folded on the table, lay down her head, loosening her hair in a spill of liquid gold. Alastair suggested again that she go home to her own bed, but she wiggled a sleepy *no* with her fingers. "Well, it won't make a bad situation worse, I suppose, if you sleep in one of the upstairs rooms." But she didn't want that either. She sat up and signed, *I don't want to be alone.*

After she washed her face and used her fingers for a toothbrush, and made a nest on the floor from a quilt and one of Alastair's pillows, she asked, with a little girl look to her, *What are we going to do?*

He had no logical answer, no plan, sound or otherwise. Throwing a full plate of food square at Lucas Donnelly was a clear statement of intent, but now he needed a scheme. He waffled instead, wishing he knew how to lie to this child. Alastair spoke the truth when he said, "I don't know. But I promise to think of something."

Some knight in shining armor he was, some St. George!

While Alastair tossed and turned, Glory slept the sleep of the just, the good, of the young. Alastair, despite his worries and fears, peered over the side of the bed at the small hump she made on his floor, and he was knotted with love. She seemed so little, curled, her legs to her chest, one hand at her mouth, as though if she needed to say something her fingers would be ready. A beam of moonlight, thin as an icicle slipped through the curtains and stroked her cheek. Alastair marveled at how still she was, a statue carved out of marble. Or a stone effigy. That image rose unbidden in his head and he shuddered.

I'm too old for this. He was past the point in his life when he should be sleeping in the same room with a female for the first time. And too old for protecting such a fragile creature. I'll need help, he thought, but who? Who was left in New Morning who'd believe his tall tale of the dragon? Who, considering the temporal benefits, would even care?

The next morning, surprisingly, Alastair awoke refreshed, feeling terrific. "Hunky-dory! A lion! Grrh!" he roared with what he considered a ferocious snarl. "Ready to eat up life!" Glory, across the breakfast table, laughed. Glory laughing was a strange phenomenon. Her face crinkled, lips stretched into a bow, and she quivered in a small quake, but of course there was no sound. Alastair's heart clattered staccato in his chest. He thought how nice it was to have a child in the house, though the child was nineteen and really a girl in distress. Oh, how much he missed, how much Omaha had taken away! How he wished they could just go on, the two of them, from day to day.

Glory made breakfast, Rice Krispies and grapefruit, scrambled eggs with sausage, and muffins burnt around the edges. He never ate so much, but she kept prodding him until he cleaned his plate.

"What a meal!" he groaned. "You'll spoil me. Besides, I'll get fat." She smiled, pleased, and got up to clear the table. "No, no. You cooked, so it's only fair for me to wash." As he jetted about the kitchen, Alastair was in a flutter. The dragon might have settled in New Morning, might himself be up already and beginning his day, washing his scales, sharpening his claws, gargling his smelly breath with Listerine, but Lucas Donnelly's early ablutions paled in comparison with Alastair's pleasure. He tried to remember when, since his father passed on, he had shared breakfast with anyone. Of all the day's meals, breakfast is the most intimate. When enjoyed in a cozy kitchen it presupposes a joint history, nights, days, preceding it in a continuous past.

Scouring the frying pan, Alastair tried to put the dragon right out of his mind. He wanted to pretend that Glory wouldn't have to go home along High Street shortly and face the music. He had no great desire to face the music himself. But the phone rang, and though he considered not answering, he knew it was silly, all make-believe. Glory wasn't his child, and lunch had to follow breakfast, dinner too. They weren't hermits, and Alastair, drooping, thought, there's work to be done.

"Your mother, I suppose. Or maybe your father," he said as they looked at each other and the phone went on ringing. "Guess I better answer it or they'll come over and break the door down."

"Alastair . . ." It was Theo. Thank God for little favors. Alastair preferred Theo to rain on his parade rather than Evelyn who would have shouted him deaf.

"Good morning, Theo. Sleep well?"

"Glory . . ."

"On her way home. Made me a healthy breakfast. A good girl, Theo, you should be proud. I had flutters and such a bad seizure, why Glory positively refused to leave. Thought I'd never see daylight if left alone. Which was probably true. Old and ailing, that's what I am. Stricken with indigestion. Gas in my chest."

"That's what I said. You were feeling poorly, and Glory . . ."

Alastair waved as she opened the back door and disappeared out into the glare of a new day. She waved back, one quick flick of her hand. "Leaving right this minute. She should be walking in by the time you hang up." He thought his heart would break. Glory, in her rumpled, party dress, with her hair pulled back and secured by a rubber band, seemed twelve. Twelve years old and lost. Her shoulders hunched, and her head hung like a broken flower. Anybody seeing her would think she was abandoned or a runaway.

Run away. Well, why not? It was the easiest answer he could come up with, and the moment he rid himself of Theo's embarrassed presence on the other end of the line, he called Farrow's. Sly, that's what I am, Alastair thought, ordering ten dollars of baked goods he didn't want and probably wouldn't eat.

By the time Jordy came around with the delivery, Alastair still rocked with indecision. What was he going to say? How much was it wise to tell the boy?

There are many weird happenings in the world today—read the newspaper, watch T.V. for proof. But who would believe the devil in 1987? *In New Morning?* In Alastair's time he couldn't even recall an encyclopedia salesman going door to door. This was a place people passed through, if they didn't skirt New Morning altogether, for more fertile fields. *The dragon!*

"Here's your order, Mr. Wayne. You want to pay for it now or put it on the tab?" Alastair was one of the few Harlan Farrow allowed to run up a bill on account.

"Oh, charge it, I guess. I've got to settle up with your father at the end of the month anyway. Com'on, sit down, have a soda pop. Take a load off your feet."

"Well, okay, but for just a minute. We're pretty rushed today. Another hired girl's hit the road. The second this week. My father's wild. But it's his own fault," Jordy said, not bothering to hide the fact of Harlan's disposition. His temper was common knowledge.

"What'd he do, overwork her?"

Jordy knew what Alastair was thinking. "No, he never laid a hand on Sarah. It's just the smell."

"The smell?"

"Yeah, he smells something bad in the bakery. Only none of the rest of us do. But that doesn't stop my old man from driving us all crazy. My mother wants him to go see Doc Trump, but she's afraid to suggest it."

Alastair hunched over the table, creeping confidentially closer to Jordy. "Harlan's a hard man, and you've got a tough job staying out of his way. Answer me this, Jordy, you ever think of up and leaving? There's a big wide world out there. Lots of opportunities for a smart young man. You could really improve your situation. Make a good life."

"You mean run off like Timmy?"

Oh Lord, Timmy! Glory was what mattered, now. If Alastair was right and Timmy burned in the pit behind Lucas Donnelly's eyes, there wasn't much anyone, Jordy included, could do about it now.

"I was just considering how you might like to broaden your horizons, see what else life has to offer. Know what I mean?"

"Can't say I do, Mr. Wayne. I live in New Morning, never lived anywhere else. Besides, there's the bakery and my job. Even if it isn't much and my father's got the temperament of a boiled owl most times. But especially, there's Glory. It's no secret how I feel about her. Though who knows if anything can come of it. With her parents wanting something better than me. I would too if she were my daughter. Glory's special."

Alastair tugged at the tip of his nose, annoyed, and cried, "Well, what are you, baked ham? You're a good boy, Jordy Farrow. A hard worker. Somebody who does the right thing. You'd make a fine . . . ah . . . mate for Glory." He made them sound like Pekinese, but he choked on the word husband, couldn't shove it past his teeth. They were so young! To Alastair, Jordy with his hard muscular arms and sturdy legs, with his square-jawed face and clear blue eyes, seemed an alien species.

"Yeah, well thanks for the vote of confidence, Mr. Wayne. I'm just sorry you're not Glory's father." He started to rise from his chair. "Guess I better be going. Have the White Bear delivery to make yet. That Badderly . . . what a pain! Goes over every little item. Would even squeeze the bread if I let him. But I said, hey, listen, you put a finger on anything and that's it, you buy it."

Alastair waved him back in the chair. "Don't rush off."

Jordy clinked the soda can with a fingernail. "I wanted to stop by Glory's. I didn't get to see her last night because of her mother's party." Jordy avoided Alastair's eyes.

Oh Lord! I wonder what the New Morning gossips are jawing over right now. My latest disrespect to the town's savior. They'll tar and feather me yet.

Alastair squirmed, muttering, "Can't stand that Donnelly fellow," as if, given his recent behavior, anybody might think otherwise.

"He's not my favorite either," Jordy agreed, ducking his head. "And," he fumbled, "there's something about him, something scary, which sounds nuts, I know." This admission had Jordy blushing, but whether from fear or embarrassment it was impossible to tell.

"Scary," Alastair repeated softly. Oh, he knew what Jordy meant all right, and was tempted to divulge who Lucas Donnelly was. Only, in all fairness, he'd then have to explain about Timmy and what he suspected, what he thought was true. That Timmy no longer wandered the world, if he ever had. That Timmy was dead.

"Throw in being jealous, too," Jordy said.

Jealousy was so normal, so ordinary, so *human*, that Alastair audibly sighed with relief. He almost smiled as he chided Jordy, "Nonsense! Why would you be jealous of an old man like him?"

Jordy laughed sourly. "'Cause he's rich and good looking, knows all about art, business, history, lots of stuff. Lucas Donnelly's educated, and me, I just finished high school. Besides, if the Crowells have their way he'll run off with Glory."

"Not if you run off with her first." At last, he'd said it.

Grinning indulgently, Jordy said, "You're some kidder, Mr. Wayne."

"It's no joke. Think about it. Lucas Donnelly can't marry Glory if she's already married to you." But he was not entirely certain about that. He thought uneasily of all the monstrous acts Lucas Donnelly could commit upon Jordy once he found out.

Alastair watched with envy as Jordy unconsciously crushed the 7-Up can in his hand. "You mean you think Glory and I should get married?"

"Idea shock you, does it?"

Jordy crashed back in the chair with such a thud Alastair worried about the old ladderback standing up to such abuse. "Never thought of it before?" he prompted.

"Hell, yes! Course I have!" Jordy was yelling. "Don't think of much else. If I've asked her once, I've asked Glory a hundred times to marry me. But she goes all moony and won't sign a thing. Not that she doesn't care, because I'm pretty sure she has feelings for me."

"Absolutely!"

"And shit . . . excuse me, Mr. Wayne . . . I'm crazy about her."

"So, do something about it," Alastair urged.

"Like what? Her mother looks daggers at me every time I

take Glory out. Her father's not much better. If they could they'd probably have me arrested. No way, Mr. Wayne, they'll ever let the two of us walk down the aisle."

"So, who says you and Glory have to get hitched by Will Austin? More romantic just to elope. They do it on television all the time."

"Mr. Wayne, you're unbelievable! You mean I should put a ladder under Glory's window and carry her off in the night?" This time when he laughed he didn't sound constricted. "You know, that's what I told Glory. Oh, not the ladder business, but us taking off for Maryland. Driving straight through. Then, before the Crowells know what hit them, Glory and I would be married!"

"That's the ticket, boy! Exactly what I was thinking myself. Theo and Evelyn will come around once it's a *fait accompli*!"

"I said we'd take Carol to stand up for us. And because it would be more proper that way." Jordy had a broad streak of New England Puritan in him. He ran his hand through his thick hair.

Alastair shrugged. "The two of you should be company enough," he said.

"Hey, Mr. Wayne, what about you?"

"Me!" Alastair sat up straight and tugged an earlobe. "Well, why not?"

"You can give Glory away."

"An honor. A pleasure." Alastair released a small smile.

Jordy tossed the soda can overhand into the trash. "Listen, this is all some pipe dream because I don't even know if Glory's interested in marrying. Me, anyway. She hasn't been so far."

"I know for a fact," Alastair crossed two fingers of the hand hidden in his lap, "that she'd jump at it." Would she? Alastair sincerely hoped so. Whatever Jordy's failings, more recommended him as a husband than Lucas Donnelly. Besides, Jordy was strong, he could protect her.

"Yeah, how do you know that?" Jordy asked suspiciously, staring Alastair down.

This isn't a boy, this is a man, Alastair realized suddenly and had a glimpse of what age would do to Jordy Farrow, how it would channel his brow and crease deep lines beside his mouth. And he will outlast me. . . . Which was in the nature of things, how life was meant to be, Alastair thought.

Jordy was still waiting for his answer, and Alastair, with the ponderous authority of age, lied. "Because she told me so," he said.

A clock ticked away in Alastair's thoughts and his intuition metronomed, *so little time, so little time*. In some manner Glory had to be gotten out of Lucas Donnelly's reach and made safe, and the sooner the better. What other refuge was there besides marriage to Jordy? A Glory married, a Glory no longer innocent would set Lucas Donnelly back on his heels. Or at least Alastair hoped so.

Alastair reached across the table and grabbed Jordy's arm, not unaware that it felt hard as cement. "Listen, you do want to marry Glory, don't you?"

Jordy smiled slowly. "That's what I've been saying, Mr. Wayne." He freed himself from Alastair's grip and moved back in the chair. "But I haven't seen her sign that she wants to marry me."

"Well for Christ's sake, drive out to The Gallery and ask her!"

Evelyn Crowell had a niggling little headache, the sort that is the tail end of a skull-splitting attack or the harbinger of a blockbuster to come. She stood by the sink dabbing her face and breathing deeply as she wondered whether to start cleaning up some of the dirty dishes piled high in the sink and on the counters or go lay down, just for ten minutes or so.

While Evelyn hesitated, Glory walked in.

Evelyn was of two minds about her daughter this morning. "Your behavior was atrocious. Rude. Surly. More appropriate to some trashy bit who hangs out at Harry's Bar than a Crowell," she lectured, forgetting for the moment that, in the strictest sense, Glory wasn't a Crowell. "I lay all the blame at Alastair Wayne's feet. He's been putting impossible ideas in your head." Swiping at the air, she moved too quickly and the motion set off a ripple of pain in her head. But that didn't stop her any more than the contrite picture Glory made with eyes downcast, hands demurely clasped at her waist.

"Ruined my beautiful dinner party, you and that crazy old man," she complained.

Glory signed nothing and Evelyn seethed; it was a trial on occasion to mother a daughter who didn't speak. While she had been spared the whines and complaints, the insignificant chatter, or the heated screaming matches, she tired of the silence. Talking to Glory was often like dropping her words down an empty well.

"Ruined," she repeated, suffering as she recalled that awful moment when Alastair had thrown a plate of her two best desserts at Lucas Donnelly. No memory lingered, however, of Lucas Donnelly's retaliatory attack. China and crystal never flew upward on the ferocious wind, nor did silver forks and spoons whiz through the air. Candles didn't stiffen in the graceful holders like soldiers to attention. It was all Alastair, unpardonable, infantile in his display of bad breeding. Or senility. If this keeps on, she thought, he'll have to be restrained. Incarcerated at the state farm, maybe, where he'll be watched full time to see he doesn't do any harm.

Though angry as Evelyn was with Glory, she couldn't escape feeling joyful imagining Glory wedded to Lucas Donnelly, living in the Tydings house. One day she might even be president of the Historical Ladies, a position, for all her scheming, that Evelyn had yet to obtain.

Lucas Donnelly had asked the Crowells if he might stay a few moments after the other guests departed into the night. So they sat, the three of them, all nice and cozy, in the living room drinking cognac. Just as if we were old friends, Evelyn remembered with a quickening of pride.

The balloon glass with its pool of amber liquid spun around in Lucas Donnelly's hands. It had seemed a crystal ball to Evelyn, in which she saw the future swimming. There would be a grand wedding, and she'd look particularly fine in a mauve silk dress. Theo in a cutaway. Masses of orchids, waiters passing canapés with white-gloved hands. Afterwards, in the years following, the pictures fluttering rapidly by continued to glow. She was the first lady of New Morning, and rode not in their serviceable Buick, but in a limousine, twin to Lucas Donnelly's. The house, comfortably and nicely done now, became elegant in the spinning cognac. All the furniture was authentic, museum quality. A Shaker drop-leaf sewing table, a meeting-house bench. Paul Revere silver and pewter. On one wall was an Erastus Salisbury Field that Evelyn would have sworn was up in the Springfield Fine Arts Museum. On another, a Hannah Cohoon ink-and-tempera that surely hung in Hancock. She had been acknowledged, she, Evelyn Crowell, stamped with approval, finally authenticated by the DAR.

"I'd like to come calling on Glory," Lucas Donnelly said in his delightful baritone. Evelyn's heart stampeded so quickly she barely breathed. "With your approval, naturally."

"Mr. Donnelly, what an honor!" Evelyn said when she finally gulped some air.

Theo, hunched over, wavered. "She's so young."

"Nonsense!" Evelyn cried, wishing it were her husband who was mute. "She'll be twenty fairly soon."

"What about Glory?" Theo countered.

"What about her?"

"Don't you think we should hear what she has to say about this? We're in the nineteen-eighties," he reminded Evelyn who dwelt, despite her dishwasher and vacuum cleaner, in colonial days. "Girls have their own minds."

At this point in her recollections, Evelyn's memory hit a snag. She thought Theo and Lucas Donnelly left the question of Glory hanging and drifted off into a discussion of investments, of stocks and bonds. She had the feeling they talked about the market, which made no sense at all.

But then, miraculously it was settled. The Crowells had formally approved Lucas Donnelly's courting. Handed Glory over on a dinner plate, Evelyn was thinking. No! It hadn't been like that. We simply promised to encourage Glory, share with her our experience and wisdom. Point out that men like Lucas Donnelly don't fall from trees. That ugly girls or uppity ones never find such husbands.

This morning, facing a disheveled Glory, Evelyn thought, we'll have to freshen her up, make her over before he changes his mind. A Christmas wedding would be perfect, snow falling and candlelight. Holly berries and pine wreaths, a towering spruce.

Glory signed, *I have to go to work.*

That was another thing. Now that she was promised to Lucas Donnelly there were more urgent things to do. She'd have to quit that job, which was piddling and unimportant. Glory would have to prepare.

Evelyn wondered if she should tell her daughter that she was going to marry Lucas Donnelly. Whether she wanted to or not. Of course she'd want to! What young girl in her right mind would turn such a man down. He was Prince Charming, after all. And she should drop to her knees and kiss the ground in thanks that he'd chosen her. Evelyn, working up steam, wouldn't countenance a refusal. Glory would go to the altar if she had to drag her there herself.

Glory was halfway through the dining room, heading for the front stairs. "That's another thing," she cried, running after her, "that job is out!"

Glory turned, startled. *What do you mean?*

"I mean you're to hand in your resignation. Quit. Today." Her fingers winged, *I don't understand.*

"There's nothing to understand. Simply tell the cousins you're unable to work for them anymore."

But I like working at The Gallery.

The headache, muffled by aspirin, flared out of control. "Glory, I've had my say on the matter, and this is simply it! Those women are the wrong company for you to keep, as a matter of fact." Evelyn wasn't sure what Glory suspected about the cousins' relationship; she was uncertain what she suspected herself. They might only be relatives, friends, business partners, two women sharing a house. Nothing off-color. But Evelyn doubted it. Her experience of independent women was limited to the cousins and Dee. But Dee was a Whittier so she didn't count. Besides, the Whittiers had all been faintly eccentric before they died out.

Glory's fingers were asking her something Evelyn missed. "What?"

What am I supposed to do with my life?

"Why just the same thing other girls do. Marry and have children." Oh, I don't want to go into this now. After dinner, with Theo, sitting quietly in the living room. That way they could explain patiently, quietly, so she'd understand how imperative it was for her to be courted by Lucas Donnelly, to marry him at Christmastime. (Though *he* hadn't specified a date.)

A wayward thought wafted through Evelyn's mind—What if she doesn't want to marry him?—but she firmly suppressed it. Why in heaven's name wouldn't she? He'll give her a happy, luxurious life.

Marry?

Oh dear, now she'll ask who. A faint suspicion nagged Evelyn that a normally acquiescent Glory would argue the idea of marrying Lucas Donnelly. Well, maybe she would—initially. But Glory was a bright girl; she'd come around. Only now really wasn't the moment to go into it. Later. Tonight. Let Theo, who always had a special way with Glory, tell her.

"Just go and change and pedal out there. But remember, you're giving notice. A week is sufficient. I hear their business is lagging so they'll probably be just as happy not to have to carry your salary. Women like that," she said, this time meaning alone and unsupported: Women who had to fend for themselves, a situation Evelyn found abnormal. Women were designed to be financed by men so that they could see to the important business of life.

Amen to that, Evelyn thought as Glory dragged the rest of the way up the stairs and she returned to the kitchen.

Quit my job! Quit! Glory, who had been so worried about possibly getting fired, was now ordered by her mother to quit. Oh, so much was happening she had a hard time thinking clearly. Bobby Pierson drowning . . . the awful dinner party . . . her own sudden clumsiness. And, always, the relentless dream. What Alastair had told her in the kitchen, over tea. She listened to his descriptions of what he'd seen. Lucas Donnelly with hell in his eyes breathing sulfuric fire. The dragon, Alastair called him. The devil, he meant.

To Glory he had been just a man in a white suit, even if he unbalanced her, worse, terrified her.

Alastair's ghosts from World War II. Poor Alastair! His dead friends were everywhere and Lucas Donnelly was responsible for them, too.

Glory trusted Alastair more than she did anyone else in the world. Never, not once, had he lied to her, and she believed him, even in this: That a man who appeared as a human was the devil. But, besides Alastair's statement, Glory had ridden in the black limousine where impossible visions appeared magically. The whole interior of the softly moving car had been transformed, and before Glory's astonished and frightened eyes, the future unrolled. Oh please! she prayed ardently, let it be only his vision, not what has to come about. Glory might not have known what she was to do with her life, but she knew she didn't want the future Lucas Donnelly offered.

Glory thought over her mother's demand. She liked helping out at The Gallery. She earned a salary, paid her expenses. Only the little things, of course. She banked most of the money the cousins paid her.

It made Glory feel important to slip the small blue account book below the teller's bars with the check Eva gave her each week inside. So much would be returned to her, the rest taken away and noted in a steadily increasing column of figures. Afterwards she'd visit her father's office and perch on the side of his desk. "Well, and how is New Morning's most important businesswoman today?" he'd ask her in jest. "Let's see your assets." And she'd hand over the book, and he'd nod his head approvingly. "Very good. Keep it up, honey. Remember, you have to support me in my old age." Then they'd laugh and Theo would take her out for ice cream, a childish treat they both enjoyed.

The column of numbers was to be stopped in its march. And what were the cousins going to say? They'd be hurt because they liked her, even Francesca who didn't like her all the time.

Glory parked her bike on the porch and tried the door. It was locked. Eva had forgotten to throw the catch. Glory knocked timidly, and when there was no Eva saying, "Oh God, I've been wool-gathering again!" she knocked again, loudly. Then she went around to the front. The main door was firmly barred, too. But from inside The Gallery she heard the cousins' raised voices. Glory peered through the pebbled glass.

Glory rapped her fist against the pane. Francesca cried, "We're closed!"

"It's Glory!" Eva said.

Francesca came to the door. "You're just in time to do a quick flutter with the duster, then lock up for the day. We're not available because we're going up to Pittsfield, aren't we, dear?" she said to Eva in a sour voice.

Francesca was dressed in designer jeans with rhinestones down the seams, high leather boots, and a tight red sweater. Eva, in funeral black, looked as if she'd slept in her clothes. Layers of makeup lacquered Francesca's plump face, but the only color on Eva were two circles of red high on her cheeks. She was flushed with unhappiness. Glassy-eyed, she turned to Glory. "We're not going anywhere."

"Oh yes we are!" Francesca rose up on her toes. "To the foreign-car dealer to buy me a Porsche. So that I can fly!"

"A Porsche is a car not a plane, and there's probably not one for sale—or one at all—in Pittsfield," Eva said in her sensible fashion. Glory, looking at an excited Francesca, could have told Eva that reason wouldn't work.

"Either you drive me," Francesca murmured dangerously, "or I'll drive myself and just abandon that old Honda of yours in the middle of the street. Well," she tapped her foot, "is that what you want?"

Glory thought she should leave the cousins by themselves. Get back on her bike and pedal home. Eva always shriveled with witnesses to Francesca's scenes, though Francesca, thrusting out her chin, never gave a damn.

Eva mumbled something into the collar of her black shirt. Not that it mattered, for Francesca, in a regal sweep, went by Glory and out the door. Eva hesitated only a second, then she loped in Francesca's wake. Her face mapped with pain, she whispered in passing to Glory, "Just lock everything up. Windows too. I forgot them last night."

Then they were gone. Glory heard the Honda roar to life and spit across the gravel, but she didn't watch the cousins depart. She walked through the empty Gallery, listening to the silence and enjoying being alone. I'll just make myself a cup of tea before I go, she thought. Then Glory waved into the quiet, as if there were someone to see what she said: *I won't quit!*

However, after her tea, which she drank perched on a high stool behind the register, Glory didn't leave. The quiet of The Gallery soothed her. Without the overhead spots lit, the big rooms were bathed in shadows, and such a moment as came between the last light of day and the night was created in the fairy-tale cottage. And this, too, was restful.

Finally she washed and dried the mug, putting it back on the shelf, but still Glory didn't go home. Rather, she drifted about The Gallery making no sound, as quiet as the anorexic ballerina wired in her arabesque to an armature. In the tranquil atmosphere where even the dust motes hung still in the air, it was difficult to imagine Lucas Donnelly out there, a worldly, or otherworldly, inhabitant.

Among the watercolors occupying the walls of the second, smaller room, a vibrant rendition of anemones hung a hair to the left. Passing by, Glory reached out and nudged the frame to straighten it. Only the barest touch of her fingers, the same fingers that so lightly flew across the piano keys, and yet they brought not beauty but disaster. The anemones seemed to rise up off the wall and plummet.

Glory, shocked, leaped back, and as she did so, a lacquered papier-mâché old woman tumbled, resulting in dismemberment, the tiny, perfect head severed from the neck. Ruin was now both front and back of Glory and she didn't know where to step, how even to move. What to do! Could the papier-mâché head be reattached, and what of the anemones? It wasn't possible to give them another frame and glass. Besides, somehow the fall had caused a blackish smudge in the sea of white.

Glory lifted up the old woman as carefully as though the figure were formed of flesh and bones rather than paper and paste. Yes, the head and neck could be glued together but there would be a visible crack, a dark thread woven through the woman's shawl.

The anemones, however, were hopeless. Glory swept up the slivers of glass and left the watercolor on Eva's desk with a note offering to pay for it. There was enough money in her bank account.

The Gallery was no longer a friendly place. How had she ever thought the big gloomy rooms, so chilly, offered a refuge? She hurried now, locking windows and doors, and throwing the last latch, she stepped out into the sunlight but felt no warmer.

For most of the day Alastair had more to occupy his time than went on in a week. Everybody might be mad as Hades at him, but the phone never stopped ringing. Jonah Enderman called to say, "I'm not just speaking as a friend, but as a member of the court. There are, Alastair, legal implications in your behavior."

"Huh! Tell me I can get arrested for being obnoxious!"

"Not arrested . . . sued."

"Who'd take me to court, Jonah?"

"Lucas Donnelly, for one. Every third word out of your mouth is slanderous. Some people don't take kindly to being called names and insulted."

Alastair laughed so hard he dropped the receiver and had a wheezing fit. Whatever Lucas Donnelly intended to do to him, or had the notion at least of trying, taking him to court would not be on the dragon's agenda.

Jonah had no sooner finished warning him about overstepping the legal limits when Howie Eumis called to say the chairmanship of the Old Home Week committee had been whisked out from under him. "We had an emergency meeting, Alastair, and decided you were crackers," Howie said.

Meeting, my eyeball, Alastair thought. The only meeting happening was in Howie Eumis's head.

Yet for half a moment Alastair felt insulted, wounded. Then his temper unwound, stretched, and he hollered, "And who did you put in my place, you groveling tabby!" Then: "Forget it, Howie." Old Home Week would just have to happen without him.

He sat brooding, worrying over these provocations and considering a New Morning of wax dummies. Lucas Donnelly was converting this little weed patch of a town into some perfect reconstruction, and in the process he was sucking the spunk out of people. Siphoning their souls. Meanwhile he had his eye firmly set on Glory, no doubt about that. Tonight . . . Jordy . . . heading south in the Dodge. Maybe with Glory gone, or otherwise wedded, Lucas Donnelly'd drive off in his limousine.

Dee came in through the back door without knocking.

"Hot damn, Dee, you almost gave me a seizure!" Alastair cried when he looked up and saw her standing by the stove. "Ever hear about knocking?"

"Fretting again, Alastair?" she said, pouring a cold cup of coffee. "I don't blame you, you've got a lot to fret about."

"If you've come over to criticize my behavior, you can meander right back on home," he said, sucking in his cheeks. Jonah Enderman might have lost a few legal screws, and Howie was surely soloing in a holding pattern of phantom meetings, but Dee seemed normal. She pulled out a chair and sat by the table, lighting a cigarette. "About to give me lung cancer by proximity, are you? Nothing like having a good friend." Alastair was cruising for a fight, a good loud long screaming match to clear the air.

Dee failed to take the bait. She said, "Misbehaving? Nope, worse. You're acting like an asshole."

Alastair sat back in his wheelchair, shocked at the coldly delivered crudity. He never had gotten accustomed to women swearing.

"As the traveling salesman said to the country virgin, there's nothing you can do about it, so lie back and enjoy. That's what you have to do, Alastair. Relax. Fighting with or about Donnelly is only going to cause you a heart attack. And it's not worth it. Lucas Donnelly always has his way."

She was as solemn as a country parson, puffing on her cigarette, sipping tepid coffee that had to taste like silt being the last dregs in the pot.

He took it back, she wasn't normal. She had the dull, drugged look of a crash victim, though he could have sworn she was younger than yesterday, rather last night at the dinner party.

"Just what's your interest in Lucas Donnelly? You've already sold him Emma's house and gotten your commission." Alastair proceeded cautiously. What did he know? Anybody in New Morning might be tainted, probably they all were. The start-up growl of Moses Llewelyn's power mower came across the yards. Moses. The least likely to be poisoned. What could Lucas Donnelly offer him? What could he be given? More to the point, was there anything in the world that old Moses hadn't at some time down the years taken a bite of already?

No one in New Morning resembled Alastair more than Moses Llewelyn. Spiritual twins in a manner of speaking, though the two men were night and day. Moses had, in one year or another, experienced all of life's varieties, while Alastair was a monk or a newly born babe. Probably most of what Moses had done Alastair wouldn't conveive of doing, yet it was just this that made them so similar. They both had spun past want and desire like stars on their way to cosmic extinction. Couldn't be bribed, probably not intimidated. Frightened maybe. Alastair at least, was scared for sure. Moses . . . he tucked the yardman away like a possible secret weapon and returned to Dee.

"Tell me something," Alastair said, settling his hands on his stomach, "just who is Lucas Donnelly?"

Dee shrugged. "What difference does it make?"

"Maybe life and death." Even to his own ears he sounded portentous.

Dee laughed, wrinkling up her face. For a moment, to Alastair's old eyes, she lost all definition and swam out of focus. "Death," she said, "is a blessing. Do you know that, Alastair? Death comes like the rain and waters the earth. A world without death is a desert."

"You're daft. You're demented." Now here, he was thinking, is a virulent brand of craziness. Too many pictures, too much gallivanting around war zones.

"Who's Donnelly?" he repeated. "Where'd he come from? Documents . . . which ones does he carry?"

Dee ignored him. "To you, sitting sniveling in that mechanical chair, death's some bugaboo. A foreign country where you don't speak the language. Customs all strange, and the food's liable to give you gas on your stomach. To the unliving what should death matter?" She was laughing in earnest now, running nervous hands through her hair.

Alastair was appalled, struck silent by her despair.

"Give it up, Alastair. Stay in bed. You can't be a fool forever. Not a live one anyway."

Maybe mortal illness afflicted her; maybe all this chatter about death was her own preoccupation. Could be why she'd returned to New Morning. To die. Alastair shuddered. She might be in her sixties but she looked much younger. Too young. To die, he meant.

"You feeling okay?" Alastair probed. "Nothing medical bothering you? Heart? Liver?"

Dee flipped the cigarette butt toward the sink but missed. The Marlboro landed on the linoleum. Alastair was stricken. "Behaving yourself inappropriately, Dorothy, like a toddler." He creaked down arthritically and picked up the butt. "Burn my house to the ground, why don't you?"

"Who cares about anything in this town?" Her voice lifted in a hot wind that flew across the kitchen, blistering Alastair. "Why should New Morning be any different? You think we're better than central Africa, Cambodia, Afganistan?"

Alastair stared at her owlishly. "What the hell are you talking about now?" But he was afraid he knew.

Dee raised the coffee cup to her lips with shaking hands. Over the rim she watched him. Softer now, rustling, she whispered, "Alastair, you're playing with plastique. New Morning's done for. The only result of carrying on will be to blow yourself into the middle of next week."

In for a penny, in for a pound, Alastair was thinking, certain he was being not heroic but foolish. "Lucas Donnelly can't just walk in here and take us over like Boss Tweed. Can't build his kingdom on the bones of New Morning . . . a colonial New England New Morning . . . which the town will be when he's finished. Just settle in and snatch Glory . . . and all the rest of it." Whatever that would be. But lightning fast he ran through the possibilities and came up with: Children. In this day and age even the dragon—especially the dragon—didn't marry without a good reason. Children. Or maybe just one. Could be, Alastair was thinking, why not son of the devil? It was about time that the dragon got around to propagating.

"Lucas Donnelly . . . Lucas Donnelly," he mused, trying

to appear ingenuous. "Big businessman, financier, can run an empire from Emma's as easily as from a glass city-tower. Believe that's what you said once. But what business is that? What kind of holdings? Iron and steel? Computers? Sow bellies maybe? Com'on, Dee, tell me!"

"Alastair . . ."

"Then let me tell you, Dee Whittier, about Lucas Donnelly." He had rolled as near to the table as he could get, so close he smelled her breath. Sour, early morning breath. Unbrushed teeth. He thought of Harlan's elusive odor in the bakery. "Lucas Donnelly is the devil."

The coffee dropped like a grenade, splattering the table, Dee, splashing on Alastair. But neither of them so much as twitched a muscle. The china cup from a set of his mother's rolled over the edge. Even when it cracked on the floor and shattered, they didn't move.

"What I want to know is how come you're pleading his case? What made you find him his house . . . handle all the paperwork after Emma died?" He had a fleeting suspicion that Emma Tydings might not have tripped on her laces despite all her years and infirmities, but because of Lucas Donnelly's desires. Poor Emma! Alastair hoped he was wrong. "Why are you acting like one of his minions?" Minion. He rolled the word around in his mouth like a sourball.

"Alastair . . ." She whimpered, puppy fashion, scared of the dark. Looked like a puppy, too. In front of his very eyes, in the minutes, half an hour she'd been in the kitchen, despite the laws of the universe, Dee had gone still younger. Age seemed to whittle off her as though Lucas Donnelly had applied a knife.

She whispered, "You don't understand."

"You know, that's what people are always telling me. But I understand enough. Besides, why don't you educate me in case I've skipped some essentials?"

Something snapped between them. Dee clattered the chair back as though she had finally realized she'd been splashed by the coffee. With her fingers she wiped at her face, leaving a brown trickle to wind along her cheek.

"I'm a mess," she said, but didn't sound seriously concerned.

"The devil, Dee, the dragon."

"The devil's a fancy. A name the priests give to evil."

"The devil's Lucas Donnelly and he's got himself a tidy berth in Emma's house. Country squire! Hell, damnation! And now he's after Glory Crowell!"

Dee seemed to calm, to be returning fast to the here and now as Alastair flared. They hung at opposite ends of a seesaw. "You've got this thing about Glory, as if you were the one who found her, adopted her, instead of Evelyn and Theo. But you didn't. And she's nothing but a girl, anyway. Pretty. Interesting I suppose because she's a mute. New Morning's own Johnny Belinda." She sneered.

Alastair had never seen Dee so snide, so deprecating. "Go to hell," he croaked both angry and offended.

But Dee only broke into wild laughter, into an old crone's cackle.

17

Despite his terrors and a loggy sadness that filled his heart, Alastair positively quivered with excitement. Sometime during the past forty years he must have left New Morning, gone further than Pittsfield or across the Connecticut line. He must have spent one night at least in a bed other than his own. But if so, Alastair retained no memory of such an event. And now, this very night, he was going on a trip. No matter how he struggled, a large part of Alastair felt like a kid, as he went about gathering clean underwear, socks, a pair of rather flashy pajamas he'd been keeping for when his blue stripes wore out. A fresh shirt, and then to be safe, a sweater. Who knew what the weather was like in the south. And just because, Alastair threw in a polka-dot tie.

By now it was only lunchtime and Alastair was left with nothing important to do. So he constructed a sardine sandwich, lettuce, tomato, and a thick slab of Bermuda onion and sat down to eat. But he strung lunch out for twenty minutes and was still burdened with the remainder of the day. Too jittery to sit quietly or take a nap, he played the entire *Ring*. He gritted his teeth and forced himself to listen as a penance, for sins, mistakes, for wrong turnings that might be taken in

the nights and days to come. Alastair absolutely loathed
Wagner.

Jordy missed Glory at The Gallery. He arrived to find a
Closed sign on the front door. Swallowing hard, he swung
around in the drive and returned to New Morning.

When Glory's mother answered the door, she threw him a
dark look like a poisoned dart. Jordy pulled away and
straightened up, suspecting Evelyn was about to say "Get
lost!" But Glory entered the kitchen and walked past her
mother and out into the yard.

"Listen," Jordy said when they settled in a pool of shade
beneath one of the backyard elms, so far from Evelyn
plastered up against a window she couldn't hear them, "let's
get married. I mean, Glory, ah, will you marry me? Not next
month or in a year or so, but tonight. Or tomorrow. Tonight I
want to run off with you, down to Maryland. Mr. Wayne and I
discussed it, and he said he'll come with us. Glory?"

Alastair?

"Yeah, he's been encouraging me. He thinks it's a good idea.
Us. Marrying. Eloping tonight. What do you say?"

Glory glanced over the hedges toward the upper end of
High Street where a slice of Alastair's roof poked through the
trees. Then she looked in the other direction. Finally she lay
on her back and stared up into the leaves. On a thick lower
branch two severed pigtails of rope remained from the swing
Theo had hung there when Glory was a little girl. Jordy had
never seen her swinging on it, but he could imagine. He lay
beside her and a ghostly Glory in gauzy memory passed back
and forth over their heads.

In a little while, when Jordy feared his heart would burst in
his chest, her fingers waltzed across the grass and whispered in
his palm: *yes*.

The New Morning telephone lines were fairly worn out with
all the gossiping about Evelyn Crowell's dinner party. People
were tied up for hours on end. Even though he had been the
star of this gala event, Lucas Donnelly—who saw all, heard
everything, and usually discerned what was going to come

about before it did—would have had a headache if he were capable of it. As it was, he simply became annoyed. Lucas Donnelly disliked chatter.

He finally climbed up to his aerie at the top of Emma Tydings's house and punched out a series of instructions on a small Apple in the corner labeled NEW MORNING. Then he sat in his executive chair and enjoyed a cigar. Almost immediately the phones across town fell silent, the receivers got hung up. Lucas Donnelly breathed a sigh of relief.

A white cat padded down the conference table. "Shouldn't you be over at the Inn making plans for dinner?" he asked as the cat hopped to the floor and Jarvis Badderly stretched six feet into the air from a patch of white fur.

"I never thought I'd be a restaurant keeper," Lucas Donnelly's man complained. "Why anyway? What's the purpose of the White Bear?"

"Because," the dragon answered. "And please don't get so familiar with me." Then he added, because Jarvis had been with him a long time, "I liked the idea of an inn. Some place to go after dinner for a tankard of ale."

"We should be in England instead of New England"—Jarvis Badderly scowled like sour milk—"if you're determined to play the country squire."

"England's boring. England's all washed up."

"Spare me the line about America being where the action is. You've used that for years."

"Jarvis . . ."

"*Mr. Donnelly!* I ask you! Why not Flynn or O'Boyle?"

Anybody but Jarvis Badderly, seeing the look on Lucas Donnelly's face, would have slunk quietly away or simply stitched his lips shut. And when the dragon hissed, "Jarvis!" again, this time sulfurically, another person—if Jarvis might be designated *homo sapiens*—would have felt a loosening of his bladder and bowels. But Jarvis Badderly just patted down his unwrinkled jacket and sneered through his nose. "What are you going to do, turn me into a toad?"

Time stopped for two heartbeats as Lucas Donnelly transformed the attic into a fiery holocaust. Flames shot up out of the floor, the rafters sparked and crackled, the table splintered into rivers of flame, and the computers exploded, but when the smoke cleared Jarvis Badderly continued brushing invisible lint from his sleeves. "The thing about being in hell," he droned nastily, "is there's nothing worse that can happen, no location more *hellish* to be shipped off to."

The doorbell rang. Lucas Donnelly, utilizing his all-seeing vision, viewed Dee on the front step. "Well, don't tell her," he said.

"I think she probably knows."

Jarvis Badderly descended to let Dee in, then led her up the steps before he went off to the White Bear, behaving, since he was in the presence of a stranger, like the perfect manservant he was.

"A visitor . . . how nice," Lucas Donnelly said, waving Dee to a chair. They stared at each other in the manner of casual acquaintances, which they certainly weren't. Even in his current guise Dee would have recognized Lucas Donnelly. It was the small tuft of hair poking out of his left ear, but especially, he was identifiable by his eyes. Dark though they were, they glittered, glassy, agates, sun-struck. By his eyes Dee had recognized Lucas Donnelly the day he arrived. He was Kurm; the Spanish grandee; a German neo-Nazi addressing a meeting in Düsseldorf. A terrorist she interviewed once in Lebanon, that was *him*, too. A weathered ayatollah in Iran. A drug dealer in Istanbul. They were all the dragon. Only now Lucas Donnelly was better looking, more urbane than she'd seen him before. He had a certain charm, a more sedate presence to him in New Morning. And Dee didn't know what that could mean.

"People are dying," she said finally.

"Every day. Every minute of every day. If you care to know how many exactly I can punch up the figure for you." He waved his hand toward the bank of computers.

Dee glanced about the room at the sophisticated machinery. "You're mechanized."

"I have to keep up with the times."

She swung back around and they returned to staring at each other. If Dee hoped to outlast Lucas Donnelly, she was being foolish. The dragon, patient to a fault, could wait forever. Time was entirely on his side. "Am I in one of those?" She jerked her head at the computers.

"Everyone is."

"No exceptions?"

"None."

Dee dug into the pocket of her shirt and pulled out a pack of cigarettes. Lucas Donnelly gallantly sparked his thumbnail, but she ignored him and used a match. When she had lit up, inhaled, and blew a trail of smoke down her nostrils in imitation of the dragon, they sat quietly, puffing, neither afraid of lung cancer, until Dee asked, "What are your plans?"

"For New Morning?"

"No. I think I understand about the town. About Glory Crowell, too."

"Really?"

Dee went on, "You want a place to settle down, to plant roots in, just like Ebenezer Symthe."

"You don't say."

"Yes, that's it. But I don't care about New Morning, or not especially. Not even more or less about Alastair Wayne. What you're up to with him."

"I thought he was a friend of yours."

"Friend!" She laughed, coughed on the smoke, and shagged at her hair with her nails. "I gave up friendship when I sold off my soul. Along with commitments and love and all sorts of ties that bind."

"Is that so."

"I suspect when you get tired of playing cat and mouse with Alastair you'll give him a heart attack. Not that he doesn't deserve one, the old fool. He just can't keep still. Mind his own business. Act the dummy like Charlie Calman. Won't be bought off either like the others. The only thing Alastair cares for enough is that silly girl." In her agitation Dee scattered her ashes. Lucas Donnelly blinked his eyelashes—long as a girl's and just as sinful—and a gray spit of ash swirled up, depositing itself in the brass uroboros set between the two of them. Dee didn't seem to notice, or perhaps certain little oddities no longer made her flinch. Perhaps she supposed anything was possible in Lucas Donnelly's domain.

"No, not New Morning. Me. What do you have in mind for me?"

"You?"

"Yes."

"You're really looking quite well, Dee. In the pink of health . . . and so young."

"Too young for a woman of sixty-two. Younger than I looked last year or the year before that."

"It's true. Younger every day," he said, puckering up his mouth as if he were about to throw her a kiss.

"That's not the way it's supposed to be! One gets older in life! One doesn't lose weeks, months, years, not in the normal scheme of things!" she cried, waving her arms, clutching at the air as if she might grasp that lost time, those moments that had passed her by.

"Ah, life!" Lucas Donnelly smiled broadly, amused.

"One day I expect to wake up and find I'm wearing diapers!" Her face mottled reddishly, and with her cheeks puffed out, she did look a bit like a baby ready to scream and wail.

"So, you want to get older, not younger. Well, Dee, why didn't you say so!" And then the laugh Lucas Donnelly had been holding in check at the back of his throat burst loose.

Doc Trump called Alastair. "I want to check your heart. Monday at two. Gracie's made you an appointment." He yelled off the phone to his nurse, "Grace! Alastair. Monday. Two P.M. An EKG . . . the works." And back to Alastair, "There, it's done."

Alastair planned to forget the appointment. Doc, too. He had no intention of even reflecting on his heart. Besides, Monday was far in the future. Who knew where he'd be. With Glory and Jordy maybe, down south, traveling. A stopover in Washington was a possibility. Alastair thought unkindly of the current administration, but there hadn't been a president he heartily approved of since Kennedy. However, suddenly ignited with patriotism, he decided every citizen should see the capital at least once. Watch the government in action as it were, drop by for a look-see at the Smithsonian. He wouldn't mind viewing The Spirit of St. Louis and a chunk of moon rock.

Glory, after Jordy left to finish the deliveries, promising to meet her at Alastair's by eleven, slipped out of the house. Evelyn kept a watchful eye, especially since Glory had been so engrossed with Jordy on the back lawn, but Evelyn, for all she assumed so, wasn't omniscient. The minute her back was turned, Glory ran down the narrow walk by the hedges, between the Crowells' and Dee's. She came out in the alley, crossed by a path to Brewster Street, and approached Alastair's from the rear.

Jordy said . . . she said to Alastair.

"Yes, yes, I know. It's for the best. A way of making sure you're safe. Out of that monster's clutches." He had a vision of Lucas Donnelly grinding her up, using her like some unholy vessel, as in *Rosemary's Baby* or *The Exorcist*.

Glory stood up. *To Carol's*, she signed, *to tell her*.

"You're not going anywhere except home. Stay in your room, lock the window, and sit with your back to the wall. The minute Evelyn and Theo turn in for the night, you sneak over here. And we'll use my Dodge to drive south. Don't forget to pack a toothbrush and some pajamas," Alastair ordered, "and whatever else girls can't live without." Then he added softly, "Carol will learn like everyone else."

Glory tipped up her face and attempted a smile, but she was more woebegone than happy. After a moment, she managed *My mother and father are going to be upset.*

"Expect so," Alastair agreed, thinking *upset* wouldn't adequately describe their reaction. "But they'll come around. Once you and Jordy make it official."

Stumbling, Glory repeated what Evelyn had said about marrying and settling down.

I knew I was right! Knew it! Thank God we're moving in time, getting her out of here, he thought. Agitated, Alastair sucked in his cheeks and blew out a thin, reedy whistle. For the first time in all his years he considered smacking a woman, except Evelyn Crowell wasn't in striking distance.

"Well," he said finally, "we're just going to rain on your mother's parade because you're not going to hitch up with Lucas Donnelly. No way!"

Oh, why is this happening? Glory asked with frantic fingers.

"Who knows! Not me," Alastair said, though it did appear to him, from his reading of the newspapers and weekly magazines, from the programs shown on television that in modern times the inexplicable was more and more the usual.

They were in the kitchen and Alastair, yearning to comfort Glory, but having no knack for such an endeavor, fetched her a Pepsi from the 'fridge instead. A good jolt of sugar might liven her up, soothe some of the willies. But Glory merely clasped the can between her palms and didn't drink from it. He wasn't sure she even knew it was there.

"You know you don't have to marry Jordy," Alastair said. "It's only a thought. A possibility. If I think on it, probably an idea or two will pop in my head." If only he were certain of that, that there were ways of circumventing Lucas Donnelly's desires.

Alastair believed that if he didn't sneak Glory out of the dragon's clutches, her parents' too, Evelyn would march her down the aisle, with Lucas Donnelly as sure as chickens laid eggs. Though Alastair would give odds the dragon had no intention of marrying in the Congregational. Wasn't the sight of the cross supposed to turn the devil to liquid Jell-O? Or was that a vampire? If he'd spent more time at the movies he'd have a better grasp on the rites and rituals of the occult. Too late for research: Alastair was forced to fly by the seat of his pants.

I don't mind marrying Jordy, Glory was signing.

"Don't mind isn't want to," Alastair said.

Glory pushed back her hair. The bones of her face jutted prominently; a smudgy grayness swathed the hallows beneath her eyes. *I think I love him.*

She didn't sound convinced. "Just think?" Alastair prodded.

My dream, she started to say, then broke off in apparent confusion.

Alastair experienced a moment of instant alarm, and then quickly quieted. Why shouldn't Glory have bad dreams?

"What about your dream?" But she only shook her head, not ready yet to part with it. Let her be. Time enough for that later.

Brahms would have been nice right then. Alastair needed the soothing; besides, it wouldn't hurt his erratic heart to be distracted. He decided, however, not to ask Glory to humor him by playing the piano. He sent her home instead.

Later, things went easier than Alastair had expected. The plan, drawn up so quickly, in such a haphazard way, could so easily be thwarted. While Alastair, however, ruminated continually about possible disaster, Jordy had little if any time to think. He was simply forced to act, and to improvise. When Harlan raged, as expected, over the slowness of Jordy's deliveries, Jordy lied. "Held up in traffic," he said.

To Harlan it didn't matter. "Wasting time!" he screamed. "I'd fire you if I had any help."

Jordy's mother ran from the bakery to the house, pleading a migraine. Jordy, who was holding his own temper on short reins, gazed after her, blinded suddenly by anger. Why, he almost cried out, didn't you ever protect us, me and Timmy? Why'd you let him do what he did?

But his anger evaporated as quickly as it flared, drying up

like a puddle in the sun. No time, he decided, not now anyway.

The bell tingled over the bakery door and Jordy went out front to wait on a late customer. Harlan always stifled the more murderous aspects of his rage in the presence of another, someone over whom he had no control. Then, before he could start in again, Jordy left also. He crossed to the house where he moved quietly. Avoiding his mother, whom he saw through the half-opened bedroom door lying down with a towel over her eyes, Jordy threw a few things together. Ready, he slipped down the back stairs, stayed on the far side of the house, sheltered there from the bakery, and circled the garage. He'd hide out in the hired girl's attic until it was dark. When Harlan couldn't see him, when nobody could, he'd walk into town.

One folding cot was made up with crumpled sheets and thread-worn blanket; the other was only a skinny mattress blotched with rusty stains. His mother hadn't been up here yet to straighten, to prepare the attic for whatever new wanderers might pass through.

It was so hot, so stuffy, the air seemed polluted. Raising the window, he stripped off his shirt so he couldn't stain it with sweat and lay down on the bare cot. The other bed held the faint aroma of Sarah lingering in its creases. He stretched out flat and stared up into the rafters where a spider spun a lazy lacy web. He willed himself to ease, loosen, to try and relax, but tension strung him out like piano wire. Is this how Timmy felt, tight and eager? Jordy wondered as he waited for darkness to arrive.

The moon was full when Jordy arrived at Alastair's to discover the old man stiff as a porcupine. "Pins and needles, plus my stomach's upset," he said, and then did something which in normal circumstances he'd never consider: he poured himself a shot of scotch. He offered the bottle to Jordy who shook his head. Jordy had to drive. The liquor burned a path down Alastair's throat like liquid fire, and his vision misted.

"You think Glory's changed her mind?" Jordy asked, nervously cracking his knuckles when eleven o'clock came and went.

"Course not!" Alastair barked authoritatively, but what did he know. It was his idea for Glory to marry Jordy and at the last minute it might not be hers.

"And if she has?" The question was ambiguous. Alastair couldn't tell if Jordy's worry was for himself or Glory. But he had, not the wide-eyed look of a kid, rather the intensity of a man anticipating pain. *Oh, what am I dragging him into?* Alastair counted on the sanctity of marriage to protect Glory from the dragon and had forgotten that real human emotions were involved here. His only concern was Glory. He considered Jordy healthy and strong, agile, and supposed in a battle he'd stand firm. Whatever happened Jordy wouldn't collapse from one or another affliction of age. However, Alastair had to admit that Jordy lacked guile. He wasn't wily either. *Maybe Evelyn would turn out to be right, that inside Jordy was strictly marshmallow.*

Alastair contemplated changing his mind, aborting this upcoming excursion before the marriage could be performed, of seeking some other solution to secure Glory's safety. But then Glory slipped through the back door and Jordy leaped off a chair to enfold her in his arms.

"All right, you two, quit the spooning. Time enough for that later," Alastair insisted when Glory didn't move, hanging on. *At least she doesn't find him offensive, probably even loves him. But what do I know about love?* Alastair asked himself, his worries scratching his insides. He thought that love wasn't the safest thing in the world, that love could lead a body, meaning Jordy, into making mistakes.

"Here, I found us a map," Alastair said, putting thoughts of love aside as he spread the map out on the table. The two lovers moved as one, Jordy's arm connected to Glory's shoulder. "It's an easy ride. Straight down to New York, crossing over the George Washington Bridge, then taking the New Jersey Turnpike. No trouble, no trouble at all."

Jordy hitched up his jeans and shrugged. "Well, I guess we better be going."

Alastair swung on his crutches between the two youngsters out to the car. They'd turned all the house lights off, but the moon still hung heavily, casting a white, chalky stream along the drive. Jordy folded up the wheelchair and stowed it in the trunk along with their bundles. *Gypsies, the pack of us,* Alastair snorted as they helped him into the backseat. Glory ran to the house and got him a pillow and a blanket, and Alastair was touched as she settled him in carefully, wrapped him up like expensive china. Though he was accustomed to a certain brief consideration due his infirm condition, plus age, the care Glory showed was special. *Ah, my heart, my heart could easily break,* he thought, and considered that this too might be a kind of love.

"Are you okay, Mr. Wayne?" Jordy asked when they were finally ready.

"Under the circumstances and because you've known me since the day you were born, I guess it's time to stop the mistering and use my first name," Alastair said, sounding sterner than he meant to.

Jordy clicked the key in the ignition, allowing the car to idle for a moment before he shifted into gear. "You don't have to go through with this, Glory," he said. "I mean we can do it properly. Ask your mother and father, then . . ." He dribbled off, perhaps hearing how foolish he sounded. Ignorance, Alastair thought. A worse handicap than a shattered spine and useless legs. But then, to be fair, he hadn't told Jordy even half the story, just bamboozled him into eloping. Alastair was using Jordy's mushy emotions to spirit Glory off, out of harm's reach—or Lucas Donnelly's, which was the same thing.

"Glory?" Jordy said again. But Glory turned and glanced over the backseat at Alastair. He couldn't see her eyes, banded by shadows, but he reached out for her hand and squeezed it. Might be me she's running off with, he thought, clattering deep in his bones.

"Jordy," Alastair ordered, "drive!"

Jordy was preparing to turn onto High Street and go around the square, passing dangerously near the dragon's, but Alastair told him to take the long way over Brewster. They drove the bumpy north route, the whiskey sloshing in Alastair's stomach making him regret the drink, then went left and headed south.

Moonlight lay over the town in snowy sheets. Through the windows it appeared as though they had blundered into winter. Just enough powder on the ground to make driving treacherous. And it felt for a moment as if the Dodge, perhaps remembering the time before the dragon, thinking back to the icy streets in its mechanical memory, did skid. Alastair heard a dull thud against the right rear fender, as if they'd tapped a garbage can or the flank of a tree, but Jordy didn't seem to notice anything, nor, apparently, did Glory. The Dodge ran on, circling the clock-tower monument, the heavy hands hanging motionless on its roman numbers, along Route 20.

The Papriakases' fruit and vegetable stand rode up on the left, prosperous, substantial, no fly-by-night seasonal operation. Even dark and shuttered, minus the burgeoning tables set in front, the stand appeared a permanent fixture, an establishment that would last the years. Alastair, turning his

head to view a last corner out the rear window, thought of
Gina, how much he missed her, how much he regretted that
she had closed the lid on the piano forever. Was the newfound
wealth true recompense for losing music? But the sacrifice
would have been made for Stanis, for their children and
grandchildren. What were Bach and Brahms in comparison
with a satisfactory bank account? To Alastair it passed understanding, wasn't a sensible trade-off; but he had no mortgage to
pay, no offspring to provide for. His expenses were minimal,
his desires few.

Harry's Bar, a scattering of angled cars in the macadamed
lot, the big spots on the roof like Cyclops's eyes illuminating
the highway, bloomed suddenly off on the left. "Not much of a
crowd tonight," Jordy commented as they drove by.

Lucas Donnelly probably had everybody home in bed
sleeping, dreaming if not nightmares of their own, then the
colonial images he so ardently admired. Alastair suspected that
Johnny Ryan who owned Harry's (the bar was named in
memory of a dead dog) would soon find himself out of business.
The roadhouse was tawdry, a tacky cinder-block establishment
with sawdust on the floor, rickety tables tattooed with gouges
and bottle rings, a loud flashing jukebox, and dusty streamers
hanging from the ceiling. Harry's was always arrayed for a
party that happened a decade ago. Johnny never bothered
taking down the Christmas wreath over the bar until the
Fourth of July.

Not Lucas Donnelly's style, not at all, Alastair was thinking.

The New Morning town lines were mysterious boundaries
and few people could tell precisely where they began or
ended. Alastair himself did not know. The unwary passed out
of New Morning supposing the town had been left two or three
miles back up the road. There was neither a sign nor a marker
to the side of Route 20 to indicate that behind this arbitrary
spot lay unincorporated state land. But it was just here that the
Dodge—legendary for reliable performance—shuddered with
a croupy cough and sputtered to a stop.

What's wrong with the car? Glory asked with quivering
fingers.

"Haven't the foggiest," Alastair replied as Jordy slipped from
behind the wheel and went around the front to raise the hood.
"It's always been the perfect perpetual-motion machine."

They hunched in silence, Alastair thinking of mysterious
conditions, such as a hairline crack in the crankcase, a dropped
rod, or a spark plug doused. He stirred with suspicion.

Finally Alastair nudged Glory's arm resting along the back of the front seat, saying, "Turn on the radio." Even for a town resident accustomed to country quiet, the thrashing of crickets, the twittering of birds, the reedy wind rustling with leaves, it was too ominously dead out here. If a slug slithered across the pavement the swish would have torn through the webbing of silence.

The battery obviously functioned because the headlights beaconed into the dark, and then suddenly, the radio blared on. But the best Glory could find was Kenny Rogers singing a blue-grass thump. Melody, yes, but to Alastair the words were asinine. All about love and waiting and going off, then coming on home where some silly woman had opened her arms. Alastair longed for a robust concerto, it didn't matter by whom.

"Doesn't seem to be anything wrong with it," Jordy, poking his head through the window, said. "Nothing I can find. Let's give it another try. Glory, shove over and start her up."

Glory inched into the driver's seat and turned the key. Nothing happened, not the slightest squeak. "Let me," Jordy said. But the engine responded no better for him. "Dead as a doornail." He sighed. Looking back at Alastair, he said, "Could be the ignition, except that doesn't short out—not in my experience—when you're moving."

"Auto mechanics aren't my specialty," Alastair said. He mulled over the irony of the Dodge's breaking down at such an inauspicious time, and was wary. No warning, nothing; the car had been smoothly traveling, nice as you please.

"Gas," Jordy muttered.

Alastair snapped. "Of course there's gas in it! Full tank. Ran it over to the pump myself. This afternoon. Had the oil checked, too. Ditto the brake fluid. And the tires. Didn't forget them either. Water's okay, besides."

"I don't get it." Jordy had a face that couldn't hide things, and right now it was lined with bewilderment. In small towns in the country, every boy becomes a man knowing something about cars. Motors are to be mastered, an essential in education as important as sex. Jordy jiggled the key, fiddling it back and forth, cocked an ear and listened though there was nothing to hear. "Beats me," he said, and in truth he did look stricken.

Alastair thumped the seat. "This car's solid as Gibraltar. Not a damn thing wrong with it!"

"Mr. . . . I mean, Alastair, it's just not turning over. So something's out of whack. Cars just don't . . . well, kick up their heels like old dogs and play dead. Even if it's a clogged fuel line there'd be some noise. Not this absolute zero."

Glory tugged Jordy's arm, and in the light of the dash, her skin was translucent. The bones were washed ivory. Her lips quaked but her fingers flashed, *What are we going to do?*

"Beats me, Glory." Jordy ran his hand down the side of her face. "But don't worry, we'll think of something. Won't we, Alastair?"

Alastair fretted. They were out in the middle of the night, stuck on the dark side of Route 20, when Glory should be home in bed. He doubted that Harlan Farrow gave one hoot what Jordy did with his time when he quit working, but Evelyn and Theo . . . oh, Lordy! After last night they'd have him up on a kidnapping charge for sure.

"Guess we better get some help," Jordy suggested when Alastair did not answer.

Help! A dandy idea, Alastair thought. Even if Glory got back in the house without waking anybody up, it would be common knowledge by morning that she'd been out in the Dodge, leaving town, with him and with Jordy. The only way to keep from hearing that would be to shoot her.

"Look," Alastair said finally, having run to the end of his silence, "you two will have to walk back to town. Not me, of course. I'll stay here with the car. Then Jordy, get on the horn and sort of anonymously phone over to the Mobil station and see who can be roused. Or maybe the Ford people."

"Com'on, Alastair, you know neither of those tow trucks will go out for anybody but Doc Trump, and then he usually has to threaten to sue. Ted Wills is probably up in Pittsfield with his girlfriend. And Grady, he's the second meanest person in New Morning after my old man. When's the last time he did a favor for anybody?"

"You're right, you're right," Alastair muttered.

"Harry's is just up the road. I can hike over there and get somebody to come on back with me. We'll shove the car to the shoulder and then go on home. Tomorrow Ted Wills can come on out and get her. Okay?"

"No, it's not okay! What do you think Glory's folks will say?" Never mind the dragon, he was thinking. "Walk Glory home. At your age those couple of miles are a short trot. Then I'll sit here until some Good Samaritan wanders along."

"Alastair, we can't leave you out in the middle of nowhere like this. Who knows what could happen?"

Who knows indeed. Alastair's chin sank down on his chest. They should have passed through Connecticut by now. He mourned the lost trip like a dead friend.

"Alastair?"

"Listen to me. I want you to take a hop-skip up to Harry's and call Moses Llewelyn on the phone. Leave Glory out in the parking lot, and don't tell Moses who you are."

"Moses? Why him? And how do you know he'll come out so late?" Jordy asked.

"Promise him thirty dollars. That'll motivate him just fine. As for why Moses, you forget he's got a pickup truck, with a winch on the back," Alastair said, not speaking the whole truth. It was his earlier intuition rather than the pickup equipped with a winch that made Alastair think of Moses.

Jordy was doubtful. Creases of worry anchored between his eyebrows. "He's probably sleeping. I don't know if he'll come out. Moses is independent."

Exactly. It was Moses's independence that Alastair was counting on. "Call him anyway," Alastair said wearily. "Go on, call him, and then get home. I'll see you both tomorrow." He ended the discussion by slouching in the corner and closing his eyes. On the back of one of his hands folded upon the windbreaker he wore, he felt the breeze of Glory's fingers. Still as a church mouse, appearing to have dropped off already, Alastair cracked his lids and saw Jordy motion her away. The two of them slipped from the car, closing the door with a quiet thud. Alastair sorrowed over the lost wedding, and hunkered down and did nap for a while.

He was up and awake, trying to decide which portion of him pained the most, when Moses came. By some stroke of good fortune, or maybe just another of the dragon's tricks, not one car had traveled the road either in or out of town all the time Alastair waited. He heard the pickup park behind him and in a moment there was Moses's carved moon of a face peering through the driver's window.

Moses opened the door and the ceiling light flickered on. They gazed at each other, a taut line stretched between them. Then Moses said with a friendly demeanor, "Warm night, ain't it, Mr. Wayne?"

"Not unusual for summertime, Moses."

"'Spect not." He wedged himself in behind the wheel and

rubbed his face. "A little birdy, a nameless birdy, mentioned you had a problem."

"That I do, Moses. The old boat just dropped dead on me."

Moses, still turned toward the backseat, said, "Uh huh. Maybe you would of had better luck if you drove her from up here." Alastair gave him one of his dumb old man looks: don't try to kid a kidder, don't con a con artist, and Moses curled up a lip and snorted, "Okeydokey, if that's the way you want it, Mr. Wayne, I'll just give it a try myself."

"Useless," Alastair muttered.

Moses flipped the key in the ignition and the Dodge sprang instantly to life, then sat purring contented as a tabby. God damn, Alastair thought, feeling the heat rise in his cheeks. Moses glanced at him in the rearview mirror with watchful eyes. He shifted into drive and fed the car a thimbleful of gas. They drove easily down the road before Moses braked and went into reverse. The Dodge performed as reasonably backwards as going straight ahead.

Alastair had a panicky sense that Lucas Donnelly was right here in the Dodge with him and Moses, that he was the power that set the car in motion or stopped it. But Moses, letting the Dodge idle with a soft hum, had turned around again and Alastair stared into his walnut eyes. Moses wasn't afraid, just curious. No bogeys, devils, or the dragon, Alastair thought, or he'd sense it, too.

Whatever had kept the car from leaving New Morning was outside, an invisible barrier, a wall of no known substance. It was an encumbrance not there now that Glory had gone back to the center of town. The barrier, Alastair supposed, trying to think calmly, was a force held for a moment by Lucas Donnelly miles behind the car. A power, a mind trick, a mental current that the dragon cast out into the night to seal off New Morning from the rest of Massachusetts and stop the Dodge in its tracks when Alastair attempted to sneak Glory away.

The wall that nobody could see was Lucas Donnelly's fortified bunker set on the ridge over the beach when Alastair landed off the assault boat. Alastair stormed through the pounding surf, weaving an erratic path, rifle raised. . . . *No, no!* That was then, this is now, Alastair cried silently, wrenching himself from Normandy and Omaha back to New Morning. His head ached and the remembered thundering of the invasion left a ringing in his ears. His jaw was so tight, he could barely wheeze to Moses waiting, patient, as a tree, "Thank you."

Alastair shuffled around for his wallet, but Moses, anticipating him, shook his head. "No need for that, Mr. Wayne. My good deed for the day . . . or the night, you might say." He climbed out of the Dodge, but hunched over so he could see Alastair flopped in his corner like a bundle of rags. "Naturally you don't have to be helped out of there and up to here, since you got yourself in that backseat in the first place. But it's late, Mr. Wayne, and I 'spect you're bone weary, so if you don't take offense, I'll give you a hand anyway."

Which was Moses's manner of implying that Alastair hadn't been the one driving the Dodge. "Who was it," he asked ever so nonchalantly, as he helped Alastair rearrange himself, "who wouldn't give me his name, all mysteriouslike, on the phone? From Harry's, I'm presuming. At least there was that garbagy music in the background."

"You're some detective, Moses. But I hate to disappoint you. It was just some stranger passing through," Alastair lied, mentally crossing two of his fingers.

"The kindness of folks." Moses sighed as he leaned in the open window, inches from Alastair. "I better follow you into town just to be sure there're no more engine problems."

Alastair gratefully acquiesced. "I appreciate that, Moses." Together, the Dodge with the pickup close behind it proceeded down the dark road, over the night-shrouded terrain, the moon tucked away, at least temporarily, in a cloud bank, right on—eventually—to New Morning proper.

18

The rains began shortly after Alastair arrived back home, weary and depressed, gripped by the feverish knowledge that the battle lines were now drawn. Lucas Donnelly as much as came right out and said, *that is it*. Splash around all you want in New Morning, but you'll go no further, certainly not south to Maryland. There'll be no carting Glory off to any secret wedding with Jordy Farrow; not tonight, not tomorrow.

Alastair had to think, but the aborted trip had tired him more than if they'd driven straight through the night. He ached too intensely even to put the Dodge into the garage, never mind consider just what he'd do next, how best to protect Glory and keep her from an eternal commitment with the dragon.

Moses' pickup kept close to his bumper, and the yardman idled until Alastair inserted his key into the back-door lock. Then he raised his hand in a limp wave, or so Alastair thought, and the headlights dipped off and on in response. Moses, dark as the night, was invisible behind the windshield as the pickup seemed to retreat out along High Street all by itself.

Good man, Moses, whatever his faults, Alastair was thinking as he let himself into the house. There was a musty odor as if the place had been empty for a long while, not just the couple of hours Alastair had actually been gone.

He deposited himself into his bed without washing up or brushing his teeth, and fell asleep in his underwear the instant he made contact with the pillow. Tomorrow is another day, was his pious, last conscious thought for the night . . . or so he supposed.

The rains woke him, the thunderous pummeling of water on the roof and out in the street. It sounded as though a dam had broken, cracked the retaining walls, and water flooded out of the heavens. A heavy battering, the pounding rain went on and on, noisy as a jackhammer. An assault upon the earth, not the slow and steady pattering that would have benefited the farmers. All runoff. Alastair imagined the Housatonic rising.

Alastair lay beneath the cascade, thankful his roof was tight, and felt abused by the drubbing blows. Fists punching at the shingles. This can't go on all night. He checked the time on the digital clock beside his bed. Three forty-five. Floods by morning. Damnation! he muttered, and still the force of the rain held steady, drummed on.

Finally Alastair worked his way off the bed, grappling with his crutches, and swung himself unsteadily to the chair near the window. He cleaned a circular patch of glass and stared out at the shimmering mist. Not much to see. The world was a dark, mysterious cave.

Alastair struggled with the window catch. The house was as stuffy as a cedar chest. Wheezing, he at last shoved the frame up, but no breeze whiffled through the screen. It was as airless outside, as stultifying, as it was within.

The rain fell straight as a plumb line. If there were any birds left alive in the New Morning trees, they'd have drowned on the branches.

The rain held Alastair mesmerized, the drumming thunder of uncountable gallons of water coming out of the clouds. He lulled in his chair, panting like an old dog, waiting for dawn, and considered the end of the world. *Not by fire but by water* . . . He slouched, slept, bounced up from unwanted oblivion, stirred, fidgeting about, then drowsed again. In this errant manner he wandered into another day—a gray, misty day, spongy, humid as a hot tub. The air felt spoiled, cheesy. It was painful to inhale, difficult to peer through the watery curtains.

Alastair was imprisoned in his house. The slick pavements held no purchase for the chair, and the crutches would be an easy ticket to broken bones. He rolled restlessly from window to door. Yet, as sapped as he felt, as achy, he continued thinking, his mind at full speed though his body was sluggish.

Alastair wondered if this rain was another trick of Lucas Donnelly's. A device to keep him home, Glory too, to strand New Morning, isolate the town from the rest of the state. Ten miles away was it raining or clear as a windowpane? Was only New Morning sinking like Atlantis?

Around ten a fist hammered at the back door, and Alastair bellowed, "Com'on in!"

It was Jordy. "I came to see if you were all right," he said, making a puddle on the linoleum. "The phone lines are down."

"Fine as I'll ever be. What about you and Glory? She get home all right?"

"Yeah, I took her right to the kitchen door, then I waited until her light went on upstairs. I thought I'd risk her mother's temper and go over after I checked up on you."

"Moses was a true savior," Alastair said.

"I see the Dodge's in the drive. Want me to get the garage to come by and tow her in?"

Alastair sighed. "Nothing wrong with it."

"What do you mean?"

"Just what I said. Moses came driving out, turned the key, and the Dodge perked right up."

Jordy was baffled. "That's not possible. She never even turned over. Stone-cold. No way the car could of gotten back here under her own steam."

Alastair was tempted to tell Jordy about the dragon, but
held back. Some warning voice inside him kept saying: *not yet*.
So Alastair simply shrugged instead.

The rains stopped just a few minutes past noon and the
clutch of soiled gray clouds, like dirty wash, began to untangle.
Lucas Donnelly stepped outside his house for a walk.

Dressed in white, as always, he crossed over to the green,
cutting through on one of the paths to Main Street. Just at the
curb, where he halted to glance up and down, he had one foot
off the pavement when Jack Boardman, hell-bent for nowhere
in particular since he'd been laid off from his job, spun around
the square on two wheels in his Toyota. The left front hit a
gulley of water and sprayed up a fountain.

Jack, going twenty-five miles over the limit, was long gone
before Lucas Donnelly let out an earsplitting roar. The
buildings throughout the core of New Morning trembled as if
seismically unsettled, the elms on the green shook to their
roots. Lucas Donnelly had been splattered with a messy
pattern of mud and water spots all over his white suit.

That's it!

Lucas Donnelly's face hardened into planes and ridges of
marble. His dark eyes smoldered with fire, and his black curly
hair leaped up from the scalp. Fortunately, or not, there was
no witness to this conniption of his. He stomped back to
Emma's colonial, smoke pouring from his ears.

It was exactly like a party that didn't come off. That's how
Glory considered the abortive elopement. For a moment, on
awakening in her own bed, she wondered if she had dreamed
it. But no, it had happened. Only things were supposed to be
different now. She shouldn't have been home, but down in
Washington or Maryland, sleeping next to Jordy.

Glory got up and touched her toes a hundred times to clear
out the cobwebs, thinking all the while, *what will we do next?*

Later, pedaling out to The Gallery, she decided not to think
at all, to keep her mind clear as the Caribbean water before
she began dreaming of the floating arms and seaweed hair. She
thought of her mother instead, bringing on a pain in her chest.

Evelyn had said, tapping her foot on the kitchen linoleum as Glory was leaving, "Today absolutely, you are going to quit!"

Glory didn't want to think of leaving her job any more than she cared to remember Lucas Donnelly or how she and Jordy and Alastair had tried to go south. But there was the crippled ballerina and the ruined anemones to explain to the cousins. In the zippered pocket of her purse was the bankbook, and that at least gave her some hope. They'll see, she thought, that I can pay for what I ruined. Everything, Glory wanted to believe, would be all right.

Worse, however, than Glory could have imagined was waiting for her when she walked in on the cousins.

Francesca stood in the big room, and when she saw Glory she screamed, "Well, how do you explain this?"

Eva might have posed for a stricken survivor of a plane crash. She looked, lips parting, as if she were about to speak. But only a sob broke loose. She had as little speech as Glory, and she cringed from her, turning her back, too, on Francesca who stood there in a silk robe, her hair loose. Most of all, Eva didn't want to face the debris, the room littered with pieces of ceramics, a mixed collection of pottery, metal sections of the wire sculpture. No one painting, gouache, or watercolor remained on the walls. All the glass was cracked into sparkling fragments. Glory put down a foot and crushed a shard. She withdrew quickly, and stepping back crunched a frame.

A particularly fine landscape that Glory loved was sliced like thin strips of meat. The two ends lay together, but the middle portion was across the room; it draped over an armature that should have held a metal dancer.

"Oh, so you've got nothing to say!" Francesca spat out, forgetting that Glory was mute. Bits of foam sprayed when she screamed, "You're just going to stand there and look stupid! Oh!" Her anger, though it seemed impossible, soared still higher. "Oh!" she cried and tore at her hair.

"Chess!" Eva moaned, coming unhinged, moving, a gangly assemblage of arms and legs. She stumbled to her cousin to offer some comfort.

Francesca wasn't to be touched. She swung out a long-sleeved arm and almost connected with Eva's chin. "Just shut up, you! Hiring this dummy was your idea!"

Glory's eyes filled with tears, and then her fingers stirred, to say: *I didn't do this! How can you think I did?*

"No, no!" Eva protested, shifting to the other side, trying to

pretend Francesca hadn't so cruelly rebuffed her. "We don't
think it's you, Glory, dear. And forgive Francesca for what she
said. She's upset since we woke up and discovered . . . We
never checked downstairs last night when we . . ." Eva
paused, grew whiter yet, and swallowed. "This. We didn't
know about this. Last night. Must have happened yesterday,
after you locked up. Or didn't."

"Of course she didn't. If she had no one would have gotten
in." Francesca's voice dropped an octave, but Glory wasn't
reassured. Now Francesca sounded dangerous.

Glory's hand wavered because she shook so. Still, she
maintained, *I locked up. I know I did. I always do if I'm alone
here.*

Francesca's nostrils flared. Yesterday's makeup still lay on
her face, now in streaks and calligraphic markings. Her mouth
appeared bloodied, like a wound. She shrilled, "How did you
get in, just now . . . hmmm, little Miss Perfect? Through
the door, right, just turned the knob. No key, no Eva opening
up. Well, you imbecile, we never touched that door!"

No one in her entire life had ever spoken like this to Glory.
She thought to draw up, to throw back her shoulders. To face
the cousins straight on with her chin raised, just as Alastair
would do. But Glory just couldn't.

She did try again, however, to say *this wasn't my fault,* but
Francesca listened not at all. Pearly beads of spit foamed at the
corners of her mouth. Her eyes were unfocused. Eva, gaunt
and shadowed, just looked sick.

"Ruined! Completely ruined!" Francesca wailed. Eva
struggled once more to reach her shoulder with a long, skinny
arm, but Francesca was having none of her devoted cousin.
She lurched instead at Glory, and would have connected, but
Glory was quick. Glory jumped aside and Francesca slipped.
She went down on one knee in an attitude of prayer, ripping a
jagged split in the robe. Now she howled, maddened.

Eva cried, "You better leave, Glory!"

I could help clean up.

"No, oh no," Eva rattled, "that won't be necessary. And we'll
put what we owe you in the mail."

I'm fired? Glory asked, feeling stupid the instant she formed
the words. Of course I am! What else can they do? Oh, how
pleased her mother would be!

Francesca crawled on her hands and knees, her rump up in
the air, tendrils of hair like lichen clinging to the sides of her

neck. Eva pleaded with her to get off the floor, but wasn't successful in raising her cousin.

As Glory backed through the door, she saw Eva's own legs fold up under her. The thinner cousin slipped to the floor and sat on the delicate remains of what was once one of Giorgio's beautiful bowls.

Glory took a shortcut home, a seldom-used rutted country lane on which she had to be diligent if the Peugeot wasn't to fly into a furrow. Jordy, on the other hand, drove the longest way around New Morning, adding miles to a trip that one could walk in ten minutes. Moses Llewelyn in his circuitous travels saw both the young lovers, and seeing Jordy Farrow got him to wondering if it had been the boy on the phone. Now that he thought about it in the clear light of day, that had seemed like the boy's voice. Moses twitched with curiosity. What was that Alastair Wayne up to? It sure was a funny business saying the old Dodge wouldn't start when it popped to life nice as a muffin in a toaster. Moses scratched his grizzled head and said out loud to nobody but himself, "Weird doings."

Moses's pickup passed down Brewster Street. All the heavy construction equipment was gone. The street ran in an even expanse of cobblestones from one end to the other. Not a car in sight, the neat houses primly fronted by small gardens—some of which were Moses's contribution—and at the curb here and there, hitching posts. Brewster Street appeared now as colonial as the square. The whole town, Moses thought, was beginning to resemble the New Morning of his fancies and bad dreams.

He entered the center of town, eased his foot off the gas, slowing, and saw Lucas Donnelly's house at the apex of the green. Despite the thick-branched, leafy trees that stood between him and the honky's house and should have blocked his view, the big colonial blazed with a blinding whiteness, like the noon sun. Moses squeezed his eyes shut, seeing painful pinpricks of light on the underside of his lids and waited for what seemed an eternity. Then he blinked and once again the elms shouldered tall and military right where they'd always been, where they belonged.

Too much gage, he grimaced, and not enough rest for a man my age. He wiped the sweat off his face with a grimy neckerchief, then spat out the window of the pickup. He was shivering and thought, goose doing a two-step on my grave.

A horn squawked impatiently behind him and somebody yelled, "Hey, Moses, get the lead out!" He was still at a dead stop, and now jerked forward, circling the green. When he rounded past Lucas Donnelly's he turned his head to the side, not daring to look at the colonial straight on.

Moses should have stopped at the manse where Will Austin expected him to trim the backyard and replace an azalea bush that had inexplicably shriveled. But Moses kept going, thinking this was a day a man was better off keeping to his bed, resting up, easing all his aches and pains.

In a few minutes Moses was back on Ridge Road, the fairgrounds coming up on his left, Bailey Cross's fields of adolescent corn unrolling on his right. High above the farm, Madder's Hill loomed darkly. Its western flank brooded thick with growth, the leafy green tangle as black as night in the shadows of late morning. At the top, where the trees sheared off, and the brush became mere stubble, Moses caught a glint of light. Something bright glared and sparkled at the narrow Dead Man's Curve. It came so fast that Moses, his foot wandering away from the gas, fumbling for the brake, almost didn't stop in time, almost drove right past. If he had, he would have missed the crash altogether, or worse, been under the airborne car when it found the ground. But as it was, Moses Llewelyn had a front-row seat to witness the sky dive of Jack Boardman's Toyota.

The hair-raising scream screeched in Moses's skull like static. It was the scream of someone imprisoned in a death sentence. Moses, an expert on the ownership of every automobile in New Morning, was so shocked, it took a second for him to recognize Jack Boardman's Toyota charging out of the shadows on Madder's Hill.

Automobile parts scattered like hailstones along the furrows and flattened the stalks of corn. His eyes tightly closed, Moses imagined blood irrigating the fields, gore splashed on the rail-split fance, a rainshower of red. His stomach unmoored at the idea of collecting the parts of what was once Jack Boardman so there'd be something to bury in a box in the ground. Thank the Lord it won't be me has to tell Mike Boardman. Moses was fervent, swiping at his nose with a fist. He had, at some moment or other, opened his eyes again, because he saw first

Bailey's son, then Bailey, racing along at the far side of the fence, toward the big fireball in the corn.

Moses reluctantly climbed out of the pickup which he'd stopped in the middle of the road. He followed the Crosses with draggy steps to the billowing cloud of black smoke. Damnation, he swore, hitching up his shoulders, I should of mowed the reverend's lawn. Right now, Moses considered, he would have given anything to be behind his machine. Instead he stomped toward an incinerated Jack Boardman, wondering if the youngest Public son had been stoked when he took Dead Man's Curve in earnest. Get away, he told himself, and thought, the honky will be pleased anyhow. Word was, he couldn't stand Jack's speeding through the center of New Morning at fifty miles an hour and playing boogie on his horn.

19

Jack Boardman's death hit people harder than Herman September's or Bobby Pierson's. Jack Boardman had been born and raised in town, as his parents before him, theirs, too. And, despite Jack's being a scalawag and a wastrel, a drinker as well as a client of Moses Llewelyn's, he had been in his right mind. None of Jack Boardman's brain cells was missing when he drove off Madder's Hill.

His father and mother, as was to be expected, took the boy's death hard. Carol, however, felt Jack's death worst of all. "My dream!" she wailed to Glory, and brooded over her bout of precognition long after the Bells of the Belwether Funeral Home put Jack in the ground. She might have missed the actual journey of the Toyota on the highway of empty space, but Jack continued to travel in Carol's sleep. If she got through a day without breaking down, she'd awaken sobbing in the middle of the night.

Glory, no matter how hard she tried, couldn't console Carol out of her grief.

Mike Boardman alternated sorrowing and worrying over his daughter's health. In front of his very eyes Carol was wasting

away. Her color changed from the rosy pink of youth to a sallow
yellow. She wandered about in a perpetual slump, her eyes
dulled, and even her shiny hair was lackluster.

Mike dragged Carol, kicking and screaming, over to Doc
Trump, but the physician found nothing physically wrong with
her. No matter how poorly she looked, he pronounced Carol
well.

Spiritual, that's what it was, Mike decided, and consulted
Will Austin. The minister, however, was less than helpful.

Will Austin had his own preoccupations these days. At last
he'd found someone in New Morning who understood the
intricate workings of his mind. The reverend hesitated to say
"a soul mate," but that was what he meant.

The relationship began innocently enough, with pleasant-
ries exchanged at various New Morning events, but then, on
the night of Evelyn's dinner party, they'd had a deeper
conversation on ecclesiastical matters. Will Austin had been
thrilled to discover that, like himself, Lucas Donnelly bent to
the right.

"Sorry to say," Will Austin had told Lucas Donnelly, "this is
an age when people are loosening all the ties that bind.
Simplifying scripture, eliminating various rites altogether. I'll
never be able to fathom their motivation." The minister had
sadly shaken his full head of white hair.

"Nor I," Lucas Donnelly puffed in agreement, "since rituals
are quite important to me."

"I'm so glad to hear that!" Reverend Austin's whole face lit
up like a jack-o'-lantern with a candle inside, and he en-
thusiastically clapped his hands.

The fragile friendship flowered, and Will Austin took to
dropping in on his neighbor at the foot of the green—when
invited, of course—for a glass of port and an interesting hour of
conversation. During these evenings Will Austin would share
his longings for an orthodoxy prohibited by his church. He also
found himself encouraged to make slight changes in ritual. As
Lucas Donnelly put it, "Who will be hurt?" On the night the
dragon offered him a harpsichord for the Congregational, Will
was beside himself.

More and more, therefore, the minister could be heard
singing the praises of New Morning's benefactor. Not that too
many people disagreed that Lucas Donnelly was anything but
the cat's meow.

The dragon also only had good things to say of the reverend, unlike Alastair who'd passed more than one scurrilous insult under his breath from time to time. But for all his deprecating the minister and the man's parochial tastes in music, Alastair decided at last that Will was the only authority in New Morning on matters of faith. For surely the dragon had to do with belief; belief in the devil's existence gave Lucas Donnelly a kind of life he couldn't have had otherwise.

Alastair knew in his heart that the dragon was ecclesiastical. Hence, he was rattling his way uninvited and unannounced down High Street and over to the manse. Will wasn't there. Alastair rolled around to the side of the church.

A low ramp attached to the three little steps off the Congregational's east flank was Alastair's usual entrance to the church. Only now, with the door slammed shut, it required adroit maneuvering before Alastair could navigate inside. But, after a sweaty few minutes, Alastair finally wedged himself into the church where he wilted in the wheelchair, sucking tired breath up his nostrils and down into his lungs. He sagged, more exhausted than he should have been, as black spots tangoed before his eyes. Finally, however, he reassembled himself, shifted into drive, and rolled into the main section of the church.

Up at the front, in the pulpit, where the light streamed through the windows in wide rivers the plump, rounded figure of Will Austin bent over in an attitude of prayer. The minister's hair feathered past his collar, and with the black academic robe and floppy red tie he resembled a Christmas choirboy.

Alastair drove over to the side aisle, and Will Austin, hearing the low rumble of the wheelchair, stopped his mumbling and stared out as though from an untenanted house. His eyes were round as dinner plates, his cheeks puffed up.

"Hello, Will," Alastair called.

"Alastair."

"What are you doing?" he asked innocently.

"Serving the people, the good souls of New Morning, which is what I usually do," Will Austin replied stiffly.

"Ah, of course!" Alastair said, as he tried out a smile on the minister.

Will stared back at Alastair sternly, hard as stone. "I'm busy right now, Alastair, so whatever you want, make it snappy."

Make what snappy? Alastair, grimly determined to hold onto his good humor, said, "Well, I just dropped by for a little chat. Maybe a glass of lemonade. We could even listen to some Palestrina. Over at the manse, I mean."

"No time," the reverend barked, shuffling about in his robe like a dark cloud. "I have all I can do to keep the world on an even keel."

Will Austin appeared reasonable except for what he was saying. That was nonsense.

"Uh-huh." Alastair, diplomatically agreeing, bobbed his head.

The reverend, souring fast, wasn't, however, to be charmed or lulled. He yelled down from his perch, "Just what are you doing in my church anyway, Alastair? Making a mess of things again, or trying to, I suppose. You and your modern improvements!" Was it possible Will meant Mozart and Beethoven?

"Now, Will," Alastair soothed, as one would the grievously moronic or the mentally indigent, "let's lock up the church and go on over to your place. Mmmm?"

Will Austin's hands had been in hiding inside the robe's voluminous sleeves, and now the right one shot out and two fingers speared at Alastair like the forked tongue of a snake. "Lead me not into temptation!" he cried in a roar that thundered through the Congregational, rattling the windows in their frames. When silence again flooded the church, a prayer book slipped from a bench at Alastair's left, exploding on the floor and almost scaring him to death.

Foolish, that's all Will is, Alastair tried telling himself. But the minister, who had emerged from behind the pulpit, didn't appear ridiculous at all.

The sun must have disappeared behind a cloud bank, because the light dimmed to a sooty gray. What illumination remained, collected at Will's back, leaving his front vague, rather vaporous. A silvery glow that had no discernible source outlined the projecting tufts of whitish hair. Alastair squinted, but he couldn't define one single feature of the minister. He might have been anybody up there in the gloom.

"Will?" Alastair said hesitantly.

The minister made no reply.

Alastair rode over to the center aisle, then slowly down it, closer to Will. As he neared, the minister's arms swept out into wings, and he stood rigidly at attention. Did he realize he mimicked the plain wood cross behind him at the far wall of the church?

The quiet, once Alastair stopped midway in the aisle, was as thick as cotton batting, so ponderous, in fact, that Alastair heard his own blood rushing in his ears. And when he spoke, softly he thought, the words crashed like falling rocks. "Do you know what's happening in New Morning, Will? You got any idea what's going on?" Alastair persisted, slipping by the Whittier family pew with its tag of brass, then the Crowells'. He stopped three rows down by the pew where the Waynes had prayed since the Congregational was built. Unconsciously, Alastair reached out and his fingertips traced the lettering of his name.

"Impossible things," Alastair was saying. "Or one big impossibility, you might say."

Will Austin's voice came like summer thunder as he rolled a string of Latin words off his tongue. Alastair, no classical scholar, failed to understand even one. Oh, Will! Alastair almost shouted, come back to the here and now. He had an unreasonable impulse to beat his fists against the minister, who in the fainter light had gone black as a crow, and howl.

Still, Alastair kept his temper firmly locked up, and said, "That Donnelly fellow, Will, he's up to no good." Oh, what an understatement, but Alastair's intuition told him to take it step by step, not to rush the minister or stampede him into some terrifying response. "As a matter of fact, that's what I came over to talk to you about."

Nearer Alastair crept on his rubber wheels, craning his neck as he closed in on Will Austin, to find some light, any glow, in the minister's eyes. But the nearer Alastair approached to Reverend Austin, still poised in his impersonation of someone crucified, the nearer to the windows, the darker it became in the church. All illumination drained away. If Alastair could have torn his attention from the minister, he would have rolled back to the main doors, and the light switch. High up in the ceiling were fixtures with banks of bulbs. But he didn't dare to glance away from Will. He couldn't trust that the minister would remain in place.

"Will, com'on and sit over here, next to me," Alastair coaxed. "It's so black I can barely see you." Outside a storm had to be brewing, because it was still too early in the day for the light to go as it was. Alastair couldn't see his hand in front of his face, and the minister was only a murky figure. "Will, listen, this Lucas Donnelly. . . ."

"No traditions left, no rituals, no homage getting paid! Man must sink down on his knees!" Will Austin said suddenly,

startling Alastair, "Lucas Donnelly. . . ." Will Austin's arms
swooped inward, and his hands met each other, colliding in a
terrible crack. "A great man!" he cried.

"False gods, Will. Don't follow them. It says that plain as
day in the Bible."

Somebody laughed loudly and Alastair jerked in his chair.
"Will?" But the sound hadn't come from where the minister
hulked. He circled around. The laughter resounded again,
hard and biting as the crack of a whip, and this time it seemed
to be over by the east door. "Who's there?" Alastair's fear made
his voice a whinny. Now whoever laughed had gotten by some
means to Alastair's left, for the thunderous roar emanated from
that side of the church. "Who's in here? Speak up!"

Alastair swung the chair ninety degrees to the left, but the
laughter moved on, circling to the right. Alastair followed in a
dizzying round, flying, though he tried to slow the wheelchair.
He threw the throttle to stop, but the little stick broke loose in
his hand as he spun even faster. Thrown about like a feather
pillow, he slipped and slid, able to only hold on, the speed tore
tears from his eyes. When he howled, "No!" the cry ripped off
his lips and trailed the echoing shriek of laughter. Alastair's
head whipped on his neck as he was hurtled and spun about.
He struggled with a plea to Will Austin to help him, but he
couldn't get the words out. Helplessly, Alastair gripped the
arms of the chair as he revolved like a top.

Suddenly he was jarred so badly he almost spilled over to
the floor. He clipped an elbow on something hard and
immovable, and the pain traveled like a runaway train up to
his shoulder. Alastair, groaning, hurt so that it took him a
moment to realize the insanely spinning chair was slowing.
Each revolution lasted longer until there was one, final lazy
turn. The only motion now was inside Alastair's head, but then
that too slowed and stopped. His chin sank on his chest, he
gulped a deep breath, two, and mewed a small, mouselike
sound.

Will still stood in the same attitude where Alastair had left
him. "Will?" he hiccuped out.

The throttle had remained clutched in his fist. Fumbling,
Alastair got it back into the proper slot. Then he rolled slowly,
tentatively, as if he didn't quite trust the earth to hold steady,
forward. "Will?" he whispered to the dark, quaking shadow.

Will Austin stirred, a man coming awake, and just enough
light remained for Alastair to see his face. And as he did,

Alastair screamed so loudly the force of his terror lifted him halfway out of the wheelchair.

Will Austin was a mass of worms. From his brow to his chin a soft, pulpy nest of nightcrawlers moved, slithered and turned in this slime.

Alastair shot backwards, thumping into a pew, smacking his arm. Swinging around in terror, he drove the chair as fast as it could go to the big double doors. He'd never remember how he had the strength to pull them open, but only seconds later he was out on the church's narrow porch about to ride the chair down the few steps to High Street. He would have crashed, flipped over, and ended up in a broken heap on the pavement, but there was Moses Llewelyn coming around the back with his mower.

"Mr. Wayne!" Moses yelled, and dropping his machine leaped just in time to keep Alastair from plunging downward.

"Home!" Alastair wheezed, tasting bile as he fought to avoid vomiting up his breakfast. Moses, not even questioning, obliged him.

It was fate that of everyone in New Morning, Alastair's confidences fell on Moses Llewelyn. Sooner or later he had to share what he knew with someone besides Glory, yet he churned anxiously, fretting that no one would believe him.

Moses was dubious. "I seen some extraordinary things in my life. Men behaving in ways contrary to common sense, or their inner directions. I know men torn in pieces by longings, by desires and needs as sure as if a lion had got at 'em. Men who has sold their souls for some White Lady, or worse, sold their loved ones. I seen men get lower than dogs and crawl like snakes on their bellies. Men in the muck, I seen that often enough. I seen men create their own disasters and then weep in the ruins. Men who has robbed and killed. I has knowed a score of such folk. Man is an animal same as the fox in the woods, only he thinks. 'Cepting those times when he don't."

Moses Llewelyn said all this in Alastair's kitchen over a cold soda after Alastair had sent him back to the church to check up on Will Austin. The minister was saying his prayers, behind the pulpit, quiet as could be. Only his lips moved and Moses swore they were flesh. Alastair, listening, pulled the afghan on his knees up to his throat.

"What did you expect?" Moses asked. Alastair, to relieve his own terror, told him.

Moses shook his head, sighing. "Wasn't at all. His head is no mess of nightcrawlers. That was you, just you, hallucinating."

"Maybe so." Alastair put up no fight to deny this, and, in fact, would rather it had been a mirage than Will Austin actually having rotted.

"You speak of the devil," Moses said. "Why I know the devil. I seen him, too. I seen him in the eyes of a man holding a bloody knife over his woman. I seen him in a mad dog, spittle on his lips, running naked in the streets. I seen the devil tending bar down in the Florida Keys, and driving a bus up in Chicago. I seen him on the street slinking like dead folk from doorway to gutter, carrying a bottle in a brown paper bag. The devil takes a toke and his eyes burn red, hot as fire. . . ."

"No, that's not what I mean, Moses," Alastair adjured. "I mean the actual Devil with a capital D, not the evil that lives in all of us." Alastair lightly fingered his own face, unaware that he was doing so. "I mean the real McCoy, Moses. Satan. Dragon he is to me. Lucifer who was the serpent in the garden. The archangel who sat at the side of the Lord when time began. Beelzebub, Mephistopheles." He pounded his fist on the table. "The one who gives us bad dreams, nightmares, calls out the demons, the monsters, and lets them loose while we sleep. That's who I mean, Moses."

Moses went to the refrigerator, and when he had retrieved another Pepsi, stripped off the tab, and taking a healthy swallow, he sighed, a long sound that seemed to travel up from his toes, down all his years. "Can't say I accept too much of it, Mr. Wayne, if you'll pardon me. Seems impossible, this day and age. Man, if you can believe them down in Washington, going to the moon. Mars . . . all them other planets. Man flies under his own steam. And here in New Morning we's got us the devil." He laughed, a big belly chuckle, a fat man's laugh, a laugh too large for Moses Llewelyn.

"That's true," Alastair agreed when Moses said he supposed the person in question was Lucas Donnelly. And when he blurted out, *why us?* Alastair tried to explain. "I think, but who am I to be certain about anything. Absolutes is a young man's game. Me, I just suppose. But supposing, I think the dragon wants a home base, that he's come out of the dark, up from whatever cave he's been hunkering in. That he's tired of moving about. A wife, children, a home. He's looking to settle down. And New England, he's got a long history here. The climate suits him you might say."

"But how come New Morning? Why not up in Vermont? Or how about Maine, out on the coast?" Moses suggested.

Alastair said, "I read somewhere that the devil is allergic to water."

"Lordy, Lordy." Moses shook himself like a dog waking up from sleep and returned to his chair. "So you mean Mr. Donnelly's responsible for Reverend Austin being strange."

"Half and half. Will was strange already." Alastair raised his cup of tepid tea to his lips.

Moses had something else on his mind. He left Will Austin to say, "I think quite a bit about Missus Emma. Most of the time, to be truthful. Supposing her living when she's dead and gone. Supposing that I can save her, which is downright silly. Stupid." He hesitated, then blurted, "You're suggesting, Mr. Wayne, that he's"—Moses jerked a thumb over his shoulder—"to blame." Alastair nodded and Moses mulled this over, questioning the revelation, chewing on it like a piece of gristle. Finally he said, "Seems strange."

To Alastair, Moses's involvement with dead Emma Tydings wasn't the least bit peculiar, not after all he'd seen this summer. "Nothing strange about it," he said. "Lucas Donnelly's got the town in a hammerlock. He's redoing us. And when you stir the pot you make more than your share of bubbles."

Moses, thinking this over too, fell silent.

Alastair was glad that Moses, who he suspected for a long time could be trusted, had been told.

Moses, unlike most of New Morning's more upstanding citizens, hadn't been walking on tippytoe since the dragon came. He hadn't these few months become suddenly affluent. Moses had remained the same: black, taciturn, old and snarly, hoary with past rage. Moses was still his own man, not the dragon's, and he said so, adding, "How come, Mr. Wayne, you're telling me all this?"

Alastair pulled at his nose, as if he might tug it right off his face. "Because I had to tell someone, sooner or later, besides Glory Crowell, and let's face it, Moses, you're past temptation. Then again," Alastair's nervous fingers climbed again to his face, "this isn't the kind of thing you keep entirely to yourself. Not if you plan—and surely I do, Moses—to make a fuss."

"What kind of fuss?"

Alastair's eyes closed and he considered in the comforting dark for a moment. Then he said, "I don't know. Except I can't just lie down and let the dragon roll over me." Like a tank across the sand, he was thinking, having feared that too when he sprawled in the Omaha muck, in a holding pattern between death and survival. "There comes a time," he ventured further, but he didn't have to go on. When he opened his eyes he saw in the liquid brown gaze Moses Llewelyn directed at him: *I understand*.

20

Lucas Donnelly came calling on Glory, though Glory didn't want him to. The night Theo and Evelyn sat her down and Evelyn said, "You're going to marry him. In December. A Christmas wedding. Cream *peau de soie*, I think and a complementary pink for the bridesmaid." Glory's hands shook, but she signed clearly, *Oh no, never!* Evelyn snapped like a guillotine's blade dropping, "Oh yes you will!"

Theo was skeptical. Something struck him as off-kilter about Lucas Donnelly's intentions. It wasn't only that the man had years on Glory. Though that bothered Theo, too, there was something else, something Theo failed to pin down. He tried to talk the situation over with Evelyn, but she said, "You'd worry about the wind. Nothing's wrong. Lucas Donnelly's the catch of the century." That might be true, but imagining the man as his son-in-law set Theo's teeth on edge. Thinking about Glory married to the tall, handsome, wealthy stranger gave Theo a constant headache. But there was nothing he could do. Evelyn had made up her mind. He simply acted as stiffly as he would when turning down a loan application.

Lucas Donnelly didn't seem the least put out by Theo's attitude. When they'd accidentally meet he'd be charming as usual.

On the Thursday before Old Home Week the two men collided by chance in the White Bear dining room. "Looks like the weather will hold for the festivities," Theo said, blowing his nose. Hay fever season was also beginning.

"That's true," Lucas Donnelly replied and invited Theo to have lunch with him.

It was as good an occasion as any to voice his doubts about the marriage, particularly since Evelyn wasn't present to throw a screaming fit and threaten to divorce him, as Theo suspected she'd do if he put the kabosh on the wedding. But Lucas Donnelly didn't want to talk about Glory. He was full of business instead. "Investing, buying and selling. The market's unstable these days. One moment climbing, the next collapsing in an avalanche."

Theo, ordering a white turkey on rye, hold the mayo, said, "Very worrisome, you know. Though, to be honest, my investments are slim. Don't have much of a portfolio." Meaning one like you have. Financial acrobatics, that was what Theo thought Lucas Donnelly engaged in to earn his money. "Wish I did," Theo, a gambler in his soul, added enviously, yearning to make a killing in the market.

"Perhaps you'll allow me to give you a tip or two," Lucas Donnelly said, sipping soda water. Lucas Donnelly never drank much, or not in public, a point in his favor.

"Of course. Delighted to hear them." Theo trembled slightly.

So Lucas Donnelly whispered at the edge of Theo's earlobe, "World Movers and Lombardy Construction. Over the counter. In, out. Be quick about it!" he admonished. "Buy before closing today, sell by next Friday."

Then the dragon went on his way, saying, of course, he wouldn't hear of Theo picking up the check. It was his inn, wasn't it. For a moment Theo remembered Herman September who'd been less than generous with his guests.

It was when Theo emerged from the men's room that he ran into Alastair. "Saw you having a powwow with Donnelly."

"Oh, nothing so monumental, Alastair. Just lunch. The man treated, which was nice of him." Theo neglected to mention the stock tips.

Alastair scowled. "Beware of Greeks, et cetera, Theo. You should know, being a banker."

"Now, Alastair." Theo smiled fondly. He hadn't seen his friend in a while. "I wish you and Evelyn would patch up your differences," he said, voicing something to which he'd given more than a passing thought.

Alastair snorted. "Come sit in the bar with me a while. I've got to talk to you." He rolled off, leaving Theo to follow.

Glory had told Alastair how Lucas Donnelly came to call, officially, and of Evelyn's insistence they marry at Christmas.

Glory also told Jordy, and Jordy wanted to shoot Lucas Donnelly dead. Alastair, who was present since the conversation occurred in his kitchen, suggested that wouldn't do.

"Listen," he said to Jordy, who had gone off his chair and was pacing the linoleum, about to wear a channel in it. "Listen," he said again, a headache creeping up the nape of his neck, "this is more complicated than you think."

"No way!" Jordy slammed a fist into a palm. "It's really pretty simple. I want to marry Glory and she—" He stopped and in two steps strode across the kitchen to grip Glory by the shoulders. "You still do want to marry me, don't you, Glor?" His voice rang loudly, insistently, but his eyes were humble. Alastair could see Jordy's look and was saddened. Too much feeling in the boy, he thought, yet Glory deserved such love.

Glory wound her arms about Jordy's neck and nuzzled into him, which was her way of answering. It was enough of a reply for Jordy who stood holding her. Alastair had to close his eyes. Then he coughed and made shuffling noises, so that when he saw again, the two young lovers had separated.

Jordy continuing his prowl said, "See, Alastair, it's easy. I mean you said that to me before we started off to Maryland. If we want to make a commitment, then that's what we do. No problem." He smiled. "We just pick some other night to elope."

It was time to share with Jordy the news that Lucas Donnelly was no ordinary mortal. As he did so, Jordy slowly returned to the table. He sat and, leaning close to Alastair, stared at the old man as if he were crazy.

Glory's fingers told the same tale, and Jordy burst out with a cry of disbelief. "You swallow this bunk, Glory? Oh, com'on! The devil's, I mean, well—" He stumbled, ran his hands through his hair, glared almost angrily from one to the other. "Bull, that's all. Maybe Mr. Austin can get away with it because it's part of his job, but for us, for real people—! The devil!" He laughed. "There's no such animal! A story or a kid's dream, like Santa."

Glory whipped her head from side to side, denying, and Jordy yelled again. "Alastair," he begged, "make her stop. You, too. I don't know how to deal with this kind of craziness. A screamer like my father, that's one thing. Even his bad smell, yeah, that I can handle. Because I think he's smelling his own rot. You know?" He rushed on, "But the devil. . . ."

It took some effort and two hours, but eventually Alastair

and Glory convinced Jordy. Somehow Jordy seemed diminished by the truth. Or perhaps he simply realized what a lopsided fight they were engaged in. Though he shouted, "God, we've got to do something!" he appeared smaller to Alastair, which depressed him. He'd rather a Jordy so macho and cocky he'd suggest taking a twenty-gauge to Lucas Donnelly. Now Jordy knew any gun was useless, that even if he hit the dragon midcenter, with both barrels, it meant nothing.

An enlightened Jordy had no notion what to do, and he grappled with his impotence. "How," he asked finally, his voice breaking, "do you get rid of the devil?"

Now, Theo yanked Alastair back to the present, asking, "How's Old Home Week coming?" They had settled at a table in the corner, by a window. The window was thick, the glass uneven, so what Alastair glimpsed on Main Street waffled. New pane, he thought, or rather, old. Somewhere Lucas Donnelly had gotten hold of originals.

"How should I know?" Alastair mumbled.

"What do you mean? You're the chairman, Alastair." Theo blinked, bewildered.

"Where have you been? Didn't you know Howie yanked the chair out from under me weeks ago?"

"No!" Theo replied, baffled. "Why didn't I hear about this?"

Alastair supposed Howie Eumis had forgotten. "Just another indication of the way things are going wrong in New Morning."

"You can't blame the town because Howie is grieving over his cats," Theo objected.

Alastair smacked the table with his palm. "Not anymore! Got the cats back, Howie did." He knew for a fact from Mrs. O'Brien, who liked cats about as much as she liked birds, which was not at all.

"He couldn't. They were dead. Or at least one of them anyway as I recall. Some feline disease. Perfectly dreadful. Howie and Rita carried on so."

Alastair laughed sourly. His parchment skin crinkled, but his eyes were worried. He zeroed in on Theo Crowell as if he were looking through the sights of a gun. "This is all your fault. In a manner of speaking."

Theo, nervously scuttling around, said, "Have you lost your mind, accusing me of killing Howie's cats?"

"Ah, Lord!" Alastair cried, rolling his eyes skyward. He had a sudden inspiration to tell Theo the truth. He had, after all, told Moses Llewelyn and Jordy, neither of whom suggested he

ought to be locked up. Maybe if New Morning discovered just
who Lucas Donnelly really was, they'd run him out on the first
bus. Send him down to Connecticut, he and that Jarvis
Badderly of his. Put a couple of firecrackers in the tail pipe of
his limo.

Theo stood up, glancing at his pocket watch. Alastair gave a
sharp tug to his jacket. "Sit down!" Theo sat abruptly. "Don't
run off."

"Business, Alastair. Things to be done."

Alastair leaned forward, his hand to his mouth, as if he were
about to pass secret information. "You can't let Glory marry
that man."

Theo glanced off. A red flush inched up his cheeks like a heat
rash. He blew his nose again. "That's what you want to talk
about?"

"What did you think, the weather? Now Theo, listen to me.
It's wrong. It stinks, as a matter of fact."

Reluctantly, Theo allowed his attention to wander back to
Alastair. He tried, "It's none of your business. A family matter.
Not for discussion," one after the other. But Alastair wouldn't
let him be.

"Theo, do you have the least idea what you're leading Glory
into?" Alastair said.

Theo wished he could turn Evelyn onto Alastair and let the
two old combatants fight it out. "People get married every day
of the week," he said.

"Not to the devil," Alastair said.

"The *who?*"

"That's who you're marrying Glory off to. The devil, the
dragon, Mephisto."

Theo's voice spiraled, then broke as he cried, "What the hell
are you chattering on about, Alastair? If this is one of your
jokes, I don't find it funny!" Theo left his chair, overturning the
candle in a pewter holder that sat in the center of the table.

"No joke. Serious business," Alastair mumured. "I know, I
know"—he waved his hands in the air, as if the shabby light in
the Bear trailed cobwebs—"it's hard to believe. The twentieth
century and all. But he's here, right over there." He stabbed a
finger in the general direction of the Tydings colonial. "And
he's got his slimy eye on Glory."

Theo's mouth opened and closed, then opened and closed
again. There were any number of things he could fling back at
Alastair, but instead he turned on his heel, his spine under-

bending as a poker, and marched with heavy steps out the front door.

In a few minutes Alastair followed, but when he reached the porch, Theo had already vanished. I tried, Alastair thought despairingly.

Alastair sat in his chair, half in the warm sunlight, half in the shadows, with no need to be anywhere, with nothing much to do today, or tomorrow. He glared across the street at Emma's house, which was just a house, and considered putting dynamite into the foundation, which was as silly a notion as Jordy's to blast Lucas Donnelly into oblivion with a twenty-gauge.

"Alastair!" A hand came out of nowhere and clamped onto his shoulder. It was a good thing Alastair stayed on his guard, prickly, too, and agitated just by Lucas Donnelly's nearness. If he'd been relaxed and loose, the sudden start up of his heart would have blown a valve.

"Jesus Christmas!" Alastair cried. "You could have given me a coronary, Doc."

Doc Trump grinned sheepishly. "You're right. Sorry, Alastair."

"How come you're in such fine fettle anyway?" Alastair asked, suspicious.

"I was just out at the hospital, and"—he smacked his lips—"you would not believe it! Why the new wing's already half up. New wing . . . ah, the old dump will be the wing when the building's all done. Will be twice the size of the original place. Do you realize, Alastair, that . . ."

Alastair, steam brewing in his insides, tuned Doc out. He didn't need to hear one more word about Lucas Donnelly's generosity, or about any of his various projects either. The man was a bog of quicksand. Every step you took you sank further into the mire. Alastair couldn't get away from the dragon for a minute. Well, an inner voice asked, what do you expect?

"I'm going home. Time for my nap," Alastair shouted in the middle of Doc's waxing lyrically about his new dialysis machine. He zoomed down the ramp, shifting to fast forward, and putt-putted across the street into the green, taking the short path, at a diagonal to his house.

Just as Alastair crossed over High Street and drew abreast of Dee's driveway, the silver Porsche pulled out of the garage in the rear. Alastair swiveled his chair so that if Dee wanted to get off her own property she'd have to run him over.

The driver's door swung open and Dee leaned half out of the Porsche. "Do I have to commit vehicular homicide to get to the Super Saver?" she asked waspishly.

Alastair rolled closer until his knees touched the bumper, his glance fixed on Dee. Just the other day, he could have sworn it, he suspected Dee of drinking the elixir of life. She had seemed a girl, young and oh so fresh, innocent even. Now, Alastair noticed her hair was graying, not in handsome streaks, but in clumps. She pushed the dark glasses on top of her head, revealing pouches beneath her eyes. Surely she'd never boasted those deep channels grooved alongside her mouth! And when she raised her hand to the edge of the door, a loose fold of skin draped from her upper arm.

Dee seemed the same generation as old Mrs. Winslow who must have had twenty years on her at least. "Feeling okay?" he asked.

"Hungry," she snapped. "I want to go buy myself something to eat." He thought he heard her teeth clatter. Could they be false? Certainly they'd resembled the real thing before. Alastair, further unnerved, swiped at his mouth, trying to think of something to say. But he did, however, retreat, slow as a snail, watching Dee all the while.

"How come," he called out finally just as she swung back into her fancy sports car, "you never come over for dinner or music anymore? Huh?"

Dee didn't answer him. The Porsche growled, and Dee stomped on the gas. The car flew by him. Alastair caught only the briefest glimpse of her profile. Even so, he saw the sag of skin under her jaw. Dee, inexplicably, had begun to shift and collapse like an unanchored mountainside.

Glory couldn't think what to do. Time weighed heavily on her now that she no longer had The Gallery to go to. If she stayed at home with Evelyn, she had to listen to more talk about the wedding. "Lucky!" her mother repeated over and over, but oh, what did she know, her eye on the genealogical chart when it wasn't on the mirror.

If Jordy hadn't been working they could take a ride in the van, north maybe, pass the fairgrounds and up toward Pittsfield, then, if as Evelyn said luck was really with her, they would keep going; but, of course, that never occurred. Glory thought of biking out to the Boardmans', but Carol, still teary and grieving, hated to leave her bedroom. Last time Glory visited, Carol had refused even to walk in the fields with the dogs.

If only Theo would give her a job in the bank, let her work up front in one of the metal cages, as a teller, handing out money and taking it in. She'd be good at that, mathematics had always been her best subject. But if she asked, at home, during dinner, Evelyn would throw herself between Glory and her father, and Theo, crumbling like a sand castle, would give in. So, dressed in a navy jumper and a pale blue blouse, a Sunday outfit, Glory slipped out of the house when Evelyn's back was turned and crossed through the green to the First National.

"Why, what do we have here, or who I should say?" Theo cried, smiling broadly when she appeared in his doorway. He stood up as she approached and kissed his cheek. "Hmmm," he said, wrinkling his nose, "my princess smells like lilacs."

Glory sat, not on the edge of the desk as she usually did when she came with her bankbook, but in the customer's chair. Theo, still grinning, settled opposite and asked what was the occasion? Were she and Evelyn on their way up to the mall for some shopping? Glory shook her head. This was serious and Theo teased her. He considered her a little girl, still that five-year-old on the southern dock, and when Evelyn had told her about marrying Lucas Donnelly, Glory suddenly remembered that Theo, his eyes brimming, had called her a child bride. Children don't get married, she wanted to tell him, and knew all at once, without his saying anything, just sitting, waiting expectantly, he'd never let her work in the bank.

Her hands stalled in the air like leaves in the stillness preceding a storm as Theo started to fidget. "Princess," he said, his smile faltering in confusion.

Glory rose and kissed her father again, leaving his office. "Glory?" he called after her, but she went right out of the bank to the summer street. New Morning slept, curled up like a tabby cat in the heat, and she felt despondent, there on the sidewalk with the heaviness of the sun beating down on her golden head. She couldn't know that she appeared to give off sparks, to flicker and burn like a flame.

At last, she crossed over into the shade, thinking she'd go to Alastair's; maybe they'd have some lemonade, maybe she'd play for him. But walking up to his front porch, she saw him sitting by the window, leaning against the pane. He was limp as a sofa pillow, his mouth agape, bubbles beading from his lips. Alastair motionless, snored, and Glory hadn't the heart to wake him.

Glory went around the back, taking off her shoes and walking barefoot on the soft grass. The air hummed, crickets fussed in a nervous symphony. The limbs on Alastair's oak drooped in weary dishevelment as Glory passed through the hedges and out into the alley. It was gloomier here—though no cooler—between the houses, interstices of narrow light slipping through the branches of the overhanging trees. She kicked up tufts of dust with her toes and walked slowly. Nothing stirred as she passed the rear of Alastair's garage and the black alley grew murkier. Glory gazed up at the sky, but the sun had vanished, displayed by clouds and foliage. The heat remained, however. She could barely breathe. She reached the Trumps' fence, almost buried in a tangle of English Ivy, and entered a leafy tunnel in which the light strained, fading into dreariness. It had never been so dark here, not that she remembered, and she couldn't see well at all. Perhaps a summer squall was approaching, a tempestuous rainstorm that would rampage angrily at New Morning before thundering south of Connecticut.

She stopped with one foot raised and listened, but there was nothing to hear. Sound had passed away and the air, thick as plaster, lay paralyzed. She knew she must be behind Dee Whittier's, but she couldn't be sure, for an early evening darkness gathered, shadows amassed and clung together. Glory searched for the earth with her foot and stepped lightly, unsure. Glancing behind, thinking she should retreat and return to Alastair's where she'd wait in the kitchen, the alley was completely shrouded in blackness, the fences and garages, the hedges, the ivy, and the Trumps' morning-glory vines lost in forgetfulness. Nothing behind her might have been, and Glory's heart quickened. Her breath sputtered raggedly, and she put her shoes back on, prepared to run, only it was no use, she really couldn't see at all now except for the vaguest of outlines.

Silly! she said to her fear as though it were a living thing, silly, go away, there's nothing to be scared of, not here. Home lay just ahead, a few yards from where she stood, and Alastair's was close to her back, but she might have been underwater in one of her dreams, so far down the light on the surface had no shimmer. She took a few tentative baby steps and thought of the long ago children's game, *Mother, May I?*

"Glory" he said, so faintly, so tenderly, she thought at first it was a breeze that insinuated its drift into the alley. "Glorious," she heard distinctly, then with a buzzing like a swarm of bees, and she came to a dead halt, her arms crossed before her breasts protectively.

The darkness neither abated, sifting down to an ashy mist, nor parted in two curtains to allow Lucas Donnelly into the alley. He was just there, suddenly, superimposed on the black backdrop like a cutout paper doll. In all that throbbing whiteness of his, he was painful to look at. Glory squinted, then closed her eyes, hoping he'd dematerialize. Maybe he was nothing more than a mirage, a configuration formed by the heat and air currents.

"You don't have to be afraid of me," he said, and his whisper was hot on her forehead.

She wiped his words from her skin with her fingertips. His handsome, swarthy face swam above her like the sun. Glory locked her jaw and struggled not to shudder as he whispered, "I've a present, Glory, a gift, from me to you." He smiled, and his sparkling teeth were sharp as an alligator's.

Go away! she cried as the storm began to rise and build around her. She smelled the clean minty odor of impending rain.

"What you want, more than anything," he said. His fingers lingered, stroked over her lips and chin.

Nothing! she swore as his touch crawled to her neck. He gently slithered over her pulse, a trembling butterfly beneath the skin. His luminescent eyes held her captive as his hands reached her throat.

Nothing! she cried again and the word rose out of the void. Glory's *nothing* came up her throat as she swam ever higher in the warm, salty Caribbean. She snapped her teeth together as the lightning cracked. She pressed full, rosy lips, firmly, one to the other, and swallowed like an indigestible lump of bread that *nothing.* The storm nipped at her shoulders, beginning to rustle, and spiraled fine silky columns of dust.

Lucas Donnelly spread his arms wide as angel's wings and smiled at her. "Nothing, Glory, nothing. Say it."

But Glory, tasting the sour *nothing* on her tongue, refused to obey him. The word was alive now, for her silent voice had become potent. She could, without question, scream at Lucas

Donnelly, I'll rot in hell first! But she didn't. Glory leaped, running instead, back through the winnowing darkness to Alastair's, where she threw herself upon the ground, not caring at all about her Sunday outfit, as the storm broke and the rain fell upon her.

Old Home Week started off normally with the Saturday parade. The weather cooperated for once by being just fine, neither sweltering nor rainy, a steady seventy-five.

The various groups gathered as in time immemorial by the firehouse at ten in the morning. The Consolidated band and the majorettes, the pompom-swinging cheerleaders, the Congregational choir decked out once again in their heavy monks' robes, the Historical Ladies and the cars to transport them, Bailey Cross riding his new tractor.

Carol, still mourning for her brother Jack, had come around enough at least to put on her graduation gown and perch upon a crepe-paper-decorated throne as Queen of New Morning. A gold crown graced the top of her head and she cradled an armful of plastic flowers. She should have looked prettier than she did, but her skin had the same hue as the white taffeta, and her mouth pulled down at the corners in what was becoming a perpetual frown.

The Belwether Brothers draped satin ribbons over one of the hearses and centered a wreath of lilies on its hood, but the firehouse ambulance went unadorned. Stanis Papriakas drove an old farm wagon, pulled by two plodding plow horses. Gina sat in the back, beside a display of fruit and vegetables. Charlie Calman remembered Herman September's 380 SL Mercedes convertible parked in the White Bear garage, unclaimed yet by Herman's heirs, and borrowed it for the event. He covered the sides with Red Sox pennants and got Teddy Myers to stand on the seat swinging a bat. The grammar school constructed their yearly float portraying in tableau Ebenezer Smythe and company arriving in New Morning.

The touchy subject of Grand Marshal had been resolved. Lucas Donnelly led the procession in his limousine. Alastair wondered who'd asked him, if anyone had. Not that there was a soul, except for himself, who'd quibble, considering the esteem in which New Morning held the dragon.

It was a sorry excuse for an opening-day parade, Alastair

thought, out on his front porch in the wheelchair. None of the neighboring towns had sent bands or fire trucks, and there wasn't a tourist in sight.

On Alastair's front porch Moses sat in a folding chair drinking lemonade. Jordy usually drove one of the Ford garage's pickups, all decorated with a pole trailing ribbons for the traditional King of the May. Nobody had ever been able to answer why a maypole and king on Labor Day. This year, however, Jordy swore, "No way!" and hunched one step down from Alastair and Moses.

Evelyn Crowell rode with the Historical Ladies and Theo marched in step with the Lion's Club. Glory, who could have had her pick of floats to travel upon, rejected all of them and sat between Jordy and Alastair.

The parade went around the square once, and then returned, sweeping back down High Street led by the creeping black limousine. Alastair recalled his vision the day it arrived. This time, however, the long car with its opaque windows stopped dead center before Alastair's front walk. All eyes were on it. Moses, a glass half raised to his mouth, froze, suspended. Glory's hand disappeared from Jordy's as the sun struck the side of the car setting off ripples of light. Of course it was impossible, but the limo seemed to stretch, to elongate and flow along the block.

"God damn!" Moses sputtered as they all sat mesmerized by the car.

"Hey! What are you doing?" Jordy's fearful cry brought Alastair up short. Glory was walking away from the porch down the narrow concrete path toward the limo.

The light glistened on her blond hair, bounced off the white dress she wore in a glare. "Glory!" Jordy yelled, panicked. He leaped up to go after her in her sleepwalker's crawl to the limousine, but Alastair, frightened himself, yelled out, "Stop him!"

Though Moses, even so late in life, had razor-sharp reflexes, Jordy, close on Glory's heels, outpaced him. Moses then made the only move he could think of. He dove straight off the porch as if leaping into the water from the dock at Garland's Pond and tackled Jordy. Down they went, the two of them, Moses gripping Jordy's legs, falling half on him, Jordy's body cushioning his fall except for one irresponsible knee, in which the concrete set off a Dixieland throbbing. Still, Jordy, seeing Glory at the end of the walk nearing the limousine, struggled, as Moses, leaning, whispered in his ear, "Boy, let up or I'll knock you out! Hear me now!" Jordy desisted, but Moses kept him pinned in place for an extra second before letting him rise.

Glory drifted, her feet not quite touching the earth's surface, as she moved ever closer to the limo. To Alastair the daze in which she glided made him think she must have fallen asleep, her eyes wide open, or been hypnotized by something he couldn't see. His chest tightening, his heart squeezed, Alastair cried out, "Glory!" But she never even turned her head. She just kept floating until she arrived at the car. The back door silently swung wide. "Glory!" he called, this time the merest breath of a whisper as she disappeared, swallowed in the darkened belly of the limousine.

Moses finally relinquished his hammerlock on Jordy as Lucas Donnelly's car led off the parade again, at a sedate ten miles an hour. The Consolidated band rounded the corner, all in step if not in tune, playing, loud and raucous, *God Bless America*.

"What did she go with him for?" Jordy cried, about to weep, with a face masked in a little boy's scowl.

Alastair shriveled, his shoulders curving, and he rubbed his hands as though he were cold, though he couldn't be. "I don't know," he whispered with dry, crinkly lips after a while.

Below, the parade continued crawling along High Street in the usual sluggish starts and stops. More than one group had been forgetful, and several of the floats looked half done. Costumes and uniforms were colorful, if confused.

Moses went into the house and slammed out a moment later with a pitcher of lemonade. "Have to keep intaking liquids with this heat," he said to Alastair, "otherwise you'd dehydrate." He fussed for a moment, a finicky old hen, worry clouding his eyes. Alastair might have been one of his own.

The parade speeded up. Will Austin and his chorus, mysteriously medieval, were indeed doing their Gregorian chants. Cowled, hands shoved up into sleeves, and barefoot, they slipped along, creatures in a New Morning dream. Behind them came a float Alastair couldn't recall from other years. This flatbed, laid with green crepe-paper grass, boasted a gibbet from which hung a swinging body dressed in colonial fashion. From the distance the deceased looked real. The spongy face purpled, and a wet stain mapped part of one pant leg. Dead or stuffed he bore a suspicious resemblance to Ebenezer Smythe, at least as the founder was depicted in the mural that covered the dome of the Barnes.

Alastair's mind stuck on Glory. Lucas Donnelly had been up front about his plans for her, and Alastair had thought there'd be no divergences, or at least not until winter. But maybe he was wrong. Lucas Donnelly was, after all, the trickster. Christmas might be as illusionary as the gallows and Ebenezer Smythe.

Moses, so jittery there was no keeping him still, went inside to make up yet another pitcher of lemonade, pink this time, and came out muttering, "Never cared for parades. Silly occasions, what with people getting blisters on their toes."

Charlie Calman, driving the Mercedes, arrived, with Teddy Myers standing atop the seat, swinging a bat. Crouched, feet apart, elbows tucked in, chin down, eyes square on the ball . . . One, two, swing! Crash!

After Charlie and Teddy in the Mercedes, not much of a parade was left. The Lions, all misstepping, and then the Historical Ladies.

"So be it." Moses let loose a sigh when the last of the parade dribbled away, though the air continued to vibrate with "When the Saints Come Marching In." Then the band marched too far away for their next selection to drift back to the square.

"Glory!" Jordy tore apart the sudden silence with her name and Alastair jerked in his chair.

Alastair said, "I suppose we should get out to the fairgrounds." Not that he'll harm her, he thought—he hoped. "We'll take the Dodge."

Alastair gave one last look to the square, empty now, and felt his head spin. The trees upended and rushed frantically around in his vision. Alastair covered his eyes, bit down on his bottom lip. The end, he couldn't help thinking, will come like this. But it was only, now, a normal attack of dizziness. From the heat and old age.

"Let's go," he said to Moses, more eager to find Glory than he let on, and rolled through the house, into the kitchen, and out the back door at high speed.

21

Old Home Week unraveled in confusion. Alastair, feeling too ill to be out and about, missed most of it. Finally, Mrs. O'Brien, without bothering to consult Alastair, summoned Dr. Thump.

"A hundred and three!" Doc read the thermometer. "Good God, Alastair!" he said. He gave Alastair antibiotics and aspirins, piled him high with quilts and ordered Mrs. O'Brien to fill him full of liquids. "We're going to sweat this out of you, or there'll be hell to pay!" Alastair tried telling Doc it was hell here and now, the first week of September in New Morning, but Doc wouldn't listen.

"Keep your eye on him, Lettie. Don't let the old goat get away. This time I'm not kidding. I'll have your hide, personally, if I find him out of this bed." Doc gave Mrs. O'Brien a steely glower, which fazed her not one bit. Nothing ever put a dent in Mrs. O'Brien's walrus skin. Through his daze, Alastair imagined even the dragon would get only a shrug.

But Doc needn't have worried. Alastair felt much too sick to go anywhere. He lay half in a swoon, so hot he longed to shed his flesh and drift through the maze of Dog Green dreams. Omaha Beach troubled his sleep with a vengeance, and bothered him almost as much when he woke up.

Alastair had come down with the flu on the first Saturday after the parade. He and Moses and Jordy had driven out to the fairgrounds and found Glory and Carol Boardman riding the carousel. Jordy jumped right on and claimed a white horse between them. When the merry-go-round stopped, Glory refused to get off and Alastair, helped by Moses—almost lifted bodily, in fact—climbed aboard to circle in dizzying turns. Alastair declined to mount a horse, however, even a wooden one, so they all crowded into a gondola.

"What went on in that car?" Alastair asked, holding tight to Glory's arm. She had to move to answer him. For a moment, her lips parting, Alastair thought she'd found the knack of speech again. But Glory said her words with wandering fingers, and there were few of them.

Nothing, and after a pause, sweeping a strand of hair behind her ear, not looking directly at any of them, but down at her knees, *wedding plans*.

"A wedding!" Carol shrieked. "Who's getting married? You two, finally?" she asked, poking Jordy in the ribs.

Alastair struggled, weary and with the first of a series of small shakes. The fever that would lay him low for days was already beginning to burn through him.

"Lucas Donnelly," he said, "is the devil. And he's after Glory. To marry her at Christmastime. He's taken over New Morning, as his headquarters, you might say, here in the USA. Besotted by the colonial, he is, and we're as authentic as I suppose you can get. And now, with his renovations, near perfect. Of course, there's been a price to pay. People trading off their immortal souls, including Will Austin, I suspect."

"Mr. Donnelly's the living end," Carol said.

"Carol, you don't understand." Alastair sighed. He reached out, and in an intimate gesture that was strange to him, took her face between his hands and rotated Carol like a mechanical doll his way. "Listen, did you hear what I said? About Donnelly being the devil? Taking us over worse than the Russians ever could?"

"Oh, Mr. Wayne, you're exaggerating!" She smiled with a big grin.

"No, I'm not. Think. Remember Jack in his Toyota." Carol's smile collapsed. "You dreamed him, dying in flames. Didn't you?"

Carol blinked rapidly. "Glory told you."

"She had to, so don't be mad. And then there was poor Bobby Pierson. I've never been convinced the boy innocently drowned."

"Jack's accident was—he did something to the Toyota's brakes?" Carol stuttered.

There would turn out to be two kinds of people in New Morning, those who struggled against the dragon for all they were worth, committed to the logical, reason, a rational explanation for whatever occurred, if not to the good; and those who—perhaps more imaginative or dumber—shrugged and said, "Oh, yes, the devil, and what's for lunch?" Carol belonged in the first group, and she flailed against whatever Alastair and Moses, Jordy as well, told her, refusing to believe.

"Ah, com'on, Carol," Jordy cried, throwing up his hands. "You don't have any trouble with vampires and ghouls, werewolves and zombies at the drive-in, so how come you're giving us such a hard time?"

"Holy Hannah! That's the movies! That's not real life. You're telling me that the devil is an actual breathing person and he killed my brother!" Tears channeled down her cheeks. Glory put an arm around Carol's shoulder, and Carol bowed her head, sobbing.

They all rode on, bits and pieces of New Morning passing on each turn. Alastair, starting to feel woozy, ventured to explain again. When he ran down into silence, Carol turned toward Glory who wrote, *It's true*, in the air. Carol's eyes welled with tears.

The carousel stopped and there, standing by the entrance, a white flame of light, was Lucas Donnelly. The gondola had come to a halt in front of him, and he waved. Before the first slide of motion, Carol flung herself off the seat, jumping from the merry-go-round.

Carol screamed in the dragon's face. "You killed my brother!"

It happened in a flash, so quickly Alastair, contending with the crutches, hadn't time to struggle to his feet. Carol launched herself like a missile, fists flying, and taking the dragon by surprise.

Lucas Donnelly dropped his cigar and hastily stepped back a few feet, but Carol charged. It wasn't for nothing that she'd grown up with brothers and knew every dirty trick in the book. Her fingers aimed for his eyes, her knee for his crotch.

Jordy and Moses leaped to the ground, carefully dancing with legs wide and arms spread. They were trying to grab hold of some part of Carol and yank her away.

Glory nervously waited for Alastair, but before they could descend, the carousel started another round, and off they went, twisting their necks to gaze behind. Carol and the dragon came up on the side, her knuckles speeding to his chin. Jordy dove for her elbow but missed, to sprawl flat in the dirt. Glory and Alastair went right on, Alastair's protest caught up in the music.

Lucas Donnelly ducked just in time. The projectile traveled on by him and Carol stumbled.

"Son-of-a-bitch!" Carol cried. Regaining her balance, she lowered her head to dive at him like a battering ram.

If the dragon was amused by a physical assault, and from a female yet, when Carol's head hit him midsection, knocking a loud puff of air out of him, forcing his arms to flap like wings so he wouldn't fall flat, he stopped thinking such effrontery funny. Alastair saw the change in Lucas Donnelly's face, like a traffic signal switching from stop to go, and cried out, "Carol, oh no!"

The devil's anger was fearsome as a tornado, swooping up everything in its cylindrical cone, slivering solid wood to toothpicks, and sucking mortar from foundations, as he let his rage loose at Carol Boardman. Up, up in the air she shot. She flipped over, flat on her back, until Lucas Donnelly turned her, spinning the Queen of Old Home Week like a majorette's baton. Alastair and Glory, holding onto the edge of the gondola while the carousel made yet another round, traveled past the airborne Carol, then returned.

Glory, distraught, abandoned Alastair in the gondola and tried running alongside the merry-go-round horses. She wanted to stay abreast of Carol but despite all her efforts, Glory raced ahead or lost ground. Alastair, thumping a crutch, yelled, "Sit down!" Sooner or later, he knew the carousel would cease revolving. But Glory kept jogging, a yellow pennant of hair streaming behind as her hands waved frantically and her fingers cried time and again, *Carol!* Alastair, wiping the tears from the corners of his eyes, flung himself about the gondola uselessly.

All at once, Glory bounded off the moving carousel, landing in a heap on Lucas Donnelly's shadow. The dragon scowled as she hulked in his shade. This reaction, so unlike his usual smily good humor with Glory, had Alastair, sailing on, press a fluttery hand to his stampeding heart. Fear rose wild and untethered along his backbone and brought further palpitations to accompany a rising fever.

Perhaps the devil couldn't think of more than one matter at a time, which seemed unlikely, but for whatever reason, his hold on Carol broke and she plummeted—deliberate as one of the dead birds to the ground—into the dust. Glory, still on her knees, crawled to Carol and cradled the limp body in her arms. The blond hair cascaded forward in a wave as Glory patted and stroked Carol's still, unresponsive face. Carol's eyes, though open, held the deadness of a Barbie doll.

If Lucas Donnelly was enraged before, he steamed now, curls of smoke funneling from his ears. The curly ringlets bristled; a feathery brow jutted up in an arch.

Thankfully Alastair felt the carousel slowing. In a few seconds it ground to a halt. He yelled for Moses and Jordy as he started to stumble dizzily forward, the world still in circling motion. They rushed to his side and between them lifted him off.

A crowd collected, curious spectators grouped about Lucas Donnelly and Glory with Carol in her arms. "Daisy" no longer ringing in his ears, Alastair heard the dragon's bellow loud and clear. "Leave her alone!" he hollered in an earthquake rumble as jets of fire flashed from his fingertips.

The earth shook as black clouds rushed across the sky. The air tightened, sequined with sparks. Alastair clung to Jordy and to Moses.

The wind rose in a wall and flung itself. People were blown off their feet. Alastair, too, would have tumbled, but Jordy and Moses bent forward, thrusting their weight as well as Alastair's against the wind.

Still Glory refused to relinquish Carol, dead or alive. Alastair couldn't tell which for the sudden hurricane tossed swirls of dust in his eyes.

"Stand next to me!" Lucas Donnelly, cracking thunder, ordered Glory. In the leaden, metallic sky, a trident of lightning fired, hurtling downward, passing a few inches over Alastair before it crashed into the carousel.

Suddenly the clouds tumbled, shrouding the fairgrounds with a cottony mist, and a torrential rain exploded. In seconds the earth was a bubbling miasma.

"Here! Now!" Lucas Donnelly howled, his command an explosion.

Glory's hair was plastered to her wet cheeks, and her clothes clung so tightly she seemed naked. But she straightened, almost rising, lifting Carol up in an embrace. She clutched her friend's lifeless body to her breasts, and her lips parted. Then, louder than anything Lucas Donnelly had yelled yet, she shouted: "No!"

Lucas Donnelly seemed to swell to twice his normal size. The Colossus of New Morning, thunderous, black as the storm itself, gigantic as a sequoia, stretched out a long, white-sleeved arm, pointing a lightning-rod finger.

He meant to draw the electricity out of the turbulent

heavens and hurl it, Zeus-fashion, at Glory, small and fragile
despite her well-meaning efforts to stand tall; or at least
Alastair presumed that was the dragon's intention. He was so
certain Lucas Donnelly, in his terrible fury, intended Glory
harm, that without considering, he wrenched free from Jordy's
arm, and though still holding Moses on the left, he lurched
further, thrusting the crutch in the way. The rubber tip
snapped hard on Lucas Donnelly's finger, and Alastair drew the
dragon's anger toward him.

Fire streaked off Lucas Donnelly's hand, incinerating the
crutch to a burning brand. Alastair, shrieking, dropped back
and was yanked clear by Moses. The crutch fell to the dirt.

Lucas Donnelly was by no means satisfied. His eyebrows
came alive and danced, breath hissed from his mouth in a river
of fire. Surely, the thought winged fast through Alastair's mind,
one of us is going to die.

In his hasty flight, Alastair had dropped the other crutch,
and now stood wholly supported by Moses. As another flare
blazed off Lucas's fingernail, Moses and Alastair lost what little
footing they had and collapsed in a jumble of arms and legs.
Jordy hurried to save them and tripped himself, the two old
men and Jordy lying flat alongside a twisted, broken Carol, her
white graduation dress a bloodstained, dirty rag. Glory
screamed that impossible "*No!*" once more and flung herself on
top of them.

The dragon's jet of fire launched in its trajectory toward
where Glory had just been couldn't be recalled. It seared a
carousel horse in the eye, struck another at the neck, blazing a
tunnel through the wood, and went to ground not in one of the
carousel's painted steeds, but in the belly of one of Stani's
Papriakas's borrowed plow horses. The poor beast, shot by the
glowing streak of liquid fire, screamed in agony, and reared,
his underbelly a nest of flames, his brown hide ignited.

Ashes to ashes . . . Alastair, having been dragged to the
side behind the ringtoss stand, covered his ears. He had his
own fever to battle with, his temperature rising with each
scream from the horse. He huddled, a throbbing jumble of
arms and dead legs, as Glory held him. If Alastair realized,
which too terrified he didn't, that she was attempting to
comfort him, as he so many times over the long past had
succored her, he would have wept the last spare drop of liquid
within him.

The tortured horse's excruciating cries seemed **to rip**

through the skin of the cosmos, then stopped entirely. Silence hurried into the void. Alastair opened his eyes, his vision fogged with the smoke from his fever, and sought to find the dragon before he struggled—again with assistance from the others—upright. He didn't want any of them to falter into the line of fire, surfacing behind the crosslines of Lucas Donnelly's sight. But Lucas Donnelly had disappeared from the fairgrounds, leaving a still-smoking stogy where he'd stood.

22

The rains fell through the rest of Old Home Week. The downpour never lessened for one moment of Carol Boardman's funeral, and Carol's coffin was a raft, her grave as watery as the rising Housatonic. The rain, mixed with tears, was salty.

Lucas Donnelly was responsible for the inclement weather. It was true, as eternally reported, that the dragon had an awesome temper. Subject to flaming fits of anger that would scorch the eyelashes, he couldn't tolerate being thwarted. When he got less than his due, his tantrums were notorious. Volcanos erupted, hurricanes blew up on the sunniest of summer days. Tornados were a favorite manifestation of his conniptions. New Morning was lucky that all Lucas Donnelly decided to do was make the rain fall.

"I hope this isn't going to be one of your longer snits," Jarvis Badderly said when he brought Lucas Donnelly coffee and a bagel up to the computer room. "Like that time with Noah."

"That wasn't me and you know it," Lucas Donnelly snapped in a steamy breath of annoyance.

"Oh, really. My mistake." He placed the silver tray in front of the dragon and dropped a napkin in his lap. "Here, have your coffee. Eat something. You'll feel better."

He hissed, "You're a regular nanny, Jarvis."

"Only one of my many jobs." He slithered about the room, straightening pads of paper, aligning pens a millimeter either way. "But I do hope it won't rain like this for long. Everything is getting soggy."

Lucas Donnelly beamed a murderous look down through the shadows and Jarvis Badderly transmogrified into the white cat. "Meow!" he howled indignantly and padded out of the room.

Returning to his labors, the dragon worked the hours away. South America was finalized for the next few days before he looked up and stretched. The rain blurred outside in the dark. Black water, the dragon thought and was amused. He considered slowing down the heavy precipitation, or alternately churning up a hurricane. Winds of eighty miles per hour, fences scattered, bushes uprooted. Ah, he rumbled, unrolling a ribbon of flame along the conference table, New Morning needs a lesson. But a hurricane would be severe.

The dragon decided to let it rain until dawn instead, and went to bed. He curled his tail about him and banked his fires, eased the hinges of his armor-plated lids loose. All this metaphorically, of course, because as Lucas Donnelly, he slept in the manner of humans, pajamaed, under a sheet and quilt, his curly head resting light as a cloud on a feather pillow. Naturally he said no prayers, or thought, in the ever-optimistic mood that characterized man, tomorrow is another day. Tomorrow, for the devil, came and went eternally. In the entire universe Lucas Donnelly was the only being for whom time was minus its terror; time, for the dragon, existed merely as a reference point.

Of course, as Lucas Donnelly, a recent guise in his masquerade that had begun at the dawn of the world when he appeared in the persona of a rather chatty snake, the dragon paid lip service to human conventions. So he wore a watch, a Tournier, and carried an ostrich-skin wallet with credit cards in its neat compartments, a driver's license, an insurance identification card, and several hundred dollars in crisp, new bills. His shirts had been hand stitched from silk—fashioned by several little underpaid Chinese ladies in Hong Kong—while his suits were of the finest, most expensive linen. Special Italian cobblers had created his shoes of soft, buttery leather, so that the dragon walked, metaphorically of course, on air. Having settled, for the moment, to be perceived as a male human, he saw no reason to be ill clad and uncomfortable. Besides, the dragon had exquisite tastes. He had, down through history, a penchant for gold and silver, for large baubles as well as masterful works of art. In his heart of hearts, however, his predilection was for the simple, the plain. Line and form, geometry and balance most satisfied his eye. In his soul—if it were possible to designate the dragon's animus in such a way—he was all New England.

"Regard that William and Mary banister-back armchair or even the side chair," he'd intoned in a recent discussion with Jarvis Badderly. "Look at the line, those beautifully proportioned baluster-shaped flats. Those restrained turnings! And are you aware of the mathematically precise dimensions?"

If he were given to such an insanity, Lucas Donnelly could have sold this piece to any of several American museums for a small fortune. But, of course, the dragon had no use for money. If he had to hand some of it over in one transaction or another, he merely flicked his fingers and a stack of bills was instantly *there*. He could also, if he wanted to be authentic, print it up in the basement in the same manner as the U.S. Mint, or have Jarvis do it as one of his chores.

Among the many reasons Jarvis resented this sinecure in New England, the most telling was that he had so much to do. "Morning to night, every single minute," he complained to Lucas Donnelly who never bothered to listen. "I'm just run off my feet, what with this mausoleum and that inn." He swore. "I wish you'd hurry up and get Massachusetts out of your system!"

That the dragon never bothered to explain to Jarvis Badderly attested to the disparity in their positions. Trusted servant, familiar, companion even, both were more than aware who held the power in their relationship, and so prudently kept their distance. Lucas Donnelly had no desire to transmogrify Jarvis Badderly into some slimy, disgusting creature. Jarvis, after all, was helpful, and they had knocked around together for so long, Lucas Donnelly had grown rather fond of the fellow. It was also rather late in the day to find and train another competent familiar. Not that he hadn't minions scattered through each of the continents, but at best they were on the middle management level. Oh, he did have some top flight executives in his system, particularly in Libya, the Middle East, and South America. There were also one or two fellows in Southeast Asia and a handful in Washington, D.C., who showed talent. None, however, with whom he'd ever want to be intimate. At close quarters, Lucas Donnelly preferred the more mundane personalities, those of rather individual sins and small, manageable desires. That was why he liked New Englanders.

It was really self-evident why Lucas Donnelly had become taken with New Morning. Even if it hadn't been for Glory, who had drawn him here in the first place, he would have been enamored with the town.

The dragon was quite pleased at how nicely things were shaping up in New Morning. But then there occurred that unfortunate business at the fairgrounds, and he'd lost his temper. Even though Carol Boardman had been the one to attack him, Lucas Donnelly blamed Alastair. Old Alastair Wayne! What an adversary! The dragon laughed. For a moment his rumble of good humor dried up the water and the rain stopped.

As essential as up was to down, hot to cold, large to small, so Alastair Wayne, with his moral imperatives, was a counter to the dragon. He had, after all, expected somebody, and received a certain enjoyment, one might almost characterize it as pleasure, from their ritualistic joust.

Wishing his weary enemy a sound sleep, though one threaded with nightmares, and deciding by dawn New Morning would be soggy enough, Lucas Donnelly settled comfortably in his four-poster. So the dragon himself slept sound as a stone in the earth. But he didn't dream. What, after all, would the dragon have dreamed about?

The next morning the sun returned to town, and it was understood, even if not plainly stated, that Lucas Donnelly should be thanked for this, too.

The dragon worked for hours with the bright sunlight lapping at his windows, then broke for lunch, which he intended to take at the Bear. A delicious rarebit accompanied by a stout ale. Ah yes, that would do, he thought, smoothing his unwrinkled, pristine white suit.

When he ensconced himself at the center table of the White Bear dining room, Lucas Donnelly found he was surrounded by a party of New Morning citizens, among whom were Howie Eumis, Jonah Enderman, his future father-in-law Theo Crowell, and the Reverend Will Austin. And, surprisingly, since he was seldom glimpsed outside the bakery during business hours, Harlan Farrow. Jordy's father wore a sour look on his face, as though a lemon jammed his mouth.

Harlan Farrow was engaged in a tour of New Morning,

wandering from place to place, from the Public to Simon's Hardware, the bookshop to the boutique. He'd also, in the past few weeks, dropped in at the Congregational (where he'd never before put a Sunday foot), and the Consolidated, the laundromat, as well as the *Eagle* office, where Charlie was so surprised to see him he offered Harlan a beer.

Harlan refused to believe that the putrid aroma was in his head, or rather lodged like impacted mucus in his nostrils, but he was making sure. If he didn't scent a whiff of his private rot in all his investigations, he swore he'd burn the bakery right to its foundations. Accidentally, of course, since he intended to collect on the insurance.

Charlie Calman came late to the Bear and made do with coffee and cake. As for Doc Trump, he had an unexpected appendectomy, though he wouldn't have stopped for lunch anyway. Not only did he have an extra-full schedule of appointments for the afternoon office hours, he wasn't a charter member of Lucas Donnelly's cabal. Though the dragon had no intention of exempting him.

Doc Trump let no moss grow beneath him as he rushed from morning to dark. The sick, the dying, the psychosomatic took up more hours than there were numerals on the clock. And wherever the two men bumped into each other, Doc wallowed up to his ears in medical thoughts, though he acted properly grateful for the new hospital. Medicine consumed Doc, and the few minutes he had free for well people he devoted to satisfying Ava.

After lunch the men drifted away one by one, until Lucas Donnelly was left alone with Will Austin. "Reverend," he said, and Will Austin smiled at him with eyes as vacant as boysenberries.

"*Mirabile dictu,*" Will Austin said.

"Glad you liked the harpsichord," Lucas Donnelly deciphered. "But now, I've been thinking, there're a few changes you might consider. Instituting them gradually, one a week, or two."

Will Austin shone even brighter. "Anything for you, Mr. Donnelly!"

"I'm glad you're so amenable." Lucas Donnelly offered the minister a cigar, and they blew intertwining smoke rings.

While Lucas Donnelly engaged in further bargaining with Will Austin, Alastair dragged through his house in a bathrobe, a dubious maneuver with the crutches, since he might so easily trip. But Alastair had slept late and awakened with a headache. Another symptom to add to his ever-lengthening list of pains.

Alastair wasn't aware of the lunchtime gathering. He hadn't dropped in at the White Bear for days, and nobody invited him. Alastair, the thorn on the stem of the rose, belonged elsewhere. Eventually, the dragon expected Alastair to join them. After, that was, his defeat in their contest. Lucas Donnelly never considered losing. Why should he? His record had more consistent wins than the Yankees, and if there were some rather startling lapses from a perfect slate, that, too, was by design, to keep mankind from eternal despair. If humans believed there was no chance to score the occasional victory, what would be the game? Then everyone would march lemminglike to the cliff's edge and say to the dragon: *Do what you will!* And Lucas Donnelly would grow fat and complacent, which would never do.

While lunch ws being enjoyed at the White Bear, Alastair, his old body sore with a medley of aches, his mind a swamp of fears, griefs, and ideas so infeasible he'd inch up on them only to blunder away, prepared for the tub.

Stripped to the scrawny buff, his spindly frame draped by flaps of skin as though he wore a garment three sizes too large, he grasped the double-winged metal bar and hefted himself like a bulky package into the warm embrace. As he did, Alastair heaved a weighty sigh, and sank to his chin, the neolithic ruin that was his mortal casing hovered beneath the surface.

His tub was one of the few physical sensations that Omaha hadn't denied him, and he lay against the plastic cushion attached to the porcelain by suckers, lulled by the satiny stroke of the water, and tried to empty his mind.

After a few moments Alastair flailed at his extremities with a washrag and soap. His remains reminded him of the mangy feline carcass in his high school biology class, passed down through the years, dragged from its cardboard coffin in the storage closet so that its leathery body could be explained.

After he scrubbed himself with no little effort, Alastair commenced the laborious process of dragging himself up from the tub and into the wheelchair that waited, a towel spread on its seat. It was then he saw Glory's face hanging in space in front of him. His hands slipped on the metal bars. Before he could stop himself, Alastair slid from the half-begun climb and thumped back, his head kissing the side of the tub. Only the hump of the plastic cushion and the fact he was so long kept him from going under all the way. Water trickled into his nostrils and he sneezed it out. His hands slapped at the burgeoning dark, and he floundered until he flung an arm over the bar, struggling himself up. As he did, Alastair, with great effort, worked breath across his teeth and calmed his stamping heart.

Hours later, after he had revived himself, rested and dressed, a goose egg the size of a shriveled peach at the back of his head, he put Haydn's Symphony no. 95 in C Minor on the turntable. But water still sloshed in his ears, and the music was wavery. He phoned Dee instead, and he knew as he dialed that he'd been working his way in a crabby side-shuffle to this moment for some while now. Dee had information; Dee knew something, and that something Alastair had to find out about. They were long overdue for a lengthy conversation. But Dee didn't answer the ringing, and Alastair, crouched in his turtle hump, fumed. He'd have to go over there, not later but sooner.

The Haydn reached a crescendo. The receiver was still gripped in his hand, the shrill ringing continuous, but above it he heard the roar and the splash. His back was burdened, something weighed between his shoulders, struggled him downward as he instinctively fought to sustain an upright position. His face was buffeted by the wind; he shivered, cold and wet. Soaked to his armpits. Alastair, at an impossible angle, holding himself an inch from the chair's seat, jumped into the water, churned through the surf. Bullets went *splat*, *splat*, all around him; one ripped through the heavy pack on his back. He felt it list and was thrown to the side. *Omaha!* Alastair cried. *Dog Green!* His few feet of spectacular hell. And he screamed, a belly-wrenching wail that came from his toes, as a face-down body drifted in and out with the tide, as he slogged through the icy salt water, rafting over that just-dead flesh, to dig into the wet, bone-chilling sand. So Alastair fell once again, but this time the chair was behind him, under him, as he went down. Only his mind churned with the surf. Yet when he lifted up his hands, they dripped; there were dark particles of sand under his nails.

23

The leaves began to change from green to yellow, to red and orange. They fell from the branches and crackled underfoot. Mornings broke crisp, and clear as glass. In the afternoons if you stood on the top of Madder's Hill you could see a rolling quilt of sun-lit gaudy colors stretching to forever.

New Morning slumbered. The renovations Lucas Donnelly paid for were all completed. Often a haze, the lightest touch of fog, drifted over the valley, and at those moments women in long dresses, men in high black boots, seemed to float on the newly cobbled street. It wasn't impossible either to hear the faint rumble of wagon wheels, the barking of dead dogs, and in the dark, when all the New Morning lights clicked off, a faraway voice would rise and cleave the silence. "Ten o'clock and all is well!"

One day Alastair noticed that the parking meters on the Main Street side of the green were gone, and there were no cars in the square. He waited, then watched from his front windows, but the only people in the square went on foot. Alastair called Howie Eumis, still council president until the next election, and asked, "What about cars, huh? What's happened to them in the center of town?"

"No cars, no trucks, either," Howie said in his singsong.

"How come?"

"At Mr. Donnelly's request."

Alastair slammed down the phone, swearing, "I might've known." But almost immediately he called Howie back. "Does anybody remember about the democratic process? You know, free choice, amendments, voting, the voice of the majority?" This time, Howie hung up on him.

The whole town knew that Lucas Donnelly meant to marry Glory Crowell when the snows arrived, at Chirstmas time, though there was no formal announcement in the *Eagle*. Still everyone had heard, in that mysterious way news travels in a small town, what the dragon's intentions were.

Theo Crowell had, for one brief moment, tried to impose himself between his daughter and Lucas Donnelly, but Lucas Donnelly could never be lured by Theo into a discussion of the upcoming marriage. Theo would mention Glory, and the dragon's conversation would veer to stocks and bonds, CDs, Fannie Maes, tax shelters, new issues, until Theo's resolve would slip, and he'd make a list in his little notebook of the investments it was suggested he look into. Slowly, but inexorably, Theo's head began to fill up with mathematical music.

As for Alastair, he was so frightened he was numb, but he hadn't given up. No, not that, not ever! He said to Glory, to Jordy and Moses Llewelyn, "There's a way out of this." But he didn't know what it was. Leaving New Morning hadn't been feasible, and getting Lucas Donnelly to shift his operations to Connecticut, his affections to another girl, was a pipe dream. Alastair was becoming desperate. Despite how perfect his town looked, to Alastair it was falling apart.

Most people now seemed to realize that Lucas Donnelly was more than he appeared. Some, like Evelyn, who knew he was the devil and didn't care, were rather quite thrilled.

Dee Whittier was different. Dee wouldn't come out of her house. Once or twice when Alastair, in the only mechanical conveyance allowed in the center of town, rode by her front walk, he saw a haggard face pressed up against the window. But, though he struggled to get her to talk to him, to tell him what she knew—which Alastair guessed was considerable— Dee wasn't in.

Alastair feared Dee was dying behind her locked door and supposed that sooner or later common sense dictated that he break in.

If Dee knew what Alastair was thinking she would have laughed. Dee had bargained with the dragon for life everlasting. The dragon, who was the devil, who was the Spanish grandee in Barcelona at the century's midpoint, now lived down the street.

In the beginning the devil had been most agreeable. He, in his Iberian guise, said, you can fly off to Majorca with the current love of your life and never arrive, or you can live forever. Who wouldn't choose the latter? And into the bargain, without her even requesting as a codicil to the parchment agreement in which she gave her soul as well as her destiny to the dragon's keeping, the devil had generously thrown youth everlasting. Dee did not age. But then she had protested. "It's not right, not the way things were meant to be!" That's what she'd cried, anguished, to Lucas Donnelly. Dee hadn't been thinking, but there was nothing much the dragon could do about that. Again, he'd been most obliging.

Dee, no nearer to death than she'd ever be, which was not near at all, was finally growing obviously older. Dee was aging. A fine webbing of wrinkles like fishnets seined under her eyes. Taut skin loosened like unfolding lap robes from the bones of her cheeks; channels grooved along her nose and mouth. A sagging was suddenly noticeable beneath her jaw, and gray hair blossomed overnight on her head. Veins popped along her thighs until her skin was tracked like a street map. Her joints ached, though not as painfully as Alastair's, and two molars fell out. Fine tendrils of hair sprouted in her nose like lichen, and spots of aging dotted the crepy backs of her hands. Looking now at the older Dee, the ever-older Dee, in her mother's mirror, this Dee witnessed a crone. The slopes of her cheeks caved in as though the supports had buckled, undermined by some shift in the earth. As she watched, her lower lip sagged.

"Damn you!" she screamed in a rusty voice, and flung the mirror across the room to the wall where it crashed. Seven years' bad luck meant nothing to Dee who could have seven times seven hundred. "Damn you!" she wailed and beat at the slippery chaise with her heels and her fists. But damn whom? In his attic Lucas Donnelly laughed. "That wasn't what I meant!" she yelled, and "damn" again. Lucas Donnelly was a practical joker. Dee should have known never to trust him. Of anyone in New Morning, her acquaintance with dragon was of longer duration and more intimate.

In fury she pulled at her hair. A hank of gray moss came out in her hand.

If Dee had tears to shed she would have cried because nothing pleased her. In all of New Morning—in the whole world, as a matter of fact—there was nothing she wanted, nothing that might make her happy. Love. . . . She had been loved more than enough, loved to distraction. Being loved bored her. As for loving in return, there hadn't occurred so much as a twinge in her heart since Jerry Holmes. What was the point in loving another when he could go down in flames? Fame, well, she had gotten her modicum of it, could have had more if she wished. Fame only engendered other people's envy. As for money, she had more than enough of that, too. What could she buy that she didn't already have, that she longed for? Nothing.

Dee was as desireless as a Buddhist monk, but found no peace in all of her not-wanting. If she could have begun all over again . . . But that, of course, wasn't to be. It made no sense to believe in the notion of karma. Dee wouldn't be granted another spin of the wheel. Her wheel, on the contrary, kept spinning everlastingly.

Now she was going to shrivel up, like a primitive's head parboiled in tanning fluid. She grabbed at the phone and punched out Lucas Donnelly's number. When the receiver was lifted she screamed, "I didn't mean this! Old and wrinkled and ugly as sin!"

She gulped for air as the mechanical voice on the other end said, "The time at the tone is—"

"No!" And she threw the phone after the mirror. "I will not . . . will not . . . will not. . . ." she kept repeating and rushed to the bathroom.

Dee crouched on the floor, cold tiles under her, and slashed at her wrists with a razor blade. Blood pumped up from the narrow canals she sliced in her skin and ran down her arms, to her lap, to pool beneath her thighs. Dee dropped the razor and leaned against the wall, waiting.

The light in the bathroom was harsh. It layered up on her like slabs of ice. In the arctic of the bathroom she chilled until her bones froze to icicles, and the rickety teeth in her jaw clattered like castanets. Dee's whole body shuddered as though the floe on which she sailed crackled, as though the floe was life itself and was breaking up. She felt, in spite of her aching and the cold, relieved.

There was an airiness to her flesh, as if once her physical self drained of blood, the spiritual Dee would rise and float. Her thoughts were translucent, and retrieving the past, shuffling the memories, the images were weightless as cellophane. Dee, drifting, never imagined that death which she feared so ardently when young, and mourned these last few years as something lost and unobtainable, would be so fragile. Death had the perfect balance of light and shadow, the conscious artistry of one of her photographs. She gazed upon her own death as if it were framed and hanging on the wall, and sighed. A whistle of breath fluted in her chest, and she lifted her arms, now washed in vermilion streams, and her arms were wings.

In the mercy of that last moment, she closed her eyes and saw, as though granted a benediction, Jerry Holmes' face.

Alastair crouched, an antediluvian relic, in his chair by the window hungering for sleep which came these days less often and stayed a shorter while. Alastair's whirling fears held sleep at the gate.

Through the window he saw nothing in the puddling night beyond the white pools cast down by the streetlights, and skeletal arms of branches slowly undulating in the wind, casting long, fearsome shadows. It was a dread night as so many seemed this autumn.

Alastair thought of Glory who'd just left him. Speak to me, he urged her, but no word crossed Glory's lips. She hadn't spoken since Old Home Week. Her *No!* hadn't saved Carol, and she grieved, perhaps thinking there was no good reason for sound. What did words mean anyway? Jordy now, Jordy had enough language for both of them. Jordy talked long and continually. Jordy brought up his fears, his own never-assuaged grief for Timmy, with language. Alastair thought Jordy knew about Harlan, suspected anyway, and that was a further cause to be afraid. Along with saving Glory, he wished to keep this boy safe. When did I get to be a guardian angel, he harrumphed at himself.

Moses, too, had been over, sitting in Alastair's kitchen drinking soda pop and talking music. Moses' memory was prodigious; he seemed to have total recall. His best remembrances were of dark little clubs, smoke-filled, off back alleys where legendary musicians played Dixie.

The two old men, one brown as a chestnut, the other bleached white as flour, had gotten to be friends, though neither would have presumed to mention it.

My troops, Alastair joked at himself, thinking of both Moses and Jordy. Was it possible to win even a skirmish, never mind a war, with them?

Alastair's thoughts eddied and flowed to Dee in her house down High Street, nearer Lucas Donnelly's, and he worried. It seemed so long since their friendship had been an everyday thing. Lucas Donnelly came and Dee slipped out of Alastair's reach. Oh, but he missed her!

He remembered the meals they shared, the music they sat

quietly listening to. Dee had taken him out into the world, thrown open doors, raised windows, and through her reminiscences, Alastair traveled far from New Morning.

How could she have given herself up to the dragon! Yet Alastair knew in his bones she had. Dee belonged to Lucas Donnelly, though to Alastair she was still his friend.

Alastair brooded. The night was warm. The last touch of Indian summer. He wiped his forehead and listened to the plush silence, straining. For once he didn't consider music to alleviate the metaphysical aches and pains, to soothe him. Bed . . . sleep . . . tomorrow. . . . But though his body was ballasted with weariness, his mind journeyed far and wide. Let Lucas Donnelly sleep where for more than ninety years Emma Tydings had laid her bones. Alastair needed all the time he could get.

The house was heavy around him, he couldn't breathe, and perhaps it was this need to fill his lungs, or to run as he'd fancied before, that forced him outside in his chair. But there he was, wheeling into the darkness, a humpbacked ghostly dwarf low to the ground. He rode the dark and the quiet where the whispering of the branches caressing one another like distant lovers crashed in drum rolls; he traveled through a somnolent New Morning, quiescent as though laid out for the grave. If he bellowed a curse at Lucas Donnelly whose lights were all out, would someone, even the dragon, hear what he had to say? He thought not, for as he went his rounds, New Morning slept the sleep of the dead. It wouldn't surprise Alastair if at the break of day he was the only human left about. For all he knew, behind the walls and doors, beyond the windows, there was nobody at home.

He stopped before the gate in Lucas Donnelly's picket. The white slats stood straight as stakes, and Alastair had a ghoulish vision of heads upon them warning him off. Not a dragon trick, but imagination, he insisted as the heads, fleshy and blood-stained, took shape.

Alastair turned, and fled, rolling on, a wetness showering the top of his skull. The sky rained blood behind him, but he wouldn't look back. Let the dead bury the dead, he thought. A Halloween trick anyway, a magic-lantern slide show. Oh what a charlatan you are, he cursed at Lucas Donnelly, as he rolled up at Dee's.

He should have known that eventually this was where he'd beach up, he thought, gazing at the big house. It loomed even larger in the darkness, a haunted castle, one of its upstairs' eyes glowing. The house was overwhelming, forbidding, as he pushed around to the side.

The door was unlocked. Alastair rode into the kitchen bathed in shadows. He rolled by the counters into the dining room. The darkness in the rest of the downstairs was solid, he could almost feel it, cup it in his hands. The air had a stickiness to it, hot yet clammy at the same time.

"Dee!" he cried out in a shaky voice, then called her again. But there was no response. Major Barnes' mausoleum out in the cemetery felt more inhabited than this house did. Yet Alastair sensed Dee was here somewhere. Her presence touched him; there was a tickling awareness in his bones, a pulse throbbing in his neck, as he wheeled through the rooms, bumping into the furniture. He smacked a table and something fragile crashed, shattered on the floor. He crunched shards of glass or ceramic to dust as he rolled over them. He met the foot of the narrow stairs to the second story with a thump, and he sent his cry, "Dee!" scurrying upward. But nothing came down to him in return.

A sane man would have rolled right back out the kitchen door, down the drive, and home to sleep, even a sleep frothy with wakefulness, and nightmares of Omaha. But then a sane man, or a more trepidatious one, wouldn't have been here in the first place. If queried, Alastair would have sworn he lacked courage, that he clung to the notion "safe and sound." He was, after all, a man of dysfunctional parts. But he knew in his heart he hadn't been tried before. Still, he failed to realize that this being in the dead of night inside Dee's dark and quiet house was a trial. Nor did he think it valorous of him to do what he did now, which was to raise his tottery self out of the wheelchair. Alastair levered himself up, and balancing his entire weight on the strength of one arm, he grabbed the newel post with his free hand and swung out. In his awkward acrobatic maneuver, the chair jerked to the side, and as he came around he smacked his brow so hard he lost his grip. Alastair sprawled on the hall floor, half hanging against the chair which threatened to topple over him. His spine screamed. A knot of air was lodged in his throat, and he was afraid to move.

There was a fan window above the front door, fifteen feet or so from the steps, and a milky light now leaked through it. Alastair's fingers, so near his farsighted eyes, they blurred, seemed in the pale whiteness fat and slimy, maggots. He jerked about in sudden horror, not caring if he cracked open like a walnut, or if one vital bone separated from its neighbor. He scrambled around until all of him was on the same plane, and there, for a moment, he rested.

It seemed to Alastair when he finally inched, so cautious, into motion, one hand then the other, that Dee couldn't have failed to hear the clatter he made. She'd have to be drowned in sleep not to hear. Or worse. It was the worse he tried not to think of.

Holding pain, that mad dog snapping, at bay, he girded himself and crept to the stairs. Turning around he lay across the steps, stiff as a board, counted to ten and then folded up so he was able to lift himself, backwards, from riser to riser. Alastair ascended the steps on his rump, grateful that they were carpeted.

He attained the second floor with the soulful relief of a pilgrim who's crawled on his knees halfway around the world. "Dee!" he rasped, then turned up the volume, sounding petulant and cranky. "Dee, God damn it, where are you?" But it was fear he felt rather than annoyance. Oh, he thought, already moving, slithering like the wounded animal he was, oh, if I were only a child I could creep into a corner and hide until daylight.

Alastair Wayne . . . oh, what are you up to now? Naughty boy! he imagined his mother, stumbling upon him in some unexpected niche, saying. It was strange, but the nearer he inched to death the closer his childhood seemed; as though eventually he'd come full circle and reenter the womb. But then, he thought, wasn't death womblike anyway? Silent? That's what he'd always believed, what he'd chosen to be convinced of until he'd had Horse, his visitor from hell, and had seen damnation in Lucas Donnelly's eyes. Now, he knew nothing for certain. . . .

Alastair had never been upstairs in the Whittier house. The second story was foreign terrain.

The first two rooms were dark except for the ruffles of moonlight hanging in the windows, and Alastair crept by them to the distant edge of the hall where the darkness unraveled in a faint radiance. A luteous spill splashed out the open doorway upon the runner. He didn't call her name again. If there was a Dee alive somewhere in the upper reaches of this old house, she elected not to answer, or she couldn't. His thoughts were a

logjam in his head, and he went forward as much afraid to
retreat and leave Dee's whereabouts unknown, as to find her.

At the doorway of what he ascertained was her bedroom he
gazed across the unblemished sea of carpeting and still caught
no sight of her. Now he did say, "Dee," but her name merely
whispered on his tongue, more in his mind than in sound.
Creeping around the bed, he rested by the chaise where, for
the first time, he noticed traces of human habitation. Ashes in
a small shell on the table, a crumpled cigarette pack. A red
shoe peeking out from under the frilly spread on the bed
stopped his heart for a half beat. Something lives beneath the
whiteness of this room, something wrong, he thought, sniffing,
thinking he could catch the badness of that sour beast on the
air.

But he saw nothing and calmed his quaking heart, biding it
to slow its capricious clanging. Resting, his face buried in the
rug that scratched at his cheek, he wondered why he was
doing this, sneaking about Dee's house in the middle of the
night, a nocturnal intruder. Only now, of course, there was no
choice but to continue.

His exertions had tired him. His body was cranky, protesting
in pain so much unusual motion. It would be so easy to drift
off, and he thought what a scandal it would be if in the morning
Lettie O'Brien—for he recalled that Monday was a Dee day—
found him on the bedroom floor. The idea of being caught for
even more of a fool than he was had him inching around the far
corner of the bed.

To the left was the bathroom from which there also flowed
light, more strident than the soft illumination of the bedside
lamps. The door stood ajar. Alastair once more expelled her
name from his throat with a sputtering exaltation of stale
breath. "Dee!" But she didn't answer. He rucked around,
trying to sense her, for she was here somewhere. He knew it.
She hadn't escaped into the night. He couldn't suppress the
fear that ticked his spine, not even when he told himself that if
Dee was in the bathroom, if Dee was injured, this procrastina-
tion did neither of them any good. That having come this
distance he must find her, the sooner the better. While he lay
on the rug, a rag of bone and skin tossed down meaninglessly,
Dee might have passed the point of no return.

From some reserve of strength he hadn't known he'd
banked, Alastair once again got himself into action and went
upstream into the river of light, pushing the door wide.

The bathroom was large, half the size of his kitchen, and the floor was tiled a shiny sea green. Light sparked off the brass fixtures in flashes of gold.

From the white shore of the bedroom Alastair gazed across the watery surface to Dee propped against the wall. She slumped in a dark pool that he recognized as blood from the bright stains on her arms and legs. Dee was dappled in blood, and Alastair, victimized by the wild horses of fright that galloped over his ribs, hooves shattering the bony cage, sending tendrils of pain over his shoulder and down his left arm, groaned: Who'd have thought a person had so much blood in the veins.

Alastair heard Lucas Donnelly's laughter, like the pounding surf, at this strange turn of events. *I only plant acorns,* he remembered the dragon saying, and now here was Dee in full growth.

Alastair swore a curse of inaudible words, trailing them along his teeth, and scuttled off the white rug onto the cool, slippery tile. He swam through puddles of blood.

"Dee," he mumbled softly, this time without strain, her name only a puff of air.

He expected she'd be stiff, rock-solid, but he discovered warmth and pliant flesh. Her hand when he touched it was living, a human thing, and Alastair snapped back suddenly, stung. Perhaps it was her name, coughed out like a curse or a prayer, or the terrible hiss of breath, but all at once her eyelids parted and Dee stared out from a distant cavern.

"Alastair!" she said in the clangy wheeze of an unoiled, antique machine.

He whimpered, pulled himself around to sit, the wetness of Dee's blood soaking his pants. "What happened?" he asked. "Were you stabbed or shot, or what?" he cried, louder. An echo bounced off the walls. Alastair had the impression of being trapped within a large aquarium, the sea-green water rising above his head.

Dee moaned, stirred, raised up bloody hands. Her hands hung before her face like Oriental sculptures, complex and unreal.

Alastair had, finally, to retrieve those bloody hands, returning them to her lap. "What happened?" he repeated. And then, "I better call Doc." It filtered through to him that Dee had survived the outrageous attack, but medical assistance was surely necessary now. He prepared his abused body by a series of shuffles and turns to crawl out to the bedroom and the phone.

"No . . ." she croaked, and one of those hands that had claimed her abstracted attention shot out to grab his arm.

"You're hurt," he insisted. "Need help."

"No . . . no help for me."

"Damnation, Dee, what went on here? Who did this to you?" Did what? There was all that blood, quarts of it, Alastair thought, but no visible injury. The blood might have been spilled from a bottle, for it didn't seem to have come out of Dee.

She groaned, but it was a sound more of weariness than pain. "Go home, Alastair, and leave me alone."

"Are you crazy!" he yelled, sitting back. "It's like a massacre in here," he said, more quietly, confronting the frayed and painful gaze she settled on him. "Dee"—he laced his fingers with hers, unaware of the humanness of this minute gesture, and asked yet again, "What happened?"

She didn't reply, just held out her other hand, and thinking she meant for him to take that too, he grasped it, but she shook him off. "No, look," she said.

"Look at what?"

She took back her arm and wiped it across her breast, leaving a path of blood on the garment she wore. Then she thrust out the limb once more. "What do you want?" he cried in sorrow and exasperation, forced to look at the arm she shoved under his nose. It was smeared with blood, pinkish, but whole. Bewildered, Alastair lifted his gaze to her spotted and stained face. She was so besmirched, and his eyes were so old—he'd seen so much tonight!—that it took him some time before he could discern the lines and gulleys, the crow's feet and the spider tracks laid down under the blood. Cheeks, once plump and girlish, settled like bread dough, and craters deepened under her lower lids into sinkholes. Dee was old!

The realization that this woman who'd had the young, wholesome appearance of a girl when he'd seen her last—had aged like Dorian Gray was more shocking than the blood. He so doubted what he saw that he crept to the far side of the bathroom where a soft fluffy white towel hung from a bar, and wetting it under the tub faucet, delicately, carefully, washed her face. Dee sat quietly, childlike, as the crone's visage emerged, its folds of ancient skin as spongy as dead tissue rotting. When he had cleaned her up and saw what a ravaged field lay beneath, could no longer deny the lines and potholed flesh, he grew tired, far wearier than he'd been after his long rise up the steps. Unconscious of what he was doing, he reached out his hand, crossed the chasms that spread between them, and trailed tentative fingers down one cheek.

"How is this possible?" he whispered, awed, not convinced that even Lucas Donnelly could do such damage in such a short while.

She shrank into herself, slipped away from the wall, and before Alastair knew what she intended, Dee had fallen across his lap. Her face, that aged relic, pressed against his pitiful legs, and she said, so softly, he had to bend forward to hear her whisper, "It was in Barcelona, over thrity-five years ago, and I was in love. . . ."

24

Lucas Donnelly made it a point to drop in on the Crowells every few days or so. He'd arrive after dinner and sit in the living room with Theo and Evelyn drinking cognac, which was what Evelyn preferred. Glory had to come down from her room and be with them, in body if not in soul. If she didn't, Evelyn would climb up and drag her out of her room. The talk when the dragon visited was always of New Morning, and after the first few times and the unoriginal chatter, Glory drifted off, even if Alastair had cautioned her to stay alert, to be watchful. Right now she was wondering what her parents would say if she just casually sighed: *Lucas Donnelly's the devil*.

"Nothing, my dear, nothing at all," Lucas Donnelly replied as he stared into her eyes, though Glory hadn't asked the question. His eyes were unremarkable, just brown and rather handsome, with gold specks swimming in the irises.

The upsetting thing, of course, was that he read her thoughts as easily as a newspaper. He did it deliberately and not by chance, like Alastair or her mother. Glory looked away, to the other side of the room, concentrating on a framed embroidery of garden flowers, and kept her mind smooth as ice. She emptied her head, but before she knew it, her mind filled up with water. There was the blue sea, the clear sky with only an occasional puff of cloud, and the sailboat lulling becalmed. There was the hand in the water, the arm, the golden hair floating like foam. For the first time, a face attached itself to this being, and the sight was so alarming, Glory faltered. Pincers squeezed her heart and tears pooled in her eyes, but nothing could obscure the vision of the woman drifting upward, searching for the light.

The cry, in a painful spasm, burst from her throat like vomit. "Mama!"

"Yes, dear," Evelyn said, but Glory had already fainted.

Lucas Donnelly carried her upstairs to bed, and Evelyn ran for cold cloths, for ice pads and heating pads, thermometers and honeyed tea, while Theo got on the phone to Doc Trump. The dragon carried her, golden hair trailing across his arms. If Glory could have seen the floating hair she would have thought, *like hers in the water*. But Glory was comatose, unaware as Lucas Donnelly laid her upon the covers and kissed a paler, chilly brow. He straightened out her arms and legs like a dead person's and stroked her cheek. He could have told her that her skin was smoother than the crepe de chine Evelyn hungered for, not that it mattered. Glory was water-logged.

Lucas Donnelly held her hand and enjoyed the composition she made, his Sleeping Beauty. He thought she was lovely, far more beautiful than her mother, but though he expected loveliness, there was the matter of genes. Science, Lucas Donnelly often snorted, was unreliable. After all, who could have known that Glory would be a girl. Glory was a dead loss, no good whatsoever, in encouraging evil. And what help might she give him with the computers? None. But oh, he mused, watching the sweet swell of her breasts as they rose and lowered, she'd make a wonderful mother, this exquisite daughter of his.

"How is she?"

"Doc's on the way."

Evelyn and Theo burst into Glory's bedroom one after the other. "Here." Evelyn put an ice bag on Glory's brow, a cold compress under her chin, a hot water bottle on her stomach.

"Something she ate," Theo said, wringing his hands.

Evelyn snapped back, "She ate the same as we did."

"She's more delicate."

Lucas Donnelly reassured them with the oiliness of a snake charmer. "She'll be just fine."

The front door slammed, and there was the rush of heavy feet bounding up the steps. Doc Trump appeared all out of breath. His tie was loose and his jacket was buttoned up wrong. "What's going on?" he asked gruffly, and immediately dragged out his stethoscope and stuck it to Glory's chest. He put a thumb on her pulse, silently counted, and then satisfied, he lifted her lids. Next he snapped open her jaws and gazed into her mouth. At that moment Glory started to come around.

Little twitches, shivers, the first trembles of a quake. "She seems to be coming out of it." Doc watched, satisfied as Glory's eyelids stirred. He sat back with a weary sigh, but his eyes were alert. "Now, you people, tell me what happened." If Doc Trump thought it peculiar that Lucas Donnelly was in Glory's bedroom he didn't say so, but then Doc wasn't much of a commentator, more of an observer. It had once struck Doc that the world could be divided into two kinds of people; those who saw and those who were seen. For his part, he was definitely a seer. Evelyn Crowell now, she was on stage, just like Ava, from dawn to dusk. He'd have bet his Buick that she never even had a dream—nightmare or otherwise—in which she wasn't the star performer. Now, beside her daughter's bed, she struck a pose like some scrawny model in *Vogue*. Only Evelyn was too old, too overweight, too pudding-faced.

Evelyn was bristling. She didn't seem to know what to do with her hands now that she'd unburdened herself from ice bags and cold cloths and cups of tea. She balled her fingers into fists and shoved them deep into the pockets of her skirt, and rocked on the balls of her feet, peering past Doc and around Lucas Donnelly to the wedge of a pallid, washed-out Glory she could see. "I wish you'd do something instead of sitting there mumbling, asking questions," she lectured Doc.

Doc attempted patience, but a pulse jerked in his cheek. "Tell me what happened," he ordered through clenched teeth.

Theo got himself under control, and in his bankerish manner, he said, "We were in the living room, sitting comfortably, drinking cognac and having a pleasant conversation on the state of the economy, when all of a sudden, Glory—" Theo froze. Ice lodged in all his passageways, and he shivered. "Oh," he stuttered. Theo, who hadn't shed a single tear in the long years since he'd been eight and got hit on the head with a softball, filled up. He glazed over wetly and sniffed.

Evelyn, stopping dead on the carpet, groaned, "She said '*Mama!*'"

"*Mama*" was considered in New Morning to be Glory's first word, since her "*No!*" at the fairgrounds had been heard only by a select few and Alastair had counseled Jordy and Moses not to gossip about Glory's sudden burst into speech. So none of the men even mentioned it to Glory herself, they simply waited and watched. Alastair thought there were more words where that "*No!*" had come from, but Glory had to bring them out by herself. But now that her "*Mama*" was on record, she became a New Morning wonder, and so hid out these days from everyone except Alastair and Jordy.

This afternoon she sneaked away and rode her Peugeot up to Madder's Hill. From her perch just below Dead Man's Curve, sequestered in the yellow grass, she gazed down the long incline, ridged and aflame with dying brush, trees burning in a small copse on the right, to the fairgrounds. She remembered the Old Home Week carnival, the flashing whip, the wide arcing of the swings, the merry-go-round slowly twirling, and Carol crashing to earth.

How long ago it all seemed now that autumn was here, and a chill lingered on the air. The last time she'd been up here on Madder's Hill it had been warm, now she wore a sweater. This morning her breath hung for a second in a white cloud, like Lucas Donnelly's cigar smoke. Oh, she thought, hugging herself, shivering, Christmas will soon be here, sooner than she even expected. If only time could be slowed down, stopped all together! Or rewound. How much she missed Carol! Tears blurred in Glory's eyes, and the girl who'd never cried that she recalled, cried now. She knew it was useless weeping, that sorrow never changed events, but she wept anyway.

She hadn't a tissue, and unlike Evelyn, Glory never carried a handkerchief. She wiped her eyes with the tail of her shirt and she sniffed.

Tilting her face up, Glory searched the sky, looking for birds. Alastair contended that all the birds had left New Morning. She wondered as she inspected the empty sky.

Blue as the sea . . . level as a tabletop, the old man had said.

He wasn't so old, it was just his hair, prematurely white and receding from the plane of his forehead. Who had he been? Glory strained to remember, seeing him arch over the side into the water. And why had he taken them out on the Caribbean? What was he to them, or they to him?

Glory's memory came and went, stirred like a slow southern current, leaving behind in its wake little bits of debris. A face, an expression, a smile, a knot or two on the glassy waters, a glimpse of a far-off island, clutched by the sea in a fist of rock and brownish vegetation. A white patch of sail unfurled, eclipsed the sky. *Her* voice, for an instant, took flight in Glory's recollections and winged off.

She no longer needed the dreams; *before* broke through the surface of Glory's forgetfulness during daylight, during waking hours.

"I am . . ." she said aloud in a rusty, unused voice. Her own voice sounded strange, cracked, discordant like Hindemith or Milhaud. Sound tasted funny on Glory's tongue. It wasn't only a sometime thing, an aberration, a mistake, like her *No* or her *Mama*.

"I can speak," she drawled slowly, released the words to the sudden gust of wind spurring the grass into agitated motion. "No more si-lence," Glory whispered, listening to the alien scratching, feeling the sandpaper motion in her throat.

She hugged her five-year-old self in the grown woman's body, and felt, once again, Lucas Donnelly's fingers on her throat. He'd touched her delicately as a flower, a touch colder than frost, and perversely, the faint stroke, numbing her skin, didn't wound but unfroze the logjam of words within.

Nobody knew, not Alastair or Jordy, not her parents, and Glory refused most of all to share her return of speech with Lucas Donnelly. "What I give, I can take away," he told her in a murmur, though it surely was a threat. Only how could she be frightened of that affliction with which she lived for all these years? There's worse, and worse beyond that, Alastair often said.

Lucas Donnelly, during the ride in the Saturday parade, had warned like an Indian giver of retrieving the gift which she refused to use but Glory wasn't afraid. And he said nothing further to her until after, when he let—no when he *made*, Carol die. Of all the horrible things Lucas Donnelly had done so far in New Morning during these awful months when he'd come for her—and come for her he had, she knew that now—killing Carol was, to Glory, the worst by far. Carol had been her friend, and again Glory cried as she had on the long-ago sail on the remembered sea. She'd cried herself into silence, alone on that boat.

All drowned, dead in the water, whitened bones.

Mama, the old man, the mate who'd tied knots in a rope for her those three days. . . . Over the side, into the sea, sucked down by the water and drowned. Mama's hair skimmed on the surface in a golden net, lacy as seaweed.

Why? The dreams didn't tell her that. Neither did memory.

It came back, but only a little of this, a bit of that, isolated stilted scenes such as leaving the marina. A different dock from the one she sailed back to as Glory Crowell, when her life started up, this life, a rewound clock. Time ticked with another beat.

Before, there had been trains, planes, a jouncing bus. They had fled in all directions. From the dragon? Glory wondered. The only life she could piece together before the Caribbean was one of running. The sun behind, the night ahead in the clouds. Baggy old women, chickens in crates. Hotels and elevators, standing by the highways.

I searched for you a long time, he told her in the black limousine.

A wife . . . a child . . . Glory's mind blanked out on that. She thought she remembered her mother once saying, *He made me promises.* . . .

Memory recaptured answered many of the questions, but not this particular one: Of all the girls in the world, *why me?*

Of the three conspirators, only Moses Llewelyn asked, "What does he want with the girl? I mean, why her and not some other female?" He tilted his Pepsi can and let the sweet liquid run down his throat as first Jordy tried to explain and now Alastair took over. But to Moses a girl was a girl. Females were much the same though some of them were better looking than others, fleshier. There were, he acknowledged, women who drove men to a kind of craziness like gage sometimes did, or more often the White Lady. But he had a hard time seeing Glory Crowell as one of those. To Moses, Glory was just an ordinary girl, not bad to look at, and a little simple-seeming because she didn't speak. Only now it appeared that she could do that, talk, he meant, even if she wouldn't. Moses shook his head. He might not have a clear picture, but that wasn't the issue. To his surprise there was something more important here. A camaraderie, a friendship, had grown between the boy and the two old men, if not a feeling even stronger.

That feeling, call it concern, or love if you will, worried away inside Alastair too, but for the moment, as he brooded more about Dee. Finally, he picked up the phone.

"Leave me alone, Alastair," she croaked. But she didn't hang up.

"Com'on over here for a while and sit with me. I'll put on some Bartók, cook up a pot of spaghetti," he coaxed. He hadn't seen her out of her house and he wouldn't go back in there for the world.

"No, I look awful. Worse. Let me be!" In her misery she meant and Alastair knew it. He thought, but never said it, you're paying the price of a pact with the devil.

Alastair never told the others about Dee, feeling a loyalty to an old friendship. Besides, they'd probably not believe him. Both Moses and Jordy had enough problems with Glory's brief return to speech. Jordy, especially, was greedy. He wanted more from her.

Evelyn was worse than anybody, as was to be expected. She wouldn't settle. "If you can say one word, you can get out another. You can speak just like everybody else."

Theo too hungered for Glory's sounds. "Please, sweetheart, do it again!" He was always after her. But Glory only kissed his cheek and went to sit in the backyard under the tree.

It was there that Lucas Donnelly found her, though Evelyn, constantly on guard, saw no sign of the dragon.

He sat beside her wearing what she thought at first was a bed sheet, then realized was a sheik's robe, brilliantly white and unwrinkled. Glory became the first person in New Morning to see Lucas Donnelly in some garb other than his usual Sydney Greenstreet suit. There also seemed to be vines growing through his dark curls, vivid and shiny as snakes. And he smelled sweet, almost musky, even his breath when he lowered his head, closed up on her, so near she strained back against the tree trunk.

His hand grazed her white throat, his fingers probed the cave beneath her chin. "Speak," he crooned faint as a far-off

radio station after midnight. But Glory held her tongue tight.
She kept the weight of it firm against her teeth, jaws secured as
effectively as her father's vault.

"Speech"—he smiled—"is my gift to you."

"You know," he said, "I can give you the lost past. Didn't I,
after all, give you the sea the other night, and just so you'd
know, I threw in the word besides." Glory tried to swerve
away but he grasped her chin between thumb and index finger.
She closed her eyes. But the darkness glowed with light. A
Caribbean sun, a smooth and glasslike sea. The woman in the
water bellied up, flat on her back, arms and legs wide, hair
seining behind her in an intricate web. It took all Glory's
powers, slight compared to his, all her concentration—cruelly
divided between the sea and the pinch of his fingers digging
into her skin—not to let the word loose again. Glory held her
breath and swallowed the *Mama* that crawled up her throat.
She kept in the word, the name, and turned away.

In another dimension Lucas Donnelly said with a fiery
whoosh of breath, "I can even take you back there. Come, give
me your hand, we'll journey together. Through time." But
Glory wound her hands into a ball, laced her fingers, and
buried them between her legs in her lap. On the boat that was
a schooner, out of Tortola five days—there on the deep Glory
suddenly remembered that—she made her way aft. There was
nobody sailing, no person up fore behind the wheel. The men
who had taken them out to sea. . . .

There, with her, down, lost, and Glory screamed at
longitude sixty-eight and latitude fourteen, screamed until the
sun banked and night rode up the scrim of the sky. After, she
went below and crawled into a bunk, crying soundlessly, cries
of air but no words, for she hadn't a voice left.

"You didn't die. . . ." Lucas Donnelly said.

"You, thank God, were left alive," Alastair echoed the
dragon later that same night. "But how did you get on that
boat? And where were you going? And why?

I don't know.

25

On the surface New Morning looked much as it always had, only better. New benches in the square, a coat of paint for the stores on Main, cobbles all along Brewster, and Moses Llewelyn felt the dragon's hot breath singeing the hair on the back of his neck so that he cut, trimmed, pruned, raked the leaves, and weeded the green, as well as the lawns on High Street, until all the vegetation appeared as lush and healthy as items advertised in the Burpee catalogue. The exterior of the Barnes had been sandblasted to the original buff color, but it was the inside of the library where the change was most pronounced.

The Barnes was an octagonal building, with each of its eight sides paneled in oak. The shelves were freestanding, running east and west, with two rows of long library tables in the center, and, opposite the front door, the librarian's desk. Overhead was a domed ceiling with a mural depicting Ebenezer Smythe's arrival in New Morning. The artist, an itinerant painter, might have been more skilled with flat surfaces, but he certainly hadn't taken into consideration the special circumstances of the dome, and so, gazing upward at Smythe and his party, the Pilgrims appeared deformed. Their legs narrowed to twigs, their arms swelled to balloons, and they all were diagnosed by Doc as hydrocephalics. These physical anomalies were now acutely apparent since the colors had been returned to their original brightness.

"A homely bunch," Alastair said, craning his neck.

Doc agreed. "Historical or not, if anybody asked me, I would have said, paint them over. They certainly don't do much for scholarship or literary endeavors. Concentration, either. I get the creepy feeling one of that gang is going to fall on my head."

They spoke in whispers, hunched close together, though there were only a gaggle of schoolchildren scattered among the tables and Cora Montrose at the librarian's desk.

When the Barnes had been minimally functional, Cora held down the position of librarian with one hand tied behind her. An ever-changing roster of high-school boys assisted her, and two of the chambermaids from the Bear came in to clean every couple of months. Now, however, the Barnes stayed open nine to five, six days a week, as Lucas Donnelly suggested, and Cora Montrose was worn to a nub. She didn't get so much as ten minutes for lunch, and had to eat her sandwich on the go in the ladies'. "It's too much!" she'd wailed, but she wouldn't give the job up. As she informed Lucas Donnelly, "I plan to stay until I drop."

Cora enjoyed being the custodian of this new literary emporium, floors waxed and buffed, windows washed, and books all dusted. New books, too. Boxes of books arrived almost every day now, and the Barnes's shelves were stuffed. If anybody besides Cora thought it a bit odd that New Morning had the largest collection of the occult in southern Massachusetts, perhaps in the whole state, it wasn't commented upon. Cora, seconded by Vera Dickson, wanted more romances, but whenever she ordered Janet Dailey or Jackie Collins she received instead some arcane tome by Wallis Budge.

Alastair, looking around the Barnes, had to give the dragon his due; the place was a beauty. It seemed, he imagined, exactly as it had when the Major cut the ribbon across the first step in 1835. This was the first chance he'd had to visit the Barnes, and Doc, who caught him leaving his walk, decided to come along. "That way I know I got you in my clutches and can drag you back with me when we're through." For the monthly examination Alastair was promised to, what with his lapses and seizures.

Doc, consumed by medical matters, hadn't stopped in at the Barnes either, and now he roamed one set of stacks while Alastair did the other. "Impressive," he said with a nod when they met at the end of the L's.

"Shush!" Cora hushed them from her command post, looking harassed. Her gray chignon, sprouting pencils, was unraveling like an old sweater, and her face, crushed velvet, wrinkled up.

One of the schoolchildren dropped a book and the resounding boom echoed through the mausoleum's dead quiet like a cannon set off. For a moment, Alastair, coming up rigid as a broom handle, thought he had retreated yet again to Omaha and Dog Green. He sniffed for the sea, furtively licked his lips in search of salt, but the boy, Simon Hooper's nephew, son of his widowed sister Syl, dived for the book and elbowed his pencil box to the floor.

Cora bore down on Simon's nephew with the determination of a locomotive, as the boy scrambled around the floor gathering pencils, in the process knocking the chair into the table for another loud *thunk*. "Miscreant!" Cora hissed, and slapped the boy on the neck.

Doc, having seen enough, was on his way out, and so missed Cora's slap. Alastair gave her a scowl of admonishment before he followed Doc to the porch.

Alastair didn't feel at all like getting examined. He was too tired and achy to be prodded, but he failed to think of any explanation that wouldn't arch Doc's brows. Besides, Doc wanted to take him over to the new hospital. "Finished, right down to the paintings on the walls, the magazines in the waiting room. You wouldn't believe it, Alastair. I can barely believe it myself. That a building could go up so fast!" Alastair believed more mysterious occurrences, but he didn't say so to Doc. Doc was a man of science, and it embarrassed Alastair to mention something so medieval, so mythological, as the devil.

Doc drove Alastair in his car, then gave him the grand tour. Doc glowed, pushed his chest and strutted like a peacock. Alastair had never seen him so proud. "This," Doc said, "is what I've always dreamed of, streamlined, compact, but with everything in it." He fairly cooed. Alastair's bad temper was scraped raw. He thought of Dee and her arrangement with the dragon, and wondered what all this modern equipment, all these medical geegaws had cost Doc. Did he hand over his soul, too, on a silver platter?

When Alastair could stand it no longer, he rasped, "Pride goeth before a fall!"

Doc's praises for Lucas Donnelly dried up in his mouth. He soured. "On your usual hobbyhorse, I see. Give it up, Alastair, before the whole town stops talking to you altogether."

"Send me to Coventry, see if I care," Alastair muttered, narrowing his eyes. "I got my principles."

"Just what do you mean by that?" Doc snapped, yanking out Alastair's arm to get to his pulse. Doc had to tether himself to something medical if he wasn't going to fly right off the handle.

They waited outside the X-ray room. Doc wanted some pictures of Alastair's lungs.

"What do I mean? You know what I mean!" But Alastair wondered if Doc did. His interest centered on diseases not metaphysics. So he added, "I don't think even this medical palace is worth an arrangement with Lucas Donnelly."

Doc sighed and dropped Alastair's arm. "There's no stopping your natter, is there."

"No more than you can stop Donnelly from sweeping over this town like a panzer division. Doc, you ought to be ashamed of yourself, getting bought off like this. So cheap!"

"There's nothing cheap about my hospital!" Doc's voice rose.

Alastair persisted. "You could've said no to Donnelly. You didn't have to agree."

"Who wanted to say no? Old fool!" He looked ready to hit Alastair. "Have you any idea of the cost of the equipment he put in here? Do you know what it means for New Morning? Lives saved, Alastair! That's what. And nothing's more important than life itself."

"What about your soul?"

"Ah!" Doc thumped his elbow. "What gobbledygook! You're going to spout that rot about Lucas Donnelly being the devil. Well, save your breath, Alastair, because I won't hear of it!" Alastair was shocked. His mouth dropped open. "Besides, who gives a hoot whether the man's the devil or not. If any such creature exists, which it doesn't."

"You don't care?" Alastair whispered. He had to sit down. He swung himself over to a chair and dropped into it. Doc hovered above him like an angry cloud. "It doesn't matter to you what he's doing to New Morning?"

Doc protested. "Just what is he doing? Fixing up the Barnes, turning that white elephant into a first-class library. Putting in traffic lights. Painting the benches. Cobbling the streets, which I grant you is a cosmetic touch and something we could all live without. But building me a first-class hospital, now that's important and I'd get down on both knees to thank the man a thousand times."

"Even if he's the devil?"

"Oh, I give up!" Doc punched the air. "There's no such animal, Alastair. You're smart enough to know that. And if there were, and if Lucas Donnelly's the creature, well, what does it matter? He's not doing anything wrong, he's only doing good. So put that in your pipe. . . . Ah, Amy's ready to take your picture. Now get in there, you old goat, and remember to

smile!" Doc laughed, but more from bad temper than anything. Alastair, shell-shocked, couldn't think what to say, and
so he wobbled to his feet, bowing his head, as depressed as
he'd ever been since the start of the dragon's reign. If Doc
refused to stand erect and be counted, if Doc could be bought
off, what hope was there? Fighting the dragon necessitated
men of good will—women, too, of course—and so far there
were only himself and Moses and Jordy.

Alastair couldn't know, as he unbuttoned his shirt and
pushed his chest up against the cold X-ray plate, that one of his
soldiers had something more pressing on his mind at the
moment than the dragon. Jordy Farrow had just decided to kill
his father.

Trees from acorns, Lucas Donnelly would have hollowly
pronounced. Had already done so, time after time.

The dragon could be held accountable for much, but even
Alastair would have had to acknowledge that it wasn't Lucas
Donnelly who had linked Harlan's hands with Timmy's neck.
In one sense the dragon was like a hypnotist. He failed to make
his subjects perform any action when under the influence that
they'd morally oppose when wide awake. Lucas Donnelly
merely lit the fire when the kindling was all laid.

Jordy's mother was behind the counter in the bakery, her
back turned. Jordy couldn't see her face. "I'm getting one of
my headaches," he heard her say.

"That's too bad, Ma." But no sympathy edged his voice.
Jordy stood in the small opening between the counter and the
rear wall, the only exit out. To escape, his mother had to push
by him, and she seemed to know that her son, this time, would
refuse to let her pass. So she had inched about, sly his mother
was, and bowed her head, exposing to him that vulnerable soft
space at the nape of her neck, the very place the executioner
always laid his ax. Jordy stared at that small patch of uncolored
skin—for his mother's hair was short, straight, and sheered up
around her ears, almost like a man's—and didn't think as he
suspected she meant him to: See how trusting she is, how frail
and slight, how defenseless. Weak woman . . . mother.
Jordy thought none of what his mother, perhaps unconsciously,
sought to foster in his mind. Jordy gazed at his mother's nape
and saw Timmy under his father's fingers.

"Did you," he cried, "ever wonder where he went?"

The woman, slight and tenuous in her J. C. Penney print housedress, sighed. That diminutive sound, intangible breath breathed into air, said, Pity me, I'm just an overburdened ailing woman, helpless and alone in this life. "Jordy," she said, and then, "I thought of your brother day and night. Not a minute did I forget him. Still," she said, "what could I do?" It was a pitiful cry, and she gave it both barrels by turning around and looking her son straight in the eye.

Jordy blinked, but to give him credit, he stood his ground. "Did you call the police?"

"What would they have done?" she asked in genuine surprise.

"Ha!" Jordy cried. "They would have searched for him. Put it out on the wire, sent flyers, with his picture, name, and size. That sort of thing. The law would of gone looking for Tim."

Despite the heater that hummed from the large unit beside the front door, it was chilly in the bakery, and his mother wore an old maroon sweater that had once been Harlan's. The cuffs were frayed, little threads dangled like worms, and a hole was torn in one elbow Jordy saw when she clutched herself, hugged that slim structure of bones. His mother was anorexically skinny and gleamed like polished ivory where her skeleton strained against skin. His mother was porcelain, but she wasn't pretty.

Yet somewhere inside, though buried deep, there was a steely core. How, otherwise, to explain her survival, minimal though it might be, with Jordy's father. One unthinking blow from his paw and she'd be crushed to powder. Harlan had weathered her, eaten her alive, used and abused her body, soul, too, but she had survived. Jordy hated his mother right then more than he ever hated anyone—meaning his father—in his entire life. His hatred flared, as intense in its power and passion as his love for Glory. It was the flip side, love inverted and laid on its back.

He hated her because she was weak, and because she was using him, playing him as deftly as Glory did the piano, working him over just as surely as though she had reached out and touched him with her hands. Her eyes, glossy, watery, brimmed to the edges of the lashes with tears. That drag to her mouth, that sad downturning of her lower lip. His mother, in a keening voice, whined about his father, how Harlan wouldn't let her do much of anything once Timmy had gone. "Wouldn't so much as let me say his name. Shushed you, too, Jordy, remember?" Jordy did, suffering again the sting to his cheek, the aching pain in his shoulder, when a week or so after Timmy had disappeared, after he'd been told "That's it! I don't want that ungrateful kid's name mentioned again. Not in this house, the bakery either. He's worse than dead, he's never been!" Jordy had disobeyed, asking, "I wonder where he is now?" And Harlan slugged him, pulling his arm far back in deliberation, putting force in the blow that sent Jordy up against the oven.

"There's no arguing with your father. He said there'll be no talk of Tim, and I never did. And he said I was to stop thinking about him, but I couldn't do that. He was able, but I'm a mother."

"That's what you did, thought of Timmy every once in a while when you had nothing else on your mind?" he asked sarcastically, which wasn't like Jordy at all.

His mother wasn't answering. Her eyes were downcast.

"Did you ever think he could be dead, might be, most probably is or we'd have heard from him by now? Did you, Ma?"

"Of course! If you were a mother, Jordy, you'd know that without thinking. Same way when you're off late at night, I lie in bed and think, he's gone, smacked into a tree or ran the van off the road into a gully. Or sometimes it's a fight over at Harry's, a knife, a crack on the head with a bottle. When it comes to worry, Jordy, I got a good imagination." She was going now, having hit her stride, confronting him, but her eyes were directed to the side. Her gaze fled not to his face, but beyond his shoulder, and Jordy knew that either she lied, or left out some of the truth. "I have imagined more horrible things happening to a boy out in the world alone than you could ever dream."

"Well, what about this one, Ma? What about Timmy never leaving, Timmy getting into a fight with Pa, one of those bad knockdown ones the two of them were always having, and maybe instead of Timmy running, he got one of your knives or bottles, or maybe Pa's hands around his neck. Did you ever think Timmy isn't off taking a tour around the world? That maybe Timmy never left New Morning?"

His mother, whose white skin was touched by the sun only when the light tracked through the windows, or during those short runs between the house and the bakery, went whiter still. It wouldn't have surprised Jordy if she slid into a faint.

"He choked Timmy to death all those years ago. That's what I think. And it's why his things were still here when he was supposed to have left. Because he didn't. Pa choked him to death!"

"What are you saying?" she cried as her hand crept to her neck, the fingers spreading. A sick feeling of horror low in his stomach rising, Jordy thought, *She knows*.

It was then, hating this woman who had carried him in her body for nine months, and who suffered to bring him, bloody, into the world, hating her so ardently he almost blacked out, hating her right to the limits of reason so that it took an effort not to throw himself upon her, to beat at her as his father had beat him, to bang her head against the floor, bounce it up and down with such force it burst open like an overripe melon, it was in that instant he decided if he wasn't going to kill his mother, he'd have to kill his father. Why this was so, he didn't stop to consider, only that he made himself such a promise, and his promise released him so that he stepped back, allowing his mother an exit.

She ran with little mincing steps, like an Oriental female whose feet had been bound, whining when she fled by him, "My headache . . . so bad." Her fist was balled up and braced at her temple. "Headache," she kept saying, prattling, sounding like a myna bird who's learned this one word and no other, or again like a mechanical toy wound tightly and playing out that high-pitched doll sound. And Jordy, feeling suddenly defeated, promise or no, slumped, not caring.

26

After the last scarlet trim of light wilted into the ragged darkness of Madder's Hill, and the thick black curtain of a moonless night descended, Dee, wearing a sweatshirt, jeans, a scarf swathing her face, and a borsalino hat, drove off in her Porsche. It was late, nearing ten when she passed along the New Morning streets, by the shadowy houses with their yellow eyes. The car windows were lowered, but the chill night air did little to clear the cobwebs in her head. Too much wine. She had drunk an entire bottle of Chateau-Margaux '69 on an empty stomach. But then she had rejected food for days, not at all hungry and besides, what was the need to sustain a body that was sinking and shifting, collapsing under the weight of time, of more years than she might have lived in ten life spans?

She downshifted the Porsche and accelerated up the short incline to Ridge Road, weaving out of town, from one side of the road to the other shoulder, pulling away from Lucas Donnelly in his colonial, a block off the left flank of her own. Dee leaned over the steering wheel, clasping it against her flaccid breasts like a lover, and felt the tug between her shoulder blades. She was a stream fighting the drag of gravity, the pressure to let go and slide downhill.

She swung the Porsche through the darkness, wandered along the fence of the fairgrounds where phantom lights twinkled like fireflies, sped out Hollow Road and past The Gallery. A Closed sign hung on the front door. She settled back against the leather seat and laid her fingers on the wheel to guide the growling beast of a car in its flight. When she climbed the final hillside before the flat run to the underpass of the turnpike, the Porsche, of its own volition, or so it seemed to Dee so drowsy and cold, took the bend on two tires and curved back toward home, toward New Morning. The fast-moving car possessed a mind of its own, and she wondered what it would do if she yanked the wheel to the side, pointed the front at one of the towering trees that edged the road like wary sentries. Would it resist, hugging the macadam despite the wrench to the axles? Or mightn't it jump the ditch and slice smoothly by the tree, entering the brush, leaping graceful as a fawn? Or again, what if the Porsche smacked against some object, squeezing metal and chrome in collapsing accordian pleats, crunching the intricate engine, and in that one moment she flew through the windshield? What would happen to a body splintered and torn, bones broken and muscles ripped apart, tendons severed, skull and rib cage pulverized, if the person inhabiting it couldn't die? How could she live if nothing of her physical being was left in one piece?

"How?" Dee cried aloud. And before she could even think twice, reconsider an irrevocable notion, she exerted pressure on the soaring car, closing her fists tightly around the steering wheel and tugging, at ninety-five, for all she was worth, to the right.

The Porsche leaped, a sleek metallic feline, leaving the road, all four wheels revolving in air. Dee traveled a millennium in that second and a half, the high beams illuminating a flattened image of a brush-and-tufted ground, not green but washed out, colorless, high-lighted black. The weeds sprung up straight as the hair on the head of a punk rocker, the vines tangled like Oriental snakes. The whole night framed in the windshield yellowed in an overexposure. The tree didn't so much as suffer an arboreal shiver, when the Porsche met it head on.

Harlan Farrow, his temper throbbing raw as a skinned knee, slept little these autumn nights. It was the smell that kept him in the double bed, stretched out, wound as a watch spring. The bad smell—worse than rotten eggs, more pungent than steaming dog turds, sour as spoiled milk, further off than Limburger gone bad—clung to the bakery, an essential element of the building itself. Once inside there was no escaping the aroma. For Harlan that was. Nobody else smelled the elusive effluvia.

Harlan persisted in his search for its source. He tore the bakery apart, painting and scrubbing, spraying with Lysol. He wasn't sure what he would do when he found the cause. Burn it out, maybe.

But Harlan had yet to discover what he looked for. All he had learned was that it smelled in the bakery and no other place. So the only relief he had was to leave the small building across the drive from his house, the business of baking breads and pastries that was his life. But though he could, in that way, avoid the actual aroma, the memory of it stuffed up his head. Even now, propped against the iron headboard, he imagined he was descending into the very center of the stink, about to drown in it, even if the smell never existed here in the bedroom he shared with his wife.

Harlan, breathing through his nose, imagined the smell right down in his lungs. He felt the hated aroma as though it were Saran Wrap plastered to his skin from toes to scalp. With one wrenching motion he left the bed where Florence lay rigidly, as if terrified of falling into some mistake while she slept. The wrong move against Harlan's arm or thigh and there would be hell to pay. Florence drowsed, out of fright, as little as Harlan himself.

What spurred Harlan Farrow into deciding he'd ask Lucas Donnelly, he couldn't say. Except what was the point of having the devil around—for of course, Harlan had heard all the speculation about Lucas Donnelly, not that Harlan Farrow really gave a damn if the devil had taken up residence in town—if he were no more beneficial than an ordinary mortal? Harlan believed all of a sudden that Lucas Donnelly could locate the source of the smell. That he might be the cause himself, or something he'd done, hadn't crossed Harlan's mind. He'd weeks before passed the last outpost of rationality when it came to the stench. Now he merely pulled on his pants, tucked in his shirt, yanked on socks, before slipping his feet into shoes, and grabbing a poplin jacket with the keys to the Tempo in his pocket.

Small courtesies such as calling beforehand, or considering the lateness of the hour, passed Harlan by. He simply drove into New Morning proper, parked at the elbow of High Street, left the key in the ignition, and strode up the front walk to ring the dragon's doorbell.

The door swung wide without apparent human intervention and Harlan Farrow was sucked into the fire. The interior of Emma Tydings's house flamed with bright orange ribbons dangling from the ceiling, searing stalagmites sprouting up from the floor. He screamed, but his mouth was a furnace as the scorching air rushed down his throat to his lungs. Harlan's hair sizzled in a nest of hissing yellow vipers; his skin glowed golden before it popped in bubbly pustules of fire and singed. Skin disintegrated, flesh boiled into lava. The Timex slipped off his wrist. Laughter carilloned, but through his pain Harlan knew it wasn't coming from him.

His eyeballs detonated like exploding cherry bombs and a white gelatinous ooze poured out of the sockets through which he never saw Lucas Donnelly in his usual white attire, though he heard him say, "My good man! Do come in," as the fires banked to a few flickers.

No flames bloomed any longer, but Harlan was drenched in sweat. He patted frantic hands along his arms and felt his own unmelted substance. The holocaust had dried to ashes and blown off, out the windows, through the slit beneath the door. Only a slightly acrid smell remained.

Harlan stood upright, on his own two feet, blinking unsinged eyelashes, as whole as he had ever been. *Oh!* was all he thought and found himself with the uncontrollable shakes in Lucas Donnelly's parlor.

"The bakery." Harlan unloosened the word at last and with tremendous effort. Then, his teeth chattering, he managed to add, "Stinks."

"Remember the dills." Lucas Donnelly, all smiles, laughed.

"What?"

"You never baked the dills for my dinner party." Lucas Donnelly repeated in his lusty baritone, blowing perfectly round smoke rings into Harlan's face, "The dills, Harlan."

Now he did hear that, and knew, back in the summer, he'd made a terrible mistake. Lucas Donnelly had wanted dills from the afternoon baking and Harlan had been obstreperous. It was only a game! he tried to tell the dragon, you needn't have gotten so offended because I wouldn't give that bitch, Evelyn Crowell, the satisfaction.

Harlan struggled to say *I'm sorry,* but the words were too foreign, too hard to spit out. His tongue stumbled, his lips swelled, and Harlan kept his remorse to himself. Besides, a wind had arisen in the parlor that nearly swept him off his feet. Lucas Donnelly began to spin away, twirling over and over in the tornado's center. As he went he called back hollowly to Harlan, "Look in the basement!"

"No!" Harlan shrieked as he tumbled out of the house. Expelled, squeezed onto the front walk where he sprawled, he made tracks on his hands and knees, fast as a wolfhound, the smell with him now, fogging the inside of his nostrils, so heavy he gagged from it.

Harlan wasn't sure how he got back in the Tempo. He lacked any memory of climbing behind the wheel, turning the key in the ignition, pulling away from the curb, and screeching off the square.

Harlan, speeding back to the bakery, whimpered low in his throat, a strange, un-Harlan sound. He drove the Tempo down the middle of the two-lane highway, right on top of the white line, and Harlan's only luck of the night was that nothing roared down on him.

Harlan's Tempo growling out of the drive woke Jordy up. He hung in the dark, uncertain for a moment what the noise was,

but when he identified *car*, he sighed and hunched down
expecting to reenter sleep. But unconsciousness eluded him.
He suffered on the lumpy mattress with its ridges and valleys,
twisting, no position comfortable until, disgusted, fully alert
now, he got out of bed and went to the window.

Leaning against the jamb, clutching the thin curtain, he saw,
glancing down, that his father's car wasn't where Harlan
normally parked it. Then, confronting the darkness, Jordy
experienced the most peculiar sensation: He felt as if the
whole house shuddered under him. A voice in his own mind
shrilled, "Well, are you going to kill him or not? Are you just
going to think him to death?"

I'm useless, he'd told Alastair earlier. Nothing new. He'd
told him that before. Uselessness was a common theme to
Jordy. Alastair had thrown his words back at him. Hadn't he
tried to drive the three of them out of town? Didn't he, with
Glory alone in the van, attempt a run out the backside of New
Morning, out the Pittsfield road. And failed that, too. The
blacktop had halted dead in the ground at the northern
boundary. Broken off, the end chewed ragged as a Milky Way.
A wall was there instead. When he'd climbed out of the van
and advanced on that concrete barrier it shimmered and
disappeared on him, and he'd crossed over onto unincorporated county land. But back in the van with Glory, headed
straight, the wall rose up again. It rose for Glory. *A prison*, he
sighed, because she couldn't walk through it either, alone or
holding onto Jordy's hand. Jordy hadn't even been surprised.
On the ride back, Glory folded up on the seat and laid her
head against his shoulder.

Unconsciously, Jordy rubbed the spot where Glory's head
had touched him, as if he could still feel the heat. It was harder
to see Glory now. Evelyn was always watching, preparing to
thrust out a hand to jerk Glory back when she walked out the
door and around the side to the van. "You can't be running off
with other men when you're engaged to be married," was what
her mother said. "People will talk." And no matter how many
times Glory insisted she wouldn't marry Lucas Donnelly, nor
how quickly or slowly she cut the words out of air, wrote them
in capital letters three spaces high, Evelyn didn't listen.
Glory's marriage was as solid as a tumor in Evelyn Crowell's
head, and as Alastair said, not even surgery could cut it out.

Christmas hung in the future, far away as the moon, but it

would rush upon all of them if they didn't do something. What? What? He thumped his head lightly against the wood and imagined all manner of horrors he and the two old men might unleash on the dragon. But to no end. Shooting Lucas Donnelly with a gun was sillier than trying to hold back the flooding Housatonic with a net.

Jordy drowsed by the window and so was in place when Harlan, going too fast, cutting through the night with his foot pressed hard on the gas, screeched to a stop. Jordy woke up. He looked down, saw the Tempo angled across the narrow drive, heard the driver's door slam closed. Harlan left the lights burning, two cones of brightness slapping into the rear wall of the bakery. Yellow currents flowed upward illuminating the gray shingles.

Jordy, watching his father rush into the bakery, thought, *Yes. I can, I will, do something about him.* Avenging Timmy was useful. It was, Jordy understood, what he had to do. There would be no place for him, ever, if he let Harlan get away with murder.

You're not going to kill him at all, the insidious voice in his head whispered so loudly that Jordy spun to the side, suddenly frightened. As if the voice had an actual presence and resided in the outer world rather than the inner. A trickle of fear stroked his neck, raising goose bumps. But he was alone in the darkened bedroom. There ought to have been moonlight, some silvery frosting creeping over the sill. Silently counting the days, he saw he was right; the moon was due. It should have been widening, emerging in the black sky as the earth turned. Yet he recalled no moon last night either.

Wide awake, Jordy lingered at the window, stalling. *Do it! Do it!* the voice clamored again, words battering against bone, striking inside his skull. He felt the throbbing seizure of one of his mother's migraines, and clutched his temples, pressing the pain back in his head but he couldn't still it completely. He knew in his heart he'd be pained forever if he let Harlan live. Some fragment of his being was ripped away each moment now that he didn't enact retribution for Timmy. He had been feeling the tearing pain for weeks, since he'd begun suspecting where his brother had gone. Into the ground or the river, out by the old quarry, anywhere except around the world in uniform.

No glimmer filled up the bakery window and splashed out on the small patch of dirt out front. It took Jordy a minute or so to ask himself why Harlan would be wandering in the dark, why he hadn't turned on the light. Nothing in Harlan's character might make him feel his way, bump about blinded, and he didn't drink. Drink would have explained a lot of Jordy's father; often Jordy wished Harlan were a drunk.

The voice quieted to a hissing, yet still insistent enough to prick him as he dragged on the jeans hanging from the bedpost, and barefoot, without a shirt, slipped through the house, the stairs creaking. The house sounded alive and in distress.

The night air struck coldly against his skin as he crept up the drive, leaning into the Tempo to click off the lights. He shivered, huddling in the darkness until his eyes adjusted and vague, ghostlike forms took shape. Then he edged around the back like a burglar, entering by the same door his father had only minutes before.

Once inside, the smooth linoleum felt cool under his feet, and he took two, maybe three deep breaths, listening. Something scraped below, then a thud. The basement, he thought, feeling his way along the counters, fingers gliding on metal, over the blank surface of the cool ovens. He moved carefully, not wanting to crash into anything and alert his father that he was walking over his head in the bakery.

Jordy inched the door open, and a pale illumination raced up the cellar steps from the forty-watt bulb hanging naked in the ceiling.

Standing still and gazing down at a rack of metal shelves pulled out from against the wall, Jordy almost retreated. He had a sudden longing to return to bed, to crawl beneath the covers. And he wished to be anywhere but in the bakery about to descend to the basement; he yearned not to have awakened.

Where the shelves had been yanked aside, bags of flour and sugar were carelessly tipped over. One of the sacks had ripped and a thin dusting of white coated the floor. The footsteps stamped in it were his father's.

Harlan was at the wall, breaking through the cement connecting the cinder blocks. One large rectangle broke free and he knocked it to the floor. He worked frantically, his motions a blur. With the noise of the pick's chopping and scraping, and with his grunts, he never heard Jordy's silent, barefooted approach.

Jordy stayed in the shadows, out of the murky light. His father attacked the wall, hurtled his pick and himself upon it.

Harlan struggled like a man possessed. The wall gave way before his fury, cracking apart.

Harlan yanked another block loose leaving a dark hole in the wall. Dust clouded up in the cellar, but Harlan rushed on. What was in there? Jordy wondered, easing himself lower on another step, silent as air. He thought he was invisible, though he stayed hidden, not pushing his luck. If Harlan gazed behind him, he might catch a hazy glimpse of Jordy. His father with a pick and shovel was a dangerous man.

An erratic pattern emerged slowly from Harlan's destruction, the black of the void and the gray of the cinder blocks. The wall, before Harlan pushed loose another rectangle, resembled a checkerboard. Then quickly the illusion changed, and appeared as a cross before that vanished also.

What's he after?

Jordy feared he knew the answer and hoped he was wrong. Yet his body told him he wasn't as a wave of sickness started in his stomach, cramping him over. He bit down hard on his bottom lip, concentrating on breathing regularly, in and out, to keep from doubling up.

He wouldn't! Not here, so close. With us . . . under us, all this time!

Hysteria gurgled in Jordy's throat and he almost burst out laughing, thinking how all these years when he'd expected postcards from Timmy, late-night phone calls, wondering about his brother far away, living the good life, living any life that was better than the one he jettisoned in New Morning, Timmy had been buried behind the bakery's cellar wall.

"Aiiiii!" Harlan screeched when his son's body came finally into full view, starkly revealed in the light. And he clamped his hand to his face, covering nose and mouth, screaming between the splayed fingers. His voice was muffled, but Jordy, sick as he was, heard Harlan anyway. "The stink! The stink!" Harlan cried.

Yet Jordy smelled nothing beyond the dampness, the faint odor of dust. No taint of putrefaction blew out of the small tomb, narrow and compact as one of the storage cabinets up above. Timmy, cast in stone, squatted. Jordy remembered learning long ago in school that some Indians were buried in just such a way. They sat in the earth rather than lying flat, entombed in wood and metal, cushioned by soft satin like Christians. But his brother sat only a moment, as Harlan in his rage lifted up a cinder block and tossed it into the upright coffin. Timmy, knocked off his perch, fell back to the far wall, his arms opening in bony wings. His head snapped up and his eyelids rose. Timmy stared straight out at Jordy. He glared past Harlan into the darkness where Jordy hung.

How could you have let this be done to me! dead Timmy said.

Dark streams slowly began to trail from Timmy's sockets, his nostrils, out and over his lips. Something oozed out of Timmy, dribbling in black rivers. Jordy, tasting bile, was sick. Yet he couldn't tear his gaze away; he was joined to Timmy.

Oh how Jordy wished it were possible to run up the cellar steps, out of the bakery, to the house. He wanted to fly into sleep, throw himself on oblivion and drown in it, but there was no sleep so deep. No sleep, Jordy thought, chilled and shaking, freezing in the airless basement. His bones rattled as Harlan, screaming, battered at Timmy with the shovel, slicing a vent in his fleshless chest. The black lines, irregular columns, shifted and separated. To his horror Jordy saw not liquid running out of his dead brother, but maggots. Timmy's whole face turned black, shimmering in a wave. Jordy, so knotted by fear he couldn't think, couldn't grieve either for *that thing* which once was his brother, buried all these years while they passed unknowingly back and forth over his head, finally screamed. Something pushed inside him, shoved, and a wall of his own broke, giving way. The sound—scream and cry and wail—mixed in one awful howl, thundered into the cellar.

Harlan spun about, the pick raised. His face was slicked with dust, cross-hatched by riverlets of sweat. A wild look fogged his eyes, and he exploded with a guttural shriek of his own, charging across the basement. But he came too fast, and tripped over a cinder block, sprawling flat. The shovel flew out of his hands.

In one leap Jordy went off the stairs. *Kill him! Kill him!* roaring in his head, crashing like the bloody tide in Alastair's Omaha. *Kill him!*

Harlan scrambled to his knees, bleating, pushing frantically away from his living room. He rolled over a flour sack, and when he brought his head up, his face was as powdery as a clown's. He looked ridiculous, except for insane, raging eyes, as he leaped in the other direction, going for Jordy now. He growled, maddened as a wounded beast, horrible bursts of foul abuse, words tangled, vomited up from his insides.

Having spent himself in that one shattering howl, Jordy

quieted, incapable of sound. He flung himself to the left for the pick, but failed to reach it before Harlan hooked an ankle, bringing him down. Jordy crashed, pain streaking along his arm. He thought he heard something snap, but what did it matter. He kept on moving, kicking, bringing a knee up into Harlan's face.

Harlan grunted and his eyeballs rolled loose in his head. Jordy went on, all the way to the back wall, and felt Timmy near his shoulder blades. A quick glance behind revealed his brother smiling out of the black beard that swayed and walked across his face. The sight of Timmy in motion set free another scream from Jordy. Fright and hysteria galvanized him so that, rushing beyond pain, he stumbled, then leaped to his feet, and grabbed for a cinder block in the wall. The block came out and Jordy crashed again, onto his side. He would have stayed down for more than a second, but Harlan, awakened from his daze, roared back toward him. Jordy's hand snaked out and found the pick. He scooted away, holding the weapon before him.

Mucus ran out of his nose and saliva dribbled from his lips. He had bitten his tongue or his cheek because there was the salty taste of blood in his mouth. He tried to yell to his father to stay away, but he couldn't get the words out. He raised the pick instead, brought it forward. It missed Harlan by an inch.

Harlan, screeching, "Youfuckingnogoodsonofabitch!" crabbed his way over the cellar floor. But Jordy also clambered to his feet, swaying, the whole of this terrible, enclosed place, this once-familiar basement, moving with him, walls swinging inward. Up went the pick again and this time Jordy tried to aim it. *Kill him! kill him! kill him!* pounding in his head.

He brought the pick over his shoulder in one clean sweep, in a graceful arch, aiming straight and true for the part in Harlan's hair. The while line gleamed like a freshly painted highway divider.

Jordy saw the point embedded in Harlan's skull, witnessed the geyser of blood spume up and fly. He saw it so vividly, it didn't seem possible he missed, that Harlan, suddenly agile as a welterweight, on the balls of his feet, leaped aside. But he did, and the pick on its downward journey carried Jordy forward. He collided with another tier of metal shelves. Jars of preserves, thick oozy jams and jellies, pitted cherries, currants in wine broke on the floor. Jordy slipped in the spillage and fell on his knees, the pick torn from his grasp. Unthinkingly he put his hands down and came away red and sticky with strawberry jelly. Sweet syrups and jams lapped at his pants, spotted his bare chest. He fought for some purchase in the mess and struggled to pull his way up the shelves, but he slipped and slid until he thought to crawl off to the side where the floor was clean.

On all fours, like some dumb beast, panting, a painful constriction in his chest, Jordy heard a terrible roaring filling up the cellar. His ears hurt and he raised his head. Timmy's remains grinned, an ugly caricature of his brother, and Jordy thought for a minute it was dead Timmy screaming. But then he glanced to his left, and Harlan swelled there, larger to Jordy than he had ever been, more massive than life itself. His father was ferocious and as maddened as a jungle animal with a bullet in him, and he howled dementedly. Harlan advanced, the pick once again in his hands. In the faded light the tool didn't look lethal, rather dull, not sharp and weighty at all. But then it began descending, arching over his head, and Jordy, terrified, cried out, trying to dodge in the tiny corner where he'd lodged himself. But he had nowhere to go. The pick drove into Jordy's back so forcefully the tip poked a tiny hole in his chest through which blood dripped. Harlan pinned him flat for an instant, then Jordy convulsed, spasmed, actually rode up the instrument. Shivering, as if only now reacting to the cellar's cold and dampness, Jordy's whimpers came softly, flowing from his mouth in a tide of red. Then he buckled again and fell flat.

Harlan stared stupidly at his dead son and looked back at the bones, the scraps of tanned flesh, having to think who this once had been. Then Harlan spat, and wiped a gummy hand over his face, leaving tracks, before he climbed up the cellar steps, hurrying because the smell was worse than ever.

Harlan ran, not from the fear that was blowing up a gale in his head, but instinctively. Some primitive sense told him to get, to flee, not from his dead sons, or because of them from the law, not from Florence either—though what would she do?—but *because*. If trapped, break free—that was the message drumming hollowly in Harlan's brain, as he took off in the Tempo.

Harlan swept around a curve barely missing the ditch off the shoulder. Some sixth sense made him flick the wheel to the left, straightening the car. Harlan, who'd been born in New Morning, couldn't have told anyone his exact location as he gunned up the road. He fled without a thought, leaving even the faint memories of his sons trailing in his exhaust. Harlan was flying.

What made him hit the brakes for the shimmering figure, gauzy, translucent as a specter, drifting ethereally down the middle of the road, was unknown. But he slammed his foot down hard, took a jolt from the wheel in his chest, felt his heart lurch and a trickle of liquid slide out of his mouth in a winding track over his chin and down his neck. It felt warm, like blood. He had bit his lip.

The Tempo fishtailed and came to rest horizontally across the road. The door, which Harlan in his hurrying hadn't shut tight, popped open, and he fell halfway out of the stalled car.

The sudden stop didn't shock his brain into working again. The smell, Harlan's torment and torture of these past months, was the one lucid memory that remained. It rose again in a virulent updraft and seemed to be sweeping in off the bloody thing by the door. The smell furled in a cloud, and so Harlan, in his panic, failed to recognize Dee Whittier splotched with specks of blood. Though it was possible Harlan had lost the ability to recognize anyone.

"Harlan, I had an accident down the road," Dee wheezed, reaching in and touching his arm. But Harlan couldn't understand; the words jammed for him like crashing chords. With the faint light from the dash, the underslung shadows, and the tracks plus the wandering threads of blood, Dee's face hanging in the frame of the window appeared to Harlan Farrow like a monster's mask. The eyes were red as rubies, set far back into bone. The eyes shone at Harlan Farrow malevolently. The blood, caked black on the lips and gums, turned the teeth to dark stumps. Harlan, staring at a countenance older than time, threw up.

Dee released his arm in haste, which gave Harlan a chance. He bolted out the other door and took off in a fast trot, carrying his own bad smell with him now. He pelted along the center of the road, and in the still, motionless night in which the leaves lay inert, the grass withered, a wind suddenly flared and winged by his ears like buckshot.

Harlan supposed somebody behind shot at him. An itch

traveled down his spine, and he had an awful foreboding. But
he lacked the courage to fling a glance into that pulsing
blackness. Nor could he stop, afraid that like an old machine,
there'd be no starting up again. So he kept going, legs
pumping, arms swinging, his heart rattling against his rib cage.
Harlan's heart begged him to slow down. Air caught in his
lungs, not going anywhere, and the swift pain struck like the
punch of a fist. He stumbled, dizzy, an aurora borealis of
sparkling spots spinning in his vision.

Harlan didn't know where he was, though all his life he'd
lived only a few miles from here, nor was he aware that he ran
away from New Morning, perhaps by instinct heading for the
town line. Harlan simply raced all out. Blood sizzled and pain
gripped his muscles. Sweat swept like rain off his brow and
over his eyelids. He ran until he stopped, slamming full tilt
into a blockage that wasn't there. Harlan rushed with open
arms and a thundering heart into death's bear hug. A massive
blowout in the left ventricle stopped Harlan dead.

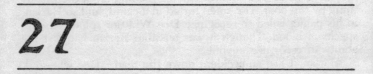

27

Florence Farrow stood alone at the graves, just as she had sat
by herself in church. No one went near her, not even to
express sympathy. She carried the plague, an awfulness people
feared would be contagious. If you closed in too near to
Florence you could catch tragedy like the Asian flu.

Even Alastair hung back, but he had his own grief to battle,
as well as Glory to support. Glory walked beside the chair with
leaden steps, her whole body as bent as an octagenarian's. One
hand lingered along Alastair's arm. Her touch was warm.
When Alastair reached for her fingers, they were hot, burning.
What could he say? Or do? Alastair, at Jordy's funeral, felt as
useless as Jordy himself had, felt older than Methuselah.
Burnt out; washed up. An ache persisted that wouldn't
dissolve and which he couldn't cry away.

Moses, too, was subdued, back in his good suit, staying
close to Alastair on the pretense that the old man might need

help. But Moses needed as much as Alastair, and he couldn't stop remembering Jordy. Now here, the poor boy, poorer even than Bobby Pierson, was gone, passed over. Sent there by that murdering maniac, Harlan, the boy's own father! Moses had seldom, in all his travels, encountered such wickedness. If Harlan were alive, Moses would have killed him.

Harlan Farrow was buried in the family plot, in a grave between his two sons. Alastair thought it would have been more fitting if Harlan had been thrown out with the trash. But Alastair swallowed his protest as Will Austin, black as a raven, dark as Torquemada, said the prayers, then changed sonorously to Latin. His *Dominus vobiscum* flew high and wide with feathered wings, the only bird Alastair remembered seeing in months. Will interred Timmy first, then Jordy, and Florence threw a clump of earth on each before she passed to Harlan. Alastair didn't care to see Harlan go into the ground, and he swung the chair around to roll across the soft slope of the Congregational cemetery. A brief wind punched out of the north in little puffs and Alastair held his coat tightly about his throat. He bumped along the back of the Wayne family plot, and he thought, *not long!* Glory kept pace on one side, her head lowered, watching nothing more than her feet, and Moses high-stepped on the other flank.

Nobody had anything to say until, in the car, during the short ride down the hillside from the cemetery, Alastair mumbled, "So young!" Jordy had been the same age as Horse Keleidas, he remembered, Timmy even younger. Alastair, chewing on his bottom lip, sorrowing, didn't know which of the lost boys he grieved for more, perhaps all of them, cut down so many years before their prime. And here am I, he thought, a worthless piece of carcass, rolling on, not doing any good. Not doing any bad either, he tried to console himself.

Doc came walking up the drive after Moses parked the car and Alastair swung out, settling himself in his chair. "Missed it, sorry," Doc muttered, "but Joe Dombrow's wife was giving birth. A girl. Six pounds, eight ounces. Healthy as a new foal. Mother and daughter doing just fine."

"Good for Joe," Alastair replied, not lightened by this new addition to New Morning. Another life, he couldn't help thinking, meant another death sometime.

Doc put his arm around Glory and hugged her awkwardly, blinking. Glory stood in his embrace like a plastic mannequin. "You people all need a drink, and you don't hear me say that often," Doc said.

Alastair snorted. "Ha! No booze is going to turn the clock back. And that's what we need most. To start time over, say from June." But he thought, no, longer than that, back at least to 1944 and Normandy, before that, too. From the thirties surely. Then the chain of inevitability broke apart as Alastair realized evil had existed from the beginning, from the days in the Garden when Lucas Donnelly was a snake. As they all reached the kitchen door, grouped close together, Alastair yelled out, shattering the New Morning quiet, "This is what your buddy Donnelly did! He's the one responsible!"

Doc stormed into the kitchen and poured himself a drink of water from the tap. He hunched by the sink, staring sightlessly out at the drab, unfriendly morning as Alastair yelled again, "He killed Jordy!"

Without turning around Doc said, and said so softly as to be almost inaudible, "It was Harlan who killed Jordy, just as he did in his other boy. Timmy was dead long before Lucas Donnelly ever set foot in this valley."

"Evil, Doc!" Alastair raged.

"Is human. Man-made, just like the atom bomb." Doc slumped, but he finally shifted so the others could see him clearly. He looked like a piece of terrain the Enola Gay had leveled.

Moses, having just poured a stiff scotch, was about to drink it down, but his glance met Doc's, and without a pause, he passed over the tumbler. Doc's hands shook as he raised the glass to his lips and swigged the whole of the scotch in one gulp. He shuddered from the unaccustomed bitterness, for Doc was no drinker, and coughed, then hacked, clearing his throat as if he planned to speak again. But Moses was already pouring another shot, handing this one to Alastair, then quickly making one for himself. The yardman didn't think to offer one to Glory, who sat by the table that Alastair hadn't cleared from breakfast, picking at a straw place mat with a fingernail. Not one of the three paid Doc much attention. Even Alastair's anger, ardent only a moment before, had dampened.

"Listen," Doc said finally, "Harlan Farrow was a lunatic. Psychotic. He . . ." But no one wanted to hear about Jordy's father, Doc realized, and stopped. He put the glass in the sink, then shuffled to the back door, where he added, "Crazy as a loon. Should have locked him up years ago. I blame myself."

Alastair, still as carved oak, barely raised his eyes from contemplating the amber liquor that he had yet to taste. "Say whatever you want to make yourself feel better, but you know, Doc, same as I do, that Lucas Donnelly was at fault. Somehow, someway."

Doc pushed himself away from his old friend, as if struggling to swim upstream against a strong current. He had only managed another step when Alastair threw at him, "You can't go on with one foot in the water, the other on the bank. Sooner or later, Doc, you've got to make a stand." He sounded so sad, Doc started to bring his hand to his ears, but then shamed, shoved them down into his jacket pockets and shouldered out the door.

Doc didn't run from the three mourners, but he moved fast, so fast, in fact, that when he reached his office he was panting.

Mike Boardman sat on the wooden bench in the waiting room, his wife beside him, both as still as characters in a painting. The couple, not surprisingly, hadn't been the same since first Jack, then Carol died. They'd aged woefully for one thing, and lost the spark of life, trailing about the Public, out in the big empty house, just two old ghosts. They spent considerable time in Doc's office too, conjuring up ailments, describing spectral aches, searching for some disease or malfunctioning organ to hold responsible for their agony. It was grief, period, but Doc hadn't the heart to tell them no cure existed for such pain. Only time, and even time wasn't a sure cure. Doc prescribed a new tonic for Mike that wouldn't help but wouldn't hurt either, and a placebo capsule for Milly. The Boardmans left no more reassured than when they came, knowing too how useless Doc's medicine would be to them.

Out on High Street Milly Boardman looked toward Lucas Donnelly's, the colonial more visible this time of year with the skeletal trees almost denuded of their leaves, and whispered in Mike's ear, "Do something! Go talk to him. He took them, he can give 'em back! Howie Eumis got that Persian of his from the grave, didn't he?" But Mike walked away, up High Street to the corner of Rowly, and around onto cobbled Brewster where he had parked the car. No cars were allowed now in the square. Mike failed to listen to his wife trailing behind him, whimpering, her whispers black-edged with sobs. He walked older than Moses Llewelyn, but he did move on. When he got to the car, Milly climbed in beside him, her voice running like rain water. "Ask him to give 'em to us, Mike!" Mike

Boardman drove off like a mechanical man, not replying, for
Milly repeated the same refrain day after day. He mightn't
have thought it was making an impression, what she said, but
it did. Milly's words were eating away at her husband like a
cancer.

Back in his office Doc tried not to think of the Boardmans, or
of the Farrows either, as he tended to a usual day's illnesses
and complaints. Nothing egregious, nothing particularly
strange. Doc was so grateful he began to feel infinitesimally
better, but when he went over to the hospital after office hours,
his spirits lagged again. Not even the CAT scanner cheered
him up. He drooped in the operating room, faltered by the
small nursery where the only baby was the Dumbrow girl, and
kept imagining Alastair Wayne at his flank, swinging on his
crutches. Alastair, faint, but oh so loud, whinnied, "What
price, Doc!"

Damn you! Doc shouted in his head, knowing all the while
Alastair stayed in his own kitchen sorrowing, maybe having a
second scotch with Moses Llewelyn, or moving into the living
room and having Glory play. But no music would soothe
Alastair's grief, or Glory's pain, Moses's too, any more than the
spanking new hospital, beautiful as a Rembrandt to Doc, now
soothed or uplifted. Time didn't pass but hung open like a
putrefying wound. Doc caught a brief whiff of Harlan Farrow's
smell and a nauseous tide rolled in his stomach. Sick myself,
Doc thought, and left his hospital, feeling further shamed, as
though he'd actually done something wrong. He climbed into
his Buick, and for a moment held his breath, then exhaled
loudly, slapping the steering wheel and thinking, I've committed no crime! Only he knew, as he drove off to his house,
he'd done nothing, period, and that was irresponsible. Alastair
was right: comes a time a man has to choose up sides.

Will Austin was crossing the grassy meridian to the church
when Doc drove back to his house from the hospital. Doc had
forgotten driving was prohibited in the square now, and took
the Buick all the way around the green. Will, his black cassock
billowing out behind him from the wind, shook a fist and
shouted at him, "Against the law!" But Doc, a swimmer in his
own sea, never heard the minister.

Reverend Austin hissed his indignation through clenched

teeth and proceeded. This won't do! he seethed, his temper prodded. Will was learning just how hard it was to get people behaving in the right and proper fashion. If he instructed in the Sunday service, "Kneel!" half the congregation stumbled. Either the worshippers sat or stood undecided as to how they were to get down on their knees. Of course, the fact that the Congregational lacked prie-dieux made a difference. The church's floor was good solid wood and made genuflecting, even for the young, a true exertion. Have to do something about that, Will Austin acknowledged, and was inspired when he reached the church's side door, to discuss the needed improvement this very minute with Lucas Donnelly.

If the dragon had a particular fan in New Morning, that distinction would fall on the reverend. He gave thanks nightly that Lucas Donnelly had come, for in all Will's years he'd never been so in sync with another person. Miraculous, that's what it was, how Mr. Donnelly—whom Will was one of the very few in New Morning not to recognize as the devil—understood him. Peas in a pod, spiritual brothers, Will prayed as he swiftly swept two fingers like a sleight-of-hand artist about his chest. Even the particularly sharp-eyed wouldn't have interpreted the scrambled motion as a cross-forming gesture.

Since it was the minister's habit to make pastoral visits unannounced, catching people with their spiritual guard down, he didn't bother to call up Lucas Donnelly and say, "I'm coming over," he just went.

Jarvis Badderly opened the door for Will and received a "My good man!" plus a smile. Jarvis didn't bother to grimace back even minimally as he ushered the reverend into the library. Waiting for Lucas Donnelly to appear from wherever, Will ran his fingertips over the smooth leather filling the bookshelves. So many of the titles were in Latin and Greek that, though he couldn't read the latter, Will felt at home. He sighed, helped himself to a cigar from the humidor, and Lucas Donnelly found him, minutes later, relaxed in a chair, his feet up on an ottoman, reading Thomas Aquinas. "Marvelous stuff!" he barked when Lucas Donnelly appeared, unruffled and shiny as always.

"I think so," Lucas Donnelly acknowledged.

Will Austin, never one to beat around bushes, launched immediately into the purpose of his visit. "Strengthening folks in their religion," was how he put it. "Everybody's so lax these days, what with television and contraception. What's a man of the cloth to do!" he cried, snapping irritably. Carried away, Will plucked at his cassock, the only Congregational minister to wear such garb.

Lucas Donnelly poured the minister a glass of port which calmed him, and in a few moments the two of them were companionably smoking their cigars. The liberalism of his denomination along with that of the world at large agitated Will Austin whenever he thought about either, but deftly the dragon steered him away from the substance to the symbol. Soon they were deep in a discussion of genuflection, and what to do about sending the flock down on their knees. Some structural improvements were decided upon, and Lucas Donnelly complimented the minister for his strictness.

The autonomy of each Congregational church, and the variety of theological opinion considered acceptable gave Will Austin much latitude for fiddling with his services. Sooner or later, however, somebody would probably notice that the simplicity of the Congregational ritual had metamorphosed into the more colorful Roman, but Will Austin didn't give a damn. He couldn't worry about everything, so he bothered about less rather than more. Alastair, just the other day, had tried to draw him into a conversation about the changes in New Morning, but Will was having none of it. To him, Alastair represented the enemy. "A modernist!" he snorted to Lucas Donnelly, looking down his nose. "Makes crude comments, don't you know, about my preference for Palestrina."

Lucas Donnelly vociferously agreed that Alastair Wayne was a cad among men, an ignorant clod, an unsympathetic busybody. "And while we're on the subject," he added, playing deftly with the minister, "are you satisfied with your usual communion?"

"Strange you mention that"—Will perked up, an almost beatific light glowing from him—"because I have a certain hankering for something a bit more traditional. . . ."

Lucas Donnelly went on to suggest certain objects—one in particular—that might adorn the plain simplicity of the church. "Nothing ornate, of course," he said, puffing, his hands steepled upon his white vest.

"Certainly not!" Will Austin chorused, wandering about his buttons, searching for some missing attachment. "Simple wood, perhaps with a touch of gold or silver. What do you think?"

"Perfect," Lucas Donnelly drawled slowly. He joined the

minister in a second glass of port, which Will raised in a silent toast. The dragon lifted his own glass. "To the future!"

"The future!" Will echoed, giving Lucas Donnelly a warm glance.

Then the dragon added, "About that item, why don't you get right on it? Order the thing tomorrow. Naturally it would be my pleasure to cover the cost, no matter how much it comes to!"

So it was that barely a week later, on All Hallows' Eve as it turned out, a large cross with a rather medievally whittled Christ figure and more than a smidgen of both gold and silver was erected behind the Congregational pulpit.

28

The ferocious battle for the Normandy beaches continued. At Omaha, "Bloody Omaha," the fight was especially savage. Dog Green, a mire of broken equipment and useless supplies, resembled, with so many wounded and so many more dead, a Bosch landscape. A human foot in a boot with a ruff of khaki pantleg stood solidly only a few inches from where Alastair lay. Wandering in a Technicolor trance, Alastair gazed at the foot dispassionately. Past thinking or feeling, he didn't consider the foot inappropriate, divorced as it was from the rest of its flesh. The lone human attachment seemed a bloody, mud-stained art object.

Behind the singular foot, in the distance, a tank exploded into the air. Pinned to the ground, unable to move once the machine gun fire off the cliffs ripped into him, Alastair had no choice but to observe.

The tide churned at his boots, foamed up his numbed thighs. He tasted salt, sand, too, so he knew he hadn't died, and he continued to drift like the dead in the waves.

Alastair, nodding in the wheelchair, was suddenly awakened by the thundering mortar explosions. For an instant he sat on the shore, the wreckage and the dead behind him, the intrepid living leaping off the landing craft to die. Before him, spread across the hideous vista of the Dog Green burial ground, were only more dead. As for those who hadn't been leveled yet, they zigzagged, half bent, for the cliffs. Alastair watched the men struggle behind the engineers as they attempted to detonate passageways through the obstacle course the Germans had left on the beach. One explosion after another.

A piece of kindling crackled and fell from the grate. Alastair sat straighter. "Hell and damnation!" He meant Omaha, that nightmare of carnage which he knew as Dog Green.

"Dreaming again," he muttered, wiping his face, staring into the fire. It was cold in the house and he held his hands out to the flames, but the piteous little blaze couldn't warm him.

The dreams weren't memorable, composed as they came to be of brief experiences plus what he'd read long after Normandy. Alastair feared them less these days, but still he was saddened by the waste. So much, so many, lost on that stretch of sand. Even more than forty years after the event, to Alastair, brooding, it was inconceivable.

He moaned, hating war and man's inhumanity to his own kind, as he finally came fully to life. The ghostly remains of the battle lulled at low tide in his mind, and he found himself yearning all of a sudden with a passion that made him lightheaded to return and save them.

Can't turn the clock back, can't! he thought, as helpless to salvage time as he had been when Jordy died. The seconds and minutes ticked on invisibly. Alastair rubbed his bleary eyes, staring at the window. He heard Mrs. O'Brien moving about the kitchen, now, and rolled that way.

"Brisk out. Winter's coming," said Mrs. O'Brien, giving the weather report.

Alastair put the chair into reverse and backed out of the doorway. "Fine mood we're in today, I must say!" she threw at him. "No good morning, no nothing!"

He muttered some pleasantry that tasted bitter in his mouth, not caring if Lettie O'Brien heard him or not. Ten o'clock in the morning, Alastair saw by the fireplace clock, as he rolled toward the small sputter of flames, and he was all washed-out. It would be a hard winter for sure, if he survived it, if any of them did. Christmas tolled in his thoughts like a death knell.

Glory came in the front door, soundless as a cat in her sneakers. The cold had put a pink blush in her cheeks. "Say something to me!" he yelled before she had a chance to unbutton her jacket. Glory's lips parted, but she didn't speak. Her violet eyes were as dark as amethysts, and when she sat down on the piano bench, doodling a short trill, her hair hung lankly on her shoulders. Glory's back hunched and in the dim light coming from the fire, Alastair thought he was looking at an old woman, somebody he didn't know.

He shattered the gloom by turning on the lamps, one at either end of the couch, and a huge shadow slipped off Glory, falling to the floor.

"We should have some music, don't you think," he mumbled, but Glory continued to toy with the piano, creating rickety sounds that were as mournful as anything Alastair had heard yet. She's not over Jordy, won't be either for a long time, if ever, ran through Alstair's thoughts. Then she began playing, of all things, Brahms's *Lullaby*.

We're all somebody's children, every man, woman of us, Alastair thought as the piece came to an end and Glory slid around on the bench. Her hands reached up in the air, and the fingers waving made words. Alastair groaned, for Glory said, *my mother . . . wedding gown . . . up in Pittsfield . . . insisting. . . .*

Evelyn was preparing her fatted calf, and Alastair, a bubble of gas rising up his chest, hated Glory's mother as much as he'd hated anyone. More in fact. The foolish woman who didn't understand what she did, moving mechanically from point to point, as unthinking as a tank. But tanks could be stalled, put out of commission, he remembered from Omaha.

"You won't marry him, Glory, so just push it out of your mind," Alastair promised. He sounded authoritative, stern even, pronouncing a statement of fact, which it was in a way, because whatever happened, Alastair would see to it that Glory and the dragon never married. Only he had no notion just how he'd stop that wedding from taking place. Jordy gone, the exits out of New Morning closed up tightly, no help from all the lemmings following along behind Lucas Donnelly singing his praises. Except for Moses no one stood with them. Alastair had even gone over to Dee's again, hoping to reclaim his friend.

His terror of entering Dee's house hadn't blown away, but he faced it squarely. "You're an old buddy of his," Alastair said to Dee, sitting in her living room. The blinds were drawn and every lamp glowed, though it was just going onto a sunny noon. Dee poured herself a cup of tea into which she put a generous dollop of brandy. "Want to join me?" she asked.

No way Alastair would have gotten that swill down. But worse than drinking Dee's concoction was looking at her straight on, when he took the fragile cup and saucer from her. Her hands, Alastair saw before he gazed off at a painting above the sofa, belonged to a skeleton. A frail pelt of skin draped over the bones. Precious little flesh clung to Dee's hands.

The skull from which Dee's voice croaked off-key gleamed. Her cheeks had collapsed, her teeth protruded slightly, but her eyes had sunk far down. Though she'd tied a kerchief around her hair gypsy-fashion, a few wisps had struggled loose. White hair, pure white as snow. Oh Lord, help us! Alastair muttered to himself, before this creature who wore centuries on her.

"Friend to no one," Dee had been saying, but Alastair hadn't heard.

"Say that again," he said.

"Lucas Donnelly's no buddy of mine, Alastair, and I'm not one of his."

"Yet you signed an agreement. There's a contract between you. Contracts are binding." Alastair had a righteous New England soul. A man's word, or a woman's, couldn't be broken, or not lightly. A signature on a piece of paper was holy.

Dee stirred the hot tea with a finger. "I suppose you blame me for being a coward."

Alastair shook his head. "It's not for me to judge," he said softly.

"Thanks for that." Dee laughed. "But I still can't help you."

"You mean you won't."

"Can't is what I said and what I meant," Dee snapped. Her temper frayed even as her body aged. She was old for sure, ancient. More years than I'll ever see, Alastair thought with relief. He feared death, there was no denying it, but it wasn't just life that was important, he saw suddenly. No, it was the kind of life, the quality of that living. Something he should have known, since he had been for so much time a man who'd never walked on his own.

Dee had sent him away, and now he sat in his parlor listening to Glory worrying the piano keys, no more certain of what he should do. He had made promises to this child, but how, how, would he ever fulfill them!

Later, long after Glory left and Mrs. O'Brien had cleaned the house, Alastair went out. The dampness assailed his joints, but he forced himself to roll up and down Main Street and along High. It was another sullied autumn day, more raw than brisk, and the soiled light smudged more than it illuminated. There weren't any shadows, but Alastair, coming back from the Barnes, saw Doc Trump at the end of his drive trailed by an elongated blackness. He started to call out, but Doc turned right away from him, hastily entering his house. Alastair almost followed him in to protest: Enough of this! Physician heal thyself! Help, Alastair meant. But that tactic would have been as futile a maneuver as soliciting advice from Dee, searching for a key in her long involvement with Lucas Donnelly. Doc had to come to his senses himself, decide for goodness rather than indifference. Though Doc now stood at a distance, seemingly oblivious, Alastair, in his heart of hearts, couldn't castigate the physician, accuse him of choosing wrong instead of right. It was more complicated with Doc and Alastair knew it.

A few nights later Mike Boardman stood in the darkness at the end of the path through the green opposite Lucas Donnelly's, thinking there's no hope for it. If he backed off now Milly would never leave him alone. She'd already driven him half crazy with her asking.

So it was that Mike parked behind the Public and let himself in by the back door to sit, lights off, staring through the plate glass at a sleeping New Morning. The big old meat and dairy case hummed away behind him, but otherwise no sound cut the nighttime quiet. New Morning went to bed early these days, and now, nearing on twelve o'clock only a few lights burned around the square. This time of year it was possible to see through nearly leafless trees from Main Street to High. The globe above Doc Trump's door cast its usual halo of whiteness, and an upstairs window in the Whittier house displayed a soft diffusion. A lamp shone in Alastair Wayne's front room, too, but otherwise the square swam in a sea of blackness. Even so, Mike finally let himself out the way he had entered and went around by the alley until he could get to Main through the narrow passageway between the boutique and the bookstore. From there he crossed to the green, and crunched over the dead leaves down the middle path.

The wind lifted, lively one minute, arrogantly whipping the branches, the next curling down, quiet as a friendly cat. Not that Mike Boardman noticed the wind. He wore over his shirt, unbuttoned, an old flannel jacket that had been Jack's and never felt the cold. Gone was the time when the weather mattered. Sunshine or rain it was all bleakness to Mike. All the brightness and clarity had vanished from Mike Boardman's world with the death of first his son then his daughter. For children to die before parents was an awesome wrongness he still had trouble conceiving of, never mind living with. As for Milly, she couldn't abide this grief at all. Mike feared for her sanity, her very life.

So, get to it, he urged himself, eyeing the unrevealing colonial, not a damn thing's getting accomplished if you just stand here motionless as a lamp pole. Still he didn't move except to fold his arms across his chest. Sleeping, both of them, Donnelly and that man of his, if sleep is what they do. As far as Mike knew, all creatures had to take a rest sometime or other, so maybe it was true of the devil also now that he walked the earth as a man. The devil, or the dragon as so many called him for some reason Mike never discovered. Not that it was of any consequence what he called himself; if he was who he was, Lucas Donnelly could do things. He took them, he can give them back, was how Milly put it. Maybe she was right, maybe not, but Mike couldn't live with his wife if he never found out. Day and night Milly refused to let up on him. *Ask him!* was her endless cry.

He took a deep breath, and squaring his shoulders, he crossed the street, pulled aside the little gate, which hadn't squeaked since Emma Tydings died, and strode up the front walk. Nothing good can come of this, Mike thought as he stepped on the porch and rang the dragon's doorbell.

"Tell me again." For the first time in a long while Milly smiled, nothing dramatic, but a definite lift at the corners of her mouth. If Mike hadn't felt so worn out, exhausted to the bone, he could have smiled himself because his wife did. One of the things Mike Boardman had learned these last few months was how much he still loved Milly. Years and familiarity had done their work blunting the peaks of his passion, so he was far from being the hot-blooded stallion he once was, but a solid bedrock of feeling definitely existed in his marriage. So much, in fact, that he gave in to Milly's pleading and had gone off to ask the dragon to bring them back, Jack and Carol. Only Mike hadn't believed in Lucas Donnelly, the devil or not. Now he wondered.

Mike sipped a steaming cup of tea, his third since he'd returned from seeing Lucas Donnelly, and said, "First, I apologized for it being so late, though he just waved that away. I think, day or night, it's all the same to him, because he said, forget it. Nicely, if you know what I mean. And then. . . ."

Milly couldn't sit still on her chair, though he'd related the story so many times already she lost count. She rubbed her work-worn hands together, then started toying with a curl of her hair. By this late hour the neat roll at the back of her head sprouted loose tendrils that fell about her face, softening the wrinkled skin and making her more like the girl Mike remembered. The haunted look in her eyes dimmed as well, and Mike saw hope stir and rise. Oh, dear God, he prayed, don't let me have done the wrong thing for her; but even as he thought the words he realized how ridiculous it was imploring the Lord when he'd just made a pact with the devil.

". . . And after I told him what I'd come for, he invited me to have a brandy with him. But I said no to that," Mike added.

"Because you knew I was waiting to hear what he said, and you wanted a yes or a no to it," Milly repeated, echoing what Mike had told her. By dawn she'd know the story so well it might have happened to Milly herself, though he had refused to let her go along, or even wait in the Public. Man's work, Mike insisted, meaning I have no notion how safe it is. Actually the whole visit had been a pleasant one, no brimstone and fire, no sulfuric clouds. Lucas Donnelly, as glamorous as an *Esquire* model, wore his little white suit and his smile, and puffed another of those little black stogies.

"Well, he said he understood about you being anxious, and I better not dawdle. So that was it," Mike said. A nerve ticked at the corner of his right eye. Mike sensed the rhythmic pulsing but couldn't halt it. Finally he put a hand over it. He ached, so weary he thought no amount of sleep would ever refresh him. But Milly waited, electrically charged, and he tried not to let her see just how close he was to dropping off.

Mike continued, "So Donnelly said it was all taken care of and it was only a matter of waiting a while." Deliberately, after the first retelling, Mike omitted the part about having to sign the piece of paper Lucas Donnelly had placed on the small endtable alongside Mike's chair. He knew what the paper said.

He had slowly read the few short lines, then read them again. But he wanted to forget about what he'd agreed to. Milly didn't mention it and must have put that contract right out of her mind. For an instant Mike quivered with resentment against his wife. He was the one, after all, who had signed his soul to perdition, if the whole evening wasn't just some big joke. Not Milly, him. But as quickly as the rancor rose up in him, Mike stamped on it.

Night was slipping toward dawn, the darkness draining from the sky. A pale faltering light began to stroke the kitchen window. In a few hours he'd have to open up the Public. "Got to get some sleep, Mill," he groaned, rising and pushing back his chair.

"No!" she cried, fright almost standing her hair on end. She leaped up and grabbed his arm. "We've got to . . . got to . . ."

"Got to what, Milly?" But she didn't know what it was they had to do. Mike rubbed her cheek gently. "Let's catch a few winks. What happens, happens, I guess." Milly seemed to have sunk once again in that whirlpool of confusion where she was so often lost now.

"But when will they come home?" she asked softly, guileless as a child. Mike hurt from her helplessness and grief.

The window was lighter now. He put his arm around her and said, "Hush now, Mill, hush." Then he led her through the cruelly empty house, so funereal even with a new day's light, and up the stairs to bed.

It was almost noon when Alastair rolled out of his house. Some days now he never budged at all, made no more effort than to change out of his pajamas and mope about, listening to music, or watching the news on the television set. Half the time if Moses or Glory or Lettie O'Brien didn't stop by, Alastair even forgot to eat. He sank in despair thinking of days passing, flying fast as the wind, so that a whole week might vanish without his being completely aware of it. Other times he'd fill with schemes to thwart Lucas Donnelly's plans, and he'd outline one or another of these preposterous projects to Moses who'd simply shake his head. Then again, Alastair found himself on certain occasions not so much denying the dragon was in town, but pretending he wasn't, that an ordinary

winter was creeping over New Morning. On those days he'd
simply read from dawn until dark. Books on history usually.
The pharaohs, or the Carthaginians, the Russian Revolution.
Alastair would maneuver himself into a different century
entirely, and when, finally, he'd come to, the truth would
strike him a cold blow in the face.

Today he'd awakened too agitated to keep still. He attempted to listen to *Figaro* after breakfast but got no further
than the middle of Act I. As a punishment for abbreviating
Mozart, Alastair got out his ledger and checkbook and paid all
the monthly bills. That boring chore set off pins and needles in
his limbs and he ran a hot bath, which failed to noticeably calm
him down. Finally, his own house a prison, Alastair left.

First he went to the bank to see Theo with whom he had
little contact now. Glory had told Alastair that he'd become
addicted to television when he wasn't reading his financial
papers. That Evelyn talked nothing but wedding plans, but all
Theo did was nod like a windup toy.

Theo sat behind his desk not straight up in his executive
chair but leaning on one elbow, tugging at a forelock of hair. A
newspaper was spread open to the stock quotations, and Theo,
reading, smacked his lips. "Theo!" Alastair barked from the
doorway. Theo looked up. His eyes, magnified behind reading
glasses, swam huge as catfish.

"Alastair," Theo replied.

Alastair realized it was useless to attempt a conversation
with Theo Crowell even before one word was spoken. He had
a lost, disjointed glaze to him. He said, "IBM is down three
points and General Motors dropped four. It's awful!"

Alastair abandoned Theo to his numbers, to the stock
quotations that played like Mozart's music in his head, and
rolled up Main Street under a sky of gray matted clouds. The
temperature hovered in the low thirties with the scent of snow
on the slight wind. Alastair's ears rang from the cold; he should
have worn his hat. A stuffed nose, congestion in the chest, he
could live without right now.

Making his way to the *Eagle* office and a soda, or better, a
cup of hot coffee with Charlie Calman, Alastair saw a crowd
gathered outside the Public. Lena Myers, Bailey Cross, one of
the Enderman boys, Simon Hooper's sister Syl, Mrs. O'Brien.
What's this? he wondered, as one by one they shook their
heads and wandered off.

"Well?" Alastair shouted at Lettie O'Brien who lagged.

"Just imagine," she said, compressing her lips in annoyance. "First time I remember this happening."

"What?"

Mrs. O'Brien jerked a thumb to the door of the Public. Alastair squinted, unable to see anything significant, anything different. Then he read Closed. The sign Mike Boardman hung each night after six and all day on the Sabbath was still in place. Mrs. O'Brien had hit the nail on the head. The Public, except for the recent funerals, kept a reliable schedule. Somebody else is dead, was Alastair's initial thought, but when he said this to Mrs. O'Brien, she shrugged and said, "Who's left?"

Glory came across the square, up to Alastair's chair. "More trouble," he said, taking her gloved hand in his. There were only the two of them now by the Public. Glory saw the sign and, stricken, turned to Alastair. Her lips began to part, moving slowly, as Alastair held his breath. But she must have seen the anticipation on his face, because she drew off her gloves and signed, *What does it mean?*

She's not ready to talk yet, he supposed, trying not to wonder if she'd ever be, and said, "I don't know. We could call Doc and ask if anybody's sick, or just drive out there." But Glory shied from doing that. She had avoided the Boardmans since Carol died. Then she'd sat with the family like some stony, dry-eyed Niobe and never formed one word.

Doc, she signed.

Alastair supposed she was right. They crossed the square through a green so sparse in mid-November that Ebenezer Smythe's marker was visible from the path.

Alastair didn't stop to take off his coat but went straight to the phone. "Public's closed," he said when Doc got on the line.

"That's strange. You know why?" Doc asked.

"That's how come I'm calling you."

"Oh."

Alastair held the receiver away from his ear so Glory could listen to Doc's half of the conversation. "Is anybody sick out there? Mike? Or Milly?"

"Not that I know of. At least they haven't called me."

"Somebody should go out and check," Alastair said, "seeing how things are around here." He waited for Doc to yell that things were the usual, which is what he always did whenever Alastair approached the subject of New Morning, or rather

Lucas Donnelly in New Morning. But Doc surprised him by not saying a thing. Alastair would have supposed Doc hung up, but he could hear him breathing. "Maybe we should call the chief," he said finally when it seemed the silence would last forever.

"No, that's not necessary. I've got a couple of house calls to make later. I'll drop by. Milly's been kind of peaked and Mike's not a hundred percent either," Doc said.

"Why should they be, with both kids dead!" Alastair shouted into Doc's ear.

"Don't blame me!" Doc shouted back into the phone.

Must feel guilty as sin, Alastair thought when he hung up. "We'll wait to hear from Doc. Don't worry before the fact," he said though he worried himself.

At dinnertime, when Doc called back, he didn't sound any too relieved, though he said, "Things seems okay."

"You don't sound like they're okay," Alastair said.

"Now I suppose you're a psychiatrist, Alastair," Doc retorted angrily which told Alastair he wasn't so far wrong. "I just said, Mike's fine, and he says Milly's hunky-dory, too."

"You didn't see Milly?"

"No, I didn't. But I don't expect a man as sound as Mike Boardman to suddenly become homicidal and chop up his wife into kindling!" he cried.

That bad, Alastair thought, and wondered just what it was that had set Doc's antenna quivering.

This time when Alastair hung up from talking to Doc, a sick feeling settled in his stomach. He poked through the pickup meal Glory had made from leftovers in the 'fridge, sending the canned peas and the scrambled eggs from one side of the plate to the other, saying all the while, "Delicious!" And when Evelyn called, pouring angry steam through the phone, Alastair didn't bother to argue with her, he just out and out lied. "Nope, Glory's not here. Haven't seen her in a month of Sundays," he said, crossing his fingers. He knew Evelyn knew he was fabricating and didn't give a damn. "And if she yells at you, tell your mother to shove it!" he suggested, knowing Glory would do no such thing.

Not my mother, Glory signed. *Not biological* she added just as Alastair wondered what she meant. He stared at Glory curiously. Of course Evelyn Crowell wasn't her biological mother. Alastair waited, fork held suspended over the plate to see where Glory was heading. But she didn't go anywhere after that unexpected riff and he had to reach across the table, taking her chin between his fingers, forcing her to look at him.

"What are you trying to say?" But there was no getting Glory to answer. In her own time she'd tell him what preyed on her mind, or she wouldn't. Perhaps it was nothing but the wedding, which was more than enough.

Then Alastair did something that, inexplicably, he had never thought to do before. He asked Glory her personal opinion of Lucas Donnelly, apart from what he did.

She froze into such an utter stillness Alastair, having released her to sit back in his chair, came forward once more, though fearful of offering the slightest touch. In that moment of shuddering silence, Glory's lips quivered and Alastair, expecting her fingers to rise as they always had before, was stunned to hear the first words he ever had from her.

"I think," she said in a rusty quaver, "maybe he's my father."

29

On the surface New Morning appeared much as it always had, but if anybody peered closely definite differences popped out. For one, the town was neater, especially in the square where all the stores were newly painted. Under a cold November sun, Main Street glared whitely. No parking meters on the square and cobbled streets were just about everywhere. Hitching posts had been erected in front of many homes. And the street lights, though electrical, resembled old-fashioned kerosene ones.

There was also a languid, sleepy air to the town, and people moved a bit slower. Time crept lazily across most watches except the moon face in the clock tower where time never moved.

Converesations, particularly those held outdoors, had a tendency to dribble off into silence. Everybody went to bed this fall practically at dusk and rose around dawn. Most people had gotten into the habit of keeping farmers' hours.

No one had the energy that was his before the dragon came.

More and more, in fact, Doc found his patients succumbing to illnesses that were minor in the extreme. Colds didn't just lay people low for a couple of days, they carried them off to the cemetery. It was some medical phenomenon that colds could kill with the efficacy of the old influenza epidemics. Stomachaches acted much the same, and the least little accident invariably turned out to be fatal. Despite Doc's fancy equipment, people died more easily now. With this plenitude of death, the Bells worked around the clock and were grateful until Bob Belwether pricked himself with an embalming needle and passed away from an unstoppable bacterial infection.

Gradually, in more peculiar ways than one, New Morning slid out of the twentieth century and into the eighteenth.

Alastair, at his front window, could see on the diagonal to Main Street, and by squinting was able to pick out the Closed sign still hanging on the Public's door. Three days now Mike hadn't opened the market.

"Nothing's wrong!" Doc protested whenever Alastair called him on the phone. "People are entitled to a holiday!" Not the Boardmans, Alastair thought. No vacation for them, not with Jack and Carol gone. Putting their heads in the oven was more like it. Alastair insisted he was going there alone until Doc gave in.

"Good, we'll go together," Alastair said, presenting himself on crutches at Doc's office door.

"You're a pigheaded old man!" Doc stormed, but he got the Buick out of the garage.

The truth was Alastair hadn't had a minute's peace since Glory spoke to him. Only once, so far, had she given him her words, but that was enough. Oh, Lord, love us! Alastair had thought. Her father, yet! But then, with her fingers, Glory related her dreams. They spun out, apparently, for the poor child, night after night, just like the old-time serials when Alastair was a boy.

Go talk to him! The command echoed in his thoughts. But what would he say? If it's true that you fathered her, why . . . why . . . why what? Alastair hadn't words enough, and besides, the dragon planned on marrying Glory, incest or not.

Her mother apparently was on the run from Lucas Donnelly (or whoever he masqueraded as then) when she drowned. Overboard in the blue Caribbean, all hands lost. Was that the dragon's doing or an accident of some kind? Glory's dreams never revealed which.

Alastair, figuring the rest out, supposed Theo and Evelyn, on their cruising, came along to find a golden-haired child adrift, sea nymph, and scooped her up. Probably the whole business was illegal and they lacked proper papers to prove Glory was theirs. Alastair could imagine Evelyn seizing her only chance at motherhood like a hungry lioness. She'd swat down any objections from Theo, not that he'd protest long. It was undoubtedly love at first sight with Theo.

Alastair, on an ebb and flow of his own, sat upon the front seat of Doc's Buick watching the familiar scenery slip by but seeing little of it. A prickly sensation at the tail of his spine warned that they wouldn't like what they'd find out at the Boardmans. Still, he struggled to keep the reins on his imagination. Reality in New Morning proved to be bad enough, no need in fantasizing worse.

It was, to Alastair's thinking, the worst time of year. The brazen beauty of autumn had faded and the snowy grandeur of winter, which covered so much drabness, had yet to fall. The naked earth, dull brown, stood out in all its vulnerability.

Alastair sighed woefully, for his thoughts had come full circle to Glory. How frightened they—mother and daughter—must have been, on the run from the dragon like two felons. Did they understand what their crime was? Not Glory, a baby then, but the mother surely. What did she think when she went into the water? Had she seen Glory at the rail, watching, unable to help? Did she suppose that Glory would die, too, or that now Lucas Donnelly would get her?

No wonder Glory wouldn't speak again. She must have screamed her way into silence, dumb finally, until Lucas Donnelly stroked her throat with those long slender fingers. It was, however, the mere fact that she owed her newly acquired voice to the dragon that kept her obstinately quiet. Alastair couldn't blame her, not even her promise that she'd never speak if Lucas Donnelly was responsible. Back to muteness for Glory. Only he hadn't wanted to tell her, but the silent time was over. It would be further foolishness to keep her lips sealed when she had the words in her mouth.

From the corner of his eye Alastair caught Doc's furtive glances. Doc was sallow, his coloring bad. He'd lost weight, too, and the skin of his neck draped in a turtle wattle. Doc wore his flesh these days like a man in someone else's suit.

"Cat got your tongue?" Doc said at last. "It's not like you to keep your lips sealed for over a minute and a half."

Alastair's implacable gaze fastened on the windshield, though the town, parting in two wings at either side of the Buick (they were on cobbled Brewster now), blurred like pencil smudges. In a minute they'd be turning off in the direction of Ridge Road, where, well inside the fluid town lines, the Boardmans lived on two acres, uncultivated and uninhabited except for the house, garage, and dog kennel.

Alastair wasn't about to let Doc get his goat. He had more serious matters, God knew, on his mind. Point of fact, he'd have given anything to stop worrying for a while, hand over his multitudinous concerns and just glide. Though he wouldn't, of course, being so responsible—for Glory, New Morning and all its souls, and for those dear dead Omaha ghosts. He would have fretted himself into a prickly rash if he'd relinquished all that worrying even for a second. Whether he was chosen or elected himself wasn't the issue anymore.

Doc tried again. "I'd of thought you'd be blathering a mile a minute."

Won't rile, won't. Alastair sucked the inside of his cheeks but then emitted a loud grunt.

"Say that again," Doc said.

Alastair broke his silence despite an intention to play dead. "Ought to snow soon," was what he said.

Doc grinned and slapped the steering wheel. "Hot dog, now you're a weather forecaster!"

"Oh, shut up and leave me alone instead of trying to send my blood pressure soaring. Fine physician you are, agitating a patient!"

Doc sighed and settled back against the seat. "That's better. Though there really was something the matter with you for a minute."

After that they rode quietly except for Doc hissing more than whistling an unidentifiable tune. No ear, Doc, so that Alastair was glad when they pulled into the Boardmans' drive through the open wire gate. They slowed past the low white-painted kennel sitting off to the side, and twenty or so yards after it, a larger, shingled garage—both doors closed—up to the back steps.

"Funny," Alastair said, frowning. He rolled down his window and listened for a moment. "The dogs aren't barking."

"Maybe they're in the house," Doc suggested, turning off

the motor. He opened the door, but looked around to say, "Dogs don't always yap, you know." Doc didn't care particularly about animals.

"These do. Heard it from Glory. Set up an unholy howling when anybody drives up. And they don't go in the house either. Outside dogs, that's what they are. Four of them, I think." Alastair opened his door too, and as if they had some unspoken agreement, both men waited. There wasn't a sound in the Boardman yard, the silence so weighty they could have reached out and touched it. Then Alastair stretched around to the back for his crutches and levered himself out of the car.

"Don't like this, damned if I do," he muttered as he swung in his crablike motion up the steps. The steps necessitated some tricky maneuvers, but Alastair made it. By the time he struggled up on the narrow porch that was a late, tacked-on addition to the big old house, Doc's fist was beating a rapid tattoo on the wood. He yelled, "Hey, Mike, Milly! Anybody home?"

Nothing stirred in the overcast grayness, not a branch or a blade of withered grass, and the prickling in Alastair's spine grew worse. Doc inched the screen door open and stuck his head into the small anteroom off the kitchen, calling out again. But the silence within was, if anything, even thicker.

"We don't have to do this you know," Alastair sputtered, his voice sounding so loud to his ears he winced.

Doc glanced back. "You're the one who just had to check up on them. Sick, or—" Doc broke off and chewed at his bottom lip. Dead was what he'd almost said. His eyes clouded thoughtfully as he moved a few feet from the door, letting the screen slap behind him. The sudden sound was a violent assault to the quiet, and they waited for the eddies to still before either spoke again. Then Doc suggested, looking about the yard, "Maybe they've gone off somewhere. Up to visit the older boy in Pittsfield. Could be." But it was a feeble attempt at reassuring himself.

"Check the garage if you're so damn sure they went off," Alastair said, as reluctant all at once as Doc to enter the house. Only it wasn't the house that put both of them off. Something was wrong here, they could sense it. Doc, unimaginative most times, was spooked, too. He made constant little motions, tugging at his hat, tightening his scarf, lightly slapping his gloved hands. Now he hopped the steps and with a purposeful stride crossed the drive to the double garage. Cupping his eyes he peered through one of the two rectangular windows in the doors.

"Both cars," he said, straightening.

"Wait," Alastair cried as Doc started to return. "I want to know about the dogs."

"Forget the dogs."

But Alastair had already swung down the steps and loped in his rocky motion toward the kennel. Nobody can get any nearer than a block without the dogs sounding off, he recalled Glory and Jordy telling him. Three shepherds and a mixed breed that Carol once found along Ridge Road. A summer resident's dog, thrown out of the car on the return to the city. It wasn't an unheard of occurrence, but Carol had been so angry. Alastair himself recalled the girl complaining. Two years or so last September, it was. That anybody could behave so cruelly to a living creature made Carol Boardman see red. And then, to think—which Alastair did, though reluctantly—how she hadn't been treated any better, worse in fact, herself.

A wire enclosure fronted the kennel, at least six feet high and carving halfway around to the side. The dogs could reach it through two holes cut into the kennel at either end and covered with rubber flaps they only had to nudge aside. Around to the right was a door to enter the building. It appeared tightly closed, but when Doc touched the knob, the door swung gently away from him.

"No dogs in there," Alastair said softly. But there was something else, he could smell it. A faint, peculiar odor that made Alastair think all at once of Harlan Farrow. He didn't know why, but he wanted to put his gloved hands over his mouth and nose. Alastair hadn't started his lurch across the doorstep yet, but Doc froze and thrust out an arm anyway as if to stop him. He knows, Alastair thought, suddenly terrified. Knows what?

Doc slowly went in, pushing the door back so it clattered. "Wait out there!" he threw at Alastair who ignored him.

He should have listened. Not curiosity, however, but fear sent him forward in Doc's wake. Like a kid, he didn't want to let Doc out of his sight. But, oh, he wished he'd paid attention and obeyed Doc's terse order.

The smell hung in the kennel like a cloud of flies. Even so, Alastair thanked God it wasn't summer. In August the stench would have shriveled a man's insides. As it was, Alastair had trouble holding his breakfast in place.

Doc, who had had all kinds of encounters with violence and death, with the horrors thrown up by life, looked awful. But at least he kept steady where Alastair trembled so violently he was uncertain whether the crutches would support him.

"Who could do *this?*" Alastair croaked. Somehow, though he was the devil, Lucas Donnelly seemed too much the gentleman and far above such wholesale slaughter. Alastair had to remind himself forcibly of all the bloodbaths the dragon had on his record. Even so . . . Alastair shook his head, trying not to look at the dead dogs. They had been split from throat to groin as if cleaved apart by an ax. Their pink entrails were gray ribbons now trailing into the wide pool of dark blood. But the worst of it was that they were laid out together, all four of them, the mixed breed at the end, neatly placed flank by flank. That little touch and their awful, sightlessly staring dumb eyes. Alastair would have bet a buck that the dogs knew who'd done this butchery to them, and they had laid down quietly for it.

"Let's get out of here," Doc hissed through clenched teeth. He spun around abruptly, advancing on Alastair as if planning to decapitate him. Only he gently took the old man's elbow and helped him over the threshold.

"The dog didn't bark," Alastair mumbled.

"What?"

The fusty light had darkened during the few moments they had been in the kennel. An ugly storm brewed in the west, already belligerently slapping the tops of the distant trees. The sky, that way, had blackened almost to night. Alastair, an iron bar across his shoulders, steadied the tips of the crutches in the rutted yard's hard-packed dirt and rubbed at his neck. But between the coat and the scarf, he couldn't ease much of the strain.

"What did you say?" Doc asked again, lightly shaking him.

Alastair's eyes came up to Doc's face slightly unfocused. "The dog didn't bark," he repeated. "Sherlock Holmes. *The Hound of the Baskervilles.*"

"Alastair, not now!" Doc cried.

"No. Listen. He didn't bark because he knew the killer."

Alastair leaned so close to Doc he felt his breath tickle when he spoke. Doc smelled minty. "And those dogs . . . ?"

The wind rose in a sudden gust as Alastair shouted, "Just laid down, trusting, and let some friend kill them!"

"Oh no!" Doc, who had seen everything and then some,

gasped. The cruelty appalled him. Together he and Alastair looked over at the big house. Not one light eased its grimness. The white paint had a yellowish tinge to it, like dead skin, because of the murkiness and the encroaching storm. Yet the nether light couldn't explain how sinister the house seemed. Just a big old house, nobody at home in it at the moment. But to Alastair staring across the yard it made him think: *Haunted*. If he'd come across the Boardman house in some other place, a location in which he was a stranger, he'd have definitely steered clear of it. It reeked, not with the putrid aroma of the kennel, but of something much worse.

Doc must have been having a similar experience because he backed off two steps—as if the house had actually reached out and shoved him. He was breathing through his mouth, and the temperature in just this little time had dropped so sharply his breath clouded visibly in the air. Alastair exhaled a whiteness of his own as he tried to straighten. More than ever now, however, his legs dropped off him like vestigial appendages. He had to glance down to be sure they still hung there and that he hadn't lost them in the few feet he'd swung away from the kennel.

"I guess we better . . ." Alastair, pulling one crutch around, didn't bother to finish. But he never got the left crutch firmly in place before Doc was in front of him. They stared at each other, and Alastair thought, I hope I look better than he does.

"There's no need for us to go in there, Alastair. We're not the police. That's who should check up on Mike and Milly, not you and me. We're civilians." Doc was pleading.

Alastair held Doc's imploring gaze for another second before he nudged him with a crutch. "Move." He had never seen Doc so frightened, and Alastair himself was certainly scared to the marrow, but he still planned on going into that house. As far as Alastair saw it, the house just waited there for no other good reason than that he should go inside and face whatever horrors it intended to throw at him. He knew, beyond any doubt, that there lurked an even more awful discovery in the house than they'd found in the kennel.

Doc stepped half a pace to the right, giving Alastair only enough room to pass him. As he went by he said, "You can wait here if you want to."

"Don't play the hero, Alastair!" Doc snapped. Alastair stopped, swinging slightly between his wooden supports. He

wet his lips which felt dry and cracked. The scent of snow was
stronger now, the storm only minutes from New Morning.
Alastair had left the living room window up an inch, and he
had a vision of returning to a drift of snow on the Oriental. So
be it, he thought, it won't be the first time that old rug's gotten
wet. He swung out another two steps. "Alastair!" Doc yelled
again, and now when he halted, Alastair half turned his head.
He desperately wanted Doc to enter the house with him. He'd
go alone if he had to, but that wasn't heroic, only necessary.
Had to meant for Alastair dropping off the LST into the surf
and charging up the beach bent double; *heroism* would have
been saving Horse and the others, or at the very least, dying in
the attempt.

Alastair failed to find anything to say to Doc. He simply
shrugged and kept going. When he reached the steps he heard
Doc running up behind him, but he didn't look back. He
lurched up the steps and struggled with the storm door—the
inside door itself Doc hadn't bothered to close—but a hand
came over his shoulder. "I'll do it. Get out of the way."

Alastair retreated, allowing Doc to open the door slowly and
hold it aside. But Doc kept his eyes averted from the darkened
interior, murky as a sea cave. Instead, he stared straight at
Alastair as if he hoped he'd change his mind. There was a
longish pause in which it seemed Alastair actually considered
Doc's unspoken request. Only all of a sudden he pushed off
from the porch into the small anteroom. He kept going, and
Doc must have too, the door thudding behind him.

The large, rectangular window above the kitchen sink faced
east, the direction from which the storm was relentlessly
blowing in on them, so that there was even less light in here,
only a dusty cast that covered everything, counters, the big
six-burner stove, the cabinets, and double-door refrigerator
with a patina of cobwebs. It draped also over the two figures
near each other on tall chairs by the kitchen table. In the
haziness the inert, lumpish bodies might have been only
cushions or giant dolls stuffed with sawdust or rags, or maybe
plastic casts, imitation people.

Alastair, at the sight of these vague, motionless shapes,
stopped so short Doc collided into his back, almost knocking
him off the crutches. Doc's breath whistled harshly; Alastair
felt it traveling past his ear. He could also swear he heard the
thundering of his own heart on a rampage of terror in his chest.

Neither man spoke in that hushed second that continued

down the long curve of time for what seemed a lifetime; neither so much as moved a muscle. Certainly Alastair knew he was unable to, that he could do no more than simply wait, just as he had on Omaha. And he felt his soul shrink even as Doc somehow pushed himself into motion, fumbling along the wall searching for the switch.

A blinding light suddenly engulfed the kitchen. Alastair couldn't see, the glow struck so jarring a blow. It was a moment or two before he understood the reason for Doc's strangled cry. But when he stopped blinking Alastair saw in glaring detail the two bodies upright on the ladder-back chairs. And he gagged as if someone squeezed a hand to his throat. He shook, too, so violently the crutches threatened to slip out of his control on the linoleum.

"Aiiiii!" Doc's cry swirled on and on, no end to it, as they stood, touching now, arm against arm, seeking some human reassurance against those *things* propped at the table as if waiting for lunch. Carol and her brother Jack, or what composition of flesh and bones had once gone by those names. Now, who could say who or what they were, dressed in shredded, purplish flesh, plum-colored hollows under their eyes and below their cheekbones, hair as long and green and tangled as the seaweed in Glory's dreams. Their eyes pitted mine shafts, filmy and clouded, pale and strange as exotic flowers. The pupils seemed to have vanished altogether and whatever color their irises had once been, now they were faded and yellowish orange.

The sight of these dead Boardman children struck Alastair dumb, but not Doc, who ceased his frightened yowling to cough, "He dug them up!" And before Alastair could find a reply, he cried, "What for?"

Love, Alastair could have told Doc. Love makes people behave in mysterious ways. Though Mike Boardman retrieving the bodies of his children from the grave was far more peculiar than anything Alastair might conjure up.

"Mike? Where is he? And Milly, what about her?" Doc asked, not taking his eyes from them.

"We better go look," Alastair reluctantly replied, not wanting to do anything but get out of here. Doc had already begun sliding along the far wall of the kitchen, as far as he could manage from Carol and Jack.

It was just at that moment when Carol raised her hand. An arm of the corpse leaning back against the chair, began to lift gradually, jerky as a mechanical part. Alastair couldn't believe what he saw.

Doc saw it too and sputtered, "Lo-ok!"

All at once other pieces and parts of first Carol, then Jack began to shudder and spasm, as if two hands had reached down and yanked invisible strings. But nothing galvanized the dead bodies into shaky motion. Carol and Jack stirred all on their own.

Doc snatched Alastair's sleeve. "Out of here!" he choked, making for the archway leading through to the rest of the house, but without loosening his attention off the dead. Alastair, jolted out of his trance, and fear burning an acid path into his brain, swung the right crutch around, hitting the edge of a cupboard. He managed to shuffle sideways to the edge of the kitchen. Like Doc, he couldn't ignore the dead who weren't completely dead at all. Half dead? Is there such a condition? Alastair wondered. And from far back in his mind a voice answered, yes. *Zombies.* Oh no, not in New Morning! But why not, the dragon is here, and with him comes all manner of creatures, the fanciful and the fantastic, many shapes and creations such as the undead. *Zombies.* Alastair's mind screeched in disbelief. He would have cried out the word to Doc, but he couldn't speak. And then he realized there was no smell; the putrefying, pustulating *things* with the savaged, rotting flesh all pulpy and soft, emitted no stinking odor. The dead dogs in the kennel stank far worse than these two.

The end of a crutch caught the leg of a stepstool and Alastair was thrown off his balance. He crashed into a counter, smacking his upper arm. The pain caused a shower of falling stars in his vision, and he must have shrieked from the sharp hurt and the fear as he slid, a crutch uselessly splaying flat out, sliding to the floor, because Doc rushed back for him. Not like me . . . oh, Lord, I couldn't move at all . . . flat down in the sand . . . so cold . . . couldn't . . . but, oh yes, if I wanted to . . . oh why . . . Alastair's thoughts reeled faster and faster, spinning in a kaleideoscope of colorful memories, all jaggedly interspersed with the horrifying image of the two ivory-skinned cadavers, gas pockets swelling them up, then collapsing. The bony dead, awkward and ugly. *Evil!*

Poor dead Carol. Oh child, Alastair wept, then realized the plaintive whimper stayed in his own head. He might have been dead himself, except for the pain in his arm and upper back like blazing knife slashes, and then his side sizzled too as he lost what little grip he had, striking the floor.

Doc was beside him, exerting such a Herculean effort to lift Alastair up again that his face broke out into a sheet of sweat, his skin slick and wet, and he puffed sour whinnies of breath, but he did manage to struggle Alastair up to some kind of position, straight enough for one crutch to be jammed in his armpit, then the other. Doc's scream slapped him full in the face, "More in the living room! Worse!"

What more could there be, and how much worse than this, dead Carol and dead Jack rising, already out of the grave, here in the kitchen. Even in these few seconds Jack Boardman had unfolded from the chair.

Alastair fled in a flurry of ungraceful motions, awkward as the living dead with their tilting, rocking steps, into the next room, the parlor, where the only light flickered off the last dying embers of a fire in the fireplace. But Doc clicked on the overhead which threw a drenching yellow glow. Milly lay asleep on her back on the couch cradling a red pillow of blood in her chest. Mike Boardman, in the rocking chair to the left of the sofa, had no head, or little of one anyway. His face was a spongy mess, a puddle of blood and mangled, shotgun blasted flesh, a shard or two of bone. And this time Alastair's breakfast rose right up his throat. Alastair threw up a sour mix of orange juice and hot rolled-oats onto the edge of the rag rug where Mike's scuffed work boots were planted. A spume of vomit flew and feathered his green chinos.

The eruption of Alastair's insides threw him once more off his precarious balance, and he spun backward, sprawling onto a settee. He kept a grip on the crutches, however, and no sooner had he fallen than he fought the grip of gravity, flailing. His mouth tasted terrible, like week-old garbage, and his ears rang, cymbals smashing in his head; but Alastair refused to give up, he struggled. No Doc rushing to the rescue. Doc had troubles of his own Alastair saw as he rose yet again, swaying like a storm-struck elm.

The *things*, rolling side to side in an almost comic parody of human ambulation, surged through the archway from the kitchen. Their arms stuck out as if they walked the high wire, and they held their heads angled.

"Get away!" Doc screamed at these two children he had delivered. He was skidding and dancing backward, flapping his hands ineffectually, as if he could shoo them off. But Carol and Jack continued their relentless forward rocking, teeter-tottering advance. Flaps of skin hung in tattered streamers on Jack's neck, and his cheek was split open to the chin. His clothes were singed, charcoaled away in patches; the jeans had burned clear off his legs leaving dark scraps; a bone poked up by his knee. And he had no ears whatsoever. Jack also missed an eyebrow. As for Carol, her nose twisted at an odd tilt it never had in life, and one arm hung peculiarly from the shoulder, the palm of her hand turned backward. Something, perhaps death itself, had eaten a black hole in Carol's chest between the slopes of her breasts, in much the same locale as Milly's flower of blood.

Were they coming for Doc, or for him, or just advancing to their parents, the old dead yearning for the new? Did they think there was some comfort in a lifeless Milly, Mike, too? Or, Alastair wondered, was there a touch that could bring the dead returning? For a moment he felt more sadness than fright. If he had had Lucas Donnelly's throat beneath his arthritic fingers, he would have pressed and committed murder no matter what effort it took. Cheerfully Alastair would kill over this, the Boardmans and their awfulness. The sin was that nothing could be done about it—or not by me, Alastair grieved. The cold chill of hopelessness stroked his cheek.

"Back!" Doc shouted.

Alastair swung to his flank, having no more idea what to do than Doc did. Somewhere behind them was the seldom-used company door. Alastair tried to remember what the front of the Boardman house, which faced the trees, looked like. Was there a porch? Steps? Narrow? Wide? Could he manage his way down them? Oh, how old Alastair felt, tempted in that one instant by the endless sleep of death that Jack and Carol had, through some dragonish device, given up. Or were snatched from. Fools, Alastair wanted to shout at the two apparitions that churned and shook the floors and the rafters of their home, the only house either had lived in before their coffins, the grave is better than this! This death-in-life equation of rot and ugly putrifaction.

Doc was so maddened he growled like a rabid dog, snapping at the Boardman children. Lost was that emotional distance that lay like a Gaza Strip between Doc and his patients. Don't get involved! was his motto, not from indifference, but because of self-preservation. Doc, the physician, however, had van-ished and Doc, the man, foamed at the mouth, spat and hissed at the *things* closing in on him. In an un-Doc-like leap he was at the fire, snatching with a gloved hand a charred though still flaming piece of wood.

"Away! Away!" Doc screamed as he backed to the door. He didn't bother to order Alastair out. It was each man for himself. Alastair saw that, and the selfishness seared another scar in his soul. What would be left of him if he outlasted Lucas Donnelly? Nothing much. A pinch, a snip of who he once was, it seemed now, as he fumbled across the living room, so shaky he skidded and careened in a crippled, old-man spasm, finally smacking against the outside wall. It was only a foot from there to the door. But the door was locked. Alastair couldn't pry it open. He pressed one shoulder into the wall, taking that crutch—the other wedged under his arm—and smashing the glass. Then, not even considering that he might cut himself, Alastair thrust his hand right through to the other side and pulled. As weird as everything else in this house, the Boardman door opened only from the outside.

"Here, here!" Alastair hollered, and Doc shot a glance back. Then Jack stretched out a dead hand and poked Doc's shoulder. Doc's scream was awful. Alastair had to cover his ears. He shut his eyes, too, and when seconds later he inched them apart, Doc had flashed his burning brand like a sword and set a chair on fire, one curtained wall. Jack, too, sizzled, his shirt and seaweed hair. Alastair turned around and pushed himself out the front door, not caring to see anymore, wishing he hadn't seen so much already.

He'd replay all this, the dogs and the dead, Mike Boardman's mess of a face, Milly's blooming poinsettia. All of it, Jack in pieces, shreds, Carol's milky eyes, her bloodless lips, them, it, all . . . forever. No number of years would be enough to forget. He'd at last gotten something so terrible to haunt him as much as Omaha. My own Dog Green, he thought, here in New Morning. He had worked his trembling body out to the porch. There were steps he saw, with narrow treads. It would be a tricky maneuver to arrive safely on the patchy grass at the foot of them, especially since the wood was wet, the first touch of the storm here. Delicate flakes began to drift, dusting the earth. Alastair's breath was clear, crisp, as he began to descend, thinking, what choice do I have? Only Alastair knew as soon as he went down one level, he was too quavery for this. Another step, then another, four more when he slipped.

The left crutch flew, cracking the last step as Alastair

frantically grabbed for the railing, but he missed, and the second crutch followed the first. He slipped, and as he fell his bones hit each of the remaining steps and he felt every one of them, screaming. Only what was his cry compared to Doc's choking screech exploding along with the fire. Doc jabbed his torch into Jack's chest where it stuck, and Jack Boardman burned, flinging an arm of fire on his sister, Carol.

Doc stumbled down the steps and grabbed Alastair, dragging him away from the stairs and the house. Flames shot up the inside of the window.

"Where are they?" Alastair whimpered, leaning against Doc, the two of them on the ground, lying together, holding each other like lovers.

"In there," Doc said, and to Alastair's surprise Doc was crying. So Doc and Alastair sat in the gathering storm, snow falling on them. They sat in the brush, cold but unmoving, until the Boardman house was a pyre of flames, a roaring, dancing incineration. Then Doc half carried Alastair to the car and got him inside and the two of them slowly drove home.

30

The Boardman house burned right down to the stone foundation. The fire department unearthed only charred flesh and bones of Mike and Milly and no more than that of the two other bodies, whose identity remained unknown. Doc Trump put it around town that they were two people in their thirties, a man and a woman, and no one disputed him. Itinerant travelers for sure. Who else could they be. Wanderers caught in passing. Everybody knew the Boardmans fed strangers, showed kindness to any stray who turned up.

Alastair in chewing over the latest tragedy about town made it a point to second Doc. "No other way it could be. Transients." Alastair said this again and again until he almost came to believe it. Oh, how he wished he did!

Only to Moses did Alastair deliver the straight and true story, in the telling of which he shook so, Moses thought he was having a heart attack. Doc, called, came racing over. But Alastair warned Moses not to breathe a word of what he'd said, for Doc's sake. No use stirring it up, the two of them just became so upset they couldn't think. All shivers and bad dreams. Doc went further. He lost weight; his cheeks began to sink in; his breath soured. Even Ava noticed and fed him more than he could eat. Each night after supper Doc threw up, but he never shared this distressing information with a soul. After a week or so, Doc took his own tests, read up, and diagnosed his disorder. Then he tried not to think about it.

Doc struggled also to forget the Boardmans and what had happened out on River Road. He said to himself in an ongoing litany: *I believe the fabrication*, but he didn't believe it any more than he believed he could transform cancer into Asian flu. In fact, Doc dreamed of Mike and Milly, the *things* the children had become, and of course the dogs. In some peculiar way the dogs were more horrifying than the others.

Lucas Donnelly's responsible. Those were the only words Alastair uttered going home in the car. Doc said nothing. Now he didn't know. This kind of demonic power was yet a third item Doc attempted to restrict from his thoughts.

Doc thought of little else than the Boardmans, his own dying, and Lucas Donnelly. Each day when he arrived at the tiny hospital, he did a tour that took fifteen minutes, no more, and when he finished he sat in the examining room and worried. He read the letters on the eye chart and considered that words were only combinations of small, insignificant little parts, and that if one never put letters into predetermined sequences, no language would ever get written down. Which translated to mean, if he kept his worries as individual elements they wouldn't depress him as well as scaring him half to death. But it was exactly this which Doc couldn't do. Then, he'd make another round of the hospital and go home.

Doc hated to see patients these days, for when he did, he'd think: *I must save lives.* Each human's mortality hung on him like a flimsy garment. Yet his own was flimsier. Doc didn't believe in a soul, but he didn't *not* believe in the existence of such a thing either. And if each person possessed a spiritual inner lining beneath the mortal casing, Doc had reason to consider his own. Again, round and round Doc would go until he'd retire to bed, where his hairy, slowly shriveling shanks would press up against Ava's plumpness for warmth. Oh Lord, Doc—a man who held dubious views on the existence of

God—would pray before dropping into the deep black hole of sleep.

So it went for Doc until one day he woke up and knew he couldn't go on like this. Many people are resolute when getting out of bed but fall back by the time they brush their teeth. Doc, rigorously trained and a true professional, was different. Doc acted. He came out of his house an hour later and instead of going around to the back to the garage for the Buick, he strode down the front walk. Turning left, he continued along High Street to Lucas Donnelly's where he rang the doorbell.

The dragon answered himself, immediately, and warmly greeted his guest. Lucas Donnelly looked pleased by the visit, in fact he said, "I couldn't be happier." Even when Doc refused to cross the threshold, the dragon held his radiant smile. Inside or out on the porch it seemed as if nothing gave Lucas Donnelly more pleasure than a few words with Doc.

Doc said, "I can't countenance this a minute longer, stuck I mean, between here and there. Not taking a position, coming down on the right or the left. Making a commitment to one thing or another, a person or a job, a family, a country, a cause, or the right way of behavior over the wrong. That is life, Mr. Donnelly, or life as it should be. For an honorable man anyway. The end doesn't justify the means you see, which means I must repudiate you. Take back the hospital. Lives saved by the devil's intervention are wrong." With that, Doc made an abrupt turn and stepped off the dragon's front porch. If Lucas Donnelly had any retort, Doc closed his ears to it. Useless barbs might have been flung at his back, but being no fool, Doc never looked behind him.

That, supposedly, was that, and he said so, relating the story to Alastair. Now he couldn't retreat from what he'd stated, not that he meant to. Having told Alastair made it a *fait accompli*.

Alastair should have been jubilant over Doc's retreat from Lucas Donnelly but however amenable the dragon had seemed to Doc, there had to be a further reckoning. He wasn't known for allowing people he counted as his own to change their minds and escape his net. Oh no, not the dragon. Nothing good would come of this, Alastair thought, but kept the dark foreboding to himself. He told neither Doc nor Moses.

There was, besides Doc's repudiation, much to think about this late November day. For one thing, Will Austin had announced at the end of Sunday's sermon that there would be a special Thanksgiving service. All members of the Congregational, and guests of course, were invited to attend. The imperious way the minister made the announcement seemed to imply they had better come, or else. Or else what? Alastair wondered, listening to Handel's *Messiah* and waiting for Glory.

Glory usually appeared right after breakfast and stayed the day. If Evelyn had an inkling where the girl was hiding out, she couldn't prove it. Count each little blessing, Alastair thought, settling in his chair by the front window. From here, in winter, he had a fairly clear view of the Crowells'. The day was cold, the house overheated, and Alastair dozed so he missed seeing Glory leave her porch and march down the block.

Glory had slept late, dreaming. The dream wasn't, for a change, of the sea and the sailboat, or of the woman with blond hair the same as Glory's, who'd been her mother and who had, Glory believed, run from the unholy alliance with Glory's father, but of a castle and a tower, and some far-off sexy voice— like James Dean's in old movies—calling.

Glory, awakened, took the scissors from Evelyn's sewing basket and went out the front door.

"What possessed her?" Moses would ask later.

Alastair entertained no logical notion, though he always listened carefully to whatever Glory said in one of the three methods of communication which were hers these days. He read her thoughts as though her mind was a slate, his ability, which had been occasional before, suddenly real. Her hands, of course, she still spoke with those. And now and again, sound crossed her lips.

Today, Glory said nothing to anyone, and even Evelyn missed her as she went, barefoot, in cutoffs and a T-shirt, looking much as she had on that Caribbean sailboat, only older, along High Street carrying the scissors. It was cold and damp, but Glory, dressed for summer, felt no chill on her journey to the front of Lucas Donnelly's house. She stood, outside the picket fence, plainly visible from any of several windows, listening to the whispers that no one but Moses— and once, poor dead Bobby Pierson—had ever heard. Perhaps the rustling voices told her to do what she did which was to lift the long hair that hung to the small of her back and to sheer it close to the scalp. Around her head she went with the clippers, snipping, not bothering to trim evenly, until she had mowed down to a yellow thatch. Golden hair fell about her. She had turned, ready to walk away, when the whole of Lucas Donnelly's house seemed to explode. Fire swelled up in a wave, singeing the bare elms. Something set off a muffled bang behind the walls, as well as a terrible, machine-gun popping, and then the dragon's outraged howl: "What did you do that for?"

Glory let Alastair know she'd cut off her hair because the dragon loved it so, that if he was determined to have her, she stubbornly determined to devalue what he so desired. *I don't want to be a princess,* she said with her hands, *I just want to be a girl!*

"Lucas Donnelly has awakened Glory with her memory returning as well as her voice, and is getting what he never bargained for," Alastair told Moses over a pickup supper that night, just as he'd told Doc on the phone earlier.

Moses left the table, going to the refrigerator, shaking his head. "Whole business is hopeless," he muttered, reaching in for another beer.

Alastair steepled his hands as he said, "We can't think that way. It's us against the dragon." Alastair, his hair mussed, his shaggy brows standing up straight, looked like a mental case, but he sounded adamantly sane.

Moses, from the far side of the kitchen, cried, "Who's this *we?*"

"Why you, Moses, and me. Doc, too, maybe. Glory for sure."

Moses chugalugged the whole Schlitz before he returned to breathing, sighing more from despair than satisfaction. "Alastair, I'm an old man. Older than you even. Old enough if it comes to it to be your daddy. And I've got to consider leaving."

"Leaving?" Alastair cried, hanging on to Moses with his burning glance.

"I can't see Lucas Donnelly giving it no mind whether I'm in New Morning or up Pittsfield way. Maybe down in New York City where I haven't stopped for a hundred years, give or take. Might be time to go another direction, renew acquaintances, listen to some Dixieland. Since he hasn't ushered me off the planet, I expect I've got more time on my plate."

Alastair was stricken. He was like a man who finds the solid ground beneath him has turned to quicksand. "Moses!"

Moses's eyes roamed the kitchen, everywhere but to Alastair's pleading face. The silence pulsated. Moses threw the empty can into the trash with a trembling overhand.

"You can't say so long and walk out of town, Moses. It's fate. It was meant," Alastair pleaded, his own fire of panic beginning to blaze. "Listen, I'll think up some plan."

"Oh, Lord, a plan!" Moses said, wandering to the 'fridge for another Schlitz. "Don't tell me about no plans. We're not a couple of kids playing cowboys and Indians. This is the devil . . . serious stuff." He deposited his skinny flanks on a chair by the table, sipping the Schlitz this time. "If he ain't burned us up, it's just dumb luck. But how long's that going to last?"

"A little longer, Moses. To Christmastime anyway." Alastair throbbed with intensity. His hair bristled from static electricity. The very air was charged.

The minutes hung, then dropped away, and Alastair shifted painfully about but his eyes glittered bright as harvest moons. He wouldn't give in.

Suddenly, Alastair had a vision, as if the future could pass before one as effortlessly as the past. And in it he saw a patch of New Morning blue sky. It was summertime, but nothing drooped and looked sandbagged by the heat. A house and a yard, children, three of them, two playing in a sandbox, one riding a bike. Glory's old Peugeot, or the Peugeot that would be old by then. She came out of the house, a modern rectangle, and Jordy, never having died, followed her. In this future time Jordy had survived and he was stouter, filled out. Glory, as beautiful as ever, had crow's feet dancing at the edges of her eyes—happy lines. It was Glory who called out in a lilting alto to the boy on the bike, "Alastair!"

Alastair rubbed a gnarled hand across his stubble, catching prickly tears on his knuckles. Oh, what he wouldn't give for such a future to fall into place. But it wasn't real; it wandered off, only a fantasy. Alastair sorrowed.

Moses, his hands running around the beer bottle in nervous motion, was broadsided by Alastair's tears and he pulled back. "Suppose you're right. Don't know what I was thinking of." Moses squirmed, as if he viewed his own visions on a screen in his head. "I guess I'm plum frightened, and the scare's worse every day."

"Why should you be different?" Alastair said.

* * *

Moses had gotten into the habit of dropping by every evening, before dinner or after. Alastair didn't know it, but Moses was ashamed. The threat he had made to desert preyed on him. Fear was a powerful prod and Moses had almost bolted and fled. This fright saddened him.

Moses also worried, not about himself so much as over Alastair. In some ways Alastair might be a hard man, but in most he was fragile. Alastair could easily break.

Moses was solicitous, offering to run errands, do the grocery shopping, drive out to the Papriakas stand for some special treat. Then too, he took to bringing over some jazz for them to hear. And the evenings, for an hour or so, came to be oases in the middle of the terror.

"Getting late," he said a few nights later as he removed a recording by Sidney Bechet from the stereo. "You need your shut-eye." Moses fretted like a nanny. He worried now over Alastair as much as he did dead Miss Emma, though he called himself stupid, and worse than that, for his worrying.

How much could the man stand? Moses wondered, watching Alastair. Alastair hunched in the corner of his chair. He looked smaller each day, each day more frail. Watching him, a tide pool of fear slogged in Moses's chest.

"Sleep, tuck in for the night," Moses encouraged.

Alastair sighed his consent. Without seeming to, Moses deftly raised Alastair up on his crutches and got him along the hall to the bedroom. Moses went off to the kitchen for a Pepsi, allowing Alastair time to perform his ablutions and get his unreliable body into a nightshirt. Then Moses reappeared, pulling up the blankets, tucking Alastair in like a child. Alastair wouldn't protest, feeling grateful, though he'd never speak of such a thing, nor would Moses. This little intimacy they performed, working it into a nightly ritual, pleased both of them when almost nothing else did these days.

Once Alastair's light was off, the door left ajar, Moses wandered through the house, sometimes staying on the couch. Tonight he couldn't decide whether to go home or not, so he drifted, finally running aground by the window where he glanced out at High Street. Through the naked branches a pale spill of light provided glimpses of the gauzy ethereal forms, the shapes of horses and hard, mean-faced honkies. In the black and white nighttime street, the ghostly shadows rode sound-lessly by, on their way to Miss Emma's.

The nape of Moses's neck prickled and he suddenly grew

frightened. His memory quivered, undulating. As a great wall
of snow would sometimes split off Madder's Hill in the first
thaw, so did his remembering break apart. Forgotten in the
slide was Miss Emma's demise, or even Alastair slumbering
behind him, never mind present time. Days, years, centuries
collided, collapsing in on one another, and in Moses's mind the
men on the horses—*white men!* sent by slavers—had been
riding hard from North Carolina and were here now, advancing on the Tydings colonial. They knew, had found out
somehow, of this station, this laying-in place. They intended to
take his people away, binding them in chains together, and
who knew what harm they'd perpetrate on Miss Emma.
Abolitionists were considered even lower than colored slaves,
were spawn of the devil. Abolitionists deserved whatever
foulness was done to them.

Moses' saliva dried up, his ears rang, and in the lifeless
street he watched the riders trot away, but still he failed to
unglue himself from the pane. He stuck fast, up against the
window, his breathing shallow. They were hidden between the
walls and back of the cellar shelves. Bounty hunters never
would move all those canning jars, never mind search all the
tidy crawl spaces. Miss Nancy was hidden under the floorboards of an upstairs closet, and Rufus Abelard, dark as an
African, was buried in the coal bin, so Moses told himself.
Time scrambled in Moses's head, for way back then, during the
slave days, no furnace had existed in the Tydings house, and
forget about a coal bin.

The bounty hunters . . . come to get 'em. . . . What to
do? Terror whiffled through Moses as he quietly swallowed his
sobs.

"Save her!" The mahogany great-grandmother materialized
at his elbow. "You is promised!"

I'm no such thing, Moses started to think, but even as he
protested, his body was in motion as he fled from Alastair's
house. On High Street his walk broke into a run. Though
Moses took the sidewalk in a loping stride, moving as fast as he
could away from her, the grandmother clung to his side.
"Hurry!" she cried. Moses didn't have to be told twice.
Already the colonial at the end of the green was alight like a
Christmas display. Each window framed a square of flickering
yellow flames. *Fire!* Moses ran harder.

The wind, having played dead most of the night, picked up
and began to rise in a gale. The trees rattled as Moses passed

them, what brilliantly colored leaves were left on the ground swirling up in spirals. A dusty curtain lifted off the ground and flung itself into Moses's eyes. Blinded, he never ceased his hurrying.

Blinking rapidly, he finally focused again, and through a watery glaze he saw that a crowd had gathered around the Tydings colonial, a hazy congregation of translucent shapes. Their cries were moans, their voices hollow sounding. Moses, in his flight, passed through the gathering, and burst without thinking into the house, once more Miss Emma's and not a place of residence for the dragon. The entrance hall had the same peeling wallpaper Moses remembered, the old rag rug by the foot of the steps. Miss Emma's ancestors hung crooked on the walls again as Moses fled by them, taking the stairs two at a time. He seemed to fly, never touching the boards underneath his work boots.

Smoke clouded the air, thickening into a cotton Moses had trouble inhaling. He choked on the acrid taste, and thumped his chest, galloping even faster. In a second, he arrived at the top of the stairs.

The great-grandmother must have left him below because she no longer sentried his elbow. Invisible, too, were the bounty hunters, though he heard the stamping of their thick-soled boots, and someone yelled, "Get the nigger!"

Not me, not old Moses who is planning to live a long while yet, passed through his head. Nobody was about to get him, take his soul and flesh south in chains. Not Moses, nor kin of his, *never!* But that was for later. Right now, the big house was a blazing Bessemer furnace. Old, dessicated, the timbers crackled, the walls melted away. The colonial was rapidly becoming ashes, and Miss Emma still waited in here somewhere.

Moses raced along the second-floor hall in a whirlwind of motion. He panicked with the heat blistering his face. His hand sizzled when he grasped a red-hot doorknob.

No Miss Emma in the upstairs parlor. Moses kicked open the next door. A fiery blast roared out at him with a flaming tongue, singeing him, but still he plunged inside. No Miss Emma in this bedroom either. He hurried on his search. To the next room, and the one after that, until he lost his way in the smoke. The whole house now was an inferno.

Slowly Moses started to falter, coughing, choking. Not enough air. Black spots dappled his vision. His legs gave way and he crawled down the Oriental runner, knowing this was foolishness indeed. Stay upright, out of the worst of the smoke! And he clawed at a doorframe, pulling himself to a standing position. He stumbled then on to the room at the front of the colonial, trying to push aside the smoke and flames.

All remembering was gone from Moses's mind now. He held one thought and one thought only: *Save Miss Emma!* He had forgotten Alastair Wayne whose condition recently unsettled his stomach; and Lucas Donnelly might never have entered New Morning. Glory Crowell and poor dead Jordy were also obliterated. The pleasures of gage and jazz music passed from memory, as did mowing and weeding. Likewise his ramshackle home and his considerable savings. Moses flung himself with all the strength he had left, into the bedroom that had been Miss Emma's.

There she sat, cross-legged on her patchwork quilt, her hair mossy. Miss Emma smiled. She was younger than Moses remembered, but then he was younger himself. It was definitely Miss Emma Tydings though, just as Moses dreamed her, up here in her bedroom where she had accomplished her solitary slumbering for close to a century.

"Miss Emma!" Moses cried with almost his last breath. "I has come to save you!"

Emma Tydings's smile widened, exposing a gaping blackness in her face. Miss Emma had forgotten to put her teeth in, but Moses couldn't wait. He hurtled into the inferno that was fast closing in on the old lady. Flames ate away the corners of the bedding, fired up the four posts. In one long stride Moses was beside her, lifting that bundle of weightlessness in his arms. As Moses held Miss Emma Tydings off the ground and the bed for an instant, held her safe from the flames, as the burning walls burst apart, all his ancestors emerged into the light. They glowed, their dark skins shining. But Moses didn't halt to watch the smiles transform their faces. He plunged through the other flank of fire to the window, gripping Miss Emma tightly.

Someone down below to catch her, that was necessary now, for a wall of fire pulsed behind them, licking up Moses's shirt, engulfing him. The flames ran wickedly along his rib cage as he thrust Miss Emma out the window, held her over empty space, screaming for a net to be stretched beneath her stockinged toes. But the old woman wouldn't let go. She clasped his wrists as tightly as bounty hunters' chains.

A lattice of shadows spread across the lawn, under Miss Emma's window. The sidewalk met the edge of that, and beyond the people. All New Morning clogged the streets in crinolines and hoop skirts, black hats and waistcoats, chanting, "Jump, Moses! Save her!"

Moses, burning, his arms bent like twigs that threatened to snap loose from the sockets with the burden of old Miss Emma Tydings, had no choice but to go out too, otherwise he'd lose her. So Moses, with Miss Emma clasped in his arms, stepped free into the void.

31

Alastair was rolling across the gravel ignoring the pathway of hard-packed earth, and up the slight rise of stiff yellow grass. Who would cut it now? He pushed into second gear, which gave the chair the little extra it needed to gain some purchase on the slippery incline, dampish from the frost. There had been a silver glaze on his own lawn just after dawn, but now, almost eleven, the day had warmed up, not much, just enough to melt the frost to a chilly dew. Glory lagged behind him. They were making an awful habit of coming out to the cemetery this fall. Alastair remembered he hadn't attended Bobby Pierson's funeral back in the summer, but he'd come for all the others. Why had he missed poor Bobby's burial? He couldn't recall, but felt guilty all the same. Just take up residence out here, save the traveling, he thought, his temper frayed, his heart so heavy it pinned him in the wheelchair.

Ah, Lord help us! Moses! Alastair still couldn't take it in, Moses Llewelyn dead, found facedown on Lucas Donnelly's front walk midway between the porch and the picket fence. Broke his neck, Doc had said, but he didn't know how.

Your business, your doing, Alastair bit his tongue to keep from yelling at Lucas Donnelly, who must be with the knot of mourners graveside, because there was his car.

Something detonated beneath the chair wheels, snapped in the quiet like a firecracker. Alastair jerked around. For a moment he thought the twig was a snake. It wouldn't have surprised him to find the dragon traveling again in his earliest disguise. But it was just a splintered branch, Alastair saw. He took a deep breath, trying to settle his nerves.

The crowd at Moses's internment was sparser than for the Farrow triple-header or the Boardmans', and that depressed Alastair, too. Not that old Moses would care. Dead is dead, he'd have shrugged, but that was before the dragon. Now dead had a different significance. Look at Dee.

Dee never came out of her house anymore, at least Alastair hadn't seen her. Yet, unless he was mistaken, there she stood, bundled from head to toe like a Moslem wife. It was colder, raw and bitter at the tail of November, winter if not officially. An icy wind promising snow whirled over the cemetery angrily. Alastair's bones ached. He shivered in his heavy coat, pulled his muffler more securely about his neck. Dee, muffled in layers of material, her face hidden by a wide felt hat and a scarf, stood lifeless as a tree, still and wooden. But it was Dee, he knew it, for the mysterious figure inched a glance his way and Alastair recognized the eyes.

Inconceivable that the mummy so hidden had appeared to him six months ago as a girl.

The wind, having momentarily died down, rose and careened across the hummocks, stiffened coats, threatened hats. It flung itself on Alastair and ruffled Glory's hair in a froth. A pneumonia wind, Doc had called it earlier. Alastair wondered which New Morning resident the breeze might carry off, and wouldn't have been surprised if it was him. After he'd gone who'd be left to protect Glory? Alastair prayed a silent prayer he'd last to Christmas, for if he died defending this child for whom he felt a father's love, death would be justified. Perhaps not a wondrous finale, but an end worth several candles lit in his name.

Alastair couldn't help feeling a kinship with Theo, the father who courageously crossed over the glassy sea in a dinghy from his boat to that other. Theo, intrepid no longer, couldn't rescue Glory a second time. Theo sat these days in the big First National office, his nose glued to the ticker tape. His whole memory was glutted with numbers. It was only a matter of time before the auditors turned up. Theo continued pledging New Morning money like a drunken sailor in a foreign port; if they ever rid themselves of the dragon, the town would be bankrupt.

Will Austin garbled the prayers which he surely should have known by heart now. He roared the usual "from ashes to ashes" and ran his Latin together in one long mumble. Lucas Donnelly had seen fit to pay his last respects as Alastair thought, and there he was, tall and straight as a Babylonian monument, his black curls uncovered to the elements. For the first time Alastair could remember, he wore something other than a white suit. For Moses's burial he came dressed all in black. Wasn't at the church though, Alastair recalled. Alastair cocked a brow for he'd just realized he'd never seen Lucas Donnelly in the Congregational. Not once. Perhaps the church was out of bounds. Perhaps! No perhaps about it, the church was the enemy camp. Alastair tucked this tidbit of information away for further thought.

The brief service ended and the small crowd broke apart. Not much of a send-off, Alastair sorrowed. But he'd paid his own respects last night all alone in the house with a glass of Schlitz and Louis Armstrong on the stereo.

Glory took Alastair back to the Dodge, then he drove to the house. Sitting once again on the piano bench, Glory took from a pocket the four-leaf clover laminated in plastic that Moses had given her early in the fall. She laid it on the piano when she played a soft concerto by Bach. That behind her, she picked up the lucky charm, rubbing it between her fingers. Her gaze was limpid, violet pools of sadness. Glory had just performed her own farewell to Moses.

"Speak to me," Alastair urged.

She tucked the four-leaf clover into a pocket of her dress and used her fingers. *He made me able which is why I don't want to do it.*

"That doesn't matter," Alastair answered. "It's your voice."

Having cut off her hair, Glory found no refuge to hide her when she lowered her head. He saw the smooth curve of her cheek, the fine curl of her ear. She looked Grecian, a face on an urn. He thought of her as Echo, as Niobe, and knew whatever chance he had to save her was minimal. More than likely, Lucas Donnelly would get him, too. The short pain in his chest reminded Alastair forcibly of his condition. Without meaning to, he glanced quickly at the clock on the mantle. Time, he thought, as his glance moved up the wall to the mounted samurai sword. It had hung as long as Alastair could remember, just there, so much a part of his daily existence he forgot it. An instrument of death and one of honor, the sword had been brought back by the seafaring Wayne. He used to wonder as a small boy if anyone had ever heaved it, the slippery blade polished to a mirror shininess. The hilt, of some dull metal, had an intricate series of designs etched in it, winding, viny patterns. The sword, so finely wrought, had a delicacy to it, yet the one time, years before—he must have been about ten—he had lifted it; he found the blade so heavy, it dove to the ground like a diviner's rod.

He wheeled over to the piano and lifted himself from the chair to the bench. My arms are strong, he reminded himself, thinking he could hold the sword and swing a killing blow with it, take off Lucas Donnelly's head. But what good would that do. Like a hydra he'd just grow another one.

His fingers poised over the keys, he tensed, then leaned forward and the first notes of the *Requiem* slipped sadly from beneath his fingers.

"And furthermore," Doc was saying, "I don't think you should go to the church at all."

"Of course I'm going!" Alastair cried from his corner of the sofa. "There's nothing wrong with me! You said so yourself."

"Nothing more than is usually wrong." Doc sniffed, snapping his black bag shut.

I'm going to kill Lettie O'Brien, Alastair thought, because his cleaning lady had decided he looked peaked and told Doc Trump. Doc came right over and took Alastair's blood pressure, listened to his heart. He even stuck a tongue depressor halfway down his throat and thumped his chest.

"Well, if I'm in my usual state of failing health, there's no reason I can't go to Will's Thanksgiving service," Alastair said.

Doc sighed. "Go ahead, see if I care. But for God's sake, keep your dander down."

Doc didn't look all that well himself, Alastair thought. His skin was the pasty color of mucilage. His hair needed trimming. The tiniest tic beat in quarter notes at the corner of his mouth.

"I expect you're going, too," Alastair probed.

Doc shrugged. "Why not?" He sounded less than happy about it. Probably Ava insisted.

Alastair wouldn't have minded a strong cup of tea, but he lacked the energy to brew it, and he certainly had no intention

of asking Doc, who probably had important things on his
agenda, though he'd made no move to be off. He sat upright in
the chair with his hands on his knees and stared off into space.
What horrors did he see? The Boardmans maybe? Or old
Moses Llewelyn with shattered vertebrae? There wasn't
enough money in the world to bribe Alastair into asking. He
simply sat still himself and brooded along with Doc. After a
while, when it became obvious Doc intended to stay, Alastair
said, "What do you think Will's up to with this special service
of his?"

"What could he be? No matter how dopey Will is, he's still a
Congregational minister, duly ordained. A leader of souls, for
Christ's sake," Doc said.

"That and a nickel, as we used to say, will buy a bag of
gumballs." Alastair had no faith in Will Austin and he wouldn't
have followed him into the Super Saver if they were giving out
free roast chickens.

"We'll see." Doc started to lumber up to his feet. The strain
in his face made him look as though he were running the four-
minute mile instead of just getting out of a chair. His arms
shook and he dropped back down. "Lemme just take a nap for
a couple of minutes, then I'll go over with you," Doc wheezed,
falling instantaneously asleep.

The church was packed when they got there. More people
than ever came to Sunday service had crowded into the
Congregational, more people than Alastair thought lived in
New Morning. Denomination or religious persuasion apparently had nothing to do with those in attendance, because the
Papriakases were there, all of them, strung out along one of
the side pews. The Myerses had come also—Teddy in his
baseball uniform, though it was long past the season—and
Aaron Stein sat in the center of one long pew with his wife and
kids. Aaron seemed right at home, not like a visitor to the
church for the first time.

Doc rolled Alastair up the center aisle. Alastair had wanted
to use the crutches, but he lacked the strength. The flesh, fine
state of health or not, drooped weakly again, and Alastair's
arms trembled. He feared he wouldn't be able to hold himself
up.

Finding a seat was no easy matter. "Doc, honey!" Ava Trump

called as they passed her. Doc stared at the rouged and painted face of his wife, wedged between Vera Dickson and Delmar Montrose. She shrugged her shoulders helplessly and smiled, the pink tip of her tongue darting out like a snake. Tried to save you a seat but couldn't, she seemed to be pantomiming.

"That's all right," Alastair barked, but Doc only gave Ava a quick nod of his head. His lips spasmed in what could have been either a scowl or a smile, and he glared at his wife with a ruffled brow as if trying to dig her name up from his memory.

It was difficult to see clearly in the Congregational with all the lights doused. What illumination pooled in a vague yellow lucency glowed from two banks of flickering candles at either end of the altar. Black candles neatly aligned in towering silver candelabra.

Except for the candles the church seemed no different. There hung in the air a weak scent of incense that Alastair supposed came from the burning candles, too. And at the center of the altar, behind the pulpit, where the big wood cross had been, far too lavish a symbol for the whitewashed, simple church, there was something else, an object draped with a black cloth. In the dancing shadows it was impossible to make out its shape. All Alastair could say for certain was that it appeared to be large.

Toward the front Doc found a seat for himself with Alastair parked next to him in the aisle. In the first row and over to the left he saw the Crowells. Glory hunched, trapped between them, and when she turned her head to look at Alastair, Evelyn sent an elbow into her ribs. But Glory rose up from the pew anyway, and before either of her parents understood what she meant to do, she had come around by Alastair. Doc, seeing Glory, hissed at the Winslows next to him to push over. "Move if you have to, but we need another seat."

In a second Evelyn was onto them, leaning over Alastair in his wheelchair as if he were no more animate than a fireplug. "You come back this very minute and sit with us," she snapped. Glory never turned a hair, even when Evelyn reached out and pinched her arm.

Alastair removed Evelyn's hand as though it were a smidgen of lint, saying, "Glory's fine where she is."

Evelyn seethed with a quick, viperish intake of air, but she pulled up, and having to have the last word, flung "Interfering old fool!" into Alastair's face. Then she marched up the aisle.

It was close in the church with so many people, and Alastair,

growing woozy, gave silent thanks that things seemed about to
get underway. At least the monkish choir, slap-slapping their
thong sandals, entered from the sides in two wings. There
couldn't be a stranger among them, but hidden under so much
material, Alastair had no idea who was who.

Doc whispered. "Where's Donnelly?"

It was true, Alastair realized, quickly glancing about the
church. Lucas Donnelly was nowhere in sight. "Never at-
tends," Alastair whispered back, across Glory.

The crowd rustled as Will Austin made his entrance. He too
wore monks' garments, but the cowl was thrown back and his
white hair shone unnaturally, as if some hidden beam angled
down to illuminate him.

Will Austin lifted his arm and the chorus began to sing. As
Alastair might have predicted, the selection accompanied by
Will's pride and joy, the harpsichord in the choir loft over the
rear of the church, was in Latin. So the only words he could
comprehend were those strung out and held taut. *Domine*,
which couldn't be right, and *infernus*, which sounded worse.

Listening to Will's chorus, their gravelly tones disharmoni-
ous, Alastair stirred with a sadness that plumbed his soul. How
silly it was, all of New Morning lumped together in this
overheated church to listen to chants in a dead tongue more
appropriate to Europe in the Middle Ages than New England
at the last quarter of the twentieth century.

True madness, these predilections of Will's, though Alastair
supposed the dragon was accountable for the minister's giving
in instead of continuing to repress. And whatever Will planned
for this evening would be not only an ecclesiastical affront, but
an insult to all of Christendom. Heresy for sure, Alastair felt
certain. And who would object? On every face there dwelt
either an expression of stupefaction or one of acceptance. If
Will elected to slaughter one of Bailey's cows on the altar, not
one voice would rise in protest.

So far the service, incomprehensible, filled Alastair with
ennui rather than outrage, but suddenly, in a bounce, Will,
agile as an acrobat, leaped to the rear and whipped the cloth off
what turned out to be the old cedarwood cross, but now set
upside down. At the center was scribbled lettering and what
might have been a twisted vine. In some magician's trick Will,
waving the black material, started a cloud of smoke swirling, as
if flames ate away beneath the floorboards. A fog lofted up,
filling the Congregational so rapidly no one had a chance to
move, and when they did, they remained as hushed, as

obedient as trained dogs, for there, in the shifting smoke, stood Lucas Donnelly.

He was ten feet tall, or seemed so in a full black flowing robe hiked up over shiny pirate boots. A dazzling light that had no source for it struck sparks off Lucas Donnelly's brightness. His olive skin was white in the glare, the white of a vampire. The focal point of everyone's attention, he looked handsomer than ever, beautiful as a god.

He hurts, Alastair heard Glory thinking and fumbled for her hand. She received his touch gratefully and held on.

The service was still incomprehensible, with the choir now silenced but Will continuing with the fluency of a Virgil or a Cicero. Then Will slid into English so skillfully that it took a moment or two before Alastair recognized his own tongue. Not that Will was being crystal clear in what he was shouting at the top of his lungs, with an echoing response from the chorus.

"Lucifer . . . Prince of Darkness." Alastair got that part as well as "obedience and homage."

Darkness swam about Lucas Donnelly except for the beam of that impossible light, and his arms spread out to the sides, disappearing. Then the right hand returned with the thickest, the longest reptile Alastair had ever seen in his life. Maybe Dee, world-traveled, might have known the name of the yellow-and-black-mottled snake, but to Alastair it was simply a monster.

Will Austin shrieked like the demented at the state farm when Lucas Donnelly produced a knife by some sleight of hand and drained the snake.

Doc grunted under his breath, "God damn!" Glory had closed her eyes. Smart, Alastair thought, and would have done likewise if he didn't fear the darkness so.

The candles burned in miniature bonfires, shooting streams of brightness up to the ceiling, and centered between their flow, Will Austin held a golden cup above his head.

Snake's blood . . .

Alastair grew nauseated as row after row of New Morning citizens trooped, heads bowed, to the front of the church, knelt, and sipped from the cup.

"Let's get out of here!" Doc cried.

"Can't," Alastair spat between his teeth. They'd have to fight the rivering tide moving along the aisles as though hypnotized.

In a little while the only ones who hadn't made the damned communion were Alastair, Glory, and Doc. Doc purpled in

rage, clenching his fists when Ava reached the rail. He half
rose off the pew and for a moment it seemed he might rush to
the front and drag her away, but Alastair leaned past Glory and
tugged Doc's coat. "Sit down!" he ordered, and surprisingly
Doc subsided.

The choir returned to jibbering their Latin, and Will Austin,
beatific in his beaming smile, made wings of his flapping robe,
as he shrilled, "To the glory of the One! Satan, Sovereign of
Death! Beholder of the glorious fire!" A chill shivered down
Alastair's spine as Will spewed his accolades. Lucas Donnelly, a
giant among men, towering in his ebony darkness, grew even
taller. In his polished magnificence he threatened to explode
the church.

Only Glory refused to look at him, even when the dragon
beckoned her to the front. There was no mistaking whom he
meant when he ordered in his authoritative bass, "Come to
me!"

The air buzzed, alive, and outside the wind howled and
struck again and again against the building. The door boomed
like a drum.

Everyone strained to see Glory. She was the focus of all
eyes, her pale hair lighting the gloom, shining iridescently.
Glory made even Alastair draw back with her white gleaming.

Glory still refused to unshutter her eyes. Off in her
darkness, on that long-ago foreign sea, the only emotion she
showed was to squeeze Alastair's hand tighter. Alastair swelled
with pride and took pleasure in the tremor of anger fluting
Lucas Donnelly's voice as he called her repeatedly.

The archfiend roared, and the wind finally flung back the
doors, sweeping in a ferocious gust through the church, flying,
slapping at hair, tearing coats, ripping the pages from a large
tome on Will Austin's lectern.

The gale tore from Glory's mouth another word, and
again her "No!" rang out clear and pure, a magnificent high C.

Blood curtained Glory's face in a sudden fountain, running
through her hair, washing the yellow strands red. Alastair
swooned, but he pulled himself back from the brink, and
throwing himself upon her, dug his fingers in the wet hair
searching for a wound. But the blood came not from some
deep slash or bludgeon injury, but from the thin covering that
sheathed the bone. It was as though, her hair still attached,
she'd been scalped.

Battered by the dragon's injunctions, buffeted with the

cutting wind, Glory opened her eyes finally, and the red film
did her in. Her nails dug channels in Alastair's knee, and she
rose off the pew. The tendons in her neck stiffened to steel
cables, and her face, wet with blood, twisted in dread. Alastair
kept shouting, "Nothing! Nothing wrong!" and Doc yelled,
too, but how could she believe them, seeing blood everywhere. It smeared the front of her, drenching her coat and her
dress. Blood puddled at her feet.

Everyone was up and standing now, screaming, creating
monsters in the slithering candlelight, and Alastair, imprisoned in his wheelchair, felt himself whirled about in a
tunnel he remembered from Omaha. And he screamed out for
them to hit the ground, to crawl on their bellies, dig fingers
into the sand, become one with the earth. But this wasn't
Omaha Beach, and he'd suffer no more crippling, and all he
could expect was death waiting at the end of a shadowy hall.
Only not yet! he promised himself and spun the wheelchair
around. "There's no pledge unless we swear it!" he screamed
and ordered Glory to grab the chair's handles. Together, with
Doc trailing, they went down the aisle.

The congregation began a dreadful humming, like wasps
under the eaves. In a second they could descend on Alastair
but he kept going. The wind, still maniacal, howled along their
route and as they passed row after row of people he'd known
all his years or theirs, Alastair lost more and more of himself.
He was as bereft as he'd been in the chaos of Omaha. Yet on
the Normandy beach he at least understood where he was. It
had been a simple situation of them and us, he thought. The
Germans lay ahead with their bunkers and guns, with the
unseen land mines and powerful mortars. Alastair, scared to
his soul, nevertheless knew his moral position. Now, among
friends and neighbors, the whole harvest of people with whom
he'd dwelt a lifetime, he was uncertain, a stranger on a distant
globe.

Hands snaked out and snatched at them as they hurried to
the door. Behind him Alastair heard the winged terror of
Glory's cries. The stench of incense and of blood was so strong
he choked. Voices rang out against them and they suffered
from curses flung like rocks.

The shouts deafened them, and they clung fast, holding
together, three against so many, driving a wedge through the
aisle. Hands came out of nowhere. Someone smashed Alastair
on the head and arms. Somebody spit in his face. Glory hung

further forward, canopying over him, her blood dripping along his chin, splotching his hands and his pants.

"Crazy! All you people have gone mad!" Doc yelled with real pain. He had either gotten his own wounds, Alastair saw, or been marked by someone else's blood. A great crowd of bodies rushed down on them from the right, and Doc flapped his hands, swatting at his patients as if they were a swarm of disease-carrying flies.

To Alastair's surprise, they finally reached the doors. He butted the doors wide, and a great black cloud swooped out of the night flinging a net over the three of them. But Alastair's chair was on high and he went down the steps, with Glory straining to hold him back. The metal chair shuddered and tipped over on its side, and Alastair was flung down the last few steps.

Later Doc would say, "I don't know how you survived that fall."

And Alastair, with Glory beside him, would reply, "It's not my time to die." But he was humbled.

32

It was cold and damp this Thanksgiving Day.

Doc Trump, lifting his shrinking body off his marital bed, had little thanks to give. Soon he'd have none at all. His skin draped off him without much muscle or fat to cling to, and the deep throbbing pain in his stomach grew stronger. Each day the fire in his belly spread. Doc caught his breath and stumbled into the bathroom where he searched the medicine chest for some Percodan. He couldn't go more than a few hours without a pill. And soon he'd have to increase the dosage. Doc had entered the spiral of his own dying. Not much left, he thought, refusing to meet his own image in the mirror, afraid he'd have that one awful moment when there'd be no recognition.

Thanksgiving was one of the few days in the year Doc saw no patients, except for emergencies, and he sat quietly on the toilet waiting for the Percodan to take hold. When it began to smooth out the pain, he dragged back into the bedroom. Ava had gone before he got up, downstairs to start the turkey. If they were eating here, Doc didn't know. He stopped suddenly. How funny, but he really didn't know if they were celebrating at home as they had last year with some of Ava's family down from Pittsfield, or going out. Friends? Family? The White Bear? Had Ava told him and he forgot?

Last night, Doc shook himself, pulling his plaid bathrobe tighter, he remembered that all right. Oh Lord! Doc's eyes rolled up and he stumbled to the window, resting his brow against the chilly pane.

Below he saw Charlie Calman hurrying somewhere and shivered with fright. What now? He pulled back in disgust, at himself, at New Morning, which had become the kind of place where just a glimpse of the *Eagle* editor moving rapidly meant tragedy. And not the ordinary sort either, the kind he could patch up. Too many people simply died on him, hospital or not.

After his bravado on Lucas Donnelly's porch, Doc had stayed away from the hospital, but finally he went out, after a week, and found everything the same. The two nurses and the three technicians hadn't much to do, but other than that nothing changed. So he continued using it, expecting any moment for the place to blow up or the walls to crumble away. Perhaps the equipment would simply cease functioning, or maybe it would be nothing more than he'd drop dead. Whatever, he'd made his statement to Lucas Donnelly and felt better.

Not enough. He heard the words in his head and screamed silently, nothing is ever enough! What else! He surely couldn't engage in hand-to-hand combat with the dragon, or gun him down as that lost boy Jordy Farrow had once suggested. Nor could he talk him to death like Alastair, or outmaneuver him, again as Alastair kept trying to do. What choices did he have left. Only to ignore him. Doc sighed as he started to get dressed, knowing he was a fool. He was halfway down the steps when he had the most powerful image of Ava in her long black coat and silver dress kneeling at the altar, receiving communion. A ritual of drinking snake's blood. Doc had remembered the terrifying ceremony, but had, until this moment, wiped Ava's part in it from his mind. She had done it, offered up her lips for that disgusting reptile blood. Taken a pledge to Lucas Donnelly. Just as everybody else in New Morning had sworn, except for Alastair and Glory. And me, Doc thought, chilled, hugging himself. He clenched his chest, holding on, counting his breaths as if by sheer willpower he could keep himself together. From dying and putrefying. *From dust*, Will Austin said over the grave, *to dust*, but that took if not forever, still a long time. First you rotted, then you—

Doc jumped up, staggered with dizziness and grabbed onto the banister. Enough of this morbidity! But the image of Ava, his beautiful wife, in her silver dress, still hung before him. He fumbled the rest of the way down the stairs.

In the kitchen no turkey was being readied for the oven; no lights were even switched on. The kitchen was sunken in shadows, dark as a cave, the grayness at the windows barely light at all. No turkey was one thing, but the Mr. Coffee hadn't been set going.

"Ava!" Doc called out trepidatiously, thinking as he often did since he had wandered into that Pittsfield ice-cream parlor, how wrong love was, how it ate into one—meaning him— worse than cancer. And now that he knew exactly how painful cancer felt, he'd stick by his original observation: love was worse.

He discovered Ava sitting in the breakfast nook. "Ava?" He inched in beside her. She gave Doc the skimpiest of smiles. "What's wrong?" he asked, taking her hand which was icy and moist with sweat. Quickly he touched her forehead. She was burning. "Ava, you're not well." It came out more a shocked statement of fact than a question.

She started to say something, then she swallowed and her face twisted in pain. Throat hurts, Doc diagnosed. Fever. He jumped up. "I want to take your temperature." And he ran for his black bag. When he came back with it, Ava was gone. "Ava!" he hollered, and he heard a strangled noise in the downstairs bathroom.

"Ava?"

She had her head over the toilet and was vomiting. Doc held her shoulders. When her spasms stopped he helped her awkwardly to her feet. "Com'on, up to bed with you."

Together they made a slow journey, Doc half carrying Ava through the house and to the stairs. "Feel so sick," she mumbled, and Doc smelled a sourness on her breath.

It took a while, but Doc got her up to the bedroom, back into a nightgown and underneath the covers. She shivered and he added an extra blanket. When he took her temperature, it was over a hundred. "The flu," he muttered worriedly and went down to his office for an antibiotic. After he returned and gave her the capsule, he pulled up a chair by the bed. "Try to sleep," he encouraged her. "I'll just sit here and read."

So Doc and Ava passed Thanksgiving. Doc never gave another thought to where they were to have turkey, and if Ava remembered she was too sick to tell him. Doc kept up a regimen of antibiotics and weak tea with sugar, but Ava got no better. She kept throwing up and ached so she lacked any energy for complaining.

The second day Doc canceled office hours to stay with Ava. Then on the third day she displayed a symptom that made Doc's blood run cold. She kept abruptly flexing her neck and when she did there was an involuntary flexion of her knees. *Brudzinski's sign!* screamed in Doc's mind. That meant meningitis. He swallowed, counted to ten, and said softly, "Let's just see if I can straighten your legs out, sweetheart, so you'll be more comfortable." Gently he threw back the covers and put his hands on her thighs. But no matter how hard he tried, Ava's legs might have been constructed of steel. *Kernig's sign!* Doc leaped to his feet.

The fire department failed to answer the call, a first in Doc's memory. He redialed and let the phone ring and ring. Line's out of order, God damn it! Doc slammed down the receiver and immediately grabbed it up to call Bob Bell. But Belwether Funeral wouldn't pick up either. My phone! Doc thought, panic unfurling inside him. He swept the phone off the night table and rushed to Ava's closet, dragging out her long black coat.

"Sweetheart, com'on, put this on. I think we better drop by the hospital for a couple of tests." Ava, lethargic, in a drowsy state, jerked at what Doc proposed. Her eyes widened, and for a moment he thought she had something to say, a plea or a protest, but she merely wet her lips, slumping as Doc struggled to get her into the coat. She sagged, a limp collection of flesh and bones, and Doc worked up a lather tugging her back and forth about the bed. But finally he got her semicovered and yanked on her boots for her. Then he tried to coax her into standing.

"Up, up and away, sweetheart," he urged, as if she were a DC-10, but Ava flopped back against the pillows.

Ava was only five-four but she carried an extra twenty

pounds around her hips and midriff, and Doc wasn't strong
anymore, or not strong enough. By the time he got her on her
feet, an arm draped about his neck, a cold sweat drenched
through his sweater and shirt. Good Lord! I'll never make it,
he couldn't help thinking, his heart pounding, his breath
sparse and sore rising in his throat. But he hammered down
his terror, swearing, *No! Got to!*

Somehow or other he hauled Ava out to the hall and to the
top of the stairs. There, he stopped. The stairs dropped away
from him in a slope like a torturous path down Everest. The
stairs had never seemed so steep before, and Doc's panic
flared. Still, he forced a foot out over empty space, searching
for the next riser. He drew back hastily in terror, for he saw
them both, on the hardwood floor below, twisted and broken.

"Now listen, sweetheart," he said, lowering his shaky
burden to the top step, "just to be on the safe side, we'll do it
the easy way. One at a time, okay?" He had moved in front of
her. The idea, to have Ava slide down on her behind, was
sensible, except she slouched, falling forward. Doc, snatching
her hand, tried to get her to hold on to the newel posts, but
the ring-ladened fingers were soft, boneless, loose as over-
cooked spaghetti.

One step at a time, bearing her weight, he struggled Ava
lower, coaxing and cooing to her, though she gave no sign that
she heard him.

The worst was yet to come. Later, he wouldn't remember
how he managed to get Ava safely into the Buick, though he
suffered various aches, in his back and shoulders. By the time
they arrived at the hospital, he was near being sick himself.

My fault! Doc sobbed, pounding his fist against the wall
outside Ava's room. If I'd seen it sooner . . . oh, God! Tears
choked up in Doc's throat, for he realized the antibiotics he
had given Ava for her flu—which wasn't flu at all, but
meningitis—now masked her condition. He had to know
whether the murderous intruder was viral or bacterial, and if
the latter, early or partially treated.

"Ampicillin," Doc whispered to the nurse, Rita Enderman's
sister Josie, and crossed his fingers. Josie, tall and spinsterish,
though only thirty-six, pursed purple lips grimly. She handed
over the latest slip from the lab and then stared down the long
empty hall so she wouldn't have to watch Doc's face crumble
like a stepped-on cracker when he read Ava's white blood
count. The air went out of Doc and he slumped along the wall.

"Doc!" Josie snapped in her no-nonsense nurse's voice, and stopped his slide to the floor with a steady, blunt-nailed hand. "It won't do one bit of good for you to collapse like a punctured balloon."

"You're right," he replied, shame-faced, and pulled up, but he was flushed and had that bad feeling in the pit of his stomach that was his personal barometer as to a patient's prognosis. He felt worse now than he ever had, because he was certain. Ava, his darling Ava, was headed straight for the cemetery, barring a miracle.

Doc Trump, physician and husband, struggled and sorrowed as Ava's fever soared.

"Let me do that!" nurse Josie snapped. She snatched the syringe out of Doc's trembling hands and drew milky fluid from Ava's spinal column. Doc sank into an uncomfortable vinyl chair and leaned his head back, staring at the squares of acoustical ceiling. Ava would die . . . would die . . . would die . . . thundered in the darkness. He'd die, too, not now but later, three, four months from now, maybe six if he were lucky (or unlucky, he couldn't decide), and he'd be alone when he'd go, no Ava beside him. Oh, how would he face oblivion with no one to hold his hand, ease his passage. Doc wept, for himself, for his wife, who was slipping from him, even as he watched. Soon, he'd have to bury her. Dear God, he'd never face that, the cold day, wind high, snow falling, a wetness, ice on his face, tears . . . no, no, no!

"There has to be a way!" he cried, jumping up from the chair, looking so wild the efficient, seldom ruffled nurse stood back, pointing the syringe at Doc as if she might stab him with it. Maddened but not crazy, Doc Trump saw the pity in nurse Josie's eyes, and growled because he knew she was right, they were doing everything possible. If Ava wasn't responding, they could try something else and some other procedure after that, but it was all up to her eventually, to dear Ava. In some unknown secret fashion her will and mind were deciding her fate. And Doc had only to wait, he could do nothing else. It was in the hands of the capricious gods and he—

Doc's internal ravings, words breaking inside his head like a rack of billiard balls, were choked off midstream and his breath

slowed. *Lucas Donnelly!* Of course! Lucas Donnelly was able
to do anything.

Doc fled from the hospital like a man on fire, burning inside,
with fear, with love. His whole life lay on an iron-framed bed,
dying! Gas rolled ominously in his stomach; his mouth was dry.
He ran out to the Buick without coat or hat or scarf or gloves,
just in his suit, and threw himself behind the wheel. He
screeched out of the narrow lot banked on one edge of the icy
Housatonic as fast and as noisily as Jack Boardman had once
driven New Morning in his Toyota. And he kept his foot flat on
the gas, doing fifty at least, right to the square. Forget the no
parking, no cars business in mid-New Morning. Doc didn't
care where he parked or whom he ran down, stopping half up
on the sidewalk, the Buick's grill kissing Lucas Donnelly's
picket fence.

"Anything! Anything at all! Whatever you want!" he wailed,
when Lucas Donnelly eased back the front door and invited
him in. Again, as he had the last time he'd come up on this
porch, Doc never got further inside than the threshold. He fell
to his knees and grabbed Lucas Donnelly's white-clad legs,
weeping as if his heart would break, was already shattering,
and begged, pleaded, as he never before had for anything,
"Save Ava!"

Alastair heard nothing of Doc's flight, and playing Mahler's
First when Doc sped wildly through the square, he missed the
screeching brakes, the slam of the Buick's door. So how was he
to know that Doc had gone back on his word. Or, rather, had
discovered a different arrangement to his priorities. He
thought, Doc had, that honor, or possibly his soul, certainly his
oath as a physician, came first, and he found, when he got
down to the nitty-gritty, to death, that Ava topped the list.
Love, poor Doc, was what he lived for, and really, he should
have known. Hadn't he, already middle-aged, gone splat in
that Pittsfield ice-cream parlor so many years ago? Silly Doc!
What did his moral position, his choosing right over wrong, his
assuming a stance on the side of the angels mean as opposed to
Ava's dying? Nothing, nothing at all. This one life usurped
every thought, idea, and ideal in Doc's head.

Alastair went to bed and got up, went to bed again the next

night, and didn't know he'd lost his last ally. For one thing, all of New Morning had closed their minds to Alastair Wayne, shut him out of their thoughts, related to him as if he were dead already. No one telephoned. No one dropped by. Therefore, Alastair no longer had his finger on the town's pulse, and never heard the gossip. So he missed Ava Trump's illness and dying, then her spectacular recovery, and Doc's jubilance. He never witnessed the light draining out of Doc through the hole Ava's dying dug in his heart, nor how he swelled and smiled widely and was revitalized (except for the pain in his gut), when she finally sat up in bed and said, "I feel all right."

Alastair simply knew that the end of November ground itself out like cold ashes, and each new December day arrived as stained and lifeless. The world, New England anyway, hibernated through the long, bone-chilling winter, and if New Morning stirred with a certain excitement at the upcoming wedding, Alastair wanted to forget about it.

Horse Keleidas, an almost constant presence now, tormented Alastair with his grin and said, "The past is always with you, Al. Can't throw it on the garbage heap like a used rubber."

"Go away," Alastair moaned to Horse, to Dog Green rising up to claim him, converting his half an acre in New Morning to the sea and the sand, the cold terror, explosions, guns racketing, rockets, planes dropping bombs, to all that death spread out on the cold coast of the Channel.

Won't I, he wondered, ever be rid of the war? And then he sought to sleep again, to slide down into oblivion, but insomnia overcame him. Alastair stayed awake except for the occasional hour when he drowsed, dreaming. He heard Sergeant Breener's screams in an unending cantata. Whiskey's blood dripped, plop, plop from the column of his neck like the softly executed scales on an oboe. And Bill Wright's torn and mangled heart pulsed, a lonely violin searching for the notes of a concerto.

Over at the Crowells', Evelyn forced Glory to try on the wedding gown, a dream of silk and white lace, of tiny seed pearls. The gown flowed on Glory like music, and except for her face, dark and cold and colorless as the December day, she was a vision.

"A little tuck at the waist, I think," Evelyn said, pinching the material. "Too thin. You're wasting away. I won't have it!"

she poured into Glory's ear, for Glory wouldn't turn her head, and if Evelyn bothered to think about it, she might have realized she hadn't seen her daughter's eyes for days, even weeks.

But it was Glory's voice that bothered Evelyn the most. She ranted to Theo, "She can speak. I know it!"

Theo, glazed, surfaced momentarily from his numbers to protest, "Oh, I don't think so!" He meant, why wouldn't she if the ability had really returned?

"Don't you hold out on us, not after all we've been through, what we've done for you," she complained shrilly. And she was right in her way, Alastair explained to Glory, for Evelyn and Theo had saved her, took her—if the dreams weren't purely fantastical—over to their boat, brought her home. They had sailed, Theo and Evelyn, out into life with Glory, and perhaps there could have been better homes and more practiced parents—no doubt of the latter—but the Crowells meant well. Even if, as Alastair put it, Evelyn was a horse's ass.

None of which obligated Glory to be offered up like the sacrificial lamb, and married off to the dragon. Forget Evelyn's ambitions (she could stick to samplers) and Theo's stock accounts! *What choice do I have?* was Glory's question. Alastair, alone in his house except for the hit-and-run attacks of Mrs. O'Brien, sequestered with the torturous memories and his ghosts, had no answer.

He crouched across the kitchen table from Glory, the remains of one of their dinners scattered on the checkered cloth. "He won't come over. His bed's been made and he's got to lie in it, just like Dee and the others. He sold out."

How do you know? Glory's fingers inquired, for Alastair, understanding her reticence, made no further attempts to coax her into sound.

"I can put two and two together." He sighed. "Lettie O'Brien talks even if she means to be quiet. Put me in a deep freeze, the whole damn town. But Lettie, anyhow, said Ava almost died." Alastair sighed again, forgiving Doc's desertion, even if he was hurt and furiously angry over it. "Doc's put love before honor. Before good."

I'm going to have to marry the dragon! Glory's cry was plaintive, her fingers shaky. Then she drove both hands through the short-cropped hair, standing the ends up in spikes. Ganymede, Alastair thought, of the perfectly shaped head, the long swan's neck. If nothing else, Glory grew more beautiful each day.

"No, never," Alastair replied, but he didn't sound convinced this time as he had in the past. Weaponless, he had no idea how to stop Lucas Donnelly from getting what he wanted. He'd take Glory away, into Emma's house, and live with her there, give her babies! Alastair winced. He'd even marry her in the old New Morning Congregational Church, built in 1765, because the church was his temple now where every other night the town went to worship. Worship him, the man in the white suit, in a newly black-painted Congregational Church! Glory told him that, how in addition to the inverted cross and the chanting, the monks' robes, the incense and smoke of no fire, Will Austin had had the white walls enameled black. Oh God, Alastair cried to himself, who's there to stop this avalanche, if now even Doc has gone, slid back, given the dragon what he wanted. Only me, Alastair thought, a hopeless cripple.

After the Boardmans were buried, Lucas Donnelly bought out the remaining son and took over the Public. The transaction was similar to the one for the White Bear, and Jarvis Badderly got to run the Public, too, when he wasn't busy at the Inn. Otherwise he hired Delmar Montrose, Cora's fifty-five-year-old baby son, who, with his fuzz of gray hair in a halo, a cherubic face like a sexless choirboy's, and the slope of a substantial potbelly, was the perfect tool for the dragon. One of Delmar's first changes involved ordering a gross of kerosene lamps, then a second, and suggesting, as Lucas Donnelly proposed that he should, it was the thing to cut down on electricity. The lamps sold out in a day.

"Got your lamp?" Delmar asked, when Alastair, bundled in his chair like a sack of clothes going to the Laundromat, rolled in.

"I'm not aiming to move out of the twentieth century just yet." Alastair sneered, shoving the grocery list at Delmar's belt buckle. "Just fill my order and let's forget all about the Revolutionary War, if you don't mind."

"You're a hard man, Alastair," Charlie Calman said, appearing between two aisles with blood in his eye.

"And you're a jackass, Charlie!" Alastair shot back. Only he couldn't leave it there. He spun the chair around and pointed a finger at Delmar, and at Cora coming out of the vegetable aisle, at Jonah Enderman picking up his lunch sandwich, at Howie Eumis just entering, the front of his navy coat lush with cat hair. "All of you," he cried, "are jackasses! Worse. Don't you people realize you're sinning, trafficking with the devil!"

Charlie puffed out his cheeks and sniffed nastily. He wanted to murder him for sure, Alastair saw, and not with a pen. A chill curled down his spine though the editor spoke in a normal voice, saying, "You never believed in sin before."

Alastair smoldered, embarrassed and frightened at the same time. Charlie was right, he'd been a humanitarian who ascribed wrongs to social malfunctions. "I changed my mind, learned from experience. Even some old dog can pick up a new trick now and then. Sin's come home to me in Moses's dying, Jordy's also. All the Boardmans'.". He shuddered. "In what Harlan Farrow did years ago as well as more recently. Maybe I was always four ways an imbecile, slow-witted like poor Bobby Pierson—and that was sinning too, his death in the Housatonic, never mind that I can't figure out how. I smell it! But I always thought before Lucas Donnelly"—at the mention of the dragon everybody pulled up, coming to attention—"kindness and consideration," Alastair continued, "love too, kept a person to the straight and narrow, except for an out-and-out rotter like Harlan. Sin back then," Alastair spoke of past time as if it lay a hundred years or more in his wake, "sin was a mistake, a kind of sociological error. Now I know better, and the rest of you should also."

Delmar Montrose handed the grocery list over the counter to Alastair. He was grim, the color of gunmetal. "All this conversation is well and good, Alastair, but I can't have you stopping commerce. Dollars and cents; life goes on. Besides, I don't want your business."

"What!" Alastair hawked.

"You're not one of us, pure and simple." Delmar smugly folded his hands over his middle.

On the Boardmans' bones, Alastair thought, and shouted, "Imbecile! Pompous ass! This is the first job you've had in fifty years, so don't play the successful entrepreneur with me!"

"You can't speak to my son like that!" Cora howled, rushing forth. It would take little, Alastair suddenly realized, for them to attack him, to beat him senseless, ground his bones to cornmeal.

"Out!" Jonah Enderman said, holding the door wide. "Before my client decides to sue you for defamation of character."

"You'll read about this in the *Eagle*," Charlie shouted after him, meaningfully, as if they'd never shared a soda in the newspaper office.

Somebody, Alastair couldn't tell who, gave the chair a vicious shove, and he flew out onto the narrow porch and down the ramp to the Main Street sidewalk. If I had two sturdy legs, nobody could have done that, he sorrowed, realizing he'd just gotten out of the Public with his life. He lowered his head, burrowing his chin in the woolly scarf, and took a gust of snowy wind full in the face.

It had started again. Short puffs of snow flew every which way, and when the wind dropped, fell steadily and straight. Swirls of whiteness covered the streets, the green, and began layering up. Alastair could barely penetrate two feet in front of his face.

The storm, surging rapidly to a furious blast, had started during the few moments he'd been in the Public. The gray overcast, which might have passed by, had settled in, and Alastair knew if he didn't hurry himself across the square and to High Street, up his own short drive, he'd get mired in the soft, treacherous snow. No one would rush to help him, and the first thaw would find him stiff as a board. Drawing as far down into the scarf and coat collar as he could go, he inched into drive. No sooner had Alastair rumbled forward than he skidded, snowshoeing at an angle down Main. He came up, midblock, with a clear view of Lucas Donnelly's colonial. Won't go in there, snow or not. And yet, he had to talk to the dragon, there wasn't anybody left. Just him. And here it was December what?—sixteenth or seventeenth.

He managed the wheelchair back on the perpendicular, up over the curb, his tires driving tracks in the snow. A humdinger, that's what the storm was building up to. A real blizzard. Cut off for days. The plow's in the firehouse. Never! That's what the dragon would say. Alastair could see him smiling as he said, Live with the snow. A natural phenomenon. Alastair remembered the devil had a thing about nature. Wood sprites and elves, dancing naked under the full moon, the witches, bonfires, all kinds of herbs. He had done more than a bit of reading in the Barnes.

On the main path of the green, he positioned himself beside

his usual bench, and tried to will himself back to last spring, in this very place, talking with Dee—a Dee as animated, as young and beautiful as any female could wish to be—when the limousine flowed into New Morning. In his daydream he knew then what he knew now, and threw a hand grenade under the front wheels. What would happen to the dragon and his driver? Would they vaporize? He shook himself, a dog scattering snow, and sneezed. That was part of the New Morning trouble, people wanting different things than what they had. It was more than the grass being greener, and nobody satisfied.

For an instant the storm stilled, and through the thin curtains of white, he had a clear view over to the Crowells'. Glory stood in an upstairs window, at least Alastair thought she did, and he waved like a fool to the child who had come to mean more to him than a daughter, a beautiful fragile being who claimed his heart. She really was the princess in the tower. She was more than just a young girl who could speak but wouldn't, had music in her fingers, and no memory of part of her life. Glory was born of the dragon and soon—horribly!— to be his wife. A new dynasty here in New Morning. A sin against everything holy. With so much evil in the world already, what would their children be like? Alastair had an instant vision of fire and burning, of cities falling, mountains crumbling apart, rivers bursting their banks, the whole earth being split asunder.

The storm swelled, closing in again and Glory disappeared from view. Up there, locked away not by dead bolts but by the whole of New Morning, Glory needed a prince. And all she has is you, Alastair chastised himself, pulling in next to his bench. It was heaped with snow. The green slats and black metal had disappeared under the soft whiteness. Deceptive snow, promising the rest of a featherbed for anyone foolish enough to lie down on it. Still Alastair remained. He needed to talk to Lucas Donnelly.

Visibility had diminished almost to zero, and through the flakes falling as close together as raindrops, Alastair glimpsed only the vaguest grayness of motion, actual people or ghosts, though his own dead returned, fleshy and dripping blood. He lulled in his chair, not as cold now as he knew in the back of his mind he ought to be, but too weary to move. For a little while, his chin down, his eyelids fluttering in a struggle to stay awake, Alastair imagined he napped under a midsummer's glaring sun, but the trickle of wetness slipping down his collar was cold not warm, and he jerked up.

Lucas Donnelly sat on the bench at Alastair's flank. He'd taken, now that winter had arrived, to wearing a white fur coat and hat like a Russian prince. "You should be in movies, like that thing I saw the other night on T.V. *Dr. Zhivago*."

Lucas Donnelly laughed, his perfect teeth whiter than the snow. "I appreciate humor, Mr. Wayne, which is why I treasure you so." He laughed louder. "And also irreverence."

"There's nothing irreverent about me, Mr. Donnelly. Not where you're concerned. I know you for what you are. I just wish you weren't."

"I beg your pardon?" Lucas Donnelly leaned forward, and the snowflakes falling on his bronze skin melted and jeweled like diamonds. His almond eyes shone warmly brown and inquiring, not burning pits at all. Could I have been mistaken? Alastair asked himself, but hadn't the strength or the courage to find out by igniting the dragon's anger.

"I only mean," Alastair said, "that I wish you were a mortal, a man just the same as me. And that you were susceptible to reason along with a human emotion or two. Then I could say—" Alastair stopped dead, his tongue cold in his mouth. His teeth ached. Whatever was it that he meant to say to Lucas Donnelly? Go away? He'd said that before and the dragon had laughed. He felt so impotent and ineffectual that it would take little effort for him to give up to the snow. But that spark of life, that obstinacy that had kept him alive at Omaha, that made him sit if not stand sturdy as a wall against the dragon's forays, wouldn't let him collapse. He finished so softly Lucas Donnelly had to bend even closer to the wheelchair. "I won't let her go, not for all the tea in China. There'll be no wedding in some demonic ceremony with Will Austin playing the mad monk, I think you should know. No children, sir."

Alastair was aware that the dragon had cut away the ground around him—Jordy and Moses and Doc—so that he'd been left desolate, a shipwrecked survivor on his little piece of uninhabited island. As Lucas Donnelly pointed out, though with a surprising touch of compassion, "You're all alone, you know."

"Too true." Alastair sighed, blowing a ridge of snow off his chin. He felt as desolate as if he were already boxed and buried underground. Even the white glaring light of the storm that took all color, all shape and form from the earth, darkened into a gray shroud. But yet again, as he had over and over in these months with the dragon, Alastair reminded himself he knew right from wrong, that he was a man of sound mind despite the fragile state of his body. He wouldn't relinquish his hold. "I won't," he said, speaking so distinctly Lucas Donnelly could not mistake his intent, "allow you to have her. It's wrong."

"Wrong, or right for that matter," Lucas Donnelly said—for once, there was not even the touch of a smile on his lips— "depends entirely on your angle of vision."

"Not at all," Alastair snapped. "And don't try to convince me. You might have gotten everybody else in New Morning to view life in a fun-house mirror, but I know what I know."

"Really!" His eyebrows arched. "And what about Omaha, Mr. Wayne? You remember Dog Green? Surely you do."

"I was injured, down in the muck. Couldn't move, not one inch. Lucky, in my own way, Mr. Donnelly, that I lived through that hell to see another day, never mind all these years." *I don't*, Alastair kept thinking even as he spoke, his thoughts counterpoint to his words, *have to defend myself to him. God maybe, if He exists*—which Alastair, moving away from agnosticism as he had from so much else this year, supposed He did, given the fact that His favorite angel, His Prince of Darkness actually sat on a snowy New Morning bench. There couldn't be one without the other.

"That's what you've always said, Mr. Wayne, what you've sought to believe and to have others do likewise. But really, I'm not someone you can lie to. I do know *all*." Lucas Donnelly spoke with sincerity.

He could sell the Brooklyn Bridge, Alastair thought, *or iceboxes to Eskimos. Only not to me. I, too, know what I know. My memories are reliable.* Alastair shook his head, setting off a snowshower. "Thanks to you," he said sourly, meaning no thanks at all, "I'm landing at Normandy most days now, every night also."

"And why do you think that is, Mr. Wayne?" he asked. "You've lived a long life. Omaha, traumatic I grant you, was only one event. There were others. . . ."

Then, as though the dragon had unwound a screen before the snow-humped bushes across the path, Alastair saw the cave on the far slope of Madder's Hill, the side most distant from New Morning. It was there, when he'd been eleven and a half to the day, that he and Johnny Winslow got trapped, sucked into the dark hole in the mountain. Inside, it was black. The air, smelly from bat dung, whispered in invisible wings about their heads. And Johnny cried out, went mad, or as close to crazy as to be the same thing, and spun off through the cave, frantic, screaming in earsplitting shrieks, while Alastair fumbled his way to the top, the air, skinning his knees and his palms. He'd been so scared he wet his pants. It took hours, nearly all of the afternoon, but he'd gotten himself out. Then he'd run, five miles without stopping, back into town. Not that it mattered, too late, too much time, all those hours for Johnny Winslow in the dark.

"They found him, bottom of a shelf. Fell thirty feet to the ground," Alastair said aloud.

He had forgotten Johnny Winslow completely, though he'd passed by his cemetery plot more than once these months.

"See what I mean?"

Alastair, returning from then to now, found Lucas Donnelly watching him as though he were a lepidopterist's specimen. "You're saying," he said, "if I hadn't run, kept a hold on Johnny, he wouldn't be dead."

"You just said that, Mr. Wayne, not me."

"Wasn't true then, not true today. He got loose from me in the dark. Couldn't see my hand in front of my face. The only thing to do was what I did. I feel no guilt for that, Mr. Donnelly."

Lucas Donnelly smiled, though not one of his toothy grins. "Ah well, there were other episodes, Mr. Wayne—"

"And why wouldn't there be?" Alastair interrupted peevishly. He was cold through the coat and sweater, down to his skin. Beneath that as well. His heart was encased in icicles. "I wasn't a hermit buried out in the desert. Some St. Jerome. I've lived a life with, granted, more minuses than pluses; still, I've bumped up against my share of people. A turtle, maybe, but I've come out of my shell more than once."

"Except," Lucas Donnelly persisted, "at Omaha."

Alastair rolled a few feet farther in his chair, disturbing the snow clinging to him. "I'm not the subject of this discussion, Glory is." It would be a struggle to get home if he waited much longer. The snow had already begun to build up into drifts.

"Glory's my daughter, not yours," Lucas Donnelly said. He crossed his legs and laid an arm on the back of the bench, not bothered by the storm at all.

Alastair spun around without taking care and the chair skidded, performed a half circle Alastair never intended, and he had to pull it right again before he could spit at the dragon,

"And you want to . . . to . . . to have illegal congress with her!" He was shouting, his fury rising up on the wind and sailing with the snow.

They were suddenly squabbling, not two fathers, but two lovers, over a girl, and Alastair felt sick. He wanted the best for Glory, by which he meant normal. If only she could have married Jordy. Lucas Donnelly read his mind and laughed. "The gold with the dross. What a waste that would have been!"

Tears filled Alastair's eyes and one round drop dripped over onto his cheek to freeze there to ice. "That was a boy you're talking about, a good, decent human being, and you shuffled him without a by your leave to the grave. A person! God damn it!" Alastair shouted so loudly his passion loosened the uneasy snow on the nearest elm's branch.

Lucas Donnelly looked bored. When the echoes incited by Alastair's yelling ceased, he said, "Have you any idea how many people have lived on this planet since way back when? Uncountable millions, Mr. Wayne. So what's one boy more or less."

"I think you're the wrong person for me to try and explain that to, Mr. Donnelly," Alastair said crisply. The snow was piling up on him again, obscuring the coat and scarf, the cap with lined earflaps Alastair never bothered tying under his chin. Only his eyes burned out of all that whiteness like two cinders. For once, it was Alastair not Lucas Donnelly who seemed to harbor a conflagration in his insides.

"Let me make you a sporting proposition, Mr Wayne, since you're so human. A worker, one could describe you, in the vineyards for his fellow man," Lucas Donnelly said, crossing his other leg. The snow was so heavy now it flung itself out of the sky, and the air was choked with it. Alastair breathed cold, wet flakes into his mouth and up his nose, but the dragon remained untouched. Whatever snow might have landed on him didn't stick. Even the elements, or so it seemed to Alastair, were deferential to the devil. Only the black curls that escaped under the white fur glistened wetly.

Alastair rolled so close to Lucas Donnelly their knees brushed. He hadn't so much lost his fear of the dragon, of being burned to a crisp, as he had put it aside. And when he spoke he gazed steadily into his eyes. "I'll have no truck with you!"

Lucas Donnelly held his gaze like a puppet-master his strings, and in the deep muddy brown a few gold flames sputtered. "It makes good sense, Mr. Wayne, to hear a proposition before you turn it down," he admonished, but not harshly, more like a friend. The tone didn't escape Alastair despite his rage. He thought, catch more flies with honey than with vinegar.

Alastair smacked gloved hands together, then folded his arms, dislodging the newest frosting of snow. "Say whatever it is you have to before I become an ice pop!" he snapped. Come what may, he knew it would be beyond him to ask Lucas Donnelly's guidance in getting home.

"You'd rather I didn't marry Glory Crowell," the dragon said.

"Too true!" Alastair interjected.

"Well then, I propose this: That in exchange for giving away Glory at our wedding, I return to you what you've lacked all these years." No smile of any kind now. Lucas Donnelly was as serious as Theo discussing mortgages.

Alastair's heart began its trapped bird fluttering, and he wished he'd brought the new pills Doc had given him before the two friends stopped speaking, Doc so ashamed he now neglected Alastair the patient. Alastair's whisper should have been lost on the wind, but Lucas Donnelly with his extrasensory powers heard him anyway when he said, "You mean my legs."

Slowly the dragon nodded his handsome head. "Precisely!" he said.

Alastair's laugh was apparently the last response Lucas Donnelly expected, because he jumped in shock. Alastair shadowboxed the snow flying in his face, he coughed, hiccuped, finally stopped and wheezed. "You think I'd trade not being crippled for Glory? Ah, Mr. Donnelly, you're a fool! What difference could it make to me now, whether I walk erect? I've gotten through ninety percent of my life in this contraption"—he thumped the arm of the wheelchair—"or on sticks. So chop my legs off at the knees for all I care, I'll never walk Glory down the aisle!"

"Oh, no! *Then*, not now. Back, Mr. Wayne, at Omaha! It wasn't just your legs you lost, it was your friends. Remember them?" he asked smoothly, his lips ruby-red as if he'd been drinking blood, his olive cheeks flushed magenta.

Lucas Donnelly was the prince of deception. Sly while being charming. Alastair, trying to slow his galloping heart, gave him full marks.

"Do I remember?" he hissed and shook the snow off his cap. As if he could forget, Horse, Sergeant Breener, the captain, Whiskey, the rest of the squad.

"Think of it! You won't go down. You'll walk or rather run. Charging through the water that drowned so many, zigzagging across the sand, taking out that particular bunker. Then, there on the left, the machine-gun nest, the gunners hanging over the cliff. You'll reach the seawall, every man one of you, Mr. Wayne, with not a single injury. Then you'll travel as safely as first-class passengers to the foot of the cliff. No lying flat down on the wet beach, afraid to move so much as a finger—"

"Unable to, not afraid!" Alastair interrupted.

"Your friends. And as an added bonus what you lost with them, your innocence, a clear conscience."

Inside the thick, fur-lined gloves, Alastair's hands were cold, heavy, almost as useless as his dead legs, so that it was a struggle to manipulate the chair into motion, to get it away from the snow-covered bench, from Lucas Donnelly, so royally imperious. But he did manage to inch it slowly, churning through the snow. He skidded more than once and the High Street curbs were mountains over which he lurched. At his unplowed drive, he slipped backward for every foot he acquired, and he couldn't help thinking, *such is life.* Nothing is ever truly gained. And one advances through time as though on a raft over the rapids. For what purpose? To simply come around and recapture what was lost. Innocence, Lucas Donnelly had offered, and even the word lay sweet as molasses on Alastair's tongue.

He groaned and strained, and supposed he'd die right here in the blizzard trying to make it to his house. Well, that would be one solution the dragon hadn't made, and part of Alastair lusted for it. To have and to have not. No one following after, laying blame, screaming you betrayed the dead. He couldn't choose if he went on the incline up the drive, just gliding back, all will and emotion, intelligence, love and desire, quenched easily as a candle's flame between one's fingers.

Only the chair's tires finally gripped tightly, and the motor whirring in a high pitch, brought Alastair up and over the hump of the drive. He gained the level, and felt a new, though no sharper, pang for not having died here and now. And as he was about to journey into the sheltering house where a fire would be laid ready for the match, Lucas Donnelly called over from the green. Alastair, looking back, saw the dragon when he shouldn't have been able to see with the thickening storm the intervening trees. The dragon smiled, and hollered one last time, "Think about it!"

33

The days were shorter now; the nights went on forever. Six inches of snow fell, then another eight followed and stayed on the ground. No thaw lowered the drifts. On the contrary, the white blanket renewed itself with sudden fierce storms that blew frantically out of the west, as if chased by a higher power, then hurried on, down to Connecticut.

The weather made it impossible for Alastair to go out and he stayed shut in, behind his windows, watching the town through the frost-covered glass. But there was little to see on the New Morning square in winter, particularly since the center of the town was closed to cars. An occasional muffled figure, faceless, wrapped like a mummy, cutting across the green.

Alastair relied on Glory for his news since still no one phoned or came to visit. If he tried to call out, most often the line was dead. Even Mrs. O'Brien stopped coming around. She left him a note in the mail box.

> NO MORE DAYS CAN'T WORK
> SCIATICA ACTING UP NO GOOD
> FOR MY HEALTH
>   L O'BRIEN

Not her, but the dragon's doing, Alastair swore to Glory. Whatever she lacked as a cleaning lady, Lettie O'Brien was fearless. Alastair just hoped Lucas Donnelly wasn't causing the poor woman too much pain.

So Alastair found himself deserted, without friends, unable to move except inside the house, which came to feel like a prison cell. Still, he wasn't scared, not until he called the

Public and asked Jarvis Badderly, who answered the phone as if the market were Belwether Funeral, to send over an order.

"No orders," Jarvis Badderly said in his sepulchral tone, and hung up the receiver.

Alastair tried the Super Saver, who'd never delivered and had no intention of starting now. He next phoned the Papriakases, but one of the boys said, "Not allowed, by law." By law? Alastair had no idea what he meant unless Howie Eumis had passed another one of his ordinances without council permission as he'd been doing most of his term—or at least since Lucas Donnelly had saved his Persians.

I'm stranded here. He intends to starve me out. OLD MAN DIES ALONE IN THE COLD, Alastair imagined the headline. And why not, it happened every year.

Alastair checked the pantry. Supplies were running short, but he supposed he could hold out, with the canned goods he had on hand. But then the furnace sputtered, refusing to send any more heat through the pipes. Either the gas had been used up, or some part had blown; whichever, Day's Gas and Heating wouldn't pay a service call. Nothing personal, they told him, but they were phasing out, business over. Their loan had been called by Theo at the First National.

There were two fireplaces, one in the living room, the other so far from his bed the warmth never reached him. And wood. He only had a cord chopped out by the garage that Moses had gotten for him earlier in the winter. Oh, Moses, Alastair thought, you'd know how to hold out in a siege. You were clever, especially about surviving, not a crippled, fumble-fingered old fool like me.

Glory brought all the wood inside for Alastair and piled it within easy reach of each fireplace. *In case something happens to me*, she signed.

"Don't be silly!" Alastair snapped, "you're going to be just fine." Only he wasn't positive about that. He grew less certain as night after night, he sat in the dark, staring out at the lit globes in the square, the other houses with their lights burning. Half the time now, the electricity was off, through only in his house. The dragon, toying with him.

I've been immobilized, Alastair kept thinking, when he wondered why Lucas Donnelly just didn't ship him into the great beyond as he'd done with so many others. Easy to have him take a bad tumble and bang his skull, or perhaps get botulism from one of his cans of beets or spaghetti; easiest of all, just to let his heart pop. Alastair's cheeks flamed when he realized that the dragon was being insulting by not killing him. It was as good as saying, you're too powerless for me to bother with, and as for your immortal soul, who wants it.

Still he had offered up Dog Green. Above all, survival meant not listening to the dragon, for over and over in Alastair's mind Lucas Donnelly presented his bargain. To change Omaha, to convert those dead into the living. *I can save them*, he'd find himself thinking at the oddest moment, washing his face (in cold water, of course), or making his bed. All of a sudden he'd see himself running. He'd leap into that freezing surf, the water frantically boiling, and he wouldn't stumble as he had then, thrown almost over by the weight of the pack strapped to him like a camel's hump. He'd step high and wide, a giant among men, darting between the dead, not struggling at all to claim the shore. Nor would he go down on the damp sand and lay so inanimate, a thing, not a man. A piece of flotsam.

Alastair led the men, the squad following him, heeding his commands as though he were an officer not just another G.I. Even Captain Murkowitz shouted, "Go to it, boy!"

Shaking away the visions that clung like cobwebs in his head, Alastair sought solace, usually in Bach. There was something cleansing about Bach, though Alastair didn't think the fantasies in themselves were unclean, that the sin—if indeed some transgression was meant—had to do with keeping the men alive, of having wanted to do so. It was simply the notion of being tempted. Here he was, crusty Alastair Wayne, a man with ballast in his soul, *considering* an arrangement with the devil. Whenever Alastair realized he was hungering for the carrot Lucas Donnelly had thrust before his nose, he'd curse himself. And yet . . . and yet. . . .

A tinny, insidious voice snaked through his thoughts, asleep or awake, whispering viperishly: only one mere accommodation, not even a life, in exchange for so many.

Even thinking over what the dragon had said that blizzardy day in the green made Alastair shrivel with guilt. He never shared with Glory that painful conversation. He was ashamed to tell her Lucas Donnelly had offered him a deal, as if the dragon knew Alastair was susceptible. So he was alone with this secret, too, locked in, chilled, not eating very well, his joints inflamed. Alone. He wanted Moses back for those nights in the kitchen, Jordy, too. He missed "toughing it" with Charlie in the *Eagle* office. And Doc, what a blow that was! Not

to have Doc making a big deal about his health in his fussy, old
hen ways. And what about the council meetings when, at the
most heated moment, everyone would turn to him as to an
older, wiser statesman! Then there was Dee . . . Even
saying her name silently brought a collapse of his insides. He
phoned her incessantly without ever getting an answer, but
just the act of dialing her number and having it ring in the
house established a link between them.

Besides dialing a dead phone and listening to Bach, Alastair
spent many an hour staring at the samurai sword over the
mantel, considering if it were at all possible to take the dragon
by surprise. One of the interesting things Alastair had read
over at the Barnes was that a real dragon could be killed by
stabbing him in the belly. Alastair wondered if this was also
true of Lucas Donnelly, but couldn't think of any way to find
out.

December twenty-first, Glory came over to say, looking ill.
The snow was falling again and a white dusting covered her
peacoat and netted in tiny diamonds on her hair. She was a
princess even if her nose was pinched, her eyes filmy.

"The winter solstice," Alastair said. "A strange disquieting
time of year. The death of the sun god, the birth of Jesus
Christ. I wonder why he picked this date to marry you."
Glory's skin shone in a deadly pallor. "No, no, I'm just
intellectualizing. I mean, does Lucas Donnelly see this rite,
this joining, as some kind of rebirth?" But Alastair dropped the
subject when Glory sank down on a kitchen ladderback.
Instead of talking, he made her a hot chocolate without any
milk and a toasted frozen corn muffin. Like a nanny, he gave
her all his solicitous attention until she finished both.

I'll kill myself, she whispered when the faintest tinge of red
washed her cheeks.

Alastair's heart flipflopped, but he managed to keep his voice
steady. "That won't be necessary," he said, and coughed in his
hand. The better, he thought, to avoid the question of what do
we do next, when he coughed again and Glory came around to
slap him on the back. He almost heard her thinking, *I want
Jordy*.

Alastair's earlier, summer vision of them happily together
gave him a burning pain in his chest now. He sent Glory to the
medicine chest in the bathroom for some Maalox and beat his
forehead with a fist, castigating himself. Dumbbell! Idiot!
Think! But whenever he did it was of Dog Green and the
invasion.

In the few short hours of the skimpiest day, Alastair's ghosts persistently hung in. At dusk when all the light—which was granular and not much—got sucked from the sky. Horse Keleidas said, "What I see, Al, is a body shop, nothing big. Just me and another guy, maybe my brother-in-law Briggs, who was alive up to seventy-six. And I'll get me a girl. No bimbo, like the kind of fluff we ran after stateside. You remember, don't you, how it was before we shipped out?"

"Horse! Please!" Alastair cried, tears in his eyes, his nose stuffing up. *It's not fair, so many dead, now, and back then. I feel like the only person alive!* Oh, how he hurt. There was no corner of Alastair's flesh that didn't have an ache or a pain stitched in it.

Whiskey Rubin appeared suddenly next to Horse carrying his head in his arms. "You know, Al," he said, turning Alastair's blood to ice water, "my boy never got bar mitzvahed." The lips moved but the head's dark eyes were still as poker chips. A ventriloquist's trick, Alastair tried to tell himself, but who was the magician? Not him.

"Because, there was this fire, out in Flatbush where the boy lived with his mother and her second husband, the one after me. This yo-yo had only airspace between his earlobes, so he smoked in bed. Well, you see what I mean." Tears trickled over the spiky eyelashes, and Alastair, swinging between fright and suffocation, remembered how Whiskey used to get teased. Sinful, to have such eyelashes, like a girl's.

"I'm so sorry," Alastair stuttered through chattering teeth. And Whiskey replied, "I coulda saved him, even with all that smoke. But if it had been me, there wouldn't a been a fire because I never smoke. Al, you're a witness, I never liked tobacco."

Another death laid on his doorstep, Whiskey's unbar-mitzvahed boy! *Oh, Lord, when will it end!* Alastair cried silently and rolled out of the living room. But Bill Wright with that fatal flowering in his chest was waiting by the bathtub. "I would have been a doctor," he said, half sadly and half accusingly.

Alastair sped into the kitchen and yanked the phone off the hook. He called Dee who wouldn't answer and cried, "You've got to help me! I'm no hero!"

"You can walk again," a voice trickled into his ear. Dee's phone rang in its endless one-note as the voice, hollow, unaccented, spoke, "Think what that would mean!"

Alastair shot into reverse and pulled the phone right off the wall. It crashed on the linoleum, but the fall didn't still the voice. "A life, a family of your own!"

"No!" Alastair howled, and beat his fists on the chair.

"Whatever are you carrying on about?" a honeyed woman's voice asked. Alastair spun around in surprise to find a female sitting in his kitchen. Or was it? The wallpaper was different and the counters weren't Formica but expensive butcher block. And light, light everywhere, pouring through the windows, a spring's luster. "I swear"—the woman smiled at someone in the distance, or off to the side—"your temper gets worse with the years."

"Aiiiii!" Alastair gargled deep in his throat, but the woman paid him no mind. She seemed young, no more than thirty, thirty-five, and wonderful to look at. Her hair, smooth and pinned-back off her face, was a darker blond than Glory's. Her eyes were cornflower blue. She reminded Alastair of one of the housewives on T.V. Selling floor wax, he thought, or maybe it was margarine.

"See here," he hawked. There was a thick pounding to the left of his chest, and at that moment the man appeared. He looked terribly familiar, like a hunch-shouldered second cousin to Jimmy Stewart. Probably watched him on television a hundred times, that part of Alastair's mind that continued to function thought.

"Kids up yet?" the almost recognized stranger asked.

"You people get out of my kitchen!"

"It's Saturday. They're sleeping-in a little late." She smiled at the man, obviously the love of her life.

"I won't have it!" Alastair cried, shaking his hands as if he could shoo the intruders out into their sunny day, or off into his own blizzard. But they weren't moving; they weren't even aware of him, Alastair suddenly realized, feeling foolish.

If they're in my kitchen having breakfast on a warmer day than this one, then where am I?

Alastair took a quick gander behind him, expecting God-knows-what fantasia on his flank, but found only the old sink and counters, the back door. He thought, as he slowly circled around again, maybe they're gone. But it, or they, were still there. The man and the woman sat across from each other at Alastair's kitchen table, the same one he planned to eat his dinner on tonight.

"The Handel album was in the wrong place, that's what I got

steamed up about. Don't mind me, sweetheart, I'm just a grouch." With that, the woman laughed, a sound like tinkling glass, and the man raised her hand to his mouth.

"Oh, Alastair—"

Alastair!

A terrible grinding sensation struck Alastair beneath the breastbone, and he bent over in the chair. He gripped the arms tightly to keep from slipping to the floor, shiny black tile and not scuffed, worn linoleum, he saw with blurry eyes. He was crying copiously now, from the pain, but more from what might have been. Could still be yet, the dragon was saying somewhere inside his head. This is you, the woman you took as a wife, and upstairs there are children. *Children!*

Alastair collapsed, finally, and hung precariously in the wheelchair, like a man on the steep edge of a cliff. His mouth dried up despite the wetness everywhere else, and he lingered half in and half out of time. When he would come to, later, in the last hours of the night, there would be blood on his lips.

Alastair took to his bed, but the mattress turned into steel spikes and he had to get up. He picked up a book only to put it down with a snap. Letters on the pages marched like ants. He tried a novel instead of history, but it made no difference. Words wouldn't sit still for Alastair's perusal. He ate, and after one meal of tomato soup and frozen lamb pie, he threw up. He switched to drinking, wine, then sherry and scotch, but he couldn't stand the bitter taste in his mouth. Nothing stopped Alastair for a minute, gave him the slightest peace. His mind never rested and his fears rubbed against his soul in a kind of spiritual prickly heat. Oh, Lord, he cried, fumbling a prayer, but that didn't soothe either.

And all the while, Alastair's ghosts of past and future, ghosts of whom or what might have been, followed him about like taunting children. His old squad begged and wheedled, tormenting him until he thought his head would split.

"Leave me alone!" he screamed in the darkened 3 A.M. living room that was, at one and the same time, a cold, bleak, deadly day on the Normandy coast. The waters churned, the LST crashed, heaving like a sea creature, and Alastair thought he'd get sick all over as he had back then.

Glory came and sat beside Alastair, but her presence

stretched his sanity and probably his very life to the breaking
point. No ghosts with Glory, he promised himself, but the
ghosts were there anyway. Even when she played the piano,
Horse and Whiskey and all the rest crowded the room.

"Don't look at me that way!" he cried when she'd asked to
spend the night rolled in a blanket on the sewing-room floor.
He ducked his head so her anguish winged over him. "We've
got to be sensible. Evelyn would just come over here and drag
you off, or call the police." It was true enough, but Evelyn
didn't scare him. Evelyn Crowell was human and ordinary.

Tomorrow after midnight, Glory signed. Then, her lips
quivering, she surprised Alastair by saying out loud, "Five
minutes into Christmas Day." Her voice was lovely, soft,
velvety. He had supposed she'd have a mezzo-soprano, but it
wasn't that at all.

"Thank you," he whispered, and long after Glory had gone
her words echoed. *Christmas Day.*

December twenty-fourth arrived bright and clear, an un-
cluttered blue sky out of which sunlight splashed. No new
snow, just the several inches from earlier in the week, packed
down now. Alastair, worn out after another troubled night,
gazed out at his lawn, at the smooth, unbroken crust like a
bedsheet on which no one had slept.

Across the green, all white and strangely unfamiliar with its
humps and mounds, he glimpsed a sketchy stick figure gliding
on Main, then a second. Business as usual at—he glanced at
his watch—nine o'clock. Some thin wraith entered the Public.
Don't know anybody anymore. Can't recognize a soul. He
might have passed through space and taken up residence on a
moon of Jupiter.

Any moment now, Glory would come through his back door,
stamping the snow from her boots, throwing open her peacoat,
even though it was as chilly as a refrigerator in the house if you
strayed too far from the fireplaces or the kitchen stove with all
burners glowing. And she'd want to know—rightly so since
long, long ago, back when this terrible reign of the dragon
began, Alastair had nominated himself to be St. George—what
his plan was. Only he lacked any coherent course to follow. He
was not even sure he could get out of the house without
landing in a drift, immobile. He imagined himself turning into
an old-fashioned snowman, with a carrot nose and coal eyes.

Down the block the Congregational bell tolled once, then twice. No one had died, he would lay money on it, just Will Austin feeling his oats. Or announcing, at Lucas Donnelly's instruction, a new world. New Morning's become the private duchy of the dragon.

Will Austin. Oh no, that would be like asking a blind man for directions. But. . . .

Alastair traveled about his chilly house considering the minister, still a man of the cloth, and under his scratchy monk's robe a servant of God's, though he had switched allegiance and pledged his loyalty to Lucas Donnelly. Probably, knowing Will, for no better reason than the gift of the harpsichord and the dragon's patient encouragement of his mad lust for Palestrina. Besides, the devil's ceremonies were far more orthodox than the plain, simple Congregational rites Will had practiced for years and years, his soul never satisfied. Will needed Latin prayers and incense like some men needed drink.

What if I suggested he raise himself up a few notches and become a Roman, maybe even joining the Franciscans? Sackcloth and ashes, masses before dawn. Down on his knees. Will would love all that, though Alastair didn't know if the order still practiced so stringently, or if they'd remained traditional and hadn't been modernized.

If Will Austin was the best idea he could come up with, they were worse off than Alastair thought. He couldn't look Glory in the eye and say we'll consult the reverend, that's my plan. She'd deflate and cry, and Alastair would hate himself even more than he did already.

Will Austin simply wasn't enough. Yet, what or whom else could he try? He was a man out in the desert, miles from any water hole.

I'll go, he decided, *before Glory gets here*, the need to move, or at least make some feeble attempt at motion, forcing him into his coat. He draped a woolly scarf around his neck, got out the warm hat and gloves, and rolled through the back doorway.

The path behind the house was flattened from Glory's visits, and Alastair made it over to the drive with no trouble. But from there down to the High Street sidewalk the snow remained exactly as it had fallen, without one indentation. Alastair, not taking even a second to change his mind, shifted into low and crunched through the snow. The thickness of it impeded his passage, but he kept going, thankful he didn't skid. What he feared was a sudden tumble, not that with all his padding and the snow he'd get hurt, but who would set him upright? He was *persona non grata* in his own home town. Alastair suspected his friends and neighbors might let him freeze to death.

He made the sidewalk, shoveled all along High Street, except for his little patch, and lurched over to the church in a bumpy ride. On its small incline the manse, with its blind windows, seemed uninhabited. The church appeared more promising, not that Alastair was especially eager to enter. The sanctuary where he had spent most of the Sundays of his life— the Congregational with its upside-down crucifix belonged to the devil these days.

Instinct, however, more than reluctance made him choose the church. He rode up to the side door unobserved, then rumbled in.

Alastair had guessed wrong. Wherever Will Austin might be, he certainly wasn't here. Damnation! Alastair thought, icy fingers tattooing along his spine and at the nape of his neck. He twitched and tingled, off in the right aisle, gazing at the cross, lumpy under its black shroud. A faint aroma of incense lingered in the air and made Alastair sneeze. Get out of here! the voice of sanity whispered by his ear, but he wasn't traveling just yet. The physical struggle from his house, so near yet so distant, to the church had worn him out. *You are an old man and one of frail condition*, he reminded himself. Besides, the Congregational was warm. The furnace was going, and hot blasts of air rose through the register by his chair. A little while, he murmured, suddenly sleepy, and unwound the scarf from his neck. And, before he could stop the inevitable, Alastair fell asleep.

The thunder of heavy steps at the front of the church, the rattle of the big door, woke him up. Who goes there! he almost cried out, then hastily spun himself to the rear, into the small room Will used as a study.

It was Evelyn Crowell, her arms filled with shopping bags, and behind her, Mrs. O'Brien. Alastair watched them through the crack in the door. Flowers and ribbons suddenly appeared, and the two women began decorating the church. Blood-red roses and black silk bows, not exactly the usual, but then Glory wasn't marrying a human. When he thought about it, Alastair was surprised that her dress was the traditional white. But Lucas Donnelly, judging by his typical attire, had a thing about white.

He did not want to watch these marked preparations, but he could not move from the study without being seen.

A good many people seemed to have something to do in the church this morning, and Alastair had no choice but to watch a bustle of cleaning and decorating, as well as to listen to the monk's choir practicing. In Latin, naturally, in a cadence vaguely similar to Gregorian chanting.

Alastair unbuttoned his coat, slipped out of the sleeves and settled in for a lengthy wait. Sooner or later Will Austin would show himself, being the officiating minister, then Alastair would get to him and say, stop this heresy, Will, not only for your own soul's sake, but for New Morning's. All these people will perish in hell's fires if you don't do something. Have an exorcism, reverse the cross, get down—for pity's sake!—on your knees and beg forgiveness. But most of all, save Glory for me!

The day wore on. By early afternoon Alastair was starving, but he couldn't slip away. The Congregational was never empty. People came and went, the choir continued its disharmony. For a while someone up in the loft played a Vivaldi piece on the harpsichord, the same concerto over and over. The musician was heavy-handed and held his chords too long. It was torturous to listen to, though Alastair, his eyes glued to the crack, saw that nobody minded.

After Evelyn and Mrs. O'Brien strung the flowers and ribbons down the center aisle from pew to pew, they built a strange little display of corn, straw, and a sheaf of wheat by Will's pulpit.

Rita Enderman arrived about two and began painting enigmatic symbols on the Congregational's walls. Alastair remembered hearing she fancied herself an artist. Once, Glory had told him, she got the cousins to put up some of her paintings, though not one of them sold. Now she slowly combined black lines with gold, dabs of bright red. Three pentacles on the far wall, and then she switched to the near, at the end of which was the study door. Alastair crouched in his chair, trying to cover himself with the shadows, but Rita passed the little room by and knelt at the top of the center aisle right where, Alastair estimated, Glory and Lucas Donnelly

would come to a halt. She drew something with long sweeps of
her arm, a circle surely, though Alastair couldn't see it.

The sun slid down the study window. Three o'clock. Glory
would be wondering where he was. Alastair shifted, uncomfortable in the wheelchair, jittery with impatience. She'd
think, he realized unhappily, that he'd run out on her. That she
was abandoned. Oh no! Yet he had a vision of that Caribbean
sailboat, as if he'd been on the water himself, and it was
memory he was reeling up. The child, clinging to the rail,
staring down at the sea, weeping and wailing . . . *Oh, Glory,
I'd never do that to you!*

If he could move unaided, Alastair would have snuck down
the side aisle, or duck-walked to the door. But once out of the
chair he was useless.

Alastair chewed on his knuckles and waited, trapped, an
observer of the wedding preparations, a watcher only, just as
he'd been in life. Always the audience, never the actor,
Alastair looked on, powerless to halt the inexorable flow, to
rush out into the main part of the Congregational and yell,
"Stop!"

There was, and always had been since Omaha, no part for
him. He traveled on the periphery, gliding in the mechanized
wheelchair, or thumping laboriously, a misshapen freak, on his
crutches. Yet it had been Lucas Donnelly who had offered him
a starring role, walking Glory down the aisle. *Walking!* He
would replace Theo for the main event, the understudy
getting a chance. Gripping his bony knees, he tried to pretend
he could feel the blood flow, the muscles stretch. Oh, how
dearly he yearned to move, to walk like other men, upright on
the earth. *Me too*, Horse Keleidas said, and for a moment
Alastair thought the Dog Green dead had joined him in the
church. But the shadows fluting about the little room held
nothing, only gray emptiness. This while anyway the ghosts
lingered in his head.

Perhaps this is meant, too, this is how it will end, Alastair
supposed as night slipped over New Morning, and the
preparers of Lucas Donnelly's most meaningful ceremony
came and went. It had finally dawned on Alastair that he was
supposed to stay, that if he left, or tried to, no one would care.
He had been just about written out of New Morning's memory.
He lacked relevance in this new life the dragon had given the
town—though it was a hellish existence or would be.

If he had been waiting, stretched out in a box, for his own funeral to begin, for his own last requiem it would not be much different from the way it was now where, watching, off to the side, he almost drowned in the murky shadows.

Parched, pangs of hunger gripping his stomach, weary and light-headed, Alastair crouched, his eyes glued to the crack through which he viewed everything. The church started to fill up. Slowly and without talking much, and then in whispers, people inched into the pews. They were all there, every New Morning man and woman, children, too, though it was past eleven. The children should have been home in bed, dreaming of sugarplums, of Santa. But no one slept this night in New Morning. Everyone had come by invitation or summons to the dragon's wedding. A current of excitement crackled through the church, stirring the hair on Alastair's arms, the fine spidery webbing on the backs of his hands. The air hummed with unseen presences. Tiny sparks darted helter-skelter like errant sunbeams. Suddenly music crashed from the choir loft. How could a harpsichord resound so loud?

The monkish chorus, journeying single file, made their way down the crowded aisle as a path opened up for them. There was a palpable throbbing, and the pulsing of harsh voices stirred a beat in the crowd, as if synchronized to each individual heart.

Alastair's own heart was near to breaking, as close to annihilation as it would ever get without forever stopping. His eye to the crack, Alastair, inventoried the well-known faces, but only Doc, cheek and jowl with a healthy, spangly Ava, looked back. Doc blinked rapidly, as if by some freak cognitive process he knew Alastair was there. What was this, a last mysterious signal?

Time ticked lavishly as the chorus held their high note. Then, abruptly, the music stopped. Will Austin bobbed up at the pulpit, out of nowhere it seemed. But Alastair's view was limited.

The minister wore a black satin robe with a white geometrical pattern on the front, triangles and circles, a scratchy hieroglyphic lettering. His face was luminescent and his hair stood straight up from his head. Even before he spoke, his lips, as rubied as Ava Trump's, sucked, pursed, drew back over what Alastair would have sworn were black teeth. The minister was hideous. A Halloween goblin striking terror from

the dark, and, in fact, there was a ruffle of gasps and cries
before the congregation quieted to listen to what he said. Not
that his words were distinguishable, for Will spoke in Latin
again, this time stringing syllables together in one long-
winded shrill.

The ceremony wore on, endless and incomprehensible.
With each minute Alastair's anxiety soared. The temperature
climbed and he was bathed in sweat. He loosened his tie,
unbuttoned the top two buttons of his shirt, tugging at the
material in an attempt to send a gust of cooling air to his skin.

In a cymbal crash, the doors were thrown wide. An arctic
wind rushed into the Congregational. The candle flames
danced wildly, almost died, and sprang to life again as the
doors boomed shut.

And Alastair caught sight of Glory.

Oh, what a vision she was! Rapunzel down from her tower,
all dressed in yards of frothy white. She didn't walk so much as
float, with Theo at one side, Evelyn locked to her other arm.
Glory's feet, Alastair could have sworn, were off the ground.

Only Glory's face was wrong. A lamb to the slaughter, she
seemed paralyzed if moving. Her eyes were blank as stones,
her mouth gaped open. Glory looked like the concussed
survivor of a terrible turnpike pileup.

When she reached the altar, standing dead-center on Rita
Enderman's painted diagram, Lucas Donnelly materialized in
a puff of smoke.

*No! No! I won't have this. I can't stand aside, peeping from
my hidey-hole, and watch this happen! No! No!* Alastair cried
and shot into drive. He swung through the door, and this time
let his voice loose, launching into another *no!* in protest at the
dragon.

The church exploded. The congregation went wild, screaming. Some, particularly those in the rear, stood up and flung
themselves against their neighbors in an attempt to reach
Alastair. Hands flew out and clutched at his sleeves, one
grabbed his shoulder, but he sped as fast as the chair would go
until he reached Glory.

It all happened so quickly it was impossible to tell who
reacted first, but all at once, Glory broke free of her intended
and threw herself at Alastair. He slammed the gear into
reverse and spun to the edge of the altar, at the head of the
side aisle. Though now where could he turn? He was trapped,

and Glory, yanking her tiny hat and veil off, crushing her dress, was crowded on Alastair's lap. Alastair backed into a corner, and Glory, free for the moment from Lucas Donnelly's hand in hers, crawled over the side. She ripped and tore the outer skirt of the dress, and savagely pulled at the pearls about her throat, breaking the strand.

Theo sank down to the floor, but Evelyn screamed, rushing toward them. Alastair howled deep in his throat, "Stay back or else!"

"Mr. Wayne!" Lucas Donnelly roared. The sound swelled in the church like a helium balloon until it almost burst and people grabbed their ears. The dragon's displeasure was agonizing but Alastair merely winced.

"You think you can hurt me! Well, you're wrong!" he shouted in defiance, though a knife slashed through his head. Alastair clenched his teeth until he cracked a molar.

Glory had slipped behind the chair, curling herself into a ball in the corner. She scrubbed at the makeup on her face with the underskirt of the bridal dress, and clawed her fingers through her hair, raking it. Black railroad tracks fled down her cheeks. Alastair, through all the awful yelling and the dragon's roar, heard her breathing.

In a sudden, unexpected moment of silence Evelyn screeched, "I won't have this, Alastair. I'll kill you myself!"

"Go to hell, Evelyn Crowell!" Alastair shot out his arm and pointed at her as if he could transform the mother of the bride into something vile.

Evelyn, however, wasn't his concern. It was Lucas Donnelly, the true adversary, whose—was human form fragmenting—. His whiteness flowed smoothly, enlarging like a photographic image on a screen, molecules separating, details erased by a melting light. The dragon's curly head butted the ceiling, and he spread his arms wide so that everything Alastair could see, near and in the distance, lapped in a white sea of eddying maelstroms. The church, the enraged worshippers, the candles with agitated spurts of flame, black satin ribbons in curling snakes, and dying flowers brown about the edges were obliterated beneath the encompassing whiteness.

Out of nowhere a wind careened, pitching and madly tossing the waves on which Alastair rode, bobbing in a frenzied, tumbling motion. A hurricane, screeching in an earsplitting soprano, rushed by, tore the breath from his lungs

and swept Alastair away. He grabbed the arms of the wheelchair and tried to hold to the corner, protecting Glory,
sheltering her, but it was too late. Gravity dissolved, unmoor-
ing him, and Alastair sailed as miraculous as Daedalus on the
tumultuous wind.

Lucas Donnelly was carrying him off, lifting him boldly right
out of New Morning, projecting him like a guided missile into
the void, the nothingness that was neither a drowning
grayness, nor a summer's blue, but white, colorless, a North
Sea churning, a cold sand beach. . . .

He stretched out, belly down, torn from the current, and
forgot in a second the vast expanse as he gazed into Horse
Keleidas's face. "For God's sake, Al," Horse croaked through
cracked lips. Alastair was so close he saw Horse's pores, like
huge craters in the moonscape of his skin, and smelled the
dead breath of putrefaction. A grimy, blood-freckled hand
crawled finger by finger to Alastair's cheek. All Horse's nails
were split and the flesh melted like wax. "I just wanted a little
more time," Horse cried, fat, gelatinous tears in the pus-filled
eyes.

*He does not exist, never did, not like this. There is no Horse,
only dead bones on this planet of illusion.* Alastair struggled to
convince himself. *And I have not returned to Dog Green. In
the Congregational on New Morning's square, that's where I
am, guarding Glory with all I have left in me, with an old
man's crippled body, and a young man's.* . . .

"Oh, Alastair, oh love, kiss me, please. . . ."

The beach slipped away from under him and he peered
down into the woman's eyes. Huge, gold-dusted, jeweled
eyes. She formed, shuddered, took soft feminine shape, the
woman from the kitchen. Moist, pink lips whispered his name,
and he lofted, lulled, floated, pulled out of the white water.
And her arms reached up to gather him in, to bring him
securely against pillowy breasts, to love and succor and
mother. She was all the Eves who had ever lived, she was
woman, about to swallow him up, and he would get lost in her,
drowning, falling forever out of time.

Alastair flailed his arms, kicked powerful legs that hadn't
been that for over forty years, only dream-flesh as the woman
of might-have-been. Alastair fought to escape her. He would
die a neverending death if he fell into that other life and
betrayed Glory in this one.

Her arms undulated, stroking, and they were underwater, Alastair and that never-never wife of his. But, his heart truly breaking, he outswam her, pushed off from the pearly nakedness, and when he glanced back over his shoulder, she was a serpent, hissing at him. Her human image shivered, waterlogged. In a deadly smile, lips dissolved revealing sharp little incisors with poisonous needle tips.

Kill me! Vanquish me! Send me from this earth to purgatory, to hell itself, but I won't give in. I will not go into the dark willingly. I will not betray my honor. Nothing, wife, lover, friend, father, mother, or even brother, Alastair screamed into the void. *None of them, the dead or never-living, will I trade this glory child for. There's no pact, Lucas Donnelly, that you can make with me. I will die as I have tried to live, honestly.*

All Alastair's music swelled to a crescendo. Sound achieved substance in a crystal bubble. Inside the delicate, fragile shell, trapped, was Moses Llewelyn as Alastair had last seen him, wearing green chinos and a work shirt, gray spiky hair, watery-eyed, a dark-grooved totem, old Moses. Oh, Alastair sorrowed, sad and caring, his hands creeping up the glass. The thin wall between them, the two men, one dead, one yet living, met palm to palm. The yardman's lips moved soundlessly. Alastair, in this phantasmagoria of the dragon's, could read what Moses was crying: *Save me! Bring me out of the fire!*

Oh no, not Moses, also! And as Alastair's hands came away, the glass cracked, spreading a map of spidery fissures. Moses flew back, sucked up on an invisible current, screaming as mute as Glory, *Help!*

No, not even you, Moses. Alastair held fast, spinning off into an inky blackness, pitched into another of hell's pits.

Lucas Donnelly pulled his puppeteer's strings, jerked arms and legs, sent the damned into paroxysms of maddened dancing. Needles, nails, stretching racks, spikes and corrosive acids, grenades and plastique, detonating land mines were all employed on Alastair's friends, his buddies, his dead loved ones. Their wails, their cries of agony, sent splinters of steel into Alastair's soul, and he bent, curved over on himself, curled up feet and hands, wound fetally into himself, heard his own lacerating shrieks ripped from his throat. And still he wouldn't give in.

His one clear thought rang out loudly in a perfect note: *Never, good for bad. You can't,* Alastair promised Lucas

Donnelly in the netherworld, *do me in. Torment me, yes. Kill me, that too. Scatter my parts and pulverize my soul, yes, all of that, but this is still true: I choose good.*

The wind roared at gale force, the darkness thundered, and Alastair's ghosts hurled themselves at him. The ground erupted as he tossed, spinning like a dervish, and the earth slipped off its axis. Alastair screamed. Glory's name . . . he tried but couldn't say it. The tempest slapping at him, pulled the skin off his face. His bones felt loose as he tumbled in black space shot through with slivers of icy whiteness, the Omaha squad in full burial dress beside him, Moses on the other flank, and he thought that dour grayness must be Jordy by his trailing legs.

Oh, God, forgive me whatever sins I've committed, prayed Alastair the agnostic. Death was speeding down on him, a monstrous, wicked-looking locomotive. He hadn't even the time to remember what he regretted, what he lacked and what he didn't. And it was an egregious lie that a dying man's life passes before his eyes, or at least that was not Alastair's last conscious experience.

Death is a clown in white face. Death is a bedsheet flapping on the line. Death is a snowy field. At any rate, death is white. Oh, he hated white, wanted blue or green, the sky, the grass, the trees. Death, on the other hand, was so bright, so glowing, it hurt his head.

"What?"

"Ssh, lie still. Oh, Alastair, thank God. I was so afraid."

"Glory?" Something flat—hard and flat. Hurt. Under him. He was lying on his back, stretched out, and the bones of his spine felt bruised. "What . . . ?" He came up on his elbows swaying, glanced right then left at the clear, cold winter's light passing through the rear Congregational windows. Whiteness bathed him in a broad splash. "What . . . ?" he tried again.

"It's morning, and you've been unconscious for hours. I thought . . . I . . . well, really, Alastair," Glory fumbled and smiled through her tears. Her face, streaked with smudges of dirt, was wonderful to come awake to.

"Where—?" He turned his head, and his neck hurt with a dull throbbing ache, up his arm and along his shoulder.

"Gone. If you mean Lucas Donnelly."

"Gone? Away? From New Morning?" he asked, stupefied.

"I think so. I mean, if he can't marry me, why would he stay?" Glory blushed. "That sounds awful, but you know what I'm trying to say."

"Evelyn? And Theo? Where are they?" And the rest of the town. He wanted to ask about everybody by name. Only not now, later, when he rested a bit more. He was easing down when he remembered Moses, and jolted forward, struck by an awful squeezing pain in his chest. He thought he'd been shot, but couldn't bring his hand up to feel for a wound. His hand was a long way off.

He caught his breath and wheezed, "Moses? Is he still dead? And Jordy?"

Glory was trying to answer every question he asked, but they tumbled out, one falling on the tail of another, until the words got all mixed up. Though Glory kept talking, about Moses, and Jordy, and the others home in their beds. She talked even though Alastair's words stayed in his mind. How strange, he thought.

"Alastair? Are you okay?" She arched over him, her hair the color of daffodils, and Alastair was surprised because he noticed, though he never had before, how much Glory resembled his mother.

Something else bothered him. He could almost put his finger on it, but then it slipped away. Oh, how hard it all is. All what? he wondered.

Glory eased him flat, gently, saying, "Careful!" and at once he knew what nagged at him. "You're . . . speaking."

How slowly the words left his lips, and he had the silliest idea that he wanted to hold them back, that language was running from him, just as the light was. Fading. Only the light wasn't inside him but out there. The light trickled slowly away from him.

"What did you say?" Alastair whispered. *If he could just stop the pain—*

Glory came down to him, so close he thought he saw his reflection in her violet eyes. Then her image escaped him, blurred into darkness. He struggled to ask Glory where the light had gone, and why such blackness now that the dragon was somewhere else, another place, a different New Morning maybe, but it took so much energy. Later . . . after that rest of his . . . when the hurting eased in his chest.

He had only the faintest glimmer of Glory's face, as the blackness closed in, and the last sensation he felt, even after the crashing pain, was her breath on his cheek. Her breath ruffled warm as a kiss and she said, at least Alastair thought he heard this, "I love you." And he smiled.

ABOUT THE AUTHOR

Diana Henstell grew up in Forest City, Pennsylvania. She has two children—Joshua and Abigail—a Belgian shepherd, Casey, and two cats—Shadow and Sunday. They all live in Los Angeles. Before becoming a writer, she worked as an editor in publishing. She is the author of *The Other Side* and *Friend*, which became a major motion picture entitled *Deadly Friend*. She is currently at work on her next novel.

John Saul is "a writer with the touch for raising gooseflesh."
—Detroit News

John Saul has produced one bestseller after another: masterful tales of terror and psychological suspense. Each of his works is as shocking, as intense and as stunningly real as those that preceded it.

☐ 26657   THE UNWANTED $4.50

☐ 25864   HELLFIRE $4.50

☐ 26552   BRAINCHILD $4.50

☐ 26258   THE GOD PROJECT $4.50

☐ 26264   NATHANIEL $4.50

Look for them at your bookstore or use the coupon below for ordering: